THE SWINDLER AND THE SWAN: HADES X PERSEPHONE

J.A. GOOD

Book Cover by Hannah Sternjakob

Edited by Rebecca Fazzio and Belle Manuel

First paperback edition June 2023

CONTENTS

To every woman who was ever made to feel like she was merely the sum of her sex. You are powerful and you are more than capable.

All of my books have a spotify playlist that was the soundtrack to writing them. The Swindler and The Swan: Hades x Persephone can be found here.

CHAPTER ONE

THE GOD OF THE UNDERWORLD IS A PETTY BITCH

HADES

S he was wearing *his* fucking color. Demeter was a blight on Olympus, the mortal world, and even the Underworld, mostly because of shit like this. It was a universally acknowledged truth that black was his signature color. None of the other immortals seem to struggle with this fact, but here she was, dressed in an obnoxious gown made of black roses. Everyone saw the slight for what it was, but no one acknowledged it because it was fucking Demeter.

"Bad mood?" Hermes asked, handing him a drink.

He knew he should probably tell him he didn't need another drink, but then he also needed to make it through this sham of a party. Zeus had called it a 'gathering for unity', but it was mostly an excuse for him and Hera to show off their remodeling work. Gold and gaudy. Hardly worth dragging him out of the Underworld for.

"Look at her." Hades held out his hand toward Demeter, who was smiling at Dionysus like she actually gave a fuck what he was talking about. She didn't. "Why is she the single worst immortal?"

"I don't know. Narcissus is fairly obnoxious," Hermes said.

"Yes, but he lives for himself. Demeter lives to make everyone around her miserable," Hades ground out.

Hermes' eyes danced as he sipped his liquor. "I'm pretty sure it's only you she enjoys making miserable."

"What the fuck did I do to her?"

"It was probably when you asked her if she enjoyed being a farmer," Hecate said, sliding next to him.

She was dressed in dark purple pants that billowed out with a matching long-sleeve shirt that hugged her body. Dark kohl ran along her eyes to match her black hair and Hades was forced to consider that she would have been intimidating if he didn't know her well enough to know she was harmless.

"Is that not what she does?" Hades scoffed.

"Well, she's a goddess, so . . ." Hermes said, swallowing another mouthful of wine.

"I cannot let this go unanswered."

Hermes and Hecate exchanged rueful glances that grated along his skin. They may think he was being dramatic, but what was next? Where would it end?

"Would it help if I said she looked terrible in it?" Hermes asked, sliding his hand through his chestnut hair.

"Probably not, considering it would be a lie," Hecate said with her eyes on Demeter. "She looks beautiful, it really shows off her shoulders well."

Hermes gasped. "Oh my gods, do you have a thing for Demeter?"

Hecate glared at him. "No, you idiot, it's just facts. I bet she would be a good fuck, though. She's feisty."

"I just threw up in my mouth," Hades said with disgust.

"I don't know, I could see it," Hermes said, contemplating.

"You both are the most disloyal friends."

Neither Hecate nor Hermes seemed affected by the declaration, but likely because they knew he didn't mean it. They were the only beings that made these gatherings, or even immortality, bearable.

"It's always you three." Zeus' deep voice cut through their easy banter.

"Brother," Hades said through gritted teeth.

Zeus was dressed in a navy suit that hugged every inch of his body as if he had painted it on. It was enough that Hades had to keep from rolling his eyes. Zeus' crimson hair was the opposite of Hades' own dark blue. Where Hades was lean, Zeus was broad-chested and imposing. Not for the first time, Hades wondered at how they were brothers.

"It's good to see you crawled out from the Underworld," Zeus said, clasping him on the shoulder.

"It didn't really feel like there was much of a choice," Hades said dryly.

"I love what you've done with the place," Hermes interjected.

Whether he didn't hear the irritation in Hades' words or he chose to ignore it, Zeus smiled brightly at Hermes.

"All Hera's doing. You know she gets bored after a while." Zeus' eyes slid to where his wife was chatting animatedly with Demeter. "What do you think about Demeter's dress, Hades?" The smile Zeus wore was enough for him to burn the entirety of Olympus to the ground.

"Tacky," Hades said, picking invisible lint from his own black shirt.

Zeus roared with laughter and squeezed his shoulder. "It's a party, Hades, try to have fun for once in your entire existence."

He was cursed. To have to endure shared ichor with his idiotic brother, who the mortals worshiped with such reverence. The worship Hades received was laced with fear and desperation. They should consider themselves lucky there was an Underworld that he tended to meticulously rather than face an afterlife of endless restlessness, or worse, oblivion. It was useless either way; the mortals saw him as a harbinger of death and trying to convince them of anything else was an exercise in futility.

"How long before I am released from my obligation and able to *crawl* back to the Underworld?" Hades sounded bored when inside he was an inferno of rage.

Zeus sighed. "Stay for our announcement and then you can wallow in self-despair once more." He turned to Hecate and Hermes. "How you two suffer him, I'll never understand."

Hecate smiled sweetly. "When we find the answer, we will be sure to let you know."

Zeus laughed obnoxiously once more and left them, shaking his head.

Hades glared at Hecate, who shrugged. "What did you want me to say? Sorry, Zeus, actually your brother just hates you and is a really decent immortal?"

"You could have said nothing," Hades growled.

"Oh dear, his mood is worsening." Hermes frowned.

"Just think, soon you will be tucked into your cold and dingy bed, cuddling Cerberus," Hecate offered.

It did sound appealing and soothed his irritation for a moment before Demeter made her way to them. She took each step as if she were showing off her gown. He hoped the flowers on it rotted before the night was done.

"Hades, Hermes, Hecate," Demeter crooned. "Imagine all three of you together."

"Hard to believe," Hermes murmured, though he was fighting back a smile.

"Demeter, your dress is positively lovely," Hecate said, running a hand over the curve of Demeter's hips.

Demeter sucked in a deep breath as her eyes dipped hungrily over Hecate's body. Disgust rolled through Hades. How Hecate could even entertain the possibility was a mystery to him.

Recovering, Demeter said, "And you look stunning as always, Hecate."

Hecate's laugh was born from seduction. "Oh, Demeter, you are too kind. Tell me, how are things at the lake?"

"Well enough. There's hardly anything to complain about," Demeter said, though her eyes flashed with something Hades couldn't name.

"You know everyone talks about that lovely swan you keep there. It's such a unique creature in that it stays when most wouldn't."

Everything in Demeter's countenance changed in a single moment. She was tense and ready for a fight, though Hecate had said nothing of consequence.

"Maybe everyone should focus on their own interests instead of being concerned with mine." Demeter wrapped a strand of short blonde hair around her finger and tugged on it, her tell that she was nearing her breaking point.

"That's exactly what I always say." Hecate smiled warmly.

Releasing her hair, Demeter frowned. "Yes, well, I should get back to Hera."

"Of course, darling," Hecate said, pressing a kiss to Demeter's cheek.

As Demeter retreated, Hermes blew out a long breath. "You are a force to be reckoned with, Hecate."

Hecate grinned with self-satisfaction. "You're welcome, by the way."

Hades was forced to concede that she had played the goddess skillfully, but he would have preferred an actual fight with Demeter. It would have been at least something to look back on with fond memories.

"What is her thing with that goose?" Hades asked, ignoring Hecate.

"It's a swan," Hermes corrected. "And I don't know, what's your thing with Cerberus? It's just a pet."

"I don't act like the world is ending any time someone mentions him," Hades said, rubbing his jaw in consideration. An idea was forming. An idea he liked very much.

Hecate burst out in laughter. "Like when Aphrodite called him a mutt? You literally set fire to her new curtains."

"First, those curtains were an abomination, and I was doing everyone a favor. Second, Aphrodite was just bitter because I wasn't interested. She should have insulted me, not Cerberus." Hades fought back a smile as his idea sprouted wings.

"Oh no. What is it? What are you thinking about doing? Not another set of curtains, Hera will know it was you," Hermes pleaded with him.

"Hades," Hecate warned. "Whatever you are thinking about, don't do it."

They wouldn't have been good friends if they hadn't tried to stop him, but they all knew he wouldn't be deterred. Hades was saved having to divulge his plans by Zeus sending a bolt of lightning into the purple sky above them. All went silent as the god of gods stood on the golden dais and held out his hand to Hera, who joined him. She had an elegance about her that set her apart from the rest of them. Tightly curled brown hair clung to her dark shoulders.

"My friends, Hera and I happily welcome you to our home, where you all are welcome any time as you well know. However, we are happy to announce that a new god will be joining us in a few short months as we are expecting."

Everyone broke out into cheers except Hades. Delightful. Another delight to add to Zeus's retinue. He wasn't jealous, of course, a child sounded like a terrible idea, but it was that Zeus had everything and was deserving of none of it.

The sun was rising over the horizon and Hades decided he'd had his fill of Olympus politics. With a snap of his fingers, he found himself blissfully free from its confines. His fingers had ached with the need to portal out of there, but decorum maintained that he had to put on a show. Now free, Hades found himself not in the Underworld, but a lake he had been to only once before. All the gods hosted from time to time and he had been forced to endure one such gathering here a lifetime ago.

Demeter's tacky gothic castle sat up on a hill over the lake, but he wasn't interested in raiding it. More important to him was the creature that sat at the center of the lake, watching him with eerily blue eyes. No goose should have that intelligence in its eyes. It was unsettling.

Hades held out his hand and called for the abomination, but it merely watched him. Fuck it. He would go get it himself. He set foot in the water and the goose flapped its wings in warning.

"I'm not going to hurt you, you overgrown duck. I just have a debt to settle with your mistress."

The goose did not like that. It took off, its white wings flapping wildly as it attempted to take flight.

"No, you don't," Hades said as he shot out his hand. Tendrils of black power slid from his fingertips, racing to where the bird had taken flight. Unfortunately for it, it was nothing, and he was a god. His power wrapped around the creature as he reined it in, bringing the squawking goose with it.

As soon as Hades held the creature in his hands, it took the opportunity to bite his forearm. He nearly dropped it but recovered enough to wrap a tendril of power around its beak.

His arm seeped with golden ichor from the wound it had made, but he felt no hurt from it. Instead, he held up the angry duck and looked into its knowing eyes.

"Time for a trip to the Underworld, my angry friend, but first—"

"Hermes!" he yelled.

In a puff of silver smoke, Hermes appeared, holding the same glass of wine he had a minute ago.

"You don't have to yell, you assh—" His eyes locked on the goose still flapping wildly. Hades wrapped another tendril of power around its wings and tucked it beneath his arm.

"I'm stealing Demeter's goose, obviously," Hades said with a proud smirk.

"It's a swan." Hermes pinched the bridge of his nose and sighed. "Also, put it back."

"No. I'm taking it for a little getaway with me. Go tell Demeter."

"I will not." Hermes glared at him.

"You are the messenger, Hermes. It's literally your job." Hades sighed, hugging the squirming goose closer to his side.

It was taking all of his godsdamn strength to keep the beast in his grasp. He needed to get to the Underworld and let the fiend run free before it gave itself a heart attack. Holding the goose close to his side with one arm, he waved the other, and a portal made of smoke opened to the Underworld.

"This thing is mean as shit, no wonder Demeter likes it so much," Hades said as he stepped through.

"Hades, Demeter is going to lose it if she finds it missing. Everyone knows she's obsessed with that thing," Hermes pleaded.

"Then she can apologize for her offense and I'll give it back," Hades said reasonably.

They stepped into the throne room and Hades surveyed the barren and cavernous space. This would do just fine for the beast. It wasn't like he used it for anything. He wasn't even sure why he had a throne room to begin with except that Zeus had insisted on it when he had appointed him god of the Underworld.

"What do ducks eat?"

The air around them shimmered in a way he knew well. Enchantments didn't last long in the Underworld, a security measure of sorts. The weight in his arm shifted and suddenly Demeter's goose was not a goose at all, but a naked woman.

"Oh, shit!" Hades yelled as he dropped it as if it were poison.

It fell with a grunt, landing on its hands, a curtain of blond hair covering its back.

"Fuck, Hades. What did you do?" Hermes said, stepping back as if he could distance himself from the crime.

"I stole a goose," he said, recovering from the shock.

"It was a swan!" Hermes shouted.

"Well, it isn't anymore," Hades said, amusement ripe within him.

"I'm not an 'it', you assholes," it said, dripping venom.

"Well, you were a goose and now you are a naked woman. Seems like an 'it' to me." Hades shrugged.

It pushed itself up and stood, showing off a lean and curvy body that had him quickly forgetting that it had been a goose moments ago. Long blond hair ran down its chest, covering the rest of it from view. Blue eyes he recognized from the lake met his with unmitigated fury.

"I was a *swan*, or are you too stupid to know the difference?" she said, cheeks red with anger.

"Shit, Hades, I think you stole Demeter's daughter," Hermes whispered, as if she wouldn't be able to hear him.

It was easy to see the conclusion Hermes had come to, given that she had the same blonde hair as Demeter and there was a faint resemblance in the shape of her face, but she was far more striking than Demeter could ever hope to be.

"Demeter doesn't have a daughter," Hades said.

"She does, and she's going to kill you when she finds out so you should bring me back to my lake," she ground out, hands on her hips as if she didn't care that she was naked in front of two gods.

Hades rubbed at his jaw. "Demeter has a fucking daughter."

Hermes groaned. "Put her back."

"Why, when this just became more interesting? Who the fuck curses their own daughter?" Hades wondered aloud.

"She didn't curse me, asshole. I've been like this my entire life."

Hades was reminded of his arm that was bleeding and thought that she was looking at him as if she would gladly bite him again. He stepped closer to her and the side of his mouth quirked up.

"What is your name?"

"Persephone," she bit out.

"Persephone," he purred. "Do you know who I am?"

"Should I?" she said with disdain, making him want to tilt her full mouth up and show her exactly who the fuck he was.

"I am Hades, god of the Underworld, and I recognize a curse when I see one. If there's one thing I know about Demeter, it's that she would burn the whole fucking world to the ground if someone cursed her daughter, which means . . ."

"That's really messed up," Hermes said.

"She wouldn't," Persephone said with less conviction.

That she was intelligent was clear enough, but his logic was sound. Anyone who knew Demeter would know he spoke the truth. The question was, why would she curse her own daughter?

"Why am I not a swan right now? It's daylight." Persephone's hands shook slightly.

"Because curses and spells don't hold up well in the Underworld. As long as you are here, you won't turn back," Hades said, watching her carefully.

She seemed to chew on his words, tasting them. His eyes nearly drifted lower down her body, but he swallowed, focusing on her face that was angular and soft, pliant.

"Which is all well and good, but you are going back so—" Hermes began.

She took a step back. "I am not going back."

Hades raised an eyebrow, a small smile playing on his lips. "No? Most people avoid coming to the Underworld and rarely wish to stay."

She fixed her glare on him. "Most people haven't been a swan half their life. I'm not going back."

Hades stepped forward slowly and watched indecision war over her beautiful face. She wasn't sure if she should attack him or fall to her knees and beg. Something in him tightened at the thought and made it hard to focus. He tilted her chin so she was forced to look up at him.

"Here's the thing, darling. As god of the Underworld, I decide who stays and who goes. You are in my domain and, as such, subject to my rule."

Fuck if the way her eyes glared at him didn't do something to him. He couldn't remember the last time someone had made him feel this way. A dangerous game. Maybe Hermes was right, or maybe it was that he was just very aware that she was naked.

"Hades!" Hecate's voice roared from down the hall.

Hades smiled and pulled away from Persephone.

"That was quick." He winked at her.

The doors flew open, and Hecate stormed in, irritation radiating off her. "Did you steal her fucking swan?"

Hades held out his hands. "I see no swan here."

Hecate looked around and seemed to relax a fraction, thinking she had avoided a conflict. Her eyes landed on Persephone and her brow furrowed.

"Who's that?" she asked. "And why is she naked?"

"This." Hades took great pleasure in drawing out the moment. "Is Demeter's daughter, Persephone."

Hecate's mouth fell open. "What the actual fuck?"

"My question precisely, dear Hecate," Hades said, eying Persephone, who watched them all, calculating, seeming to shift her countenance with each moment.

"Hades is putting her back," Hermes said desperately.

Hades smirked. "Hermes, go tell Demeter I stole her daughter."

"Hermes, do no such thing." Hecate held out her hand as if she could stay him.

Hermes glared at her. "Like I would actually do it. I'd take one of Zeus' lightning bolts before I did that."

Relaxing a fraction, Hecate seemed to put the pieces together. "Wait, why were you a swan?"

"Because my own mother cursed me apparently," Persephone seethed before she turned to meet his eyes, fire alive in them. "And I'm not going back."

Fuck, if he wasn't inclined to agree with her.

CHAPTER TWO

HOW TO STRIKE A BARGAIN WITH THE DEVIL

PERSEPHONE

P ersephone's life had been a series of cruel jokes, one on top of
another. Cursed to spend her days as a swan and her nights
as a woman, it was all she could remember. Yet, the moment Hades
laid the accusation at her mother's feet, there had been no doubt
in her mind it was true. Her mother was fierce in every way. It was
a trait that Persephone admired in her. From the very start, her
mother instilled a fear of the outside world in Persephone. She had
told her of the cruelty of men, gods, and the unknown.

A life of solitude with only her mother and her lake for company.
Her days were spent at the lake, sleeping and trying to survive in a
body that felt wrong and confining. Nights at the castle with her
mother had been her only consolation. Nights that she had always

looked forward to and enjoyed. Her mother was tenacious, clever, and made Persephone laugh. And it had all been a lie. Thirty years of lies.

"I am taking her to get dressed and then I will meet you two in the dining room, which had better be well stocked with wine and liquor," the woman he had called Hecate said, reaching for Persephone's arm.

Reflex made her step back and draw her arm close to her. She wasn't used to touch from others. Only her mother and now the dark man with the strange blue hair had ever touched her. Doubling her number was more than enough for one night. The woman held up her hands as if Persephone were one of the feral animals that visited the lake during the day.

"It's all right. I won't touch you. Just come with me and I'll help you find some clothes," she said soothingly, though it sounded more patronizing than anything else.

"How do I know you won't take me back to my mother?" Persephone said, eyeing the woman.

The question was meant for Hecate, but Hades answered instead. "Because while I grant Hecate and Hermes the freedom to come and go from the Underworld as they please, no one except I may bring or take from my domain." His voice reminded her of midnights with only the light of the crescent moon above to illuminate. "Which means, darling, that you will remain in the Underworld until I say otherwise."

He held her gaze and she knew he meant every word like a dark promise that she was happy to lean into. Nodding her head, she stepped towards the way the woman had come from. She wouldn't ask any of them for help. Her mother may have been a monster, but she hadn't raised her to be anything except capable.

A dark chuckle followed her as she threw open the door and the small pattering of feet told her the woman followed. The room opened up to a large cavern with what felt like a thousand stairs that ascended, illuminated by torches on either side of its path. It was more stairs than she had ever seen in her life, but she wouldn't show weakness to any of them. She began the climb and wondered how long her strength of will would hold.

"Persephone," Hecate called.

Every muscle in her body was coiled and ready for a fight as she twisted to look down at the woman. She was pretty in the way women in all the stories Persephone read were. Tall, dark, with a body that her unique outfit accentuated.

"Let me show you the shortcut." Hecate smiled warmly.

She was trying to be her friend. Despite the fact that Persephone had never had a friend, she wasn't about to jump into this woman's lap. Her mother had taught her that everyone was after something and unless their wants aligned with yours, they were your enemy. That made this woman her enemy because she wanted to send Persephone back and that was not going to happen. She never wanted to feel her body compacted into the swan's body that was wrong and too small.

Hecate put her hand on one of the stones and it glowed beneath her touch before groaning and giving way, sliding to reveal a passageway that had not been there before.

"The stairs are for those who Hades doesn't like," Hecate said, holding her hand out to the pathway.

Persephone said nothing as she passed the other woman and came into a hallway lit with blue flames. There was the occasional door that was carved from stone, only the faint outline giving away its otherness.

"Here," Hecate said, pushing open one of the doors. "This is my room."

"You have your own room?" Persephone eyed her.

Hecate shrugged. "Do you know anything about the other immortals?"

This was information Persephone was sure she shouldn't give up. The more ignorant they thought her, the less they saw her as a threat. Persephone had known the moment she had seen Hades at the lake who he was. Her mother hated him more than any other living creature. Whenever Persephone dared to ask what the god had done to earn her ire, her mother would say that he took what was not his to take. It was a puzzle that Persephone was happy to find answers to while she was here.

"I knew there was a world outside our lake, but my mother always told me that no one would understand me," Persephone said slowly as she stepped around the woman and found herself standing in a room that took her breath away.

It was cavernous like the rest of the Underworld, but this felt like coming home. A large canopy bed lay at the center dressed in white, fluffy blankets and endless pillows. A dresser sat at one end and a fireplace was carved into the cave wall across from the bed where a long crimson couch sat with a table in front of it. All along the walls, a flowing blue light cascaded and intertwined as if following its own path. At the far side, a massive window stood.

Curious, Persephone went to the window and gasped as she took in the sight below.

The curtains pulled over it and Hecate shoved her out of the way.

"You're naked, anyone can see," she explained.

"I don't care," Persephone said as she pushed the curtains back open.

She didn't care if the whole world was watching her; she needed to see the beauty outside the window. A thousand lights twinkled out below where a river ran through a town that was bustling on either side. A waterfall cascaded far in the distance and boats came and went down the river. Row after row of balconies looked out over the river, much like this one did. People littered the streets looking no larger than ants.

"What is this? Who are they?" Persephone whispered.

Hecate pressed along the glass and it slid open, revealing a balcony that was open to the night air. Persephone stepped out and looked up, seeing the same blue thread of lights running atop the cave ceiling.

"They are the dead that aren't ready to move on to Elysium. Grief, love, loss, passion, all of it hold them back from reaching peace. So they live here with each other until they are ready to let go," Hecate said the words solemnly as she surveyed the city.

"What happens when they are ready?" Persephone asked, a million questions bubbling up within her.

"Hades senses it and he guides them to Elysium. His job is to shepherd souls to where they belong."

Her mother had told her that the god of the Underworld passed judgment on souls and condemned them to an afterlife of torture, but that was not what Persephone saw in the people who roamed freely and openly.

"What is Elysium?" Persephone asked.

Hecate turned to her and her eyes narrowed. In a single moment, Persephone knew she had given up too much. Her lack of knowledge was information Hecate could and would use against her. She would need to be more careful moving forward.

"It is one of two final resting places for souls. Most souls. The truly vile souls that pass through the gates of the Underworld are judged and sent to the River Styx, where they swim for eternity, having forgotten who and what they were. Their existence is merely a consequence and nothing more. Those not found guilty wind up either here in Asphodel or in Elysium, where they may find peace until they are reincarnated once more."

"And Tartarus?" Persephone asked.

Hecate turned towards her. "How do you know that name?" Suspicion laced each word.

The truth was that her mother used to say that it was a good thing she was immortal, else Hades would throw her in Tartarus with the Titans when she was dead.

"I read it in a book once," Persephone lied.

The only books in their home were the ones her mother deemed safe and not full of lies told by other immortals. With that being said, there were few to choose from.

There was a knowing in Hecate's eyes, but she sighed. "It's a place of suffering for the vilest of souls. Souls that not even the River Styx and the punishment of no reincarnation could suffice. Few actually end up there, but the ones that do very much deserve it."

Hecate clapped her hands together and smiled. "Clothes."

Going to the dresser, she took out a dark teal color that instantly appealed to Persephone. It was her favorite color and most of her dresses were made of it. It seemed a small comfort in the face of such upheaval.

"I'm taller than you and the top will definitely be tight, but it should work well enough until you can get home."

Persephone stilled. "I'm not going home."

Hecate sighed and set the clothes down on the bed, facing Persephone with quiet patience that made Persephone want to scream.

"Do you know how I knew you were gone? Your mother is on a rampage up there. In all the thousands of years I have known her, I've never seen her this way. She's scared."

"She cursed me," Persephone ground out.

"I can't help but think there's more to the story. Why would Demeter do that?"

"Honestly? I don't know and I don't care to find out. I am not going back, so unless she comes to the Underworld, I'll never know." Persephone grabbed the clothes from the bed and started to pull them on.

"Aren't you curious?" Hecate pushed, averting her eyes.

The shirt was absolutely too tight and while it would have clung to Hecate; it was glued to Persephone, leaving nothing to the imagination. The pants that were meant to billow out were tight against her legs but also sagged with the loss of height.

"I don't care why she did it because there is no reason she could give me that would make what I've been through okay. Do you have any idea what it's like to be a swan? Trapped and uncomfortable every single day? To fear daylight because it meant losing your form? The dark has been my only comfort for my entire life, so now that I have found somewhere that's shrouded in it and will never make me into a swan again, I'm not leaving. I'd rather die than go back."

Hecate sucked in a long breath and when the air left her again, it was with a slump of her shoulders as if defeat had claimed her.

"I can't pretend to know what you've been through, but I do know that your mother will destroy everything to get you back. It's a dangerous game you and Hades are playing."

When Persephone said nothing, Hecate ran a hand through her short, dark hair. "I am going to go talk to him and figure out what to do about this mess. Stay here and help yourself to anything. I'll be back."

The fact that Hecate thought she would stay locked away was laughable at best, but she smiled and nodded all the same, making a show of settling into the bed. Though there was still suspicion in

Hecate's eyes, she left her all the same. It took all her patience to count to five hundred before she let herself get up and follow the way they had come. She had no idea how to go about finding the dining hall, but she would be damned if she didn't try.

Sliding her hands along the cavern walls in the stairwell, Persephone felt the satisfaction of victory when one finally gave way. Shouting was the only encouragement she needed to keep going. The hall was much like the other one with Hecate's room. Following the sound of discord, Persephone leaned towards the room, careful not to activate the door.

"I agree it's messed up what Demeter did, but you have to give her back," Hecate said, despite what Persephone had just confided in her.

"Or I can make this into something even better than it already was. This is an opportunity, dear Hecate."

She could practically hear his smirk.

"Whatever you are thinking, let me be the first to tell you it's a bad idea, which by the way I would have told you if you had told me you were going to steal her swan in the first place," Hermes said.

"Which is precisely why I did not tell you," Hades said.

"Hades, this isn't a game. Persephone is a person—"

"Half of the time," Hades corrected, and it was all she could do not to open the door and strangle him.

Two loud sighs echoed through the wall as if they agreed with her.

"If Demeter finds out you have her, she will call Zeus to intervene," Hermes said.

"And what will my dear big brother do? Send me to Tartarus and saddle someone else with the dead? It seems like too much work for him to bother with."

"It was just a dress, Hades," Hecate said, frustration leaking through her calm.

"And it's just a goose," Hades said.

"Swan," they yelled in unison.

"Either way, what is the only thing that would make Demeter even more angry than stealing her goose?" Hades asked. "Very well, I'll tell you. Breaking the curse."

Everything in Persephone stilled. Break the curse. There was a way to end this half-life, and let her be in the real world? She hadn't ever thought it was possible.

"Even you can't argue with that, Hecate. You are too noble to let a curse like that stand when we could help," Hades said.

"How?" Hecate asked, considering.

"The Fates," Hades answered.

"Shit. They never actually tell you anything," Hermes said.

"They do if you know what to listen for."

A moment passed. Persephone barely breathed.

"What do you say, Persephone?" Hades called, and the door slid open, revealing her attempt at espionage.

How long had he known she was there? Her gut told her it was the entire time, but how he knew was a mystery. Summoning the courage to act as if this were entirely her idea, she strolled to the long table littered with fruit and wine. The room had a window that went the entire length, overlooking Asphodel. Flames flickered all around and a massive fireplace roared along the far wall.

Hermes and Hecate sat to one side of the table, while Hades sat at the head of it, his cool gaze assessing her. Taking the seat next to Hades, she reached for a pomegranate, but Hades' hand came down on hers, pushing it towards the table.

His eyes were a shade or two lighter than his hair and they bore into hers. "I would not do that if I were you. While you may want to stay in the Underworld right now, eating or drinking from the Underworld would bind you to it forever. Unless you are sure that is what you will always want, I would exercise restraint."

"Won't I be hungry while I'm here?" she pulled her hand from beneath his and he leaned back in his chair.

"Things work differently in the Underworld, you will be fine for the time being." He seemed unconcerned.

"You said you would help me break my curse," she reminded him.

"I assume that is agreeable to you. Unless you were attached to being a goose." He took a long sip of wine.

"Swan," she bit out.

"It feels like the same thing," he said with a shrug.

She had the impression he enjoyed getting a reaction, so she ignored him. "My mother said The Fates were useless and prone to theatrics."

"As per usual, your mother was wrong except for the theatrics part. They do love to put on a good show," Hades said with a smirk.

Persephone found herself wondering if he was perpetually amused. It was an exceedingly annoying trait. Yet, at the same time, there was a darkness that clung to him, that rippled over him occasionally. It made her think she should appreciate the amused side of him lest the darkness be freed.

"What did my mother do to you that you are so determined to anger her?" Persephone asked.

He considered her. "She annoyed me."

"She wore his color," Hecate said, drawing Persephone's attention.

"Excuse me?" her mouth fell open.

"That's right." Hermes groaned. "She wore his color, and that was enough for him to steal you and now apparently break a curse she put on her own daughter."

"That seems . . . dramatic," Persephone said.

"Some crimes cannot go unpunished," Hades said with a sigh as if it were all very taxing on him.

So the god of the Underworld was deranged. Did it matter if he helped her break the curse? She knew the answer before the question had even formed. It didn't matter why her mother had placed the curse, only that she would never go back to it again.

"I accept your bargain," Persephone said with her back straight.

"I don't remember making an offer of a bargain," Hades said, leaning forward.

She matched him, leaning forward till their faces were even. "You want to piss my mother off and I want to break the curse. You help me, I help you. Seems like the definition of a bargain."

His smile faded till he was watching her with an intensity that made her toes curl. "Very well, Persephone. Consider our bargain struck."

And so it was that she made a deal with the devil.

CHAPTER THREE

THE FATES ARE TESTY OLD HAGS

HADES

Sleep left him wanting. Blonde curls and piercing blue eyes filled his mind until he eventually gave up and set about wandering as he usually did when sleep eluded him. Still, it couldn't be his conscience that made him think of her, he hardly had one. Besides, he was doing the woman a favor. This was something else. Something dangerous.

When he realized where he was going, he felt his muscles contract as if stopping had physically offended them. He couldn't remember when he had last been to the library. It was a necessary part of his home, but one he rarely visited except to grab a book and retreat. That he was here now was enough to set his blood roaring in his veins. Anticipation had him opening the doors and his eyes were immediately drawn to the high-backed red chair where Persephone had curled up with a book open, her finger moving eagerly across the words. The fireplace carved into the wall flared brightly, shifting the light, but the luminescent blue that followed along the underworld's ceilings seemed to grow brighter, as if heeding her command.

Interesting. She never looked up from her reading even as her finger moved with increasing franticness, as if she would be unable to read without its guiding movement. Hades wrapped his hands around his back and clasped them as he moved quietly to the bookshelf in front of her. Even as he passed her, she hadn't noticed him, though her breathing was fast and irregular. Her blonde hair spilled over her shoulders, and he had the sudden urge to wrap his fingers around it. Unsettling.

"Aren't you supposed to be sleeping?" he said, quietly.

She screamed. The mesmerizing creature in *his* chair let loose a shrill cry and threw *his* book on the floor. Hades bit back a smile as humor danced through him. She was looking up at him with helpless, wide eyes that were so unlike her usual ferocity, as if he had truly caught her in a world of her own.

Bending down, he lifted the book and felt the smile take the side of his mouth before he willed it back down.

"*Daphnis and Chloe*, an interesting choice," he said as he handed the book to her, which she quickly took and held to her chest as if it would ward off bad spirits or maybe just him.

He saw the moment she overcame her shock and her blue eyes regained their wariness.

"I couldn't sleep. I've never actually slept in this form before."

The words were hesitant, trusting, and he found himself sobering at the offered gift.

"Why not?" He busied himself by moving to the liquor cart and pouring himself a drink, giving her the time she needed.

"I guess because I didn't want to remember my time as a swan. So I forced myself to sleep. Now that I am only ever this, it's like my body doesn't know how to do something that should come naturally."

Demeter was a fucking monster. Who would curse their own child to live a life of misery? A half-life. Even if he weren't interested in helping her to spite Demeter, he might have been tempted just because it was monstrous to allow her to continue with such an existence. However, since the former was his motivation, it allowed for less complications.

"So you explored my home, unchaperoned?" he said, tossing back the liquor and enjoying the way it burned his throat, reminding him of who he was.

"I didn't think you would throw me out for the offense and when I found this room—" Emotion caught her words. "It felt like a safe place."

If it wasn't maintained meticulously by his staff, it would have been covered in dust, long forgotten. It was interesting that a place like this could inspire such feelings in her.

"Does Demeter not have a library? She does seem like the uneducated type,' he mused, swirling around the amber liquid, careful not to look at her.

"She's still my mother, you know. You don't have to insult her any chance you get."

The anger and conviction in her voice made him raise his eyes to hers against his better judgment. There was a fire there that was dull, as if years of repressing it had made it into less than it was. His own fire lit in his veins, an urge to kindle hers into everything it always should have been. Anger. He was angry.

"That you would defend her when she fucking cursed you is not a good look, little goose," he said, tampering down the rage building in him.

He had spent centuries crafting his emotions to be easily pliable and fit what he needed to be, but this woman had him slipping into habits that were long dead. Dangerous.

"Are you always this irritating?" she asked with a huff of breath.

"So I've been told," he said, dryly.

She shook her head, but her luscious lips curled up a fraction before she pulled her bottom lip between her teeth. Hades' hand tightened on his glass. What the fuck was this? He knew lust, debauchery, general wanting, but the way her teeth held that lip had him thinking the most debased thoughts. Had him wondering what she tasted like.

"We have a library, but there are only fifty books or so. I've read them all a hundred times each and certainly none of them like this." She held the book up and then pulled it tight to her, her cheeks going crimson.

Hades threw back another glass, knowing it wouldn't dull the effect she was having on him. Maybe he needed to get this out of his system. Maybe he should call Minthe and make him forget the lost blonde looking at him with curiosity.

"The story of two naïve lovers? Hardly seems like Demeter's cup of tea." He was even impressed by the way he managed to sound disinterested.

Persephone bit her lip once more and he resisted the urge to tell her to stop. It was very distracting.

"You've read it?" she asked, curious.

That curiosity was its own curse. He could see that she craved knowledge. Knowing. Demeter had denied her what she needed to thrive on top of cursing her. Fuck Demeter.

"Once. Their idiocy was annoying enough that I never desired to read it again."

"You fault them for their inexperience?" she asked, her words faint.

Hades told himself he shouldn't do it. Shouldn't toy with her emotions, but he was a bastard, so he set down the glass and positioned himself over her, hands on the armrests of her chair. Her chest heaved with effort and he allowed himself the pleasure of slowly running his gaze over her. Her lips were parted and the hollow at the base of her throat rose and fell in time with her breasts as if she were starved for air. Starved for emotion. Fuck if he didn't want to satiate her.

"No, Persephone, I fault them for not taking what they wanted," he said with lethal quiet.

Shit. This was a mistake. He should move and leave her alone. She was curious, but he was also a bastard. That she longed for connection was obvious and he had enough morals that he wasn't going to take advantage of that.

A knock on the door nearly had his eye twitching, but he didn't remove himself from her proximity as her eyes ran over him, searching.

"My lord Hades, The Fates have arrived," Minos, his servant, said.

Hades pulled himself back as if struck. Never. Not in all his millennia of life had The Fates responded to a summoning in less than twenty-four hours. They took pride in making the gods wait on them. What did it mean that they hurried to his call?

Persephone was still breathing heavily, Hecate's shirt tight along her body. Pushing down this need in him, he held out his hand.

"Well, best not to keep The Fates waiting."

She slid her hand into his and her touch was molten, her doe eyes lifting to meet his. She was dangerous. This was dangerous. The thing about immortality was that it made you forget. Forget what it meant to feel something intensely. Everything was dulled until you were forced to chase feeling just to know you could, but this woman. She made him feel.

"Could it really be this easy?" she whispered.

Hades shook his head, "Let me tell you something about The Fates. They are testy old hags and rarely give you what you are looking for."

When she turned her head up to him, it was like she had steeled herself and determination shone through in her eyes. "How do we make them give us what we need?"

Not despair, not anger, not tears, but sheer determination governed her. Maybe that's why Demeter had hidden her away all these years. Her own tenacity would bring Olympus to its knees. It would bring *him* to his knees if he wasn't careful.

"Luckily for us, I get along well enough with The Fates. Just let me do the talking," he said.

She snorted. "I'm fairly certain you would say that even if they didn't like you. I get the feeling you like the sound of your own voice."

Raising an eyebrow, he met her gaze, humor masking her nerves. "I would take offense to that if it wasn't true."

Persephone laughed and fuck if it wasn't the most intoxicating sound he had ever heard. Fucking dangerous.

He led her to the throne room and gave her a small wink as he pushed open the doors.

"Clotho, Lachesis, Atropos! What a monumental delight to have you three lovely ladies in these hallowed halls!"

They were as hideous as ever, but that was beside the point. The Fates thrived on flattery and he was always willing to play their games when the price was right. Honestly, he didn't even know which of them was which. They all appeared as haggard beggar women with thin white hair and noses that were too long for their faces. The only difference was in the sizes of the humps in their backs and Hades had never gotten around to learning which was hunched over more.

"And so the Prince of Darkness and the alabaster Anatidae found their way through the haze of retribution," one of them said, the mild hunch.

Honestly, he thought it was Clotho.

"I can only assume that I am the Prince of Darkness in that statement, given how devilishly attractive I am in black. It's my signature color, you know." He winked at the one with the worst hunch. Lachesis? When this was over, he was finally going to commit to learning which was which.

"A slight of color and a fate to empower," the third said, clearly Atropos.

"Ladies, may I formally introduce you to Persephone, daughter of Demeter." Hades held out his arm toward Persephone, who came up next to him and inclined her head.

If she was taken aback by the appearances of the fates, she didn't show it. If he hadn't been so godsdamn distracted by her, he would have warned her.

"The child of two, we know well." They said as one in their eerie way.

"Lovely. Makes this easy. I'm sure you are well aware, but Demeter laid a rather nasty curse on her," Hades said lightly.

The three looked at each other in silent conversation and, not for the first time, he wondered if they could speak into each other's minds. It was like they were one entity divided into three. It was creepy on the best of days. Annoying on the worst.

"A fate sought to be avoided only strengthens the thread that binds it," one said.

Understanding gathered at the corner of his mind and he grabbed it like a dying man with one last request.

"Demeter cursed her to avoid another fate," he said slowly.

The one with the largest hump squealed with delight. This was why they liked him. The Fates, whether by design or their own volition, made a rule of not speaking plainly. If you could grasp at their riddles and hints, then they were more inclined to speak to you.

"What fate could be worse than this?" Persephone growled.

That wouldn't do. Hades put his hand on her lower back and pulled her into his side, where she fit like a puzzle piece against him. Pushing down the thought, he bent down and said quietly, "Easy," before raising his most charming smile to The Fates, who watched with eager eyes as if they were consuming them slowly.

"Fate entangles and strangles when the bargainer bears ill will," the unhumped one said.

"Delightful." Hades smiled, though he would have much rather told them all that they were next to useless. "As it so happens, we are interested in breaking Persephone of her little duck curse."

"Swan," Persephone gritted out.

Good. Let her be distracted with irritation for him rather than at the fates who would cease being helpful the moment they decided this wasn't entertaining.

"Right, anyway, any helpful tips? Suggestions? Detailed directions?" His hand was warm on her back, distracting.

The fates exchanged glances once more. "Those who wish to break a fate must give up memories innate."

Hades went completely and utterly still. Fuck no. His hand tightened on Persephone's back.

Despite the rage that was gathered in him, he said lightly, "Surely you can do better than that, ladies."

He knew it was a mistake as soon as the words left his mouth and as one the Fate's lips turned thin, their eyes narrowing.

"If the darkness seeks to keep what belongs to it, then the test of will reclaim it," they said before disappearing in a swirl of dust that smelt of rot and decay.

Persephone whirled on him. "What did you do?"

"Saved us from enduring more of a waste of time," he ground out.

Persephone shoved him, anxiety and anger warring within her. "You know what they said and you didn't like it. I felt it in you, so tell me."

Her words caught him off guard. She *felt* it in him. What the fuck was that supposed to mean?

"I told you The Fates rarely give you the answers you want. It wasn't all a waste. At least you know that your mother was trying to save you from a different fate."

Her cheeks were flushed and her breathing was ragged as she glared at him. "Tell. Me. What. They. Said."

"No," he answered, before turning away.

He wouldn't entertain the possibility of what The Fates suggested because it was the same thing as a death sentence. He wanted to fuck with Demeter, not kill her daughter.

Her footsteps were as loud as the night as she followed him, each as solemn as a death drum.

"Hades, you asshole, don't walk away from me!" she shouted.

At least Hermes and Hecate had left, or else her shouting would wake them and he'd have to deal with them on top of this little tantrum.

"Last I checked, ducks don't give orders to gods," he said, entering the dining hall, which, as always, was littered with fruit and wine.

"I was a fucking swan," Persephone yelled.

He turned and gave her a placating smile. "Alas, I'm almost positive swans don't give orders to gods either. I'll have to double-check that though, it's less clear than ducks."

She was a fury incarnate. A goddess of rage and retribution. If he wasn't immortal, he might have even feared for his life. There was no use denying she was beautiful, but it was her spirit that called to him like a beacon in the night. So dangerous.

"This isn't a joke. You have no idea what it's been like for me. I've been isolated and forced to be an animal for half my life. There isn't a cost that's too steep. I will pay it. Whatever they said, I will pay it."

Hades held his own anger in a firm fist that threatened to give with each heaving breath she took. He wanted to go find Demeter himself and ask her what fate was so fucking terrible that she would curse her own daughter. He shouldn't have lost his patience with The Fates. This was on him.

Throwing back a glass of wine, Hades set it down and turned to face Persephone, who was only a few inches from him. He could easily grab her and tell her that some things are worse than even curses, but instead, he took a long, steadying breath.

"Is your life worth an eternity of your soul being trapped, never remembering who you were or what you cared about?" He hadn't meant the words to come out with such venom, but he felt on edge and ready for a fight.

The anger that had been boiling in her a moment ago seemed to recede. Her hands clenching and unclenching.

"What do you mean?" she asked slowly, as if she didn't want the answer.

"'Those who wish to break a fate must give up memories inna te.'" He quoted the words that were seared into his mind.

"So I lose my memories. I won't remember anything?" She mulled over the thought and he could see her battle as if she were voicing it aloud.

She was angry with Demeter, but she didn't want to forget her. Even though Demeter didn't deserve it, Persephone loved her. The rest of her memories she would happily sacrifice, but she hesitated for a woman who cursed her. It didn't matter, though. The answer was always no. He had intended to fuck with Demeter, but even he had lines he wouldn't cross.

"It isn't just your memories The Fates want, Persephone. What do you know of my domain?"

She swallowed and he tracked the movement carefully. Something in him coiled and waiting, watched from within.

"Only what Hecate told me last night. That there's Asphodel, the River Styx, Elysium, and Tartarus," she breathed out the words in a way that made her sound winded.

Fucking Hecate saying whatever came into her godsdamned mind.

"And what do you know about the River Styx?" he said with lethal quiet.

She watched him and he could see the hint of fear in her eyes under his scrutiny, but she never once backed down from him.

"That souls who are unworthy of reincarnation are sent there for eternity. They don't rem—" Realization ran over her beautiful face. "The River Styx."

He pulled away from her and filled his wine once more. "That's right, Persephone, The Fates would take away your curse for a small swim through the River Styx, which you would never survive."

"It must be possible else why would they offer it?" she insisted, determination its own curse.

"I told you why. The Fates are testy old hags who are just as bored with immortality as the rest of us, so they play the games that keep them from falling into despair."

"Is that what you are doing with me? Playing a game in order to forget?" she asked, stepping into him, invading his personal space.

Hades very carefully set down his wine and turned to her, their bodies nearly touching. He wrapped his finger and thumb around her chin and lifted her fiery gaze to his. Gods, she smelt like champagne and cinnamon.

"What do you think, Persephone?" he purred.

She was clay in his hands, ready to be molded into something fearsome and undeniable. That fire in her called to his and he was loath to deny it, but she was also cursed. While the cursed part didn't bother him, the years of isolation and loneliness did. Her fire called to his because she was desperate. Lost. She wanted connection and he was the first opportunity. He was a piece of shit, but he wasn't in the habit of taking advantage of vulnerable women.

"Yes," she whispered, her eyes fluttering.

He dropped her chin and turned back to the wine, downing another glass. He should probably put a limit on how much alcohol he consumed. While it took a lot to get him drunk, he was likely pushing the limits.

"Then you would be correct," he said nonchalantly, even though everything inside him screamed it was a lie. It wasn't a fucking lie. That's exactly what this was. He was fucking with Demeter and that was the end of it.

"How do you know I wouldn't survive?" she asked, still fixated on the damn Fates.

He met her fiery gaze. "Because no one has ever survived it."

The woman didn't even flinch. "I could."

"Are you so eager to die?" he threw the words back at her as if they were poison and maybe they were.

"I'm that eager to live," she countered, and he had never been more confident that if anyone could do it, it would have been her. However, it still wasn't an option.

Hades walked away from her, hating each step, but needing it more than he needed air. "You can stay for the time being, but you are stuck with your curse."

He shut the door and when she didn't follow him, he breathed a sigh of relief that was laced with regret. Maybe this was one of The Fates' games after all. Damn Fates.

CHAPTER FOUR

THE GOD OF THE UNDERWORLD IS A DOG PERSON

PERSEPHONE

Whether it was grief or despair that eventually claimed her for sleep, Persephone couldn't have said. All she knew is one minute the tears were endless and the next darkness took her. They had been so close. The Fates, terrifying as they were, had given them the answer, but it wasn't what she had wanted to hear. Even still, she knew she would try it.

Hades might have said that no one had survived, but she could do it. The thing about Persephone was that she was desperate to live. She had spent her entire life in the confines of one lake and one castle, never truly living. Now that she had a taste of the Underworld and the freedom it offered, she had no intention of going back.

The only problem with that was that she was here as long as Hades found enjoyment in the game he was playing. Which meant she was prepared to do whatever it took to keep him interested. The plan was simple. Keep Hades interested and find the River Styx.

Not simple when you've been a cooped-up virgin your whole life. There was no mistaking the heat in Hades' eyes when he watched her, and despite her limited experience, she knew what it meant. He was attracted to her and she would use that to her advantage. Of course, she felt the same pull to him, but there was no way for her to know if that was just the product of years of isolation. There was no denying he was attractive. Dark blue hair, chiseled features she longed to run her fingers over. What was that?

She held her hands to her chest, refusing to acknowledge the ache that had settled into her. No, she knew what the god of the Underworld was. He used until he couldn't use any longer. Anything she felt would be a waste of time, but what he felt was a different story. If there was one thing Persephone had to her name, it was determination.

Throwing on one of Hecate's more simple outfits of dark green pants that were loose along her legs and a matching top that hugged her body, ending an inch above her belly button, she opened her door. She had been given the room across from Hecate's and it was the twin to hers, except without the large balcony.

First things first, she would need to get her bearings. A few trials and errors led Persephone to a series of stairs that led downward and followed. Elation filled her as they dumped her down in the middle of a street. She had done it. This was Asphodel and exactly where she needed to be. Elation quickly gave way to trepidation as she realized she had no idea what to expect from the city of the dead.

Hecate had said souls who weren't ready to pass on made their home here and the idea slid across Persephone's skin like a phantom in the night. Even still, she wouldn't let fear of the unknown hold her back. She had waited her entire life to live and she had no intention of cowering now that she had been given the chance.

Of all the things Persephone might have expected, the scene before her hadn't been it. The city was alive with people coming and going, working and playing as if it were any other day. Nothing about them gave any clue to the fact that they were dead, enough that Persephone began to wonder if Hecate had been telling the truth.

"Hello there, can I help you with something?" His voice was foreign and yet the accent was familiar, itching at the back of her mind.

Given that Persephone had only met a handful of people, it didn't take her long to pinpoint the memory.

"You're Minos."

He tipped his broad-brimmed hat and smiled brightly. "Yes, Lady Persephone, it's an honor to meet you officially."

He appeared for all the world like a living, breathing person, making it hard to rectify that he was most likely dead.

"You know who I am?" she asked.

Minos laughed and she thought he might be in his fourth decade of life with a thin frame and tanned skin. How did one get tan in the Underworld? Did the dead appear as they had in life? Questions littered her mind, making it hard to focus.

"I serve Lord Hades and as such, I make it a point to know new faces. Would you like me to show you around?"

He offered her his arm and she took it despite her trepidation. This was an opportunity and she couldn't afford to not take chances.

"Do all the dead serve him?" she asked while suppressing a shiver.

Minos turned to her, wide-eyed, before he broke out in laughter, his hand resting on his stomach. "Gods, I am not dead, Lady Persephone. I serve Lord Hades willingly in life. The dead do not serve him. What an outrageous idea. The dead are simply dead."

Persephone was quickly finding that she did not like Minos very much. It was one thing to laugh at her, but he had a way of making her feel very small and foolish. She knew it was easy to do, but not even Hades had done that. He had made her feel—well; it had just been different.

"How long have you served Hades?" she asked as they walked.

"A few months. My father served before me and he only recently died. Straight to Elysium, he went." Minos said with a bright smile.

As they came further into the city, people emerged, walking to and fro. Talking to each other and some sold goods, while others seemed to just wander. Boats filled the river with ferrymen rowing. It was an entire city settled on a river that expanded as far as she could see. Lights twinkled from many of the rooms as if to say they were occupied. The cobblestones that separated the river from the city were irregular and uneven, as if they had been there a long time.

"Are all these people dead?" she asked.

"Of course they are. Not ready to move on yet, so they gather here. Some like to pretend they aren't dead, like Anatole here." He gestured to a man with sun-kissed skin who was selling a wagon full of fruit.

"Good day, Miss. Would you like something from the cart?" he asked her with a wide smile.

Nothing about him told her that he was dead, except that maybe the light in his eyes was slightly dulled.

"She don't want nothing from you, Anatole. Leave the lady alone." A woman in a bright red dress said.

Her hair was the same red as her dress and her lips matched. She was stunning, but when Persephone looked closely, she saw the same dullness in her eyes.

"Aye, I am one of the dead, too. We all are except for Minos. It's rare to see another down here except for the occasional god or goddess, of course. My name is Basilia, Lia for short. It's a pleasure to meet you, Lady Persephone."

Persephone wasn't even sure the woman took a breath that entire time, but the smile she gave her felt genuine and that was worth something.

"Very nice to meet you, Lia."

"Not that you asked, but I can see you are curious. I've been dead for going on twenty years, but I can't bring myself to go to Elysium and await reincarnation. You see, life was difficult as a woman. I was tossed around from man to man. First, my father, then my husband, then another husband when that one died and it just was terrible. I think part of me thinks if I hold out a little bit longer maybe life won't be so hard for us women though that's assuming I'd even be a woman. I suppose I could come back as a man and wouldn't that just be a laugh? Though I wouldn't remember being a woman, but then I have to believe we hold on to some things, don't you agree?" She was watching Persephone expectantly.

"Are all the dead as self-aware?" As soon as she asked, she cursed herself, thinking it was likely very rude.

Lia laughed. "We come in all shapes and sizes. The only way to find out is to talk to them. These are good folk, but you'll find life was hard for most of them."

Persephone bit her lip as she considered. "Thank you for being so open with me. I'm very grateful."

Lia's smile was radiant as she inclined her head. "If you ever need someone to talk to, I own a hat shop down the way. I'm always up for a bit of company."

Persephone's eyes watered. She reached for them and pulled her hand away, looking at the liquid. She was crying. Why was she crying? Yet there was a foreign sadness that felt heavy inside her, along with something she struggled to name.

"Oh, you sweet dear, it's just as I suspected. You are starved for kindness. Minos, I'll be stealing the lady from you, after all." Lia said.

Minos rolled his eyes but continued along the path as if nothing had occurred at all. Persephone wished she knew if the man was actually strange or if she was just not used to people.

Lia put her arm around her and squeezed her. "Let's go find you a hat."

Persephone nodded and gladly leaned into the woman. Maybe she was starved for kindness, but the heaviness in her seemed to subside slightly under Lia's calming chatter. She led her to a shop that was a dark green with gold lettering. *A Hat For Any Occasion* was written on the top.

"I loved hats when I was alive, so it made sense to own a shop in death. The nice thing about Asphodel is that whatever you need is there for you. Take Andole, for example. He was a farmer and sold fruit, so it brings him comfort to do so now. One day when he's ready to move on, that might not be the case, but for now, it's exactly what he needs. Me, on the other hand, I need to know that I am independent and so that comes in the form of my shop. I take good care of it and it takes good care of me."

Persephone felt at home the moment she entered the shop. It was small, with only a small counter, two chairs, a full-length mirror, and a litany of hats of every shape, size, and color along the walls.

"Now let's see. I suspect this headdress would be exactly what you need." She lifted a gold and dark green cloth that was nearly identical to the color Persephone wore. "May I?"

Persephone nodded and Lia got to work on manipulating her hair so that it was tied and fell over her left shoulder. She reached up and placed one part of the headdress over the top of her head and the other one underneath her tied hair. When she was done, she gestured for Persephone to go to the mirror.

Her breath caught as she took in her own reflection. She hardly looked like the woman who had existed in days and years, never truly living. Here, she was thriving. Her skin seemed more luminescent, and her eyes were brighter. Was it that she wasn't forced to be a swan, or was it something to do with the Underworld? Either way, it was another reason she needed to make sure she never went back.

"See, even Asphodel gives to you, my lady," Lia said with a smile, though her eyes were lined with silver.

Persephone turned on her heels and reached for the woman. "Did I upset you?"

Lia shook her head even as fresh tears bloomed. "These are happy tears, my lady. Something about having you here just feels right, you know. Makes me think of my own children. How much I loved being with them. They are all grown and old by now, but I hope they've lived good lives."

Persephone didn't think, didn't plan. She wrapped her arms around the other woman and rested her head on her shoulder.

"I think if they had you as their mother, no matter the amount of time, then they were very lucky," Persephone said quietly, her own tears coming freely.

Lia pulled back and pressed a kiss to Persephone's cheek. "Thank you, my lady, I think it's about time I get on with it and get to going, don't you?"

Persephone had only a moment to register the words as she stumbled forward, the weight of Lia gone. Staring with wide eyes, she peered around the shop that had once been full of hats and found nothing but the stone of the caverns that made up the Underworld. Lia was gone. A terrible sadness threatened to overtake her, quickly followed by a sense of rightness she couldn't explain.

Persephone made for the door, but a series of black tendrils appeared from the ground and wrapped around her, gentle and yet demanding. Her panic was quickly swallowed as they pulled her down onto the stone floor, only to deposit her into an unfamiliar room.

"What did you do?" Hades asked.

Persephone spun and found him seated at a desk in a room that was about the same size as her room. It had the same balcony along the length of it overlooking the city and a similar fireplace as Hecate's room, but this was composed of a desk and a small sitting area. Hades was leaning forward, rubbing his jawline as he so often did, though she had yet to determine what he was feeling when he did.

"I didn't do anything," she said unconvincingly, still trying to adapt to the knowledge that he could easily pull her from anywhere at any time.

A low whine sounded behind Hades, followed by a groan.

"Are you all right?" she asked, genuinely concerned as the sounds seemed to be coming below him.

As soon as the words were out, a dog appeared from behind the desk. It was all black with a square face that might have been intimidating if its panting didn't make it appear as if it were smiling. It trotted over to Persephone and after one of two sniffs, laid a very wet kiss on her hand. Persephone laughed and kneeled, running her hands over the dog's soft, short fur.

"And who are you?" she asked with a smile.

"A terrible guard dog. Cerberus, if you keep that up, I swear I will replace you," Hades said dryly.

The dog seemed unconcerned about its master's threat and curled up in a small ball at Persephone's feet.

"He doesn't seem too worried. Maybe you are losing your touch," Persephone said, humor chasing away whatever had been threatening to cave in around her.

"Maybe," Hades mused, watching her.

Hades pushed up from his chair and walked leisurely to the front of his desk and leaned on it, his dark gaze consuming her.

"Do you have any idea how long Basalia has been in Asphodel?" he asked.

Persephone's hand stilled on Cerberus. "She said about twenty years."

"Two hundred years, Persephone. She was a resident in Asphodel for two hundred years."

Her breath caught and the way he was watching her made it hard to take the next breath. She couldn't tell whether he was displeased with her or not. Everything she had thought she had gathered about him fell away beneath that knowing gaze.

"Are you angry with me?" she asked, though she wasn't quite sure why she cared.

Hades snorted and his lips quirked up in that half smile that he only did when he was truly amused.

"I know every soul that comes and goes from my realm. I can see the lives they lived, what they wished they had done differently, their hopes, their grief, their despair. All of it belongs to me the moment they enter the Underworld. I can guess from what I see how long they will remain in Asphodel. Basalia was born a princess. She was married to a man three times her age who used her and abused her. When she found out she was pregnant, she took matters into her own hands and killed him. Smothered him in his sleep. To the world, it looked like an accident, but instead of being free, she was married to his brother who was just as old and just as cruel, but more cunning. He never gave her a chance to do to him what he suspected she had done to his brother. If she was pregnant, he was careful to avoid her stomach in his beatings. After bearing him five children that she loved and tried to protect from him, he got drunk and beat her to death."

Cerberus whined and nudged Persephone's hand where it hovered over him, but it was difficult to see through the tears that blurred her vision. Lia had been kind and gentle. That life had been so cruel to her was a tragedy.

"That's terrible," Persephone managed.

"It is," Hades agreed. "It's also why I expected her to be in Asphodel for at least five centuries, if not double that. Yet in a single meeting with you, she felt ready to leave for Elysium. So forgive me for repeating myself, but what did you do?"

Persephone sniffed and stood, wiping at her tears. "I only talked with her. She helped me pick out this." She reached for her headdress. "Hades, I don't even remember exactly what we talked about. She told me about how Asphodel worked and—and when she showed me my reflection I thought about how healthy and different I seemed. It made me emotional and when I looked back, she was crying. I hugged her. She told me about her children and I told her they were better off for having her as their mother and then she just—she left."

Hades was silent as his gaze consumed her. He was three feet away from her, but it felt for all the world as if he was right in front of her. It was intimate and searching.

"What do you think happens next, Persephone?" he asked, darkness in his voice.

"Excuse me?"

"In this game we are playing. What do you think happens next? The Fates won't give you more answers and the one they did was a nonstarter. As far as the world is concerned, you will always be cursed. So what do you think happens next?"

Persephone straightened. "I'm not going back."

Hades pushed from the desk with the kick of his foot and whistled, making Cerberus jump from where he was napping and crawl back behind Hades' desk. Persephone sucked in a breath as Hades circled her, his hand drifting to take a piece of her hair and wrap it around his finger.

"You wish to live out your days in the Underworld with only the dead and myself for company?" his eyes were on the piece of hair he twirled around his finger, running his thumb over it. It sent a shiver through her, and his eyes jerked to hers. Something warm and dark lurking in them.

Persephone swallowed. "Yes."

Hades drew in a sharp breath. "The living don't belong in the Underworld."

"You are here, Minos is here," she said, breathless and with significantly less conviction than she had meant to.

"We come and go. None of the living truly stay in the Underworld, but you would." His words were silk.

"Yes," she breathed.

Her body ached in a way she had never felt before. It was as if she was on fire and she suspected he was the cure, despite the fact that she was entirely sure he was the reason for it.

"What if your life here would be worse? You would never see the sun, stars, or moon again. You would be unable to come and go. The moment you leave the Underworld is the moment the curse finds its way back to you."

"I could go at night."

It was the wrong thing to say. He dropped her hair and walked back to the desk as if the heat that had been building between them had all been in her imagination. It hadn't been though and gods help her, but she wanted more. More than that, she needed him to want her. To not get bored and send her back.

She stepped forward, and even with his back to her, he stilled. Sucking in a breath of air, Persephone crossed the distance and placed her hand on his arm. His muscles were taut beneath her touch, as if he were ready for an attack.

"Hades," she whispered, and she thought she saw a subtle shiver run through him.

The door burst open, and Hermes appeared, worry etched on his face. The moment he took in the scene before him, he groaned and slid into the chair.

"Demeter is really fucking mad," he said.

CHAPTER FIVE

HOW A GOD LIES TO HIMSELF

HADES

I t was unlikely that Hermes had ever had such good timing in his entire life. As it were, had he entered the room much later, all of Hades' good intentions would have crumbled. He had been two seconds from giving in and throwing Persephone on the desk and teaching her everything he knew. She was in his fucking blood, and he couldn't carve her out. Everything about her called to him and it only grew with every fucking encounter he had with her.

What did it mean that she had eased a soul effortlessly into Elysium? There wasn't a precedent for it, for her.

Thankfully, Hermes' interruption had made her pull away from him. He needed the distance to clear his head. Taking a quiet breath, he situated himself at his desk, his cock hard from the thoughts that burned in him. Of all the ways he wanted to taste her.

"People know by now it wasn't just a swan, but oddly enough, no one has guessed correctly. She's lost her damn mind."

Hermes' voice was like ice on his skin, soothing the fire in his veins as he droned on. At least there was that.

"Are you even fucking listening, Hades?" Hermes practically yelled.

"What do you mean, she stopped the harvest?" Persephone said, her hand clutched to her chest and worry playing over her face.

What did it mean that he wanted to take it away? To ease her worry and reassure her. This was getting out of control. He needed to get it together.

"I mean exactly that. The mortals can't grow anything. There's a frost over the land, and she says she won't restore it until she has you back."

"That's manipulative as shit," Hades ground out.

"That sounds exactly like her." Persephone frowned.

"Either way, you need to go back. Before long, she is going to get Zeus involved and they are going to find out you took her and war is going to break out and it's all going to go to shit." Hermes groaned.

"She's not leaving," Hades said the words before he even realized what he had done.

Persephone and Hermes jerked their gazes at him in unison.

"You've made your point, Hades, it's time to give her back," Hermes pleaded.

Hades turned his gaze to Persephone, who was watching him with those intense blue eyes he saw every time he closed his eyes. "She leaves when she wants to leave."

Persephone's mouth turned up in a devastating smile. It was enough to nearly bring him to his knees. Fates, he should send her back. This was a fucking mistake, and yet he knew he wouldn't. He was a selfish bastard.

"Are you fucking serious?" Hermes shouted, running his hand nervously through his hair.

Hades kept his eyes on Persephone. "Do you want to leave?"

Two dimples shone on either side of her smile as she shook her head slowly. "No."

Hades shrugged, turning to Hermes. "Then she stays."

"You are going to get us all thrown into Tartarus," Hermes whined.

"I would very much enjoy watching Zeus try," Hades said with amusement he barely felt.

"He could do that?" Persephone asked.

"Yes," Hermes said.

"Theoretically," Hades corrected.

He watched her as she warred with herself, but much to his pleasure, she didn't beg to be sacrificed for their freedom. No, Persephone was made of something stronger than self-sacrifice. She had been denied her life for long enough that she was desperate to seize it at every opportunity.

"Would he actually intervene?" Persephone asked, and he was impressed she knew the right questions to ask.

"No," Hades answered. "Zeus is self-absorbed and only interested in what immediately benefits him. The only reason he is in charge is because he is stronger than Poseidon and me. Other than that, he's fairly easy to figure out."

"Then why are you worried, Hermes?" she asked.

Hermes ran his hand over his face and sighed dramatically. "Because Hades is partly correct. If Demeter becomes enough of a problem, Zeus will take note enough to intervene just to get some peace."

"And I will handle him if that should happen," Hades said, irritation making him short-tempered.

"And what about Hecate and me? We can't just handle your big brother like that."

"Hermes, if you keep worrying you will get frown lines," Hades said, shuffling his papers.

"Hades," Hermes begged.

"Goodbye, Hermes," Hades said as he waved a hand, and Hermes disappeared in a black ring of smoke.

"What did you do to him?" Persephone asked.

"Similar to shutting the door to the Underworld for a short while. Hermes is the messenger of the gods and by definition can come and go as he pleases, but I can deter him for a little while, at least."

Persephone stepped forward and hesitated. "Why did you tell him I could stay?"

"Because you can." Hades' eyes ran over the report in front of him, but fuck if he actually knew what it said. Her presence was too consuming.

"But why?" she insisted, looking at him for all the world as if he were the prey and she the predator.

He found he didn't mind that notion nearly as much as he thought he would. Fuck, he needed to get it together.

"Because it suits me for now," he said and raised his hand, depositing her safely in her room.

His cock was hard again with need. What he needed was to get this out of his system. Unbuttoning his pants, he took his cock in his hand and pumped it once, twice. He closed his eyes and imagined that he had been depraved enough to throw her on his desk and taste her. He would have taken his time teaching her how to let him into her mouth, first teeth, then tongue. The sounds she made would have him wanting to bury his cock in her, but he would wait. He would take his damn time, even if it killed him to do it.

He would have run his hands along her chest and down that perfect stomach until she begged him for more. She wouldn't beg long. Instead, he would rid her of those tight pants and take in every curve of her. The memory of it wasn't enough, that was before he knew her. Knew her fire and her strength. He would memorize every part of her with the knowledge that she was more than just beautiful. She was powerful.

She would have spread her legs for him and he would have worshiped her as he buried his face between her thighs, tasting and learning her. She would beg him for release and he would give it to her, crying out his name as she came hard enough to see stars.

His own release came with the vision in his mind and he lay back in his chair, breathing heavily. That was enough. He just needed to get it out of his system and now he could go back to being a morally gray god with decent intentions.

That was enough.

CHAPTER SIX

HADES IS A LIAR

PERSEPHONE

Two days had passed since the god of the Underworld unceremoniously threw her out of his office. Two days since she had last seen him. According to Minos, Hades had things to see to that were strictly Underworld business. When she pressed him for more information, she got nothing in return. Hecate and Hermes were nowhere to be found and overall, she was already feeling bored.

Persephone relegated herself to the library, where she had found books on every matter she could want to know. She dove into the history of the gods, needing to know everything her mother had denied her. She was absorbed in a story about Athena losing a weaving contest and being vindictive enough to tear her opponent from death, only to make her a spider when the door to the library opened. Her heart leapt thinking it was him.

Instead, a man with a broad chest and curly brown hair down to his shoulders was appraising her. "*You* are not my brother."

Poseidon. He was easily recognizable from the portraits in the books she had been devouring.

"Can I help you?" she asked, unsure what she was supposed to do with the third most powerful god in Hades' library.

Even if she hadn't been raised in isolation, she suspected she wouldn't know what to do.

"You are also not dead," he said with his head tilted to the side as if she were some puzzle he wanted to solve.

"You are correct on both accounts," she said, shelving the book she had been reading.

There was one thing her mother had taught her, and that was that fear was a weakness. Never show fear to someone who could use it against you. The glint and upturned lips on the god said he wouldn't hesitate to use it against her. So she would become immovable. He would grow bored with her and move on.

He stalked towards her, raking his eyes over her body as if it were his to enjoy. Rage burned in her and she wondered what it would feel like to slap someone. Maybe she would learn soon enough.

"You know, I have a theory," he drawled.

"I'm sure I would be delighted to hear it, but as you came to see Hades and Hades is clearly not here, I will let him know you stopped by."

Undeterred by her words, he stepped forward until her back was pressed against the bookshelf and she had nowhere to go. Her mother may not have taught her enough, but the other lesson she imparted was that men were dangerous. They would covet and use your body as they saw fit if given the chance. Persephone was determined that would not be what happened here.

"If you've been down here for a spell, you might not realize what a mess it is up there. Gods fighting, accusing each other of crimes, the mortal world wasting away. It occurred to me though who was glaringly absent in all of this. My brother. Very unusual for him."

"Was there a question?" she asked, her hand gripping one of the books as he raised his hands above her head, pinning her to the shelf.

"Actually, there was. Who are you and what do you have to do with Demeter and my errant brother?" He ran a finger down her chin.

Persephone acted. She jerked the book from the shelf and slammed it across his head. Ducking beneath his arms, she made to escape, but he grabbed her around her waist and pulled her against his body. With no options left to her, she screamed. Kicking and shoving, she tried to get away, but he was a god and she didn't stand a chance.

"Put her the fuck down right now, Poseidon, or I will throw you in Tartarus myself."

His voice was the sweetest sound she had ever heard.

Poseidon laughed, but he released her, and she ran, crashing into Hades, who ran his hands and eyes over her, looking for signs of injury.

"I'm all right," she said, as he placed his hands on either side of her face.

There was a wildness in his eyes she had never seen before, like a storm in the night.

"Hades, I'm all right."

Despite his nod, he didn't believe her, or rather couldn't.

"I'm not. She clocked me with a damn book," Poseidon grumbled.

It was as if his voice was all the reminder Hades needed and he turned, black tendrils of magic snaking out and wrapping around Poseidon, throwing him against the bookshelf. Books tumbled out from their resting places, but Poseidon merely stood and dusted himself off.

"Fascinating." He smiled.

Another wave of power shot from Hades, but Poseidon was ready this time. His own power was made from the ocean itself and it cut through Hades' ropes easily.

"If you stop throwing a temper tantrum, we could talk about this, you know," Poseidon hummed.

The two gods dueled with evenly matched strikes until Poseidon sighed. "I'm bored. Also, since when does Demeter have a daughter?"

Hades stilled, his power retreating back into him.

"Also, I have other questions," Poseidon said, righting his gray shirt.

"Leave, Poseidon," Hades ordered.

She craned around his body to see Poseidon smirking, looking between them with growing amusement.

"I only just got here and I promise to behave, plus she did more damage than I did. I'll probably have a headache, eventually." He threw himself into one of the chairs and sighed dramatically.

Hades ignored him and turned to her, his eyes still held the stormy night sky, but they had settled slightly. "You should go."

Persephone put her hand on her hip as if she hadn't just run to him for help. "I'm not going anywhere and can't you just do that thing—" She waved her hand. "—that you did to Hermes."

"Shit, Hermes knows too? That explains why he's been sweating more than usual." Poseidon laughed at his own joke.

Hades glared at her, and she realized her error.

"Sorry." She mouthed, and she actually was, mostly because she didn't like Poseidon and anything Hades didn't want him to know was something she didn't want him to know.

He just rolled his eyes and walked to Poseidon, taking the chair opposite him. Hades seemed absolutely unbothered by his presence as he crossed his ankle over his knee and leaned back in his chair.

"What will it take to keep you quiet about this?" he asked.

"Resorting to bargaining already? I hardly recognize you, brother. Usually, there are threats and glaring before this point. Does Hecate know too?" He turned his head towards Persephone and she bit her lip, stilling any words from leaving her lips. "Damn, Hecate didn't give away a thing. I'm almost impressed."

Persephone groaned, and Hades pinched the bridge of his nose. "You are a blight on my existence."

"And yet I hadn't pegged you for one to steal feral damsels in distress."

"I didn't." He sighed. "I stole a goose."

"Wasn't it meant to be a swan?" Poseidon asked, turning to Persephone and nodding. "Yeah, that's what I thought."

"Dammit, Persephone, if you are going to shout every little detail to him, could you please leave," Hades growled.

"I'm not! I'm literally not doing anything!" she wasn't. She wasn't even blinking more than usual.

"It's all over your damn face." Hades ran a hand over his face and through his hair.

"I can't help how my face looks." Persephone crossed her arms.

"It's a very pretty face," Poseidon offered.

"Do you have a death wish, Brother?" Hades growled.

"It's like a delightful free for all in here. She tells me whatever I need to know and you give away the rest by being an overbearing asshole. You two had better hope none of the others happen to wander down here or you both are done for," Poseidon said with grand amusement.

"What do you want, Poseidon?" Hades asked, his thread of patience dangerously thin.

The door opened and Hermes walked through. "Bad news. I think Pos—Oh, shit."

"What took you so long? Have a seat!" Poseidon gestured to the empty chair next to Hades.

"A little fucking slow, don't you think, Hermes?" Hades spat.

Hermes, who was in fact sweating, huffed out an irritated breath. "I shouldn't have to be a part of this at all. I was merely a witness to the crime."

"When Hades stole Demeter's swan, who is actually her daughter, Persephone." Poseidon summarized.

Hermes cursed and slid into his chair.

"Why was she a swan? Never mind." He twisted in his chair to look back at her. "Why were you a swan?"

Persephone stilled her features, careful not to give anything away.

"A curse? How about that?"

"How do you do that? I made sure not to do anything that time," she asked, holding out her arms.

"You did very well. I actually was just guessing because you didn't give anything away, but thank you for confirming," Poseidon said with a bow of his head.

"Persephone," Hades warned.

"I've been a swan half my life, I don't know how to do this—" She gestured between all of them. "Whatever this is."

"Half your life. Interesting," Poseidon said.

"Which is why I told you to leave," Hades said.

"Well, I want to know what's happening." She frowned.

The door opened and Hecate surveyed the room before walking over to the liquor cart. "Poseidon knows."

"Thanks, Hecate," Hades growled. "Could you all be less incompetent for even a minute?"

"Rude," Hecate said, winking at Persephone before she downed her glass. "Are you sick of him yet?"

Persephone opened her mouth to tell her absolutely she was, but Poseidon spoke. "No, she's not. When's the last time either of you were here?"

Hecate looked at Hades and then at her, then back to Hades again. "Are you fucking kidding me? As if this wasn't bad enough?"

Persephone had the feeling she had missed something important as Hades glared at Hecate.

"It's not a thing. Poseidon is just being an asshole," he said, as if he were bored.

Hecate narrowed her eyes. "It had better not be a thing."

"It's a thing," Poseidon said.

"What's a thing?" Persephone asked and Poseidon choked on the liquor he had just swallowed.

"Nothing is a thing," Hades said. "Is there a purpose to all of you being here? Unlike you all, I actually have a job to do."

"Like what?" Hecate asked, leaning against the bookshelf.

"Like maintaining the barrier on Tartarus. The Titans have been in an especially foul mood lately. So unless you would like them roaming around free again, can we get on with whatever this is?"

"Have The Fates answered yet?" Hecate asked.

"Oh, they are testy old hags," Poseidon said, with a knowing nod.

"Fuck, Hecate, do you want to give him the layout of the Underworld while you're at it?" Hades shot out.

"He already knows. There's no point in pretending he doesn't." She shrugged.

"Between you and Persephone, he will know every godsdamn thing that happens down here."

"It's not my fault." Persephone frowned.

"How could it be? It's not your fault you've been sheltered in isolation your whole life with only Demeter for company," Poseidon said.

"Thank you," breathed Persephone, begrudgingly grateful for someone to finally understand, even if it was him.

"Persephone!" Hades growled and three black tendrils shot around her and dragged her over and into his lap. "Next time you think about saying anything, you look at me first and I'll tell you if it's a bad idea, all right?"

Persephone swallowed, aware of everywhere their bodies touched and the ache that built in her once more. She thought about arguing or asking to sit somewhere else, but all that came out was a nod.

"Excellent," Hades said, voice tight. "The Fates were useless as usual and gave us nothing."

"What about the witch, Circe?" Hecate asked.

"No," Hades answered quickly.

His hand rested on her knee and tightened a fraction. Understanding dawned on her. He was helping her to filter what she gave away and didn't. She settled into him slightly and felt him stiffen beneath her.

"They didn't tell you anything?" Poseidon asked skeptically.

"Nothing actually useful," Hades said, his thumb running in light circles over her thigh.

How was that part of the game? It was very distracting and Persephone found herself drawn to each movement and wondering what it would feel like if he—No. She banished the thoughts. Unhelpful.

"What were you asking The Fates, by the way?" Poseidon asked.

"You ask a lot of questions for someone who was uninvited," Hades said.

"Yes, but I also talk a lot when I feel left out, so please include me lest I have to go elsewhere for friends," Poseidon sulked.

"I don't think I like you," Persephone said, assessing the god before her.

Hades' thumb stilled, and she felt a slight chuckle move in his chest.

Poseidon winked. "I bet I could change your mind."

Hades' hand tightened around her leg possessively. "Make another comment like that again, and I'll feed you to Cerberus."

Persephone was about to point out that Cerberus was as harmless as a fly when the shattering of glass drew her attention to Hecate, who stood with her mouth wide open.

Poseidon held out his hand to her and then gestured to Hades and Persephone. "See, I told you."

"Shit," Hermes groaned.

"You said it wasn't a thing, Hades," Hecate accused.

So they were back to this again. She doubted she would get an actual answer this time, either.

"I lied," Hades said, dryly.

Hecate's slim face flashed with panic. "Oh no, no, no, we are putting her right back where you found her."

Persephone understood that well enough and made to stand, but Hades pulled her back down.

"She isn't going anywhere. Like I told Hermes, she leaves when she wants to leave," Hades said, soothing her panic.

Hecate glared at him, but she turned to Persephone. "Your mother is destroying the mortal lands looking for you. People, real people, are dying, Persephone."

"Don't guilt her into leaving just because Demeter is a manipulative bitch," Hades growled.

"The least she can do is go talk to her so she can stop killing innocent people," Hecate said.

Hades scowled. "Yes, and I'm sure the woman who cursed her for her entire fucking life will happily have a heart-to-heart and let her live her life as she sees fit."

"That's not our business, Hades," Hecate shouted.

"The fuck it isn't," Hades shot back and Persephone could feel the storm raging in him.

"This is my decision," Persephone said, looking at him, and there was frustration and anger in the eyes that met hers. "It's my decision to make. That's what you said. I get to decide when I leave."

"Persephone," he warned. "You walk out of here and she will never let you go. You know that."

"There must be a way," she tried.

"There's not. I didn't know what—who I was stealing when I took you, so I would be granted leniency for that, but if I knowingly took you again, even Zeus would have to intervene. It's part of what makes immortals able to function together for millennia. There are unwritten rules and breaking them has consequences."

"What if I told them I wanted to leave?" she asked.

"It wouldn't be enough. Demeter is a goddess. Her wants weigh more than yours in the eyes of Olympus. So know that if you choose to leave, because make no mistake, it is your choice, it'll mean you return to the life you had before with no hope of reprieve."

The thought of going back made her want to hide behind him and let him scare off anyone who tried to take her, but Hecate's plea was ringing in her ears.

When she spoke, she was surprised at how calm her voice sounded. "I need time to decide. I know what that means, but I told you once I wasn't going back. I don't want to be the reason people die, but I also am not a good enough person to go back and sacrifice the freedom that I've found."

"We could convince Demeter to come here," Hermes offered.

"It's an option, but ultimately a last resort," Hades said, resuming his gentle exploration with his thumb.

"Hades, you are a fucking idiot," Hecate said.

"Can we go back to the part where Persephone gives away why you called The Fates?" Poseidon said.

Persephone turned her gaze to Hades, who raised a single eyebrow. Her choice. He was giving her the room to make her own decision, which after a lifetime of being denied felt amazing. She turned to Poseidon.

"Like you said, they are testy old hags, so there really was no point to it," she said sweetly.

Poseidon shook his head in disappointment. "And you were so helpful before."

"I'm a quick learner," she said and Hades' finger stilled on her a fraction before he continued.

"I bet you are." Poseidon winked at her and the next moment, he was gone in a wave of black smoke.

"Hades!" Hermes and Hecate yelled at once.

"He won't say anything. He's an asshole, but he likes the promise of drama. He will want to draw it out as long as possible," Hades explained.

Hecate bit her finger, looking between Hades and Persephone with growing anxiety. "This is really fucked up on so many levels."

"Hardly helpful to state the obvious." Hades ground out.

It was in that moment Persephone decided she would start keeping a list of questions she needed answers to. The first of being how they always seemed to know what the other was talking about without actually saying it.

"You need to make an appearance or more than Poseidon will get suspicious," Hermes urged.

"Fine. Is there anything else you two need?" Hades said with ripe irritation.

Hecate frowned, indecision playing over her face. "I just think—"

She disappeared in a puff of smoke, Hermes followed a second after. With only Persephone and Hades left, she was acutely aware of how they were positioned. She wasn't sure what to make of it except that she didn't hate it.

"Where do they go when you do that?" she asked curiously.

"Outside the gates to the Underworld. From there they can get themselves to wherever they please," he answered, all his irritation dissipated as he watched her closely.

"Will they be mad?"

"I don't care," he answered.

Persephone bit her lip, considering. "But they are your friends?"

Hades' eyes dropped to her lips before lifting his eyes to hers. "Hermes and Hecate are. Poseidon is more of an obligation, though right now I can think of several ways I could torture him."

"Because of the thing that isn't a thing, but is?" she asked.

Hades stilled beneath her, his eyes taking on a heat that reminded her of a fire. The intensity made her second guess the confidence that had made her ask and she brought her hands together, feeling the soothing way they rubbed together as if the motion could ground her. Hades reached up and took her hands in his.

"You're nervous," he said.

"There's just a lot I don't understand, but that I *want* to understand," she said, feeling as if the honesty left her exposed.

Hades' lips turned up a fraction. "Ask me."

"What is the thing?" it was the one question she needed to know.

His smile fell and his eyes searched hers. "That I feel very—protective of you."

Her chest felt tight. "Why?"

There wasn't a way to be prepared when he raised his thumb to run over her bottom lip. Her entire body seemed to hone in on the sensation as if she were locked in time. A chill ran down her back, and it was something entirely consuming.

"You bite your lip when you are nervous." His voice was made of midnight and dark things.

Persephone was confident that she wasn't breathing, but that it was perfectly fine. "That doesn't feel like the answer to my question."

The side of his mouth quirked up. "What do you think the answer is, Persephone?"

The way he said her name felt like a caress, and she shivered. His hand trailed from her lips and down her neck. It was tantalizing and thrilling. She should have been nervous and maybe she was, but mostly she just knew that she didn't want him to stop.

"Because you want me," she said, knowing it was the truth.

His hand paused as if he hadn't expected her to name it. "Does that scare you?"

"No," she breathed, because the truth was that something about him called to her. It felt almost like she imagined a siren's call would be. Beautiful, demanding, encompassing.

Hades drew in a sharp breath as his fingers trailed further down toward her breasts.

"Do you want me to stop?" he asked.

"No," she pleaded.

"I should." His fingers slipped inside her shirt, and she gasped.

"But you won't," she prayed.

He teased and rubbed at her nipple, and she threw her head back. It sent pulses through her body to pool low in her. An ache grew with each flick of his fingers, making her clench her legs together as if it would dispel the need building there. All the while, his gaze consumed her every movement, every sound. She felt on display for him, and it only made the ache grow.

"Not unless you tell me to stop," he said with a touch of breathlessness.

She shifted and felt him hard beneath her. It shot a thrill through her.

"You want me," she repeated.

His eyes were an inferno. "Very fucking much."

The heady way he said the words had her whimpering. He withdrew his fingers, and she thought maybe she had done something wrong, but then he was trailing them lower, and anticipation built inside her.

"The things I could show you, Persephone."

She wanted that very much. All of it. Her mind felt murky at best, but she knew that whatever he wanted to show her, she would gladly learn.

Her body ached, and she squirmed, needing more, but he pulled his hand from where it was running across her stomach. Taking her chin between his thumb and forefinger, he tilted her head down. His lips were parted, and his eyes were hungry on hers.

"Persephone." Maybe it was a question or maybe an answer.

It didn't matter. She had spent her entire life waiting for something to happen, to be free, and she was done waiting. Persephone brought her lips to his, and the surprise in him was quickly extinguished by desire as he opened for her, inviting. She might have been clumsy, but he knew exactly what he was doing.

His mouth moved over hers, finding a rhythm that left her feeling hot all over. She twisted in his lap so their chests were pressed together, her hands on either side of his face as if he would decide this was a terrible idea and pull away from her.

His hand threaded through her hair, sending shivers down her back, while the other held her tight against him as if he had the same fear. His tongue slipped into her mouth, hesitant, asking. Persephone hadn't lied when she said she'd always been a quick learner. She pushed her own tongue into him, and he moaned against her mouth.

The pure heat that ran through her was enough to convince her she would do anything to coax that sound from him again. This was more than she ever thought kissing could be, and it was all she ever wanted to do for the rest of her life. Except her hips seemed to shift of their own accord, and she knew there was more that she wanted. More that he could give her. She ran her hand down his chest and to his hard length.

His hand shot out, gripping hers, and he pulled away. "Best not to run before you walk."

He was breathless, and his eyes were heavy-lidded with lust all because of her. She made the god of the Underworld come undone with just her mouth. It made her feel powerful and only made her crave more.

"I told you, I'm a fast learner." She nipped at his bottom lip for emphasis.

"You are a damn prodigy, but you are also not thinking straight."

"My thoughts are just fine," she said, taking his mouth with hers once more.

He consumed her a moment before he pulled away. "Make no mistake, Persephone, I want you enough to strip you and show you just how fucking much I want you."

"But." She knew there was a but.

"But I'm already a bastard for letting it get this far. You know nothing about pleasure, and everything I take from you is taking advantage of you." His eyes were clearing, as if the lust in him was receding.

"It's not taking advantage if I'm willingly giving it," she argued, irritation replacing some of the ache.

Hades gave a bitter smile. "Tell me, Persephone, have you ever touched yourself? Ran your fingers over your clit and deep inside you?"

The words were molten and dirty, reigniting the ache within her.

"Yes," she whispered.

Though even when she had, it had felt nothing like the way it did when he touched her or kissed her.

His eyes widened in surprise as he lifted his thumb to her bottom lip before slipping it inside her mouth. Unsure, she ran her tongue along it, and his shiver and shifting hips told her she had done it right.

"How did it feel when you touched yourself?" he asked, his thumb exploring her mouth in a powerful and commanding way that made her feel as if he owned her. He pulled out and ran his hand back over her neck, lower and lower.

Gods, she was afraid to say the wrong thing. Afraid that he would stop. But still, she met his gaze. "I think it would feel a lot better if you did it."

His hand stuttered to a stop over her breast, and he stared at her with disbelief.

"You are a damn siren," he murmured in awe.

Surprising him would likely be her second favorite thing to do with him, but then again, there was only one way to know for sure. She lifted her hand and cupped his over her stomach, and pushed him down. He let her.

Their hands dipped below her waistband, and she shifted, allowing them more room. The moment their hands ran over her aching center, she moaned. It was already better, and she wanted more. Guiding his movement, she rubbed at that spot that elicited pulses of pleasure and fell into it until she was panting. Hades' eyes feasted on her as they pleasured her together.

She had no idea where this would lead, but she only knew that it felt incredible. When he pulled his hand away, her eyes shot open, and he watched her as he pushed his fingers into her, an entirely different sensation. He waited, as if seeing what she would do, and

Persephone knew in that moment she never wanted to disappoint him.

She shifted her hips, and the place deep inside her that he was touching spread throughout her body, the pulses more urgent. All she knew was she needed to keep moving. She rubbed at the center of her while she rode his fingers.

"Take your pleasure, Persephone, and let me watch you come undone," he ordered.

She nodded because that was all she was capable of and when his fingers curled inside her just as she hit the right spot; she unraveled. The pulses in her exploded, and she chased the feeling of falling apart as if she were made of the spasms of pleasure that moved through her.

Hades held her against him as she fell through whatever was happening to her and when the intensity passed and her mind was only a beautiful haze, she settled her head on his shoulder.

Her breathing settled, and she sighed contentedly in his arms.

"You are entirely singular," he said, his lips against the top of her head.

"How so?" she asked, snuggling deeper into his chest.

"You are fearless and bold when I expect you to be timid and scared." There was an element of awe in his voice.

She pulled away and met his gaze because she wanted him to understand what she was about to say next.

"For the first time in my life, I am free. I will never hesitate when it comes to the things I want."

"And what is it that you want, Persephone?" he said, never shying away from her intensity.

"Everything," she answered.

Chapter Seven

OLYMPUS IS TACKY AS FUCK

Hades

Olympus was a fucking mess. No one enjoyed gossip and chaos more than an immortal. Hades stood against one of the infinite pillars in Zeus' meeting hall. Ostentatious was a poor word to describe the tacky gold and marble that made up every surface. It was something far worse. That he was here at all put him in a bad mood. When he had left the Underworld, Persephone and Cerberus were curled up on one of the couches while she devoured what must have been her third book of the day.

Her thirst for knowledge and experience was voracious, and it was all he could do not to show her everything he knew. He knew he was a bastard, but taking advantage of her desperation was low, even for him. There was no doubt that Persephone was tenacious and knew what she wanted, but at the same time, he had to recognize that he was the first person she had ever been around. The first man.

"Who pissed in your wine?" Ares chuckled, coming up to his side.

Shit. Just his fucking luck.

"Don't you have wars to arrange or something?" Hades drawled.

Also, why was Ares always wearing that ridiculous golden helmet with the red plume adorning the crest? Hades had always had a strong urge to rip it off and see what he was hiding beneath there. Maybe that would be his next stunt.

"What do you think I'm doing here? This all has promise, don't you think?" Ares smirked.

"Because Demeter lost her goose?" Hades rolled his eyes.

Ares roared with laughter like a drunk man high on his own self-worth. The god was arrogant and stupid, which made for a dangerous combination in his line of work. How many mortals had Ares convinced to fight his wars and sent to the Underworld? Greed and ambition fueled his motivations. All the gods enjoyed making the mortals fear and love them, but some took it to a place that left the Underworld overcrowded with lost souls.

"I think we both know it's a bit more than that, but even so, with her starving out the mortals, desperation is building and that's always a good sign. It's only been a few weeks and already they are at each other's throats." Ares said cheerfully. "Oh, look, we are beginning!"

Time worked differently in the mortal realm. What had only been a few days for them had been likely more than a few weeks, as

Ares had said. The mortals were already starving. The souls in the Underworld were a testament to that.

Zeus and Hera entered the room and took the head of the table, Hera to his right, practically glowing with the energy her pregnancy gave her. As if that was all the sign they needed, the immortals fell into place. All thirteen were gathered, which was rare enough for an unmandated meeting. Usually, it was Zeus that ordered everyone out of their holes, but now he understood why Hermes had said he needed to make an appearance. Every immortal was invested in Demeter's temper tantrum.

He dragged his eyes to her, though he had been careful to avoid her. Knowing what she had done to Persephone made him want to strangle her and feed her to Cerberus. He would enjoy watching her scream and beg. He might have done it if he had been sure that was what Persephone wanted. She was angry about what was done to her, but she also clearly loved her mother. A mother who didn't deserve her.

Even still, there was no denying the toll Persephone's disappearance was having on the goddess. Her eyes had dark circles under them and while she appeared haggard, there was rage beneath the surface in her white-knuckled fists and poignant glares.

"All right, Demeter, you have all of us here," Zeus said, half bored. "It's about time you tell us what the damn swan really is."

Hades fought to keep his interest hidden. If she was honest, then she would have to tell them what she had done to her own daughter. Would the immortals forgive her for the crime she committed? Probably. There was little they did that gave them pause. The symptom of immortality, or at least one of them.

Demeter stood, her place in the middle of the long table making it easy for everyone to focus on her. Hermes tensed next to him and Hades had half a mind to kick him. The problem with Hermes was that he was too open and too easy to manipulate.

"What I did—" Demeter began, her voice hoarse. "You are correct that it wasn't just a swan. In fact, it was my daughter, Persephone."

Gasps rang out along the room and Hades made to arch his brow as if he were mildly surprised. It took several moments for the room to come to order and Zeus banged his hand on the table, commanding the room.

Demeter swallowed. "The Fates—"

"Testy old hags, they are," Poseidon said with a grin.

Humor dripped from him and it was clear he was enjoying watching this play out while he knew all the moving pieces. He was a threat. His amusement would only take him so far before ambition or greed had him singing to the highest bidder. Hades would just need to make sure that he remained as that bidder.

Demeter glared at Poseidon but continued. "They told me that my daughter would be stolen from me. That I would search the world and never find her. That darkness would swallow her whole and the seeds that spread throughout her would remain her prison."

Demeter shivered and choked on what almost sounded like a sob while Hades held back his rage.

"I thought that if no one ever knew about her, I could avoid her fate, but—"

"You turned your own daughter into a swan?" Athena said with open disgust.

Demeter's head shot up. "Only during the day! At night, she was who she was meant to be, but it doesn't matter because she's gone."

"You cursed and isolated your only daughter?" Athena growled.

Of all the immortals aside from Hermes and Hecate, Athena annoyed him the least. With the way she was glaring at Demeter in Persephone's defense, he might even tolerate her.

"To protect her!" Demeter shouted. "I will do whatever it takes to get her back."

"Clearly," Hades muttered and immediately regretted it.

Demeter's eyes shot to him, and there was fire and accusation in them. Shit.

"We all know which one of us had motivation, and who would be base enough to do such a thing."

Hades smirked. "Do you feel as if you've made some sort of transgression that would warrant such an act?"

Ares chuckled. "She did wear that black dress."

Fucking Ares. Maybe they could replace him somehow. Any mortal would do a better job of it than him.

"Is that why you did it, Hades? Give. her. Back," she yelled.

Hades sighed as if this were all very taxing on him. "Even if I had your goose, Demeter, I wouldn't give it back just for your tone. As it so happens, the Underworld is currently free of geese."

"You think you are better than everyone else here, but there's a reason you live in the Underworld instead of Olympus. No one can stand your arrogance and self-righteous bullshit," Demeter spat.

Hades winked at her. "Go on."

She let loose a practically feral scream, and even Zeus seemed taken aback.

"Demeter, what proof do you have of the accusations you are throwing at Hades?"

"I know he did it," she growled.

"A very convincing argument," Hades said.

"*You* are the darkness. I never knew what they were talking about, but now it makes perfect sense," Demeter snarled.

"Are you accusing me of swallowing your goose?" he asked.

The room broke out in poorly concealed chuckles, but if only they knew how right Demeter was. No one knew what The Fates meant when they spoke, not even The fucking Fates knew. Yet the pull to Persephone was stronger with every day, every smile she gave him, every time she surprised him, every time she took what she wanted.

"Hades, stop antagonizing her. She's clearly upset," Zeus said with a wave of his hand.

Hades sighed and leaned back in his chair. "I don't know where your goose is, Demeter, but if you could stop starving the mortals, it would be appreciated. I doubt any of them stole it, anyway."

"I will not stop until I find her. Nothing grows till I have her back," Demeter vowed.

Hades stood and met her cold gaze. "Then if you will excuse me, I seem to have more work than usual."

His power deposited him back in the library and Persephone sat up, Cerberus growling in protest at the movement. She was stunning with her hair deliciously messy and her too-tight shirt slightly askew. The thought crossed his mind that he should get her clothes that weren't Hecate's, but then again, he selfishly enjoyed the way they clung to Persephone.

"What is it? Was it terrible? How was she?" The questions came one after another as if she had been waiting for hours to ask them.

"It *was* terrible, though that was to be expected." He moved to the liquor cart and poured some whiskey. "Demeter was—"

He didn't know what to tell her. It wasn't as if he would lie to her, but he also didn't think telling her that her mother was practically unhinged was helpful.

"Upset," he finished.

He threw back the glass of whiskey and was grateful for the burn it elicited in his throat. When he turned to face her, she was biting her lip and running her hand over Cerberus, who nuzzled his head onto her leg as if he sensed her distress.

"I'm angry with her. Livid really. Knowing she did this to me, but never told me the truth, is enough to make me happy that she's miserable. Then in the next breath, I remember how much I love her and I never want her to suffer." She frowned and wiped at her eyes. "I know it doesn't make sense."

Leaning against the bookshelf, Hades considered. It didn't make sense to him, but he was sure there were those that did. In all his immortality, he never cared about another enough to elicit those feelings, but the way his stomach twisted knowing she was hurting was enough to make him pause.

"Love rarely makes sense," he offered.

Persephone gave a small snort. "I think you might be right."

"Of course I am. I'm always right." He smirked.

The small laugh she gave was one of the most delightful sounds he had ever heard. More than that was the way her lips curled up in a half smile. She truly was devastating.

"What's Olympus like?" she asked.

Hades sighed and took the spot at the end of the couch. Cerberus lifted his head to eye him warily before settling back down on Persephone's leg.

"It's gaudy and loud. Gods and goddesses coming and going."

"It sounds terrible," she said with a small smile.

"I told you it was," he said with false irritation.

"Hades?" she asked quietly.

"Yeah?"

"Have you been avoiding me because of what happened between us?" She was biting her godsdamn lip again.

"I've been busy," he said.

She hesitated as if she wasn't sure what to say and he hated he didn't know what would make it better. Making people feel better wasn't something he did. It wasn't something he had ever even wanted to do before.

"Is it because you regret what happened?" she asked, as if she had forced herself to work up the courage.

"Fuck no. Yes. It's complicated," he said.

"Explain it to me." She didn't shy away from him.

Hades ran a hand through his hair and sighed. "You haven't been around people, Persephone. Everything is new to you."

Persephone's lips quirked up. "And you think I only want you because I would run to anyone at this point?"

"Would you?" he asked, knowing that he didn't want the answer.

Persephone narrowed her eyes, watching him as if she saw more than he wanted her to. "You know I've met other, more agreeable people by now?"

Hades choked out a laugh. "Hardly."

"Fine. Would it make you feel better if I asked Hecate or Poseidon to teach me?" She tilted her head in challenge.

The very visceral jealousy that coursed through his veins told him he would very much not like that.

Persephone wore a self-satisfied smile. "You seem irritated."

"That was an irritating question," he countered.

She tapped her mouth thoughtfully. "So you don't want me to learn from anyone else, but you also don't want to teach me."

"I never said I didn't want to teach you, Persephone." The words grated out of him.

"Oh? Only that your morals won't allow it?" She slid her gaze over him, and he felt his control fracturing.

"Are you—Are you trying to bait me?" he asked as he finally realized what was happening.

Persephone beamed. "I'm getting better at it every day."

Fuck, if he didn't want to wipe that smile off her lips with his and then be the reason it returned.

"That's the thing about me, Hades, I enjoy learning and I would really like you to be the one that teaches me." She licked her lips and his cock grew hard.

He was a piece of shit. "What do you want to learn today, Persephone?"

"You," she said as she set down the book and shooed away Cerberus, who shot him a glare as if he were the problem.

"Me," Hades repeated.

She crawled across the couch, her breasts in full view, making his hands itch with the need to touch them. He wanted to learn her every sound and coax it out of her in every fucking way. Instead, she kneeled next to him and, while meeting his eyes, began slowly unbuttoning his pants.

Fuck. He wasn't some Greek hero with high morals. He was gray at best, and his intentions were questionable. If she wanted to use him, he was damn well going to let her because the desire in her eyes was too fucking much for him not to take every damn thing she gave him.

The moment his cock was free, Persephone licked her lips, studying him. He kept his hands carefully on the couch, not willing to rush her.

Her eyes lifted to his. "What do you like, Hades?"

His body felt like it was on fire and he knew exactly what he liked, what he wanted her to do.

"Tell me, Hades," she urged. "Tell me how you take your pleasure, just like you told me to take mine. I want to be the reason you come undone."

Fine. She wanted to be taught, then he would teach her every damn thing he knew.

He placed his hand over hers and wrapped it around his cock. With his eyes on her, they pumped his cock slow and steady. It was an effort to keep his eyes on her as tension coiled in him. This felt good, but he wanted more. He wanted her confident and taking from him. He showed her a few more times before taking away his hand.

She watched her hand work him and she pressed her thighs together as if watching him fall into her touch was making her equally aroused. It made the pleasure building in him even more intense.

"Now your mouth, Persephone," he said, sounding breathier than he had intended.

"My mouth?" She licked her lips, and he watched every movement with need distorting his vision.

"Yes. I want your perfect fucking mouth on my cock."

He expected her to be taken aback by his demand, but she took in a deep breath and leaned forward. His fingers caught her chin and he tilted it up to look at him.

"You don't have to do anything you don't want to do, Persephone. Just say the word and this is done. No judgment." It was an odd contrast to the demand he had just made, but he needed her to know.

"Hades?"

"Yeah?" Her hand still around his cock was distracting.

"I've spent my entire life never choosing. Never picking what I want. So whatever I do, you can know it's for me. That I want it. That I want this."

The conviction in her voice was followed by her taking his cock in her mouth with all the confidence of a lifetime of experience. She moved her tongue around the tip and he moaned at the course of pleasure that ran through him. She was fucking incredible.

He held himself perfectly still while she worked him, even though what he wanted to do was wrap her hair in his hands and fuck her mouth. At least he still had some restraint when it came to her.

She pulled away and eyed him warily. "Hades?"

"Yeah?" His chest felt tight.

"You—you don't seem like you are enjoying this. Am I doing it wrong?"

He met her gaze so she would understand. "There is nothing you could do that would be wrong, Persephone. Everything you give is perfect. It just takes a bit of concentration to not give into my baser instincts."

Her eyes darkened, and she dipped her mouth, running her tongue along the length of him. Fuck.

"Hades?" she asked.

"Fuck." He had not meant to say that aloud, but his blood was rushing at the way she was watching him while tasting him.

"I would really like it if you gave in and showed me *exactly* what you like," she said.

The way she spoke called to every dark part of him. "You tap my leg if it's too much. Do you understand?"

She swallowed and nodded, eagerness and trepidation warring within her.

"Say you understand, Persephone," he ordered.

In answer, she rolled her eyes and tapped his thigh. "See? I understand just fine, Hades."

There was that attitude he craved in her. "Open your fucking mouth, Persephone."

Despite the dark tone, her lips lifted in a smile as if she knew just what she did to him and loved every second of it. Eyes on him, she lowered her mouth to his cock and sucked.

Fuck.

He wrapped her hair in his fist and pulled her closer. Urging her to take more of him.

And she did.

She let loose a low moan that vibrated over him, reassuring him. *She shouldn't be so damn perfect.*

Everything she gave him only made him want more like the greedy bastard he was. His hips thrust, the movement uncoordinated. Tears pricked at the corner of her eyes as she took each in and out. Her hands were soft on his thighs. He was so close, and she was stunning.

"You are incredible," he said through a rushed breath.

When was the last time he had felt like this? Ever? He might have thought on it longer if it weren't for the sensations building in him, clouding his mind. She looked fucking divine, kneeling in front of him with his cock in her mouth.

"I'm going to come," he panted.

She didn't hesitate and when he shattered in her mouth, her eyes widened, but she swallowed him down. When she pulled away, she licked her lips, making him see stars.

"Fuck, I'm sorry. I should have warned you," he said through the spasms that still worked through his body.

When she didn't respond, he opened his eyes to see her pushing up to stand and coming to snuggle herself into his side. Was it the orgasm that was making his chest hum or her? The urge to kiss her was overwhelming. He lifted her chin up, and the soft smile she gave settled over him.

"I enjoyed that. It made me feel powerful. Commanding," she confided.

"You are both of those things," he answered, honesty in every word.

He dipped his mouth to hers, and she instantly opened for him. A quick learner indeed. His tongue swept in, searching, claiming. Her soft moan had his cock already hardening. Lifting her into his lap, she straddled him, making him wonder what it would be like to have her like this. First things first, he had other lessons for her.

"I'm going to make you come so hard they will hear you all the way in Olympus," he said against her mouth.

The shiver that ran through her gave him great satisfaction even as a small smile worked on her mouth.

"Wouldn't that tell them exactly where I am?" she smirked.

He devoured her mouth. "That's the idea."

Before he could explain in vivid detail what he was about to do, an awareness filled him, chasing away all thoughts from his mind.

"Hades?" she asked.

The mood that overtook him was dark as he gently set her beside him and stood. "I have to go."

"Go where?" she asked, standing.

"It doesn't matter."

He was about to portal when she grabbed his arm. "You aren't okay. I can see it all over you. What is it?"

The reminder of what he hated most about this job Zeus had given him. The thing that made him want to level all of Olympus and tell them all what pieces of shit they were. Something she should never have to worry about.

"It's fine." He pried her fingers from him and stepped through the portal, but he was too slow. At least that's what he told himself afterward.

CHAPTER EIGHT

A QUESTION OF HOW

PERSEPHONE

The change that came over him was sudden enough that she knew it meant nothing good, but she hadn't expected this. The portal opened to massive black gates that were slowly closing, the iron of them something ominous and permanent. At the center, an ornate "U" and "W" overlapped each other as if anyone wondered where they had ended up. On the other side, a body of water lay and a hooded figure dragged his oar through the water, retreating into the darkness behind. Even as the gates shut, they opened once more and a person walked through. She had graying hair and wrinkles around her face while she walked with a slight hunch on her back.

Persephone's eyes dragged back to where Minos knelt down on cobblestones, talking to a small figure. When he saw Hades, he stood and nodded, before going to the old woman. Confusion burrowed in Persephone, but all it took was one look at the small figure to understand what this gate was and what this meant. Her blood ran cold.

Hades, god of the Underworld, knelt in front of the small boy.

"Hello," he said, quietly.

The boy sniffed, a never-ending trail of tears down his gaunt cheeks. "I'm scared."

"I know you are, Petre," Hades said gently.

The boy looked up and rubbed at his tears. "How do you know my name?"

"It's my job. It's also my job to make sure you are safe here."

"I want my mama," he said.

Persephone's heart felt heavy in the worst possible way. Almost like she couldn't breathe. Even still, she came to Hades' side and bent to face the boy. Hades went still beside her, but he didn't tell her to leave.

"My name is Persephone," she said, wiping at the boy's cheek.

The boy swallowed and let loose a long sniffle. "You are really pretty."

Despite the sorrow within her, she laughed. "That's very kind of you. Do you like flowers, Petre?"

He nodded. Persephone reached for the small patch of white flowers that appeared next to them and shot Hades a grateful look, but he was staring at her as if he had never seen her before. Maybe it was that he was forced to bear this burden for so long he hadn't expected her to want to help, but the call in her blood couldn't be ignored. She wanted—no, she needed to help this child.

She lifted the delicate flower to him, and he hugged it to his chest.

"What do you like to do, Petre?" she asked quietly.

His body was frail, too thin. Whatever had caused his death had slowly taken from his body till all that was left was a shell of a person. It made her want to scream and rage.

"I like playing with my dog, but he died." There was sorrow in his voice that should never have existed in one so young.

"Well, I have someone I'd like you to meet then," Hades said with a small smile.

As if summoned, Cerberus barrelled through all jowls and drool as he ran between them and licked the boy. Persephone might have thought the boy would be afraid of such a giant dog accosting him, but instead, Petre laughed and threw his arms around Cerberus. Underneath the sorrow burying her, there was an undercurrent of joy in the boy's laugh that echoed throughout her.

"He's so slobbery." Petre giggled.

"He is," Hades said with a smile that didn't reach his eyes.

Persephone reached over and took his hand in hers and his eyes jerked toward hers, something unreadable but undeniably fragile echoing in them.

"Do you think my mama is all right?" Petre asked, pushing Cerberus' incessant kisses away. As if he understood, Cerberus sat next to the boy, who ran his hand over the top of his head.

Persephone pulled the boy into a hug. "Let me tell you something about mothers, Petre." She met his eyes and ran her hand across his cheek, wiping at fresh tears. "Mothers only want one thing. Do you know what that is?"

Petre shook his head.

"Well, that's all right, because I do. All they want is to know that their children are safe and happy. So I think your mama will be more than all right because you are very safe here and you can be happy too."

"Are you happy here?" he asked.

Persephone stilled underneath the question, hesitating a fraction. Tucking a stray piece of hair behind his ear, she nodded. "Yeah, Petre, I'm happy here."

His smile was one of confidence only the young know. He reached up and tucked the flower behind Persephone's ear and pressed a kiss to her cheek, making her heart swell. He wrapped his arms around Cerberus and looked at Hades.

"Will my mama know where to find me when it's time?" he asked.

"Yes, Petre. I will bring her to you myself," Hades said solemnly.

Petre nodded and squeezed Cerberus one more time before disappearing. If Persephone hadn't seen it once before, she would have been concerned, but instead an unmistakable sorrowful peace fell over her. One she thought must be unique to those who witness peace after suffering.

The gates opened and two more souls walked through, a young man with sallow eyes and a middle-aged woman whose bones were tight against her skin. Minos stepped forward and bent his head, talking to them.

"What's wrong with them?" Persephone asked as she stood.

Hades' voice was thick with emotion. "Persephone."

She turned to look at him, but the way he was watching her was as if she were a beautiful mystery.

"Yes?" she asked, wiping at an errant tear.

His eyes searched hers, and he held out his hand. "Come with me."

There was no hesitation as she slipped her hand into his and stepped through the portal, Cerberus at their heels.

The portal opened to a dim room lit only by a single candle. Shelves upon shelves of books lined each wall. At a small desk at the center sat a man who appeared to be in his mid-fourth decade, with black hair that was long down his back and an unruly beard and mustache to match. He hardly seemed to look up from the book that was open before him.

"Hades," the man said.

"I've brought someone to see you," Hades said, nodding to Persephone in encouragement. She didn't know how she knew what he wanted of her, only that she did.

"My name is Persephone," she said.

The man looked up from his book, eyes searching hers, before turning to Hades.

"What is this?" he asked.

"Just a visit. You can't expect to allow me to let you hole up in here without bothering you occasionally."

"Isn't that the purpose of Asphodel?" the man countered, irritation in his voice.

"What are you reading?" Persephone asked, edging closer.

The man heaved a great sigh and leaned back, waving to the book. "I was attempting to read the tale of Odysseus."

"You've read it before?" she asked, somehow knowing the answer.

"Yes." The man eyed her suspiciously.

"Do you think Odysseus was terribly foolish for sparing Polyphemus?" Persephone asked, taking the chair that appeared in front of the desk.

"That's a rather broad question," the man said with a huff of laughter. "I suppose the answer lies in why you think he spared the cyclops."

"Are you asking me?" Persephone smiled.

The man threw up his hand as if in defeat.

"I think it was not foolish," Persephone said.

The man barked a laugh and shut the book, leaning forward. "One choice made in hubris cost him and his men years away from their home and loved ones. It was not only foolish, but selfish."

"It is never selfish to choose life. To choose to spare," Persephone answered.

"Except had he killed him and Polyphemus not prayed to his father, Poseidon would not have made it impossible to return home for Odysseus and his men."

"Or he would have mourned the loss of his son and learned it was Odysseus and killed him and his men instead of delaying them," Persephone countered.

The man shrugged his shoulders and leaned back. "Or had he not told the giant his name, maybe none of it would have come to pass."

Persephone shook her head. "To maim and not take ownership of one's deeds does not courage make."

"To brag about one's achievement at the cost of another does not honor the victor," the man countered.

She was aware of Hades behind her as he seemed to disappear into the stacks of books, as if he didn't want his presence known.

"He saved eight lives as well as his men still on the ships. There is honor and courage in that," Persephone argued.

"Whatever honor is achieved in the act is ruined by the need for acknowledgment," the man countered.

"I disagree. What are we if not stories?" Persephone gestured to the hundreds of books surrounding them. "We live and die a million times beneath these words. We love and we mourn. We grow and become more from the stories gifted to us. You and I can sit here and debate honor and courage because of the examples given to us in stories through the pages that mark each victory and devastating loss. That is not worth nothing. You and I say Odysseus' name because his story matters. His sacrifices matter. His mistakes matter."

The man's eyes flicked to Hades behind her and then to hers. Emotion blurring the rims of his eyes. "Who are you?"

Persephone took a long breath. "I told you. My name is Persephone."

The man smiled knowingly, despite the sadness clinging to him. "Not just Persephone, I think."

Before she could ask him what he meant by that, he ran a hand along his beard.

"Not just Persephone, do you know the story of Prometheus?" he asked.

"Of course. Everyone does." She gestured to the flame flickering between them.

His gaze locked onto the flame as if he hadn't noticed it was there before. "And what do you make of his story?" he asked, his gaze wary on the flame.

"Where would humanity be without his sacrifice? Of course, he should be honored," Persephone answered easily.

The man gave a bitter laugh born of resentment and grief. "Why did Prometheus bring fire to the humans?"

Persephone rolled her eyes. "I already see your argument, and it is foolish. You want me to say that his hubris in tricking Zeus was the reason humans were punished, warranting his action to bring fire to humans. Just like Odysseus, you argue that hubris is vanity and a fatal flaw."

The man tilted his head. "Is it not?"

Persephone heaved a sigh of frustration and tapped the book in front of him. "It is what makes these stories real. What compels us to keep reading? No one would read the story of Odysseus if he had made every right choice. No one would speak of Prometheus with wonder if he had been free from flaw. We need to see ourselves in the stories to become them, to appreciate them. None of us are perfect, but we live when we read about other flawed beings who inspire us to do better. To make the next choice without shame or fear, even if it is the wrong one."

Her chest heaved from the emotion building in her. She may have grown up and lived her life without human contact, but she had her stories. Her mother had let her have the stories of Odysseus and Prometheus because she saw them as this man did. As lessons against vanity and betrayal of the gods, but they were so much more than that. They were the lives she longed to live, the mistakes she longed to make, the love she longed to know. Stories were her salvation.

The man gave her an exhausted smile. "And Prometheus' fate? Was that a fair trade for his hubris?" Seeing her instant rejection, he waved a hand. "His actions?"

"You want me to say whether his gift to humanity was worth the eternity of torture Zeus condemned him to?" Persephone asked.

The man nodded. Solemn.

Persephone considered. "I think only one who has endured that level of injustice can speak to that answer, but if you are asking, would I do it knowing that was the eternity that awaited me? I want to say yes. I don't know that I am good enough for self-sacrifice, but for him, I hope each night as he awaited the next day he would at least know that somewhere someone was telling his story because he made that possible. That not just his sacrifice, but his name would live on. There's something comforting in knowing your legacy is secured, be it in hubris or sacrifice."

The man went very still, his eyes locked onto hers with the intensity of a man starved. "And if rest were an option? Do the infamous and those afflicted with hubris deserve rest?"

Persephone was many things, but in this, she did not hesitate. "More than anyone or anything deserves it and everyone and everything are deserving of rest."

The man stood from the chair, his black shirt torn at his right upper abdomen where a long angry scar lingered. Persephone sucked in a breath and stood, the chair beneath her crashing to the ground.

"Oh, gods." She brought her hand to her mouth. Shock and mortification mixed together until she wasn't sure where one ended and the other began.

Prometheus stepped around the desk and took her hands in his and pressed a kiss to them. "Don't call to those who are beneath you, Lady Persephone. I believe someday your name will be remembered, but I doubt it will carry the scars of Odysseus and mine."

He reached up and took the flower from her hair, pressing it into her hands. She saw now that his eyes were ancient and haunted. The torture he had endured well and alive in the shadows around him.

Prometheus looked behind her and nodded. "I believe you have found your equal, Hades."

"Far more than that," Hades answered, thick with emotion.

Prometheus gave a knowing smile. "Thank you, Persephone."

The Titan and legend she had fought sleep to read about was holding her hands in his and thanking her. It was enough to nearly bring her to her knees. Instead, she nodded, blinking away the tears that gathered.

He leaned forward and pressed a kiss to her cheek before the weight of his hand on hers disappeared, as if it had never existed. In a blink, the room returned to the cavern it was just as it had when Lia had moved on.

Persephone bent down and set the flower at the center of the room where the desk had once been. When she stood, she wiped at her tears and found Hades leaning against the wall, something unreadable in his eyes.

"How?" she asked.

He inhaled a sharp breath. "How indeed."

CHAPTER NINE

WHAT BELONGS TO THE GOD OF THE UNDERWORLD

HADES

Hades' entire body hummed with restless energy. On one hand, he wanted to fall to his knees and worship the woman before him. On the other, he wanted to fuck her against the wall and make her feel an ounce of what she gave him. How fucking indeed. She shouldn't be. Nothing accounted for the how of her. No precedent for who she was.

"That was Prometheus," she said, shaking.

"It was," he answered, kicking off the wall and coming to stand in front of her.

"Zeus sentenced him to be tortured for eternity. A vulture to eat his liver every day, only to regrow it at night and begin again." She winced as she recited the punishment his brother had put on Prometheus.

"And he suffered that fate for thousands of years, but Zeus is not infallible and I have cleaned up and kept quiet enough of his mistakes that I am able to call in a favor from time to time." Hades shrugged.

"And you asked him to release Prometheus." She finished the thought as if there were no doubt in her mind.

Hades reached up and ran his hand along the side of her face, unable to restrain himself from touching her. He didn't deserve the way she leaned into his touch.

"Do you have any idea how long he has been in Asphodel, living with his shame and guilt for his own perceived failings?"

Persephone shook her head.

"He was the oldest soul here, Persephone. The most restless. The most deserving of peace and the most unwilling to allow it. I have spent thousands of years trying to convince him to take his due and in one conversation, you did just that." Hades hardly recognized the awe in his voice.

"But he was a Titan, immortal," Persephone said.

"He will live forever in Elysium, but in peace," Hades explained.

"I didn't know." Her lip quivered and he ran his thumb along it.

"No, you didn't. Just like you didn't know that Petre, by all accounts, should have stayed in Asphodel until his mother met her own demise. It is rare for children to move on without a loved one to guide them."

"Are you angry?" Persephone asked, searching.

The words knocked the air from him. "Am I angry?"

Well, he hadn't been before, but now that she asked such a stupid question like that, he was definitely considering it. He stepped forward, allowing for no distance between them. He stared down at her, wondering how much of the truth she knew and hid from. How much, she wondered, but wouldn't ask.

"You have done two, really three, things that should be impossible," he said, his eyes searching for any sign that she was hiding from a truth she knew. "You know you aren't merely a demi-god, don't you, Persephone?"

Eyes widening, she took a step back from him, but he placed his hand on her back, pulling her back into him. There wasn't a scenario where he was letting her get out of this. The need to know what she was burrowed into him, consuming him from within.

"Hades," she begged.

She begged him as if he were hurting her, but she was the one cutting through him like a knife. There was no way around this. Damn him, he cared about her, but he wouldn't let her hide from what she was and what that meant to him. Maybe that was selfish, but he had never claimed to be anything else.

"Souls leave Asphodel in one of three ways. One, they come to the conclusion of peace of their own accord. Two, they are reunited with a loved one and make the ascent together. Three. Three is that I guide them, push them towards that peace."

Persephone swallowed. "I just talked to them."

"Do you think Hecate and Hermes don't talk to the dead when they are here? Never once has one ascended to Elysium after talking to them."

"Maybe they weren't saying the right things?" Persephone whispered.

The growl he let loose was one borne from the god of the Underworld. "You are intelligent, Persephone. Do not insult yourself or me by pretending to be anything but." With his free hand, he lifted her chin up so she couldn't hide from the truth. "Flowers don't grow in the underworld."

She tried to turn to see the flower that lay behind him, but he wouldn't let her. Some truths had to be acknowledged.

"I don't know what you want me to say," she murmured, voice distant as if she were retreating.

"Say what you are, Persephone," he ordered.

"But why should I be able to do these things even if that's true?" she asked.

"Say it, Persephone," he demanded.

Her eyes locked on his, irritation and fear warring in her, but she was made of flames and steel. "A goddess."

He imagined the smile that broke out over him was predatory as satisfaction welled inside him. There. That wasn't so fucking hard, was it?

"A goddess who can create life where there is none," he purred.

"I created the patch of flowers." It was more of a statement than a question.

Hades released her chin, satisfied that she wouldn't hide from who she was anymore. "You did when you gave Petre one. There are no flowers in the Underworld. You created them because you wanted them to exist."

"What does it mean?" she asked, acceptance already in the way she held herself, shoulders high.

The fuck if he knew, but then again he had some ideas. "Currently, it means a few things. One being that Demeter can go fuck herself if she thinks I'm giving you back."

She should have been afraid of the cold promise, but the wicked creature before him smiled with self-satisfaction. It only encouraged his next thought.

"Second, I intend to worship you like the goddess you are." He dipped his head to run his mouth the barest breath over her jaw and neck. She shivered under his touch, and it was like a match to his blood. He craved her, longed to possess her. The Underworld answered her, as did he.

"Will you make me offerings?" she murmured, her hands coming up to his hips and tightening on him.

The air hummed around them as he portaled them to his room. Persephone gasped and pulled away to look around. He gave her the time to register where they were and what he intended in case she changed her mind, but he really hoped she didn't. The need to touch her and show her what pleasure was burned in him.

When she stepped away from him, his heart sank into his stomach. He knew it was too much for her, too fast, but this longing in him was nearly unbearable. Yet he would bear it because he had to. Just as he had resigned himself to his fate, she took three steps back, eyes locked on him, and lowered herself onto his bed.

"Persephone," he warned.

He wasn't an immortal that was a slave to his base needs, but he also had his limits. Her on his bed was one of those limits. Her body, tight beneath her restricting clothes, begging to be released and touched.

Her lips turned up in a sly smile. She knew exactly what she was doing to him and she was enjoying it.

"I want you to touch me, Hades," she said with all the confidence of a siren.

"Thank fuck," he said, his voice hoarse from drinking in the sight of her.

Her body fit perfectly beneath him as he lowered himself over her. She sucked in a breath, but ran her hands over his hips and sides, sending need throughout his body.

More. He wanted more.

The kiss was consuming, claiming. Ever the quick learner, she opened for him, allowing his tongue to sweep in. As if there was any doubt in his mind where he intended this to end, this kiss would have reminded him.

"Hades." His name on her lips was an aphrodisiac more potent than Aphrodite's power.

"I am going to taste every godsdamned inch of you, Persephone, do you understand?"

She whimpered in need, but nodded in understanding. Not enough.

"Tell me what I'm going to do to you." He ran his hand down her chest slowly for emphasis.

Her eyes locked onto his, fearless and brave. "You, Hades, god of the Underworld, are going to taste every godsdamn inch of me."

The sass in her did something to him. That she would throw his own words back at him. He would make it so that she struggled to remember her own name by the time he was done with her. She tasted of champagne and cinnamon, her skin smooth beneath his tongue and hands.

"Take off your shirt, Persephone," he ordered.

He wanted her to bare herself to him. To be the one to choose this so that he never had time to doubt how much she wanted him. He practically vibrated with the need to be inside her and take her, but that wasn't what this was. First, he would give her pleasure that only she would know.

He watched with hunger as her fingers carefully undid each lace of the front of her shirt until she rose on her elbows and slid it off one arm and then the other, no hesitation in her movement or the eyes glued to his. She was stunning in every way.

He allowed himself the singular pleasure of taking in her form. Her breasts longed to be tasted and taunted.

"Now your pants," he said, holding himself back.

"Am I to do all the work?" She arched an eyebrow.

In answer, he placed his hand on her thigh and pushed the slightest power through, her pants disintegrating into nothing as if they had never existed, leaving her bare before him.

"That's a nice trick," she said breathlessly.

"Wait till you see my next one," he said with a wicked grin that instantly wiped the humor from her face to be replaced with heat.

Hades lowered his mouth back to hers before exploring her perfect neck and lower to her breasts. Eyes on her, he lowered his mouth to her nipple and flicked out his tongue. Her breath caught and her eyes fluttered. It was a start, but he wanted more from the goddess in his bed. Taking her nipple in his mouth, he ran his tongue over it before teasing it with his teeth, light when he was maintaining all of his restraint. She made a soft moan as her hand threaded through his hair, pushing him against her, demanding more. He happily obliged her, licking and sucking until sounds of pleasure came from her perfect mouth.

As he lifted his head once more, she began to protest, but he winked at her. "I swear to you, Persephone, I will not leave you wanting while you are in my bed."

"Am I to just take your word on that?"

If it wasn't for how raspy her voice was and the flush in her cheeks, he might have thought her unaffected.

That she was talking at all was problematic. He had intended to take his time with her, but now it was quickly becoming a matter of principle. She arched an eyebrow in challenge, and he wondered how the fuck she existed as she was. Reaching between them, he ran his hand between her thighs and smiled as satisfaction wove itself into him.

"Your body betrays you, goddess. I can't fucking wait to taste you," he growled as he lowered himself further down her body.

Persephone bit her lip as she watched him, her legs spreading for him. Fucking perfect. He buried himself between her legs and used the flat of his tongue to lick up the center of her. Her cry was made for him, and he wanted more. He lapped at her, tasting the sweetness of her, exactly what he thought she would taste like. Fucking delicious.

Her moan drew his attention, and he found her with her head back on the pillows, her eyes closed and her mouth open. All her bravado lost beneath his mouth, just as it should be. At his pause she raised her head to look at him, the lust and need in her a beautiful symphony.

"Do you like when I'm buried between your legs, Persephone?" he asked.

"Yes!" she panted.

He might have asked her for more, made her beg him, but he wasn't strong enough. He wanted to feel her unravel beneath him. He lowered his head once more and teased and licked the center of her, swirling his tongue and finding the movement that elicited the most pleasure from her. Learning her was fucking incredible. She was incredible.

He pulled away to watch her as he dipped one finger into her, her body soft around him. His aching cock twitched with the idea of how he would feel burrowed inside her. Persephone threw back her head and cried out, her breasts arching above her body. Fuck. He could come just like this, watching her.

He withdrew and added a second finger, pumping in and out of her in gentle strokes. Her hands clung to the bed, seeking purchase, but he wouldn't give her the chance.

"Come for me, Persephone. Come on my fingers while you ride my face." He hardly recognized his own voice.

"Yes!" she answered.

"Good girl." He smiled before flicking his tongue against her while he curled his fingers inside her.

Persephone cried out a mixture of his name and nonsense. He was all satisfaction and need. He curled his fingers and with the flat of his tongue slowly ran up the center of her. Her body spasmed around him while she called his name. It was everything he hoped it would be, but he didn't stop, wouldn't stop. Her thighs tightened around his head and he felt like if he wasn't immortal, this is how he would like to die. He waited till the tension left her body and slowed his pace. Mourning the loss of the taste of her as he lifted his head.

Persephone lay in a perfect disaster against his dark satin sheets. Her blonde hair was a mess as if she had run her hands through it in her pleasure, her body twisted and spent under his interrogation. Her plump, swollen lips were parted as she drank in air, her chest rising and falling with the effort. He would fucking commission a portrait of her if he wouldn't have had to send whoever did it to Tartarus for the crime of seeing her like this. This was for his eyes only to feast on. He would show anyone who dared to touch what was his just how the god of the Underworld got his reputation.

"Hades."

His name on her lips ripped him from his dark thoughts.

She held out her arms to him and he smiled as he slid up the bed and she wrapped herself around the side of him, pressing her head against his chest. The darkness in him receded at her gentle touch as she sighed contentedly on his chest.

Moments stretched as they took the comfort the other one offered. A perfect balance of give and take. When she yawned, he ran his hand down her silk hair and pressed a kiss to the top of her head.

"Sleep, Persephone."

She murmured her agreement and just as he thought she was asleep, she said, "You won't let me go?"

He jerked his gaze down to her beautiful form wrapped around him. "No. You are mine."

"Good," she murmured as sleep took her.

Chapter Ten

THE TIDE OF
MEN

Persephone

There were a million ways Persephone had woken up before. One time, she had forgotten to be up before dusk and woke up in the middle of her lake, fumbling for purchase beneath the water. Another time, she had woken on the lake shore when she was eleven to her mother telling her she wouldn't be allowed any more nighttime sweets with the way she was filling out her body. Mostly, she had woken up on the lake's edge cold and exhausted. Never had she woken up in another's arms feeling safe and . . . happy.

Persephone lifted her head the smallest fraction, hoping he didn't realize she was awake. He sat with one arm curled around her and a book open in his other. His hair was still chaotic from her hands running through it and he was more relaxed than she had ever seen him. He had a habit of clenching his jaw, but now it was as if he were at peace.

"You are staring," he said without looking away from the book.

"What are you reading?" she asked, snuggling deeper into his chest.

Somewhere along the way and very quickly, she had lost sight of her goals. She had meant to keep Hades' attention and by all accounts she had, but it wasn't in the way she intended. Where she should have been disquieted by the thought, she only found peace.

"I am reading about born immortals. You are rare, but not impossible," he said.

Persephone pulled away and sighed. "Does it matter how I came to be?"

She didn't know why trepidation filled her and made her clench her hands, only that it did.

Hades eyed her and closed the book before placing it on the nightstand. "Why do you fear the answer?"

Her first instinct was to deny it, but he saw through her in a way that was singular to him.

"I don't know. It's not as if it will change anything, but it's just that—" She struggled to find the words. "The only person who ever showed me love or kindness was also the reason I never had the chance to be loved by anyone else. I've known my mother was complicated. Her moods were swift and the smallest infraction led to her either not speaking to me or reminding me of all the ways I was a burden to her. When her mood finally settled, she would pull me into her arms and tell me that she loved me. That I was her greatest achievement."

Hades barely breathed as he considered her and let her work through the emotions building in her.

Sucking in a deep breath, she let it out, shaky and slow. "I thought I knew my mother. Her flaws and her strengths, but I could never have imagined that she would have been the one to curse me. My world, though it was small, has been fractured irrevocably. I don't want to know the answers to how I came to be because a small part of me wants to preserve what's left of that small world. Maybe it makes me a coward, but—"

Hades lifted her chin and his vibrant eyes bore into hers. "I have thought of many things to call you, Persephone, but coward is not one of them. Admitting and asking for your needs is braver than accepting a fate."

Part of her wanted to fight against the compliment as if it were a trap. Her mother's were so often wrapped in barbed wire and pointed at her deepest failures, but Hades had never done that to her. Had never made her feel small or less than. If anything, he had only ever empowered her. Taking a steadying breath, she nodded.

He released her chin and pressed a light kiss to her forehead, which left her feeling vulnerable in a way she had never felt before.

"I would like to take you into the city today if you are not opposed," Hades said, voice thick.

A thrill shot through her, but she eyed him suspiciously. "Is this another test?"

His lip quirked up in amusement. "Yes, and no. I won't deny I am eager to test your power, but also I would really just like to spend the day with you and show you my home."

Honesty. It settled against her skin, reminding her she chose what happened next.

"You disintegrated my clothes," she said with a tilt of her head.

"Two things," he said, holding up his fingers. "First, technically they were Hecate's. Second, I regret nothing."

Her cheeks heated at his words despite the laugh that built in her chest. "Well, can you reintegrate them?"

He arched an eyebrow. "That's absurd, Persephone, I am a god, not a magician."

Persephone rolled her eyes. "It seems impractical to ruin perfectly good clothes."

"Yes, because it's so difficult to get new ones. It was time you had your own, anyway. You can pick out whatever you like in the city."

"Made by the dead?" Persephone asked.

"Much better quality than the living. Souls like Basalia create because it pleases them to do so. They don't do it for profit or survival, but because they wish to," he explained as he flicked his hand and a teal ensemble appeared in his hand. "One last Hecate outfit."

Persephone reached for it and shot him a rueful glare. "Don't pretend like you don't love the way the tops hug my breasts."

The god of the Underworld choked, pounding his chest as he fought for air. She could die happy with the satisfaction that rolled through her.

***

With her arm threaded through the god of the Underworld's, she walked Asphodel's worn cobblestone streets. He knew every name of every soul they passed and spoke to them easily. She loved the city. The city rose up next to the river with white buildings, some with large columns and some with stone structures. It built upon itself, rising higher with buildings on every level until at the peak there was a massive white building with eight columns stretching the width. On the other side of the Acheron River, Hades' manor sat. It sprawled over the landscape, but its columns led to open terraces and stairs that fed into balconies that went through the whole length of the house. The peaked roof was made of red brick to contrast the white.

The city was busier than last time and it was hard to believe it was a city of the dead. Life seemed infinite among the open streets and people conversing without ire or ulterior motive. It was peaceful.

"What do you think of Asphodel?" Hades asked.

The smile that lit her face was genuine. "It's wonderful. Everyone seems so at peace, even though none of them are."

Hades' lips thinned. "Asphodel is whatever they need it to be. There are more unsavory parts on the outskirts. Fighting rings and gambling spots, but all who are there choose to be. Some never come out of their homes and choose solitude. Some crave social interactions. Every soul that comes to Asphodel is unique and how they find peace is never the same."

He led her into a dress shop run by a man with a long gray beard who knew every fabric and every style there was in vivid detail.

When she had pointed at a blouse and leggings, he had insisted she try it on. That led to a long road of her trying on outfit after outfit and the man, Origen, would pull out a tape measure and go through all the ways he could improve the outfit. He seemed to glow with purpose and all the while Hades sat in a chair, watching with the faintest smile.

When Origen finally released her, he promised to have the orders done and to the manor by the end of the day. As she waved goodbye to him, a single tear slid down his cheek.

"Can you feel anything from him?" Hades asked as they began walking.

Persephone shook her head. "Only a faint feeling. Like regret, almost."

"He spent his whole life pretending to be who he thought he should be. His regret keeps him in Asphodel," Hades explained.

"Maybe I'm not as singular as you thought if he didn't move on to Elysium like Lia or Prometheus," she said, nudging his shoulder playfully.

Hades stopped and ran his eyes over her. "I wish you were able to sense how close a soul is to ascending so that you would know what a difference you made. Origen is more at peace after an hour with you than he has been in his entire time here. That is not to say that I expect you to have such an exponential effect on every soul, but never believe for a moment that you are anything but singular."

Maybe it was the lightness of the day or the way he made her feel that made her do it, but Persephone reached up on her toes and pressed a light kiss to his lips. When she pulled back and settled onto her feet, she had only a moment before he dipped his head and captured her lips with his own.

It was a heady and intoxicating kiss. One she could easily lose herself in. He kissed her as if he had waited an eternity for her.

"Well, this is certainly new," a delicate voice said from behind her.

Persephone made to pull away, but Hades gave her one last lingering kiss before releasing her and running his finger over her lip.

"Helen," he said in a way of greeting.

"Hades," the woman answered.

Despite the fact that she had just been kissing him, an irrational jealousy ran over her that made her feel out of control and volatile. When she twisted, she found a woman with a narrow face and a body that curved in and out almost perfectly, but where she should have been breathtaking, her face was scarred with small red blotches that marred her tanned skin.

"I haven't seen you in a while," Hades said. "This is Persephone."

Reaching out with whatever ability lay inside her, she searched for something, anything. A burst of rage strong enough to make her lose her balance broke from the woman in front of her. Hades gripped her waist, steadying her in front of him. In all the times she had fought with her mother or even when she had found out what her mother had done, she had never felt a rage like that.

Helen merely cocked her head of frizzy blonde hair. "New indeed. Are you afraid of what you feel from me?"

It wasn't a question born of insecurity but of challenge. Persephone had never been one to back down from a challenge. She stepped from Hades' grip and walked towards the woman who watched her with muddy eyes.

Persephone reached out her hand. "May I?"

If Persephone had never backed from a challenge, she got the impression neither had this woman who nodded sharply. Dropping her hand onto Helen's wrist, she closed her eyes and allowed herself to feel.

Sorrow and loss danced over her, but it was rage that consumed each small emotion, as if it would not tolerate any other feeling. Persephone pulled away and met the woman's eyes, who watched her with coldness.

"Are you afraid?" Helen repeated the question.

Persephone felt a chill over her body and longed to wrap herself up in a blanket and retreat by a fire, but she did not feel afraid.

"No. I only wonder what could have been so terrible to leave you with this burden," Persephone said honestly.

Helen's jaw tensed. "The most unforgivable crime. Men."

She closed her eyes for a fraction of a moment, her mother's cautionary tales playing in her mind. When she opened them again, she bowed her head.

"I'm sorry for what you endured," Persephone said.

"But you don't even know what it was," Helen said sharply.

"I don't need to," Persephone answered.

Helen narrowed her eyes. "What are you?"

"A goddess. My mother is Demeter," Persephone said.

"And your father?" she asked.

"I don't know."

Helen clicked her tongue. "That's probably for the best."

The woman was harsh and straightforward, but Persephone was inclined to agree with her.

"What do you think of Asphodel, Persephone?" Helen asked.

"I love it." The words slipped through, earning the faintest smile from Helen.

"But you haven't even seen the best part," she said, holding out her arm.

Without turning back to Hades, Persephone threaded her arm through hers and followed her lead. Most of the residents of Asphodel watched them with weary eyes and averted their gazes. It was a stark change from when she was walking with Hades and insecurity bubbled up within her unbidden.

"It's not you. They don't look at me because I do not wish it. Asphodel is whatever we need it to be," Helen explained.

Despite her scars, there was still a profound beauty beneath them. That she should be insecure enough to need absolute solitude was heartbreaking.

"It is not for the reason you think," Helen said as they neared the top of the city where a massive pantheon stood before them. Souls parted for them as they went. When they climbed the stairs and made it past the columns, a whole new world opened before them. There was music and art of every shape and size. Laughter and chatter took up every space. It was a beacon of life in a city of death.

"This is where we come when we need to feel," Helen said, surveying the open space.

Marble statues and detailed paintings lined the walls while music danced around them.

"It's wonderful," Persephone breathed.

"For some, I can see why," Helen said dryly.

Persephone turned her head to find Hades leaning against one of the columns, watching them.

"Do you seek his permission to enjoy the art before you?" Helen asked though it felt like more of an accusation.

"Why does it bother you that I might?" Even if that hadn't been her motivation, she found herself wanting to know more about the woman next to her.

"Everything bothers me," Helen said dismissively.

She said it with the air of someone used to their sharp tongue shredding connections, but Persephone was persistent.

"You approached me, Helen. As you said, Asphodel is whatever you need it to be. Why speak to me and then try to push me away?"

Dark brown eyes considered her before Helen snapped her fingers and the city center melted away to reveal lush gardens surrounded on all sides by a sprawling villa. Fresh lilacs filled the air, and a small pond with a soft waterfall sat to their left.

"This was my home," Helen said.

The urge to tell her it was beautiful was on the tip of her tongue, but somehow she knew what fragile truth Helen had placed in her would be gone. Instead, Persephone kept quiet and waited for her to speak.

Helen surveyed the garden and the home before turning to Persephone.

The air ripped from her lungs as she took in the transformed woman before her. Her tanned skin was smooth and unmarred, her eyes an enchanting emerald, and her hair fell in loose ringlets down her back and shoulders. She wore a white dress that showed off her shoulders and hugged her narrow hips. She was the most beautiful woman Persephone had ever seen.

Understanding dawned on her. "You are Helen of Troy."

Helen clicked her tongue. "That is my crime, yes."

A million thoughts passed through Persephone's mind. She wanted to tell her she wasn't a crime, but at the same time, she knew her story well. Married to Menelaus, she ruled Sparta and bore him a daughter, Hermione. Yet, she ran away with Paris, Prince of Troy, and started a war that killed thousands over the course of years. So much life lost and families ruined over one choice. Yet, even as she ran over the story, she felt the rage that stormed in Helen's soul and took a seat on one of the many marble benches.

"I would hear your story if you would offer it," Persephone said, folding her hands in her lap.

Helen met her gaze, unflinching. "Everyone knows my story. Oh, but wait, which version? The one where I am an unhappy wife and elope with my lover knowing that my husband will start a war and death and carnage will follow in my wake? Or perhaps that one where I am the helpless queen, kidnapped and her husband comes to her rescue, starting a war if only it means seeing her safe in his arms."

"I would hear the truth," Persephone said, not shying from the venom in the Queen's words.

Helen watched her like she couldn't decide if she wanted to see her burn or hug her. It didn't matter. She knew by now that Asphodel was whatever they needed and, right now, Persephone was part of Asphodel.

Helen clenched her teeth and snapped her fingers. The world shifted around them once more and Persephone was standing in a hall of marble and silk couches. Helen stood at her side, her eyes focused to the right of them. A small girl sat with her heels crossed and her hands folded in her lap.

Towering over her was a man with a short beard and a youthful face. "Would you like to play a game, Helen?"

Helen nodded, her lips pursed. Even at what could only be seven years old, she had the bearings of a queen.

The man smiled. "That's a good girl. We are going to go on an adventure."

He held out his hand, and Helen took it.

"That was the first time. Theseus. He came into my home and ate in my father's halls before he stole me to be his bride. I was a child," Helen said with no emotion, as if she were reciting her own story.

"Did he hurt you?" Persephone asked and immediately regretted it.

"Not in the way you think, but he would have. I was found before he could marry me, but it taught me my first lesson. Beauty was a curse, and I was afflicted."

The room shifted once more and Helen was older now, a teenager. She had grown into her beauty with grace. There was nothing awkward about her. She was the most beautiful woman Persephone had ever seen. Maids fussed over her as she sat in front of a mirror in her bedroom, draping jewels over her and setting her hair so it fell just right.

A short man with choppy blond hair and a round belly walked in. "Helen, my sweet, you look divine. The man who ends up with you will be blessed by the gods themselves."

Helen dipped her head but said nothing. There was a sparkle to her eyes that spoke of youth and hope, even if her body was tense and guarded.

The world shifted once more and Helen stood to the side of her father's throne while he surveyed the row of men before him. Ten men of varying ages and stations stood before them, all darting their eyes over Helen as if they could consume her. One after another, they knelt and swore an oath. If Helen was ever stolen from her chosen suitor, they would answer the call for war. When it was done and every oath secured, a grizzly man with dark hair stepped forward.

"Agamemnon. Menelaus couldn't even be bothered to come ask for my hand himself. He sent his brother," Helen said, beside her, but for the first time there was less anger.

The scene flashed and Helen sat across the table from Agamemnon tossing a die in the air and cheering when it landed. The gruff man smiled fondly and Persephone got the impression it was a rare sight. He grabbed the dice and said something that made Helen laugh, a melodious and light sound.

Persephone blinked, and she was in a bedroom with a large bed at the center, terrace doors thrown open, and the sea breeze billowing over the white canopied bed. Instinct had Persephone wanting to turn away, but if Helen was showing her, she would not insult her by being weak. Agamemnon had his fingers laced through Helen's as he slowly thrust into her. A thin sheen of sweat covered their bodies and Helen met her lover's eyes with trust and . . . love.

"He told me he loved me. That when Menelaus arrived, he would tell him that he couldn't give me up. That he would die for me. He made me feel seen. Like I was more than my beauty. He laughed with me and told me I was even more clever than I was beautiful. At seventeen, I knew I had found my soulmate. That was the first and last time I wanted a man to touch me like that."

It was as if Persephone could feel the betrayal and hurt even before she witnessed it. Could feel every unwanted touch like a hoard of insects crawling over her skin. It made her want to scratch her body clean, as if something like that could ever be wiped away.

Helen reached out and clasped Persephone's hand in hers. "It never goes away."

The words were heavy and poisoned, just like the acts that gave them life. Without even seeing the rest of Helen's story, she understood the rage that lived in her. The air between them blurred and stretched. Menelaus and Agamemnon forming and falling to shreds over and over.

"You would take from me the very purpose of Asphodel, Hades?" Helen called out, her voice low and predatory.

"She does not need to see what you would show her," Hades' disembodied voice seethed.

Helen gave a bitter laugh. "And I did not need to live it."

"I will see what she wants me to see, Hades. Do not interfere," Persephone ordered, voice thick with emotion.

She could practically hear his argument, but since the first day she had met him, he had allowed her the space to make her own decisions. The images fractured before the cracks ebbed and flowed together, becoming one again. Menelaus, tall, dark, handsome, everything a Greek hero should be stood before her. He reached out his hand and a young Helen stepped through Persephone and placed her hand in his.

Helen shot a nervous look at Agamemnon, whose smirk was colder than it had been before. A moment later, Menelaus broke out in laughter, leaving Helen's cheeks red and tears staining her cheeks.

"Menelaus found it amusing that his brother had . . . 'sampled' me as he put it. He said it was a just price as any for fetching me. When I begged Agamemnon to tell Menelaus, it was more than that he laughed in my face and called me a gullible bitch. As if it had all been some sort of game."

The urge to tell Helen she was sorry was strong, but somehow she knew it would not be welcome. There was nothing that could be said for what had been done to her.

Images flashed in quick succession. Helen laying on the floor with red handprints on her cheeks and blood staining her white tunic. Menelaus looming over her with dark intent. Helen crying in the middle of the night, biting down on her hand so as not to wake the sleeping brute beside her. It dragged the breath from Persephone and made it hard to be anything else than the emotions Helen channeled, but then just as the pressure threatened to end her, relief. The world shifted, and there sat Helen with a small bundle in her arms. Even exhausted and sweaty, Helen was stunning.

"Hermione. She was everything. A chance for me to do better. I vowed to protect her. To be stronger for her," Helen said, quietly.

Images flashed around them. Slowly they watched Hermione grow from a small babe to a ten-year-old with a knack for making others smile. Her joy and happiness were infectious.

"You succeeded. No one with that much joy and kindness could know the cruelty you did," Persephone said.

"So I did," Helen said, but it was mournful.

Helen raised her hand out as if she could touch the smiling Hermione, but the image dissipated into nothing. In its place was a strong blond man with a youthful face and a dreamy stare.

"Paris," Helen explained. "The night everything changed."

Paris reached out his hand, and Menelaus met him with a firm shake. A deal was struck.

"Menelaus was many things, but most of all, he was clever. Paris was ambitious. He wanted more than being a second son. So Menelaus proposed Paris steal me, knowing that all my suitors would be oath bound to answer his call. A war where Paris' brother Hector could be neatly disposed of. Menelaus knew I would not come willingly. Would not leave my daughter. So he drugged me. When I woke, it was on a ship to Troy."

Paris reappeared, holding a knife to Helen's neck while she stared at him with wide, hazy eyes.

"He told me that if I did not cooperate, my daughter's life would be forfeit. I told him he was stupid for trusting Menelaus. That he would not stop with only Hector's death, but he was young and arrogant."

Persephone sucked in a breath. How could one woman's story have been told so inaccurately for so long?

As if she had heard her thoughts, Helen met her gaze. "Because it is the men that do the telling. We are merely adornments for their great acts, or worse, excuses. Paris paid the price for his greed but so did many Trojans and Spartans. The war lasted ten years and took so much from so many."

They stood in a garden and tears rolled down Helen's face as she took in her daughter. She had grown into a woman just as beautiful as her mother, but where there had been a light in her eyes, there was only a distant dimness.

"I could not save her. She was married off to a man who did not want nor deserve her. He died soon after, but she was remarried to her cousin, who was dull and cold. The one thing I wanted to protect, I failed. How stupid I was to think that I could stand against the tide of men."

It was intrusive and made her sweat with the effort, but Persephone pulled at the image before them. Pulled at what she knew lie just beyond. When the image finally gave, she heaved out a sigh. Hermione fell to her knees while Helen ran to her and wrapped her in her embrace. The two women kneeled on the stone ground and cried, finding comfort in one another.

"But she knew you loved her. You gave her comfort in a way no one else could. You did not fail her, Helen."

Helen watched the image with fresh tears. "I could have done more."

"Where is Hermione now?" Persephone said, somehow knowing the answer.

"Elysium." Helen's voice was stronger when she said the word.

"Her life was hard, but her mother taught her what love meant. That is worth very much indeed," Persephone said, holding back the way the words stung and burned.

"So it is," Helen said, waving her hand once more.

Her world fell apart and once more they stood in the Pantheon. The life and hope Persephone had felt when she had first entered was gone, and there was only a heaviness left. Even still, Helen's rage had dimmed to a soft kindling, and she met Persephone's eyes.

"Thank you for hearing my story," Helen said.

Persephone raised her hand to her heart. "I am honored that you would share it with me. You are an incredible woman, Helen. It is a shame your story has been tainted by lesser men."

"It is," she agreed. "For now, this is enough."

Helen turned and walked from the Pantheon as if nothing had happened. A hand pressed to her lower back, and she turned to see Hades watching her with searching eyes.

"She didn't move on," Persephone said.

"No," Hades answered. "Hers is a burden that is heavier than most, but she is closer to Elysium than she was before. That counts for something."

Persephone ran her hand over her chest. "It's so heavy."

Hades wrapped his hand over hers and some of the pressure eased. "It is."

CHAPTER ELEVEN

FAMOUS LAST WORDS

PERSEPHONE

W hen Persephone awoke, it wasn't to the god of the Underworld, but instead a stack of books. Grabbing one off the top, Persephone held it above her head, too lazy to roll over and sit up. As she flipped open the cover, her blood ran hot, and she sat up in a flurry. Depicted on the first page was a man and a woman in a scandalous position, each one tasting the other.

A note next to the books grabbed her attention, and she set the provocative book down in exchange for it. Heat curled her toes as she read the words.

Persephone,

I will be busy the next few days, but here is some homework I expect you to busy yourself with. Stay within the house and don't go into Asphodel until I return. Clothes in the chest.

-H

"Asshole," Persephone murmured, even though a small smile played on her lips.

That he thought to cage her with his little homework was a poor use of his time. Now that she knew she was more, knowing wasn't enough. She wanted to see what her power could do. However, every time she tried to focus on what should have been her power, nothing happened. Not a whisper, not a murmur, nothing.

Irritation flared bright in her. Was it possible that the curse was holding her power at bay? Things may have changed between her and Hades, but she needed to remember that her goal was to cure herself. It didn't matter that Hades said it was impossible. She knew what she was capable of and what she was willing to sacrifice.

Opening the chest, she found an array of clothes, from pants and shirts to dresses in varying colors, though all were dark in nature. Finding a dark green blouse and black pants, she tugged them on and was happy to see that they fit her perfectly. It seemed she would no longer be relegated to Hecate's tight clothes. The smile that worked its way onto her face was foreign and unfamiliar. He had clothes made for her.

What was she to the god of the Underworld? What was he to her? A means to an end? An experiment? Persephone was not a coward and yet she found herself wanting to hide from the question. It felt like if she pried too far into it she would find an answer that hurt or made her feel too much. It was dangerous territory.

Instead, she would do exactly as Hades had told her not to and go to Asphodel. That seemed like a far better use of her time. Opening the door, Persephone made her way to the entrance. The dining area was open and inviting, the feast that was always there ready for the taking. Laying a hand on her stomach, she thought it was odd how there was only the barest whisper of hunger despite having been in the Underworld for weeks.

Ignoring the uncomfortable concept, Persephone went to open the front door when a hand slid in front of it.

"I was told you would not listen to orders, so I've been sent to babysit you," Hecate said with a frown.

A sigh broke loose from Persephone. She should have known he wouldn't make it that easy. Hades was many things, but most of all, he was clever. He would have known exactly what she would do.

"You don't seem pleased about it. Tell me, do you always do his bidding?" Persephone said with a tilt of her head.

The smile that formed on Hecate's face reminded Persephone exactly who she was dealing with. Hecate was the goddess of magic, witchcraft, and sorcery. Many mortals feared her while some threw themselves at her feet, hoping to feel an ounce of her power.

"Cute. I can almost forget you are Demeter's daughter until you say antagonistic shit like that." Hecate placed her hands on her hips, assessing Persephone.

This felt like a battle of wills and Persephone wasn't prepared to lose. "You know, you are one of the few immortals my mother had anything nice to say about."

Hecate waved a hand dismissively. "That's because she's been hoping to be invited into my bed for centuries, but I've always felt like she would be the clingy type and that's not worth it."

Persephone wrinkled her nose as an image of her mother and Hecate formed in her mind. "Gross."

Hecate laughed and it was light and endearing. "She is going to be livid when she finds out about you and Hades."

Something in Persephone ran cold at the thought. Not because of what her mother would think. That was probably lowest on her list of concerns, but because it made that nagging question of what they were come to the forefront of her mind again. There was no doubt that she enjoyed being with him. Not just in his bed, but just being around him. He was clever and his humor made everything seem lighter.

"I thought you didn't approve," Persephone said, trying to banish the thoughts.

Hecate's eyes roamed over her face, seeing something more that Persephone wanted to hide. It was uncomfortable, like being stripped bare.

"I don't." She frowned, considering her next words. "This started as a game, and it's quickly becoming something else. I wonder if I told you the truth, what you would do."

"The truth?" Persephone asked, feeling like she didn't want the answer.

Hecate opened her mouth and made a choking sound, her face went red, but as soon as Persephone went to her it was as if nothing happened.

"Fuck Hades," Hecate swore, the promise of vengeance on her beautiful face.

"You can't say what you want," Persephone said, understanding.

Hecate swore. "He's an asshole. I should have known he wouldn't make it that easy."

"Is there a way around it?" Persephone asked, finding that as scared as she was to know what Hades was hiding from her, not knowing was worse.

Hecate shook his head. "Not unless we leave the Underworld, which I'd be happy to help you with."

"No." She didn't have to think, didn't need to consider.

Hecate sighed and turned away. "You can't actually leave the manor either, by the way. You are essentially trapped in a new prison. Doesn't that bother you?"

Even though she knew Hecate spoke the truth, she tried to open the door and found that when she opened it, there was nothing except darkness on the other side. She slammed the door as rage poured through her.

"That fucking asshole," Persephone seethed.

"But you can leave the Underworld. He's an asshole, but he does have some lines and you are free to leave when you wish it," Hecate said quietly.

Persephone saw the game as it unfolded and smoothed out her face. "You were manipulating me, but you forgot one thing. Demeter is my mother and all she knows is manipulation. I have spent my entire life being made to feel as if my needs were a burden and now that I am free from it, I'll never go back. You can save your time."

Hecate nodded. "All right. If we are going to be stuck here, we might as well have some fun."

She tossed a small package to Persephone. Unwrapping it, she revealed a small leaf rolled delicately.

"Scythian Fire," Hecate said, waving her hand and producing a small flame.

"Teach me how to use my power," Persephone said unceremoniously.

"Your what?" Hecate stumbled as she took the small leaf from Persephone's hands.

Hades didn't tell her. Her body filled with warmth at the knowledge that he hadn't shared her ability. He was still an asshole, but this meant something.

"I made flowers grow in the Underworld," she said matter-of-factly.

Hecate stared openmouthed at her. "You aren't a demi-god."

"No," Persephone answered.

"And you want me to help you learn your power?"

"That's what I said." Persephone met the other immortal's gaze.

Hecate nodded slowly. "We are going to need more of this." She lifted the leaf from Persephone's hands and used her small flame to create a slight burn at the tip.

Persephone watched as she brought the leaf to her mouth and sucked in deeply. Handing it back to Persephone, she gestured for her to the same thing.

"What is it?" Persephone asked even as she took a deep inhalation of it and held it in like Hecate had showed her.

When she couldn't stand it any longer, she let loose the breath and coughed as it burned her throat. Hecate laughed as Persephone coughed violently, grabbing at her chest.

"You'll get better at it. Now follow me," Hecate ordered.

They came to the library where Hecate made her sit down and stood over her, occasionally handing the leaf back to her.

"Your power is a part of you. Like your life force that will never deplete. You shouldn't have to think about using it, but you are likely an exception, having been a swan half your life."

"I didn't think about it when I used it before. I just did," Persephone said.

"Maybe it would help if you told me how it happened," Hecate said, one hand on her hip.

The hesitation in her made her pull the leaf from her lips as she considered. It felt like it was a truth she didn't want to share and yet her desire to learn was greater than her fear.

"There was a boy that crossed over into the Underworld. He was scared and I wanted to make him feel better. So I gave him a flower. I didn't realize I had created it until Hades told me."

Hecate's eyes widened and she brought her hand to her chest, rubbing it almost anxiously. "He brought you to the gate?"

It felt like an accusation, but the disbelief in her voice made Persephone feel as if she was missing something.

"He didn't let me. I grabbed onto him before he portaled," Persephone explained.

Hecate's eyes burned like coals. "Hades did *let* you, Persephone. He could have sent you back in an instant. What the fuck is happening between you two?"

An excellent question. "That seems like a personal question."

Hecate narrowed her eyes. "I honestly can't decide if I like you or hate you."

Despite the sentiment, Persephone smiled. "Well then, maybe you can just teach me and figure out the rest later."

"Fine. It's not like we have anything better to do down here," Hecate said, giving in.

***

Hecate and Persephone settled into their own routine over the course of the next few days. During the day, they would practice Persephone's magic, which she had learned enough of to be able to conjure a small carnation. Hecate would berate her and tell her she was deliberately holding herself back and Persephone would tell her that made absolutely no sense. At night, Persephone would find her way to Hades' room and read the books he left her.

Eventually, need would coil in her and she would find herself exploring her own body, but nothing felt as good as he felt. Even in his bed that smelt of him, she tried to imagine it was his fingers touching her, but she felt his absence too much. If that was the only time she had missed the god of the Underworld, it might not have been concerning, but she found that she missed him even when laughing with Hecate.

She should have felt like she was trading one prison for another, being stuck in the manor, but it never felt that way. Hecate kindly reminded her every day that she could leave and that was more than she ever had on the surface. If this was a prison, it was of her choosing.

On the third day, Hecate produced another leaf and they shared it while Persephone tried to access the power she now recognized within herself. At least that was something. A soothing calm fell over her as the leaf cleared her mind.

"Stop overthinking it," Hecate said, bored from where she was sprawled along the couch, tossing a ball up in the air and catching it.

"Easy for you to say. Your power is literally magic," Persephone grumbled.

Shock ran through her as something hit her in the head. She jerked her head to the goddess who held out her hand to the ball at Persephone's feet, which easily answered her call. Hecate's eyebrow rose in challenge, and Persephone stared open-mouthed.

"Did you just throw a ball at me?"

"I did," Hecate said, resuming her game.

Persephone focused on the ball and pulled at the center of her, the very core of who she was. To her delight, the ball slipped through Hecate's fingers as it turned into a single black rose. Hecate sat up slowly and held up the rose.

"You did it!" she shouted, a smile breaking out over her face.

Persephone stood up and held out her arms. "I did it!"

The two immortals squealed and Persephone unthinking trotted over to Hecate who handed her the rose.

"Now do it again," Hecate said with a wicked grin.

Holding onto the rose and clutching it to her side, Persephone focused on the book that lay on the side table. Pulling on the source inside her, she projected until at last she felt the form of the book give way and it turned into another black rose.

Both women erupted in cheers and to both of their surprise wrapped each other in an embrace.

"What is happening here?" drawled a midnight silk voice.

Persephone's heart leapt at the sound and she broke from Hecate and held out the rose to him.

"I made it," she said, proudly.

He kicked off the wall he was leaning against and strode to her, eyeing the rose. It was hard to say what she had imagined his reaction would be, but it certainly hadn't been the darkness that fell over his eyes. Taking the rose from her, he eyed it as if it were a worm he could crush before lifting his eyes to hers.

"You told her." The words were sharp, his body tense as if expecting a fight.

Persephone narrowed her eyes at him, unaffected by his dark mood. She had made her decisions and she wouldn't apologize for it even if he disapproved.

"I wanted to learn. She's a good teacher," Persephone said.

Hades glared at Hecate behind her. "You tell no one. Not even Hermes. Do you understand?"

"Hardly," Hecate scoffed. "But I'm beginning to."

If she hadn't known they were friends, she would have been worried about a fight breaking out between the two immortals.

Persephone lifted her hand to Hades' cheek and made him look down at her.

"You look exhausted," she said, running her fingers over the dark circles under his eyes and seeing the way his cheeks were drawn in.

He relaxed a fraction under her touch as he raised his hand to cover hers. "I'm fine."

"Yes, Hades, tell us why you are so very exhausted. I'm sure we would love to know," Hecate said, coming up next to Persephone.

"Hecate," Hades, growled. "I'm not in the mood."

"I'm sure we could change that." Hecate lifted a strand of Persephone's hair and twirled it around her finger.

Hades' eyes locked onto the gesture and the darkness she thought she imagined hovering over him leaked out from his side like smoke.

"You know I'm not the jealous type, but we could share her, you know. It's not like we haven't shared partners in the past. I mean—she really is stun—"

The words were ripped from her as a tendril of black wrapped around her throat, Hecate dropping Persephone's hair.

"Finish that fucking thought and I swear you will find there are thousands of ways to torture an immortal." Hades' eyes flared with black flames.

Panic ripened in her at the bulging of Hecate's eyes and the fear as she grabbed for Persephone.

"Hades! Let her go!" She put her hands on either side of his face and forced him to look at her. "She's your friend, Hades, and she's mine as well. Let. Her. Go."

The flames in his eyes receded, along with the black smoke that returned to him as if it never were. Hecate released a breath, gasping for air. Persephone released him and went to Hecate, pulling her into her body.

"What the fuck, Hades?" Persephone ground out as she ran her hands over Hecate who had a slight bluish tint to her lips.

"It's all right," Hecate rasped, patting Persephone's arm. "I knew what I was asking for."

Persephone shook her head, not understanding, but turned to Hades to see his eyes widen a fraction as he stared at her. Nothing made sense about what was happening, but all Persephone knew was she couldn't stand to see either of them hurt.

"You are really fucked, Hades," Hecate said, finally reconciled to her previous well-being.

"Don't—" Hades fought for the words. "Don't pull something like that again, Hecate."

"Yeah," Hecate agreed. "Despite how it may seem, I don't actually have a death wish."

"What was that?" Persephone asked, her eyes darting between them.

Hecate groaned and threw herself onto the couch while Hades sniffed the air. "Have you two been using Scythe?"

"Yes. I am an excellent influence. You chose your babysitter well." She picked at her nails, bored once more.

Hades pinched the bridge of his nose and sighed. "Three days, Hecate. It was three fucking days and you are already annoying me."

"Yeah, before you throw me out, let me be the first to tell you that while I am fond of you, I'm not going down for this, so count me out. I also like her. She's kind of bratty and really stubborn, but I like her."

"Thanks?" Persephone said with narrowed eyes. "I would really like to be part of this conversation."

"Exactly. Which was my next point. You need to tell her all of it. Putting a mute spell on me was a shitty thing to do." Hecate glared at him.

Hades slid into his chair and a glass of liquor appeared in his hands, "But apparently necessary."

"Not if you wouldn't be such a territorial prick—"

"Bye, Hecate!" Persephone called as the goddess rolled her eyes while being thrown out of the Underworld.

"I shouldn't have left her with you," Hades said, throwing back his drink and setting it down.

Persephone watched him and wondered what could make one of the most powerful immortals exhausted enough that it began to show.

"I need to talk to you," she said, crossing her arms.

She wanted to touch him, to climb into his lap and tell him it would be okay, but that wasn't who she was.

"Oh?" he said, arching an eyebrow.

"Yeah. It really was shitty to put that spell on her, but also to just leave with only a note—"

"And homework," he corrected, running his eyes over her.

Her core tightened at his appraisal, but she steadied herself. She would not be distracted.

"Focus, Hades," she snapped, pointing up to her face. "Stop keeping things from me. I want to know where you went, why Hecate is worried, and what *this* is." She gestured between them.

"Do I get to choose the order in which those are answered?" he said, rubbing his jaw.

Rolling her eyes, she threw up her hand. "As long as they all are answered."

Hades leaned forward. "And what if I don't? Are you going to go back to your curse and your mother?"

"No," Persephone answered. "But whatever *this* is ends, which would be a shame because I did a lot of homework."

His eyes darkened, and she knew she had hit her mark.

"What if you don't like the answers, Persephone?"

"Then so be it, but I'd rather know. I've been kept in the dark my entire life. I won't do it again."

"No," he said, watching her carefully. "I don't think you will."

Silence stretched between them, waiting for one of them to give in. Surprisingly, it was the god of the Underworld who spoke first.

"Things are not going well in the mortal lands. Your mother has ceased all harvest, and the mortals are dying at a rapid pace. Asphodel wasn't prepared for as many as there are. Minos and I were expanding to make room while I tried to push souls that were nearing Elysium to move on."

Persephone felt like the air had gone from her lungs. She clutched her chest as her mind thought back to how gaunt Petre was. It was a truth she couldn't hide from. He had died from starvation, and it was her fault.

"And if I go back, she will stop?" The words were steady despite her rapid heartbeat.

Hades' hands turned white where he rested them on the armchair. "It is likely."

The darkness that clung to him seeped out, a small haze of smoke stretching out.

"What is that?" She gestured to the smoke.

Hades tilted his head. "That wasn't one of your questions."

"Well, now it is," Persephone shot back.

"You are exceptionally difficult," he said with mild irritation despite the way his body was coiled tight.

Persephone stalked forward and leaned over his chair, their faces inches apart. "Here's the thing, Hades. I am naturally inclined to be selfish. A normal person would have heard what you just said and ran home, sparing lives, but I'm not."

Hades was hardly breathing. "No. You are not."

"Answer my questions."

"It's a manifestation of my power when I feel particularly strong emotions, that are . . . darker in nature. Hecate is worried because the longer you are here and the more mortals die, sooner or later, Zeus will intervene. She won't risk his wrath. *This*—" He leaned forward, his breath mixing with hers. "Is whatever you want it to be."

"That's not what I mean, Hades, and you know it." Persephone's voice was raspy as she fought the urge to kiss him.

"I feel . . . very possessive of you." His eyes darted over her eyes and to her mouth.

"Because you want me?" she asked, quietly.

"Yes," he answered, his hand glided up to slide across her chin and jaw.

"Do you usually find yourself . . . possessive of your lovers?" The thought made her feel slightly sick to her stomach. She didn't enjoy the idea of him being with others.

"No," he said, trailing his hand down her neck and chest.

A thrill ran through her that she thought she was better off not exploring. "Let me try to break the curse."

It was the same as ice water pouring over him as he jerked his hand back and cold eyes met hers. "No."

The urge to scream her frustration was blinding as she pulled away from him and stalked across the room. When she was satisfied with the distance between them, she whirled around and saw black smoke seeping from him.

"That would fix everything," she said, irritation tight in her voice.

"Because you would be free to return to the mortal lands and your mother," he said, lethally quiet.

It was at that moment that she realized it wasn't as simple as it used to be. Maybe before breaking the curse would have been enough, but not anymore. Now that she knew him, wanted him, cared about him, it would never be enough. Even if she broke the curse, her mother would keep her and never let her back into the

Underworld. Demeter hated Hades and the fact that she had been in the Underworld with him would only increase her ire.

All her bravado deflated at once. "No. I guess that won't be enough now."

The darkness retreated back into him as he stood and strode toward her. Her legs felt shaky as he came to loom over her, a dark promise in his eyes. His fingers trailed along her jaw and down her neck as she leaned into his all-consuming touch.

"And why won't that be enough, Persephone?" he coaxed.

Because she wasn't a coward, she met the god of the Underworld's eyes as she said, "Because I wouldn't have you."

And that was all she saw as the world blurred around them.

CHAPTER TWELVE

YOU ARE MINE

HADES

Hades didn't think, didn't hesitate as he opened the portal into his room, taking her with him. All he knew and needed to know was that she wasn't content to be without him any longer. Somehow that knowledge burrowed into him and it was all there was. She was all there was.

When his power settled around them, Persephone was standing, circled in his arms with a small gasp on her lips. Need coursed through him, but he was better than that. He would let her decide what this was and he would take the scraps she gave him.

"Hades, we should talk about what to do next," she said, even as her mouth parted and her eyes drifted to his lips.

Amusement drifted into him and her attempt to fight her desire. "Is that what you want? To talk?"

Persephone licked her lips and he bit back the need to taste her.

"I said it's what we *should* do, not what I want."

"Mm," he murmured, running his finger over her bottom lip and enjoying the way she shivered under his touch. "Then talk, Persephone."

She was fire incarnate as she glared up at him, though there was no real anger in her eyes. "I can't think when you are like this."

"Like what?" he crooned, his free hand pulling her into him.

She bit her lip as he languidly dragged his thumb down her chin and neck. "You know what you are doing to me."

He bent his head close to hers and whispered in her ear, "Would you like me to stop?"

"No," she breathed.

Satisfaction rolled through him. There was part of him that thought she might fixate on the worries that lingered around them, but her desire was palpable. It made him feel more like a god than he ever had before.

He lifted his trailing hand up and threaded it through her perfect hair. "And what would you have me do to you, Persephone? Should I taste you once more?" He leaned down and ran his tongue lightly along her bottom lip to remind her how good it felt to have him between her legs. Her gasp told him his message had been well received. "Should I let you fuck my fingers and feel you come around them?"

Persephone whimpered and grabbed his shirt with two fists and consumed him with a single kiss. There was urgency in the way she instantly parted for him and allowed his tongue to slide in, tasting her, claiming her. Fuck. His cock was pulsing with the need to be inside her.

She broke the kiss with a sharp bite to his lip that had heat tearing through him. "I don't want your mouth or your fingers." Her voice was breathless.

Part of him wanted to toss her onto the bed and claim her right then, but he could be patient when he needed to be. "Oh? And what do you want, Persephone?"

"I want you to be inside me." For emphasis, she ran her hand over his hard cock, fighting for purchase against his pants.

His eyes fluttered against the touch and the wicked smile she threw at him said she knew damn well how she affected him.

"How would you have me take you?" he asked, restraint breaking as she stepped away and slowly began unbuttoning her shirt.

Her eyes locked on his. "You choose. Do what you will with me, god of the Underworld."

His control snapped like one of The Fate's threads and he reached for her, easily lifting her while she wrapped her legs around him. So fucking eager. He should have taken his time with her, but all he could think of was this need to claim her. To make her his. Her hands tangled in his hair as he gently laid her down on his bed, rumpled and smelling of her.

"You slept in my bed while I was away," he said, settling his body over her.

She ran her hand over his cheekbones and down his jaw. "I missed you."

Something stirred in him, long since dormant and forgotten. "I missed you too."

And he had. He had thought about her every fucking second and it had been torture. This wasn't supposed to be how this went, but it was hard to make himself care when she was in his bed, looking at him like he was all she had ever wanted.

Unable to stand the thoughts, he captured her mouth with his and kissed her like he had wanted to for the past three days. Languid and consuming. His hand roamed down her body and over her breast, where he let his power consume the barrier of her shirt to what he wanted. In a moment, her breast gave under his hand and he claimed his prize.

"Hades," she breathed out.

His name on her lips was fucking amazing, but when she said it with lust in her eyes, it was intoxicating. She was intoxicating. He dropped his mouth to her breast and teased at the small peak of her nipple. She whimpered under his ministrations and wrapped her hands in his hair. He let his hands go lower, ridding her of her pants until she was naked beneath him. Pulling away, he took in the sight of her. Every curve and angle perfect.

"This seems a little unbalanced," Persephone said as she reached for his shirt.

He bent down and nipped at her ear. "All you have to do is ask, Persephone."

She turned her head, catching his mouth with hers. It was hungry and teasing as she lightly bit at his lower lip and pulled away. His whole body felt as if it was made from heat and need.

"Take your clothes off, Hades," she ordered, meeting his eyes.

She was likely the only person he would take an order from, but either way, he was happy to comply. With a thought of his power, his clothes were gone and he was hers to do with as she wished. His body was tense above her as she drank him in, swallowing hard as she ran her hands over his chest and stomach.

In one swift movement, he picked her up and flipped over so he was on his back and she straddled his legs. The small shout of surprise quickly swallowed by the desire in her eyes as she took in her new position. Here he had learned a fundamental fact about her. She loved taking control wherever she could find it. It had long been denied her and she craved it more than life.

Her eyes darkened as she understood what he was giving her. He was hers to take and he would worship whatever she gave him. Persephone shifted, rising on her knees before slowly lowering herself onto his hard length. The anticipation had him holding his breath while he forced his hands to be light on either side of her hips. The darker part of him wanted to grip her hips and slide her along his cock, but this was about her and what she needed.

Persephone placed her hand on his chest and lowered herself onto his cock. She was fucking ethereal with her blonde waves wild over her shoulders and back and her head lifted, eyes closed.

"You are a goddess. Fucking perfect," he said hoarsely.

A smile curved on her mouth as she met his eyes and she slid onto him fully. A soft moan escaped her lips and despite his efforts, his hands dug into her hips. She felt incredible around him and it was all he could do not to move his hips.

She bit her lip as she adjusted to the feel of him inside her and when she was satisfied, she nodded.

"Are you all right?"

Her eyes flashed and she leaned down to hover her mouth over his. "I've never been better."

Fuck, it was hard to hold himself in check when her voice was sultry and provocative over him. He thought he had already reached the limits of his self-control, but for her, he would be whatever she needed.

"Hades?" she asked, quietly.

"Yeah," he grunted.

"Show me everything."

So he fucking did. He lifted her up before sliding her back down on his cock and she gasped, righting herself so that she could control the movement. As always, she was a quick learner and moved her body, learning what she liked and didn't. Picking up on her rhythm, Hades allowed himself to move his hips with her and she cried out, the sound the most beautiful thing he had ever heard.

"Take what's yours, Persephone," he ordered as he brought his thumb to her clit and pressed against it.

She cried out. "Yes! You. You are mine," she panted.

If that didn't shatter whatever control remained in him. He bucked his hips beneath her and ran his thumb along her clit, just the way she liked it.

"I'm fucking yours," he growled, coming undone at the sight of her riding him and claiming him. Fucking hers.

"Hades, I'm, I'm-oh gods . . ." she pleaded.

"Don't call out to them," he said with all the authority that came with being a god. "You are *mine*."

"Hades!" she shattered around him, her warmth convulsing around his cock, as she took her pleasure from him.

It was all he needed to follow her over the edge, his own pleasure spilling into him. She was his. She looked wild and untamed above him with his clouded vision as the pleasure coursed through him. It was heady and consuming in the best way.

Persephone collapsed on top of him and he brought his arms around her, loving the way their bodies felt together, sweat and all. He shifted his head to allow hers to cradle in against his neck and the flash of white on skin caught his eye.

He lifted his head and saw the markings of a tattoo along her back. Shifting her hair, he traced the lines even as his thoughts just peaceful turned murderous.

"Hades?" she asked as she lifted her body from his, a question in her beautiful eyes.

"Your tattoo," he said, his voice rough. "Every curse leaves a mark."

Her lip quirked up. "I hated it for a long time because it reminded me of my prison, but now that I've been free down here, I don't mind it as much."

She twisted her body and pulled her long hair over her shoulder exposing all of the white tattoo. Two swan wings blossomed from her spine and formed around her shoulder blades. He traced the lines of it and she shivered under his touch.

"Would they go away if the curse broke?" she asked.

"Sometimes," Hades answered, disliking where this conversation was going.

There was no point in even discussing her curse ending because the payment of her life wasn't worth it. Would never be worth it. Instead, he would deal with Demeter. The how of it wasn't clear yet, but he would figure it out.

"You're mad," she said, her lips turned down into a frown.

The rage in him dimmed as he remembered that everything else could wait. All that mattered was that she was here with him. He shook his head and held out his arm to her. She immediately curled into his side and rested her head on his chest. Her body warm against him as a foreign sense of peace fell over him.

"I'm happy." Persephone sighed contentedly against him.

The words felt sweet and consuming. "Me too."

A command shot through his blood that was unwelcome and intrusive. "Fuck."

"What is it? What's wrong?" Persephone said, sitting up, her eyes running over him as if she thought something was wrong with him.

He almost wished there was. It would be a better alternative. He disentangled himself from her and threw on a shirt and pants.

"Fucking Zeus," Hades growled as fury lived in him.

Persephone brought her nails to her mouth as if anxiety were claiming her. He quickly strode over to her, the call in his veins growing by the second. He grabbed her hand from her mouth and gripped her chin between his thumb and finger, forcing her to look up at him.

"It will be fine, Persephone."

Maybe it was a lie. There was no way of knowing until he answered the summons. The fucking nerve of Zeus to summon him like some dog. That it was happening was enough to convince him he was lying to her. There had only been two other times Zeus had summoned him and neither had ended well for him.

"Hades, your veins are turning black and look like they are trying to rise from your skin," she said, as her hands ran over his forearms.

Despite the fact that he likely appeared terrifying, there was only concern in her voice.

"It's because I'm fighting the summons," Hades said, twisting his neck against the strain in his body that was bordering on painful.

"Why would he summon you?" A tear slid down her cheek.

He ran his thumb over it as if he could take her worry away. "I don't know how long I'll be gone, but promise me you won't leave the manor. You won't go into Asphodel."

He wouldn't even say the River Styx, wouldn't even put the thought into the universe. Into her.

Fuck, it felt like every cell in his body was on the verge of exploding, too tight and too much.

"You're in pain," she breathed.

"Promise me, Persephone," he said through clenched teeth.

"I promise!" she gasped out.

With a roar, he gave in to the summons and let it take him. A moment later he was standing in Olympus, his jaw tight as he bit back the pain those few minutes had cost him.

Zeus sat on his gaudy ass golden throne surrounded by marble pillars and the illusion of open blue skies surrounding them.

"What the fuck?" Hades ground out, his whole body tense with the urge to punch his brother.

"That's the longest anyone has fought my summons, which begs the question of *why*," he drawled as he tapped his fingers on the massive armrest. A clear indicator he was annoyed.

"You could have sent Hermes. Summoning me like some dog is uncalled for." Hades brushed at his sleeves, tampering down the instinct to level all of Olympus.

Anger would only encourage Zeus. Indifference and levity tended to work better to set him off balance.

"That would have taken too long and the less involved, the better," Zeus said.

"And what exactly are we involved in?" Hades asked, schooling his face into boredom.

"Give Demeter back the girl," Zeus ordered.

Hades' blood ran cold. "What girl? Wasn't Demeter looking for a swan?"

Zeus slammed his fist on the throne. "Enough! Normally I tolerate your little schemes, but this one is costing far more than it's worth."

"Two points to make," Hades began with a sigh. "One being that can't you just order Demeter to fall in line? Second, are you so worried for the mortals suddenly?"

Zeus stood from the throne and strode down the dais. It was enough. Hades felt his aura the minute he drew close.

The chuckle he let roll from his chest made Zeus' temper grow with each step. "I should have known it wasn't the mortals you were concerned for, but yourself."

The thing about being the god of the Underworld was that mortals feared him. They never revered his name or made sacrifices to him. His power was entirely his own, not imposed by any outside factors. Every other god could not say the same.

"Have the mortals lost faith in you, brother?" Hades smirked.

Now that Zeus was closer, he could see that it wasn't just his aura that had dimmed, but there were lines on his usually smooth face as if he was aging.

"Demeter is gone. She fled to the mortal realm and in doing so, is immune to my summons," Zeus seethed.

Shit. That was problematic. "And you want me to, what, go fetch her?"

While in the mortal realm, Demeter's powers would be unusable or faint at best. It was why her connection to Zeus couldn't be used, but one of them would be able to track her down if they tried hard enough.

"I want you to bring her daughter back so she stops sulking and does her damn job," Zeus yelled, and the blue sky turned gray and lightning zipped through its atmosphere.

This was far worse than Hades could have imagined. Without worshippers and sacrifices, the other gods would slowly drain their power because that was the secret of the gods. They needed mortals just as much as the mortals needed them. The balance was delicate, but Demeter had tipped it a little too far.

Either way, there was no point in mincing words.

"No," Hades said, meeting his brother's eyes.

Zeus' brow furrowed, unaccustomed to the word. "No?"

"No," Hades answered.

The sky was now black around them and Zeus lifted his hand, a lightning bolt appearing in it.

Hades refused to be intimidated by his brother's theatrics. "Send Athena or Ares to track Demeter down. That is the solution."

"The solution is whatever the fuck I say it is," Zeus roared, his power running over Hades.

Even dulled, his power was still the strongest of them all and it attacked him with a viciousness that spoke of desperation. It wasn't as much pain as a battle of wills that brought him to his knees. Zeus loomed over him and held the lightning bolt to his neck. His pulse driving his vein closer to the bolt with every pump of his immortal heart.

"You will release the girl or I will make you suffer, brother or not," Zeus said, fire dancing in his dark eyes.

"Then get on with it because I will not bow to Demeter's tantrum," Hades said.

Zeus held his gaze a minute as he considered keeping good on his word, but then the storm cloud receded and the sky turned blue once more. The lightning bolt at his neck vanished. The compulsion lifted from him and he fought the need to gasp for air as he stood, attempting to look more unaffected than he felt.

Zeus shook his head and ran his fingers through his red hair. "I understand the need for your games, Hades, but you push me too far this time. I will send Athena and Ares to track Demeter, but if she is not back in three days' time, you *will* surrender her daughter even if I have to torture all the blood from your body. Do you understand?"

"Perfectly," Hades said with an arched eyebrow. "Though if you could send a reminder so I don't forget, that would be delightful."

Zeus chuckled and clasped his hand on Hades' shoulder. "I know the others find you annoying, but there's something to be said for your fortitude. The rest of them would have crawled and begged me to let them go. Even Poseidon."

"If that is all," Hades said, lifting his hand to create the portal that would take him back to her.

The power blew out in his hand as Zeus exerted his control once more. His own power smothering Hades'. "Three days, Hades."

Zeus' power lifted and Hades wasted no time summoning his portal and stepping through. Persephone, who had clearly been pacing, jumped when he entered. Just like that, all the distasteful interaction with Zeus faded as she stood before him, wearing one of his black shirts that were far too big for her and looking at him with relief. She barreled into him and wrapped her arms around his waist.

"Are you all right?" she asked, squeezing him tight enough that if he were mortal, he might have been concerned.

He chuckled and ran his hand down her hair and back, pulling him tighter against him. "I'm fine. Zeus just likes to remind us where we stand from time to time."

"What did he want?" she asked into his chest.

The urge to lie to her, to protect her, was there, but he knew she was strong enough and would want to know. "Your mother has fled to the mortal realm and the mortals are rebelling by not worshiping or making sacrifices. Zeus has sent Athena and Ares to find your mother and drag her back to Olympus, but if they don't find her in three days, Zeus expects me to deliver you."

Persephone pulled back to look at him, searching him for something. "What will he do to you if you don't?"

Hades shrugged. "Torture, maim, the usual things."

She shot him a wary gaze. "It's not a joke."

He pressed a kiss to her forehead. "It'll be fine."

CHAPTER THIRTEEN
THE PROMISE
PERSEPHONE

T hree days. That was all the time she had to find a way out of this. Yet even if she broke the curse, there was nothing she could do about finding her way back to Hades. Because that's what this was about now. There was no world without him in it. She craved every part of him and she wasn't prepared to give him up.

She snuggled closer into him and tucked the cover over her shoulders. Hades pressed his face into her neck and she shivered even as she laughed. They had slept very little last night and somehow she was awake and feeling better than she ever had, even with the deadline looming over them.

Persephone twisted and wrapped her arms around his neck and pressed her lips to his, smooth and coaxing.

"You are insatiable," Hades murmured approvingly as he shifted his body over her, eager to give her what she asked for.

Her body warmed and her toes curled with anticipation, but Hades stilled above her and a heavy sigh left his chest. He slumped down beside her and rested his head on her chest.

"Hermes and Hecate are here," he said with annoyance.

Persephone was surprised to feel a pulse of happiness to know Hecate was back. She had come to like her. However, she didn't appreciate the interruption.

"Can't they wait?" she asked, running her hand over his head.

"Normally, I would say yes, but they might have word from Olympus," Hades said.

Persephone conceded defeat at the bloom of anxiety in her chest. Leaving his bed was a loss she mourned, but as she threw on clothes, she wondered at what it all mattered. She needed to find a way to earn her freedom, not just from the curse, but from her mother.

They found Hermes and Hecate in the library sitting on the couch, Hecate with her legs propped on Hermes' lap. The fireplace was burning and the room exuded a warmth that had Persephone rolling up the sleeves of her shirt.

"Zeus gives you a deadline and you sleep it away? That doesn't sound like you, Hades." Hermes frowned.

Hades rolled his eyes and took one of the large-backed chairs. Deciding she didn't want to be far from him, she propped herself on the side of the chair. His eyes widened a fraction before he gave a small smirk and lifted his hand, which she gladly took.

"Shit," Hermes said, looking between them.

She saw the wicked glint in his eyes as he lifted her hand to his mouth and kissed it.

"We are fucked," Hermes moaned.

"Stop torturing him," Persephone said through her smile.

"But it's very easy to do," Hades said with a wink.

"You know who also enjoys torturing from time to time?" Hecate asked. "Oh, right. Zeus."

That ripped the humor from them easily enough. Hades didn't let go of her hand, but he settled back into his chair. "I have an idea."

Persephone's heart beat faster. "You do?"

His blue eyes met hers and she felt like she was drowning. Persephone didn't have a lot of experience with people, but she couldn't imagine the sway he had over her was common.

"I was thinking of throwing a party," he said, running his thumb over her hand.

Hecate choked on her own surprise, coughing until she regathered herself. "You want to host a party for the gods? Here in the Underworld?"

"You've always refused," Hermes said, open-mouthed.

"I think it's time I reminded them all who they are dealing with," Hades said with dark promise in each word.

"This feels like a bad idea," Hecate said.

"Hermes, send a message that I will be hosting two nights from now."

"The day of the deadline," Persephone said quietly.

Hades' eyebrow rose. "So it is."

Persephone narrowed her eyes. "What are you planning?"

"I suppose that depends on your answer," he said.

Persephone threw back her head, sighing before glaring at him. "Stop being evasive and ask me the question."

Mirth gathered in his eyes as he nodded his head towards Hermes and Hecate. "You want me to ask you in front of them?"

"Please don't," Hecate pleaded.

"Ask me." Persephone didn't shy away.

"I want to secure your position and make it more difficult for you to be traded like cattle. To show that you are not only powerful in your own right, but have the backing of the Underworld at your beck and call."

Persephone swallowed and it was as if the world narrowed down to him. Her heart beat rapidly in her chest, but she wouldn't hesitate with him. Never with him. She wanted everything he offered her and more. Deep down, Persephone knew she was reaching a boiling point, a place she needed to make a choice.

Her conversation with Prometheus floated back to her and she thought about how she had been quick to tell him that a life of sacrifice was a life worthy of remembrance, but how many had died while she lived and found happiness? No, she wouldn't hesitate with him or her truth.

"What happens to you when you do this?" she asked.

"Torture," Hecate said.

"Imprisonment," Hermes offered.

They might not have existed at all for the way he watched her. He ran his thumb over her hand, ocean eyes feasting on her every movement, as if desperate to understand her. Yet she had never been anything except when she was with him.

"Does it matter?" he said dryly.

She reached over and grabbed at the front of his shirt. "You know it does."

His free hand reached up and covered her own and for all the world, they looked like two desperate lovers. And maybe they were. Cleaving to an idea they could keep what they had found, they barely had time to understand.

Hades waved his hand and she didn't have to look to know that he had sent Hecate and Hermes away.

"It would be worth it. Whatever the cost, it would be worth it," he said.

Persephone's heart fractured at the vulnerability he let show only for her. Standing, she straddled him and ran her hands along his face and neck, down his chest.

"Hades," she said his name with all the worship he deserved.

He brushed the side of her jaw with his knuckles. The gesture sweet and somehow heartbreaking.

"Ask me your question," she whispered.

Hades swallowed and it was the first time she had ever seen a flicker of nervousness in him. The god of the Underworld, the second most powerful immortal, was nervous only for her.

"You're scared," she said quietly.

"Terrified. I've never felt anything like it," he confessed.

"Why?" she asked, even though her own heart raced with her own fear.

His face twisted as if he was in pain, but he was more than his fear. "I'm terrified that I am no better than Demeter and that if I ask you and you say yes, I'll be chaining you just as she did. I'm afraid that *this* is a symptom of your imprisonment and that you will wake up one day and realize you want more. Part of me wants to make you experience everything and everyone the world has to offer, but a much larger part of me knows I would slaughter anyone who touched you. That I would enjoy torturing anyone who brought you an ounce of happiness or pleasure when I could not."

Persephone's throat felt too tight. Like emotion was swallowing her whole until she was only consumed by it. Despite the way she felt as if she was drowning, she relished the way her heart beat for him. The way he made her feel.

"Ask me the question, Hades," she said, stronger than she felt.

Hades searched her eyes and whatever he found made him run the back of his finger down her neck. "Marry me. Be the goddess of the Underworld and rule beside me."

A smile broke across her face and she gave a small laugh. "That wasn't a question, Hades."

His lips twitched, but his nerves kept him tense beneath her. "I am not used to asking for things."

"Try again," she teased, leaning forward to run a trail of kisses down his jaw and neck.

He took in a sharp inhale. "You are distracting."

"Then you must not want to know my answer enough," she murmured against his ear.

"Persephone," he said, running his hand through her hair while gripping her waist. "Will you marry me?"

She pulled back and smiled sweetly at him. "That wasn't so hard, was it?"

His lips thinned, and his eyes locked onto hers. "You are more than any torture I could conceive."

Persephone cupped his face with her hands, forcing him not to pull away from her. "I'll marry you, and you need to know that even if this were a new prison. Even if I never left the Underworld because of this choice, then I would still be happy because it was my choice to make. I am choosing this. I am choosing you."

Emotion broke out on his face, and he squeezed his eyes shut. Persephone ran her hand along the back of his hair and rested it on his neck.

When he opened his eyes, there was a new conviction in them. "What if you end up resenting me?"

Persephone shook her head. "Never lie to me and never suppress me and I will be happy."

"You have my word," he said and she believed him.

He tilted her chin down and claimed her with his lips. It was slow and beautiful, as if they knew they had all the time in the world. The kiss deepened and she could feel him harden beneath her as the need between them grew. Persephone shifted her hips, an ache growing in her core that sent languid heat down her entire body.

Hades pulled her closer against her and stood, his arms supporting her even as they continued the kiss, teeth, tongue, and lips moving with relentless need. He stepped, and in the next moment, they were standing in his room. He set her down on the bed with a gentleness that left her heart aching.

As he positioned himself above her, he trailed a sweet kiss down her jaw and neck and she clung to him. Even though she knew he could rid her of her clothes with a simple thought, he worked his fingers into the laces of her shirt.

"Hades," she pleaded.

She didn't want his patience. All she wanted was him inside of her, filling her and reminding her who she belonged to. Who he belonged to.

"As you command, but know that I intend to take my time with you, Persephone."

In a single thought, their clothes were gone and it was just skin against skin. The hard length of him ready and glistening with his desire for her. He ran his hand over her breast and bent down to lick and nip at her. Her body shot with pleasure with each tantalizing movement as she arched her back, begging him to take more of her. Never one to deny her, he sucked hard on her nipple and she cried out, digging her hand into his hair and holding him against her.

Her core ached and she didn't want to wait for him any longer. She wrapped her hand around the length of him and pumped him just the way he liked it. He moaned against her and claimed her lips with his even as she continued working him. The feel of him in her hands was pleasure itself. She loved that she could make him moan and his breathing turn shallow. His hand wrapped around hers, taking her away from him and she nearly objected, but his eyes were determined as he slid into her entrance, ready for him in every way.

Persephone threw back her head as his cock brushed against her clit. She thought she might resort to begging, but he gave her exactly what she wanted as he thrust into her, slow and purposeful. She loved the way he filled her and when he withdrew to enter slowly once more; she thought she might go mad.

"Hades," she breathed, needing more and yet having more than enough.

His arm wrapped around her waist and he sat up, holding her against him. This new position made him hit deeper inside her and she cried out, burying her face in his shoulder as they worked in tandem, their pace slow and sensual.

Persephone lifted her head and cupped his face in her hands. His eyes were heavy-lidded with lust, but there was a clarity in the blue of them that made her want to bare her soul to him.

"I love you, Hades," she said the words without reservation or regret.

Somehow, he had become her truth in a short period of time. Her body and her very blood answered his call and his alone. There was nothing that could convince her that she wasn't made for him. The way they fit together and the way she was his had long since been ordained by The Fates.

He stared at her with wonder, as if he thought she might be a conjuring of his mind, but the same conviction she felt was written all over him. "I love you, Persephone. I am entirely at your mercy."

Their kiss was a sealing of words and promises and when she rocked her hips, a gasp broke from her. Pleasure rippled through her and her body clenched. She was already breaking against him. And when she rocked her hips against him and his cock hit just right, she broke with his name and her love on her lips. Hades drank in her release like a man starved, fueling his own as he followed her, her name a prayer on his lips.

Even as they worked through their haze of pleasure, they clung to each other. Their bodies warm and made for one another sealed for an eternity. The Fates' foretelling sealed.

Chapter Fourteen

A Shit Party

Hades

It was hard not to convince himself that this had been a terrible plan. It felt as though one moment he was convinced it was the best option and the next he knew it would all end in flames. Which was not an option.

"This is a bad idea," Hermes muttered, running his hands together.

"You say that about everything," Hades said, fussing at the cuff of his shirt to hide his nerves.

"Because your plans are always bad ideas," Hermes said.

"Name one," Hades countered.

That had been a dumb thing to say. Hermes lifted his hand and began ticking off fingers. "When you burned Aphrodite's curtains. When you stole all of Narcissus' mirrors. When you dyed trout green to make Poseidon think there was something wrong with the ocean and, oh, when you stole Demeter's fucking swan."

Hades cracked a smile and clasped Hermes on the shoulder, "See, that's where you and I disagree. That was the best plan I ever had and probably will ever have."

Hermes stared at him with wide eyes and an open mouth. "I don't even recognize you anymore."

That made two of them. How could it be in just a few weeks everything had changed for him? Now he just needed to make sure he kept what was his.

Hecate appeared next to them wearing a form-fitting red dress that hugged her body until it flowed out at the bottom, trailing behind her. Her lips were painted to match and her hair was done up in an ornate pattern.

"You look nice," Hades said with a wink.

Hecate crossed her arms and glared at him. "One. This is a terrible idea. Two. Don't get me in trouble with Persephone. I begrudgingly like her."

Hades laughed and the sound was warm and entirely foreign to him. A side effect of Persephone. "A high compliment coming from you."

Hecate rolled her eyes before her face softened with unmistakable concern. "What are you going to do when this goes wrong and she goes back to the mortal realm, because Hades that could very well happen."

Hades stilled. He was an immortal who prepared meticulously for all outcomes, but in this, he had struggled to formulate a plan. It was as if his mind refused to consider the possibility. Either way, soon it wouldn't matter when they secured her place at his side.

Ignoring the question, Hades said, "It's time."

Hecate watched him a moment longer, but he didn't give her time to voice her concerns. With a thought, he transported them to the site of the night's festivities. It was beautifully monstrous as he took in the image before him. He had chosen to host the gods in the Underworld's east. The walls of Tartarus rose high above them, a mixture of black and red bricks with no apparent pattern that shed black smoky mist. The evidence of his power held the wall in check.

To the side of his venue was the River Styx, where condemned souls swam and reached out to anyone who got too close to their banks. Yet opposite it sat the ethereal promise of Elysium, marble steps led up into a beautiful pantheon of pure white. The doorway cast an amber glow. It was where three out of the four parts of the Underworld converged. All reminders of the realm he ruled. At the center of it all was a large pavilion, set with flickering candles suspended in the air, that gave the river an eerie glow.

Gods and goddesses gathered at the center, their excitement at something entirely unprecedented, palpable despite their unease at its location. All dressed in their finest, they drank and ate to their pleasure. The thirteen were cemented in their power enough that they could eat and drink and not be bound to the Underworld. It was those that came after the original immortals that fell victim to the prison that came from consuming the Underworld.

Hecate and Hermes went first, dispersing into the crowd with ease. His nerves had him nearly clawing at his shirt to make space around his throat. He could hardly breathe. He should have seen her one more time before they did this. Delayed his coming to spend a few more minutes with her.

But this was for her and he would not fail her. An awareness filled his mind and it settled among the crowding already gathered. The Underworld had too many souls in it as it was, but adding the awareness of the immortals was distracting. Even still, he smiled with satisfaction as the awareness found its place. His plan was already succeeding. Hermes would need to apologize for his lack of faith.

Removing his veil, he strode into the pavilion as if it were Olympus itself. At the top was a group of nymphs wearing scantily clad black dresses dancing with sensual purpose to a song of longing and desire that rang throughout the air. They had the crowd's attention, but Hades sent out a wave of his power that shifted throughout the room. All heads turned towards him and he set his face in cool amusement, hiding his worry.

"Welcome to the Underworld. I hope tonight is a night you all will not soon forget," he said in way of greeting. "However, I hadn't expected to see you tonight, Demeter, though if you don't mind me saying, you look terrible."

And she did. Demeter stepped away from Athena and glared at him with all the hatred her immortal heart was capable of. She had dressed for the occasion in a navy dress that was loose around her and her eyes were slightly sunken with dark circles beneath them. Where once he could see Persephone when he looked at her, that time had passed. There was nothing left of Persephone in Demeter except for their shared blonde hair. The room was ripe with tension as all the immortals watched the show they had come for.

There hadn't been a doubt in his mind that if he announced he would host that Demeter wouldn't show herself. The question was whether that would work in their favor or not.

"I've come for my daughter," Demeter shot at him.

Hades sighed. "Hardly a way to start a party, Demeter. Try to keep up."

Poseidon's shoulders bounced with light laughter, but even his eyes were wary with the question of what Hades was doing. Zeus had his arm slung around Hera, whose lips were pursed in disapproval.

"You've managed to coax Demeter out from her hiding place, but why should I exert my will over her after the distress you've caused her?" Zeus said, with a slight uptilt to his mouth.

He enjoyed the role of a benevolent overseer. Pretending to be just and fair, as if they were all his errant children in need of redirection and guidance.

A few shouts of agreement broke out among those loyal to Demeter, which in fact was most of them. As if they had forgotten she had cost them sacrifices and worship with her tantrum. Only Hermes, nervously running his hand through his hair, and Hecate, who looked bored, were silent. They all thought him the villain in Demeter's story, but maybe it was time they learned.

"An excellent question, Zeus. Though I believe I am not the right person to answer it." He sent a nudge through their connection and it was as if she slid her hand down his back in answer.

A cloud of inky black smoke laced with the smell of champagne and cinnamon appeared next to him, filling the room with gasps. In a moment, it dispersed, snaking its way throughout the room around the immortal's feet. In its place at his side stood Persephone, and she was enough to bring him to his knees. Her blonde hair fell in waves down her shoulders and back while she wore a tight black dress made of lace that showed her skin below in tempting hints. It hugged every aspect of her body, leaving her shoulders bare and running down her hips and legs to where it split in the front, opening to pants that clung to her. She wore heels that laced and crossed in a pattern that had its own mind. Dark kohl lined her eyes and her lips were painted black. Most noticeable was the ink that flowed along her collarbone, vines with small flowers laced throughout. She was terrifying and made of the Underworld.

He held out his hand to her and she slipped hers into it. Running his thumb over, he could feel the rapid beat of her pulse that betrayed her nerves.

"Persephone!" Demeter gasped and made to run toward her, but Persephone held out her hand and a wall of immovable black roses appeared before Demeter, locking her in place.

His blood caught as he took in the look on Zeus' face. His eyes roamed up and down Persephone as if she were something to catch. It was all he could do to not make his attempt to throw Zeus into the prison behind them.

"I would say it's good to see you, Mother, but that would be a lie," Persephone said calmly, commanding the room.

Demeter's face fell. "What I did—"

"Was for you," Persephone said, unflinching from the pain he knew seeing her mother caused her.

Demeter's face twisted with pain and she stepped forward to go to Persephone, but the wall of power prevented her. She turned, glaring at Hades.

"Let me go to my daughter," she seethed.

Hades chuckled, taking the utmost joy in delivering the truth to her. "It is not I who holds you in place."

Her eyes widened with an echo of shouts and murmurs behind her.

Poseidon glanced between Persephone and Hades.

"Shit," he said, rubbing his hand over his face, his former delight replaced by trepidation.

None of them mattered except for one. Zeus' eyes hardened and he released his arm from Hera's shoulder. Standing to his full height, he met Hades' gaze.

"What is this?" he asked, but he already knew.

Hades gave a small smirk despite his heart's pumping that told him he was anxious. The hand in his tightened and he looked at her, finding strength in her. They had made this decision together and they knew the consequences if this failed. Persephone inclined her head slightly as if deferring to him, but he knew she was giving him the space to get his nerves under control. The thought of losing her was consuming.

Instead, he turned to Zeus. "The Underworld answers to her authority. She is both its queen and my wife."

Demeter let out a wail of mourning while Zeus clenched his fists at his side. Hades had anticipated this. Zeus coveted his authority and his power. He would see this as a threat when it didn't have to be, but Hades would damn well make it one if he needed to.

"You've overstepped," Zeus said with dark malice.

Hades shrugged, unconcerned. "Perhaps. However, now you see why Demeter's claim on her is void. She belongs to the Underworld."

"You fucking monster," Demeter snarled at him before turning to Zeus. "I demand retribution."

Zeus nodded, as if considering it, but Persephone stepped forward.

"I realize my desire for my autonomy in the hierarchy of Olympus is low, but I would speak for myself if permitted."

Fuck. That was not in the plan, but he should have seen it coming. She was done letting others speak for her, but she didn't understand Zeus. He had thought he had made the threat clear, but apparently, it had been lacking.

Zeus drank her in and crooked a single finger at her. The instinct to grab her and pull her against him was consuming, but he held himself perfectly still as she strode towards Zeus, the immortals parting for her. When she walked past Demeter, who reached out for her, Persephone shot out a tendril of power that locked her in place. She was using too much power, too quickly. The power they shared was locked by the bond they had created in their marriage pact and amplified by her own natural power, but it was not limitless.

She stopped two feet from Zeus, putting necessary distance between them, but Zeus was never one to learn boundaries. He prowled forward, circling her like a predator. Hades' blood roared and he could feel Hecate's own power nudging him, reminding him to still.

"It's not hard to see why my brother stole you. You are enchanting," Zeus purred.

Persephone inclined her head. "Thank you. I wish to plead my case."

Zeus smiled with hunger and waved his hand in acquiescence.

"My mother wronged me when she cursed me to a half-life. I do not wish to return to the mortal world with her. My place is here in the Underworld." Her voice was strong, commanding.

Zeus nodded, watching her. "Yet to be able to rule the Underworld, you must be more than a demi-god. Something your mother and Hades were remiss in not sharing with me."

Power hummed in the air as Zeus' promise of ire filled the space. He was angry, despite the way he spoke to Persephone casually.

"I cannot speak to others' decisions. Only my own," Persephone said.

"And yet, you must know they will both be punished for their lack of judgment."

She knew it well enough. Hades had warned her he would face retribution no matter the outcome of tonight and that she was not to intervene. That it would be a small price to pay.

"As is within your right, as the god of gods." She bowed her head.

Zeus snorted. "Was it your mother or Hades who educated you on the hierarchy of the gods?"

"Both," Persephone answered easily.

Zeus kept his eyes on Persephone. "It's time you explain, Demeter. Who is her father?"

The question was more of a command and Demeter's veins bulged as she fought against it. She fell to her knees. Hades hadn't concerned himself with who Persephone's father was, but the way Demeter fought made him suddenly curious.

The word was ripped from Demeter's throat. "Aeetes."

Fuck. That was unexpected.

Zeus whirled toward the fallen goddess of the harvest, and if she was mortal, his eyes alone would have killed her.

"You dare to lay with a sorcerer!" he roared.

Everyone was quiet, knowing the crime Demeter had just been forced to confess. There was very little Zeus feared, but he feared sorcery. There were four. Aeetes, Perses, Pasiphae, and Circe. The latter being powerful enough to have turned a mortal into a god and transformed a nymph into a terrible monster. For her power, she had been banished to an Island to live in isolation. The others had stayed within their power and not earned Zeus' wrath, but everyone knew they were capable of more.

"She does not have any sorcery in her. He tested her himself before placing the curse." Demeter covered her mouth as if she hadn't realized she was giving away more than she meant to.

"You had better fucking hope not," Zeus growled.

Persephone was locked in a head spin. He could see it in the way her fingers curled at her side. In the way she steeled her shoulders. In the briefest of moments, she had learned the identity of her father and her curse's orchestrator.

As if he no longer cared about Aeetes and Demeter's betrayal, Zeus turned towards Persephone and reached out his hand to trail his finger along the black ink of their marriage contract. Hades didn't think. All reason left his mind. All his calculations lost in a single moment. He lashed out his power and wrapped it around Zeus' hand, lifting it from his wife.

"She is not yours to touch," Hades said with dark intent.

Zeus didn't show any surprise, as if he had anticipated it. His own power tangled with Hades'. A battle of wills, but Zeus was weaker than he had ever been. The mortals lack of sacrifice and worship, leaving him less than he was. Yet Hades had never been the recipient of their love, only their fear and respect. His power was not dependent on them and so his power held.

Zeus' face quickly turned red as understanding dawned on him. Persephone turned to face Hades with her features furrowed in concern. She shook her head while Hecate's power clawed at him.

"Hades," Persephone said quietly.

Her voice cut through his rage and he released his power. The Immortals in the room breathed a sigh of relief. All except Zeus, who met his eyes, a promise in them, a moment before his power landed over him. It was a crushing weight, forcing him to his knees. Hades' breath was ragged as he fought against the suffocating weight. He could feel Persephone's consciousness press against his mind in comfort, but it wasn't enough against the pain that followed the pressure.

Zeus loomed over him. "I can't decide if you are stupid or just drunk with lust that you would challenge me."

That hadn't even been his challenge. Zeus was a fool if he thought that was all the threat Hades presented. He had been too long in power to remember that he was only slightly more powerful than Hades and Poseidon. If they ever worked together, Zeus would be left with nothing. Yet, the discord and mistrust among the gods was enough that none of them would trust another long enough to work together.

"You forget that you are replaceable. That I could throw you in the walls behind us just as easily as I could let you live. Speak," Zeus commanded, lifting some of his power.

It was an effort not to vomit at his feet as the pressure receded. Yet he met Zeus' hard gaze, all familial bonds forgotten. "And who would you saddle with the Underworld in my place? Who would have the power to hold Tartarus while managing the dead? I am not as replaceable as you would like to believe."

Power slammed into him, but this time he was ready. He held Zeus at bay as he stood. The fury and promise of retribution in Zeus' immortal face would have brought the rest of them to their knees. He was more than that. At all times, his power spread in many directions. His hold on Tartarus, Elysium, Asphodel, and each soul in his realm. Even with that, he still had enough to stand against Zeus while he was weakened. It was the reason he had always suspected Zeus saddled him with the Underworld and not

Poseidon, whose well of power was less. Zeus wanted Hades busy so that he couldn't threaten his rule and until now, Hades had never had a reason.

Now he had every reason. Releasing the barest breath of the control he exerted over Tartarus, the wall behind them groaned, and dust released as the bricks shifted. A roar said the Titans were well aware of the strength of their prison. Shouts around them broke out as the immortals realized what was happening.

Zeus' eyes widened and Hades leaned forward. "I suggest you reconsider your stance."

"You wouldn't. Even you aren't mad enough," Zeus seethed.

Hades laughed, a low and off-setting sound. "I would rather let the Titans have their fill than see you lay a hand on her."

The brick wall shuddered as the Titans seized their opportunity and rammed their bodies into it.

Zeus bared his teeth. "She will suffer the same fate."

Hades met his eyes so that there would be no questions between them. "So be it."

The scowl on his brother's face was born of a promise of death. "This was your ploy? I wondered what you were planning, but this exceeds even my own expectations of you. You forgot one small fact, though."

All of Hades' confidence faltered at his brother's relaxed countenance. A miscalculation somewhere along the way. It was impossible. The plan was that if Zeus forced his hand, he would remind him why he was the god of the Underworld. Why he was the greatest threat to Zeus. His brother would be livid and take every opportunity to remind Hades of the hierarchy, but over time, he would relent. They would settle into the same pattern and Hades and Persephone would be free to live as they pleased.

Yet he knew Zeus saw everything and still he gloated as if he had not been out-maneuvered. It made Hades want to grab Persephone and throw them all from the Underworld, but remaining ignorant wouldn't serve them.

"Reinforce the prison and I will allow you to know how The Fates laugh at you, brother," Zeus said.

He could feel Persephone against his mind, comfort and yet not enough. Something in the words Zeus spoke settled over him like an infection. Working its way into every corner of his body. Maintaining the hold that would prevent Zeus from exerting his will over him, Hades forced the wall behind them back into its impenetrable state. Even the sound of the Titans fighting for freedom receded.

Assessing the room, he had never seen the immortals shaken as they were. They had come for a show and gotten much more than they bargained for. Athena and Ares stood together, shoulders pressed together as if prepared to fight for one another. Apollo had his arms around Artemis. Aphrodite, Hephaestus, and Dionysus were exchanging quiet words, likely whether to stay. Hermes and Hecate were watching him carefully. Hera stood beside Persephone, saying something to her that had her biting her lip. Demeter was wringing her hands, but there was more clarity in her eyes. Poseidon just stood with his arms crossed, his lips in a thin line.

"Demeter!" Zeus called. "Tell Hades what he has failed to consider."

Demeter reached for Persephone, but his wife shook her head.

"What did you do?" she asked, understanding something Hades didn't.

Demeter's face fell. "I did it for you. To protect you."

This was more than the curse that bound her in the mortal realm. This was a threat. It was the reason Zeus wore a small smile as he turned to Persephone.

"There was a reason your mother risked my wrath by fleeing among the mortals. Desperation. Time working against her. Against you," Zeus intoned.

Persephone's chest rose and fell rapidly as she met her mother's gaze. "Tell me."

Demeter cringed against the harshness in her daughter's voice. "The Fates—they told me you would be stolen, so I knew no matter how I tried, this would come to pass. So I asked your father to make the curse to protect you. I didn't know the cost would be that you would live half your life as a swan."

Being a swan wasn't the curse. Hades wrapped his power around Demeter's neck and forced her to the ground before coming to stand over her. "What was the curse he cast, Demeter? Speak quickly or I swear I'll snap your neck myself."

He released his hold on her throat and a tear streaked down her face, but her attention was only on Persephone. "You are bound to the lake. You will die if you don't return in swan form to its waters within a month."

Persephone paled and her eyes snapped to his, but he couldn't think straight. Everything they planned. They had made their move without knowing all the pieces and now they were fucked.

"Hades," Persephone said quietly, but she didn't need to say what he already knew.

He had nearly killed her. She would have died and it was all his fault. The one thing he had wanted to protect and he had nearly doomed her.

"So you see now that this was all for nothing. She will return to the mortal realm with Demeter and you will be left to deal with the ramifications of your treason."

"You wanted to see what I would do, knowing that I would still be forced to give her up," Hades said with mortification.

Zeus smirked. "I always win, Hades. You know that."

"The seeds," Persephone breathed.

The smirk fell from Zeus as he tilted his head, his mind working through the puzzle in his mind. "That *was* clever, Hades. To bind her to the Underworld." He turned to Persephone. "How many?"

Persephone looked to Hades, panic making her clutch her hands together. Hades let loose a long sigh of defeat.

"Three," He breathed.

Demeter was cursing his name, but he only cared about Persephone and what he had cost her.

"So she belongs to the Underworld three months of the year. You are lucky you did not do much more or she would have died," Zeus said, enjoying his victory.

Even though he was gloating, Zeus gave him hope. "It doesn't matter which three months."

Zeus shrugged. "I would think not. As long as at the end of the month she returns to the lake, she will live. Both contracts honored."

"I have to go back," Persephone said, despair clinging to her like a second skin.

Hades was tired of the audience. He banished all but Demeter and Zeus. He crossed the distance to Persephone and cupped her face with his hand. She leaned into his touch.

"But you will live," he said, quietly.

She locked her eyes onto his. "Not if—"

"We were outmaneuvered," he said, silencing the damning words she would have spoken. Not only would he not allow her to attempt to break the curse, but they also didn't need their enemies knowing there was a way to.

"Come home with me, Persephone," Demeter said as if she were rescuing her.

Persephone twisted her head to glare at her. "I have one more week."

Zeus laughed as if it were all very amusing and his heart wasn't ripping from his chest.

"Persephone," Demeter said as if she could not believe her daughter, even after everything.

"She will return in one week to Demeter," Zeus decreed. "This is almost a fitting punishment for you both. One who thought to keep secrets from me and one who thought to challenge me. May you both find misery in your conniving. In the meantime, know that there will be consequences for you both. I would think very carefully about your next actions. Demeter will decide the three months Persephone spends in the Underworld."

With that, Zeus left the three of them in a prison of their own making. Demeter reached for Persephone and with tears streaking down her face, Persephone slapped her mother. Demeter pulled back and held a hand to her face, staring wide-eyed with disbelief.

"Fuck you," Persephone seethed. "You have made a mockery of my life and now you take me from the life I choose."

Delusional still, Demeter shook her head. "You are confused. He has muddled your mind-"

"Get. Out," Persephone breathed.

Hades answered her call and took great enjoyment in throwing Demeter out of his home. When she was gone, Persephone fell into him. He ran his hands over her hair and pressed his lips to the top of her head.

"It'll be all right, love," he soothed.

"You know it won't. You are worried, Hades. I can practically feel it. Don't placate me. It was all for nothing."

Hades lifted her chin with his thumb and forefinger, forcing her to look at him. "Not for nothing, Persephone. If you hadn't taken the seeds, they would have taken you tonight and you never would have been able to come back. This is still something."

"Three months. Three months with you and the rest forced to endure a half-life made even more miserable because I know what it means to live now. To love."

"I'll think of something," Hades said, but it was a barbed promise.

Their hands were tied. Outmaneuvered and outsmarted. Fuck.

CHAPTER FIFTEEN

EVERYONE SHOULD HAVE A DOG

PERSEPHONE

Persephone could list her mistakes for hours, but the biggest one was not jumping in the River Styx at that disaster of a party. It was the only way now. She would have to swim to earn her freedom, but then, it wasn't as simple as that. Hades was sure she would die and once, that wouldn't have been enough for her not to try, but now there was him. A life with only a little of him was better than no life.

Even still, she was greedy. She wanted more with him and the river offered her that chance. With the curse broken, she could fully bind herself to the Underworld. It would be her choice.

It had been a punch to her stomach to learn who her father was. Hades had told her of his experiments with controlling men and making them do his bidding. How he was known for his cruelty. When she had suggested asking him to relinquish the curse, Hades had told her it was a non-starter. He could have simply bound her to the lake, but he had added the layer of making her a swan as a level of cruelty. There would be no aid from him. She was better off never meeting him.

"You look like shit," Hecate said, coming up behind her.

"You always say the nicest things," Persephone said, patting the soil into a tight formation.

The past few days, she had busied herself with setting up a garden at the edge of Asphodel. Since binding herself to Hades, accessing her power came more easily. No matter how much they both wanted to hide away, the duties of running the Underworld were persistent. Persephone was at least able to help alleviate his burden by guiding souls, but maintaining Tartarus was outside her new abilities. Since he had loosened his hold on the prison, it had required more maintenance. So while he was there, she had taken to setting up this small area in order to feel like a part of her would still be here when she left.

"Have you slept at all?" Hecate asked.

Persephone shrugged. "Seems like a poor use of my time."

In truth, she had slept very little. A few hours here and there. She didn't want to waste a minute of her time in the Underworld or her time with him. Even when Hades would insist she slept, she would lie with him until he fell asleep and then make her way to the library. Even though she knew he disapproved, he said nothing.

"I'm sorry, Persephone." There was uncharacteristic sorrow laced through the words.

Tears pricked at her eyes that she wished would go away. "Me too."

"Hermes and I will still come visit you in the mortal realm," she offered.

Persephone nodded. At least there was that. It was more than she had before. It wasn't enough, though. Could never be enough without him.

Silence stretched between them as Persephone called to her magic and a small flower took shape among the soil. Something to grow while she was away. It was worse not knowing when the next time she would be back was. Her mother could make it months. It didn't matter how the three months in the Underworld were satisfied as long as they were.

"How is he doing?" Hecate asked cautiously.

She flinched at the question before correcting herself and focusing on the next plot of soil.

"That bad," Hecate murmured.

"I'm worried about him," Persephone said, her movements stilling under the weight of the confession.

"I would promise you that Hermes and I will look after him, but you've seen how easily he throws us out of here," Hecate said dryly.

"How did it all go so wrong?"

Hecate snorted. "How could it not have gone wrong? He stole you. It was never going to end well." Seeing Persephone's glare, Hecate threw up her hands. "It's just the truth."

She felt his presence like a warm breeze wrap around her. "Hecate."

Persephone stood, wiping the dirt off her legs, and found Hades assessing her as if something could have happened in the last hour he was gone.

"Just being a good friend and checking in," Hecate said too casually.

"Unnecessary," Hades murmured.

"Hades," Persephone chastised.

He arched a brow. "What do you want me to say, Persephone?"

"Thanks for being a great friend, even though I always put you in shit situations would be a good start," Hecate offered.

Despite her bad mood, Persephone's lips curved up. "A bit excessive."

"Under no circumstances will I be saying anything like that," he said, rolling his eyes.

"It was worth a shot." Hecate shrugged.

The banter died as the weight of the next day fell over them. Hecate shifted uneasily. "Hermes will come tomorrow to escort you."

Dark shadows gravitated from Hades' body as his jaw clenched. The sight didn't startle her in the least, as it happened multiple times a day.

She turned to Hecate and clasped her arm. "Thank you for checking in."

The goddess nodded before casting a wary glance at Hades. "You know how to reach me if you need anything."

Hades didn't bother to reply, but Hecate knew him well enough and saw herself out. When she was gone, Persephone crossed the distance between them and wrapped her arms around him. His body was warm beneath her as his heart beat too quickly.

"It will be all right," she said quietly.

He pulled her tight against him with one arm and ran the other down her hair. "You know it won't. What will it cost you every time you go back? I keep imagining every time you leave, a little more of your light will be dimmed. Worse, what will Zeus do or any of them when you are vulnerable and I can't protect you? My threats mean less to them after losing to Zeus. Even then—"

"Hades," Persephone interrupted. "Stop worrying."

Hades gave a bitter laugh. "That isn't possible."

Lifting her head, she peered up at him. "Remind me what I have to look forward to when I come home."

The flash of emotions on his face made her heart fracture. The broken joy when she referred to the Underworld as home, the reminder that she was leaving, and the knowledge that she would come back washed over him rapidly. He ran his hand over her cheek and dipped his mouth to hers with blinding reverence. In a tendril of darkness, he brought them to their room, where he laid her down with a tenderness she doubted anyone had ever witnessed from the god of the Underworld.

Her body yearned for him in a way that was consuming and fundamental. He was in her blood and she was happier than she had ever been, even on the eve of their temporary separation. In a moment, their clothes were gone and it was just them. Bared, body and soul for one another. Running his hands along her skin, she arched her back, needing more.

Never one to deny her, Hades pressed his body against hers as he ran his tongue over the seam of her lips, urging her to let him in. She complied happily and he took her as he entered her, eliciting a soft gasp from her. She ran her hand over the mark on his left chest of vines that wrapped around each other in a large swirl. The mark he carried of their marriage contract.

Wrapping her arms and legs around him as if that could make them closer, she murmured into his ear, "I love you, Hades."

His movement stilled and for a moment Persephone wondered if that had been the wrong thing to say. That she had been caught up in the moment and it was all too fast. That she was desperate and in one moment she could have ruined everything, but Hades pulled back to run his gaze over her. She let out a sound that was more akin to ruination as she saw what she felt reflected back at her.

His hand caressed her cheek and he tilted her chin up, placing a languid kiss on her mouth. "I don't know what I've done to earn your love, but I swear on my crown and my life that I will honor the gift you have given me. I love you, Persephone, as I have never loved another in all my immortal life."

The kiss deepened and she loved all of him. As they made love, Persephone felt for the first time in her life that she was where she was meant to be. How could she give up something that was a part of her very soul? Their movements were slow and patient. As her core tightened, it was in the same tantalizing steady way until she could no longer focus on their kiss or anything outside of the way he fit inside her.

Hades buried his face in her neck as the pleasure brought them to the edge, his breath hot against her, sending shivers along her body. Wrapping her hand in his hair, she held him against her while she called out his name as the dam broke. Her body pulsed with what he did to her and she knew there would never be anyone else for her. No matter how long she lived, it would only be him. The sound of her name on his lips as he followed her over the erased whatever doubt lingered that he loved her. Brought together by The Fates, but cemented in love.

**

The level of concentration it took Persephone to not fall asleep cuddled up against Hades while Cerberus snored at the foot of the bed, was record-breaking. Everything in her body told her to take the comfort offered to her and let sleep carry her away from what loomed in a matter of hours. She reached up and brushed a strand of blue hair from his face and tucked it behind his ear. The fact that he didn't react at all told her he was fast asleep, which meant that this was her only chance.

Disentangling herself from him, she slipped out from under the covers and threw on one of his shirts and a pair of leggings. Some part of her wanted him with her while she did this, even though she knew there was no way he could be. He would stop her and drag her back the moment he even suspected her. Grabbing her shoes, she tip-toed out of the room, but Cerberus jerked up his head mid-snore as she neared the door. Shit.

Uselessly holding out her hand, she mouthed the word, 'stay,' but Cerberus merely tilted his head before hopping off the bed and plodding over to her. Persephone pointed to the bed and whispered, 'Go lay down.' But he sat in front of her instead. Groaning silently, she tried walking back to the bed and gesturing for him to get up, but he just watched her with a tilt of his head that said he thought she had lost her mind. This was not one of her concerns when she thought out her plan. Fine. She would just go.

Cracking open the door, she slipped past, but Cerberus butted his head in an attempt to follow her. She pushed his head back in and tried to shut the door, but as soon as it was done, he whined and scratched at the door. Her heart raced as she opened the door and looked at the bed, but Hades hadn't stirred at all. This was already a disaster, but none of it mattered if she got what she needed.

With an exasperated wave, she let Cerberus out, who walked by her as if he hadn't almost ruined the plan she had spent a week fine-tuning. Shame on her for not accounting for the dog, though. Cerberus followed at her side as if he knew exactly where she was going, as a long string of drool fell from his jowls.

"You are a mess," she told him with mock irritation.

He didn't even look up at her as if her opinion mattered nothing.

"I'm going to remember this next time you ask me for belly scratches," she warned.

Apparently, he suspected she was bluffing, which she absolutely was. Coming to the front door of the manor, she stopped and crouched down towards him. In a motion quicker than she could react, he sent a slobbery kiss onto her cheek. She wiped at it as she gestured for him to sit.

"You are staying here. I'll be back in a little bit."

Hopefully.

As soon as she stood, Cerberus stood and nudged himself toward the door.

"You know I know you are intelligent, right? I'm ninety-nine percent sure you can understand me, so stop being so difficult. Stay," she said sternly as she opened the door and slipped out quickly.

The howl that erupted from the other side of the door made her heart fall into her stomach. She wrenched open the door and Cerberus walked out as if he weren't the cause of the adrenaline rushing through her blood.

"We are going to talk about this later, just so you know," she told him, even as she started to walk.

Hopefully, that didn't wake Hades, but if it did, she would still make her attempt. She knew it was futile and that he would find her instantaneously, but at least she would have tried. Since marrying Hades, Persephone found that her bond with the Underworld was a small bundle at the back of her mind. It was like she was aware of it, but that awareness didn't have any purpose. She knew Hades was connected to his realm at all times and could sense every soul that resides in it, but she couldn't do anything like that.

However, she could feel a sense of rightness, or rather a general sense of ease, when she was where she wanted to be. It had made navigating the streets of Asphodel significantly easier and allowed her to not rely on Hades as much. So each night when Hades slept, Persephone had gone to the library and searched for maps and anything that would help her give a general sense of direction to the River Styx. Though she had been there the night of the party, Hades had been careful to portal her so she wouldn't be able to return on her own.

She had spent the last week careful not to let on to her new ability, but the way Hades watched her, she wondered if he knew. No, if he knew, he would never have taken his eyes off her. The other change that had occurred with their joining was the little ball beside the Underworld that was him. A similar awareness of him allowed her to sense when he was close, but it was more of a comfort than a tool.

With every step, she felt a rightness settle over her. This part of the Underworld was barren and lay as an empty stretch of land, with only the light of the bioluminescence above for comfort. Even still, when she spotted the white marble of Elysium in the distance, she knew that she had been right to follow her instincts and the knowledge she had worked to gather. For the first time since the night before the party, she felt real hope settle into her chest.

She could use her magic to portal a short distance, but then she would use up the limited store she had. Better to save it in case things went wrong, although if what Hades and The Fates said of the river was true, then it wouldn't matter. She would soon forget who she was and what she could do. Yet she had to believe The Fates wouldn't have given her the answer if there wasn't hope in it. Hades had said that was the way of The Fates and that they delighted in cruelty, but she refused to believe that. Couldn't believe it.

So instead of calling on her power, she ran. She ran because she couldn't stand to be close and not make it. Because she couldn't tolerate a life without her home and her family. He was her family now. He was her home. She would not throw away such a precious gift. So even as her legs ached and her lungs screamed in protest, she ran.

The river formed up ahead and her eyes hungrily drank in its shifting black waters, where silver tendrils shifted beneath its surface. The air hummed around her and she felt it too late. Persephone ran harder, Cerberus next to her, keeping pace. The river was only ten feet away, but the awareness in her mind shuddered before it exploded around her. Arms wrapped around her and she let out a scream of frustration. She was so close. So close.

"Persephone," Hades warned, his tone darker than she had ever heard it.

He was pissed, but not even one cell in her body cared. Instead, she lifted her foot and slammed it into his. He let out a small grunt, but there was enough surprise that his grip loosened and she freed herself and ran. Five feet. In a flash, the river was blocked from her as he appeared in front of her. She couldn't slow her pace enough and she barrelled into him as he caught her easily.

"Persephone," he growled.

She looked up and met his gaze, letting him see the determination barreling through her, motivating her. She kicked up her knee and hit him right in the crotch, which was all the element of surprise she needed to get past him. She used her own portal magic born of spring to get on the other side of him and then she was there, just a few feet separating her from her freedom and the life she wanted. Not hesitating, she leapt. Just as she expected cold water to greet her, she was held in place just above the water. Frozen in time, she let out a scream that sounded feral and broken.

The world shifted and she fell onto the soft carpet of the library floor. Fuck. Tears streamed down her face and she didn't know if she was more heartbroken or angry. His hands reached for her, but she slapped them away. Instead, she lay on the carpet and sobbed for what had almost been.

In that moment, she hated him. Her grief was a living thing inside her and she cursed the day he took her. Loathed him for showing her a beautiful life and then denying her. It was the cruelest form of torture. She didn't know how long she lay on the carpet grieving, only that Cerberus stretched out next to her, head on his paws. Wrapping her arm around him, she mourned the loss of everything she had found. Her chest felt fractured and torn to shreds as the dawn above loomed over her.

She could feel Hades' presence, but he didn't try to comfort her and for that, she was grateful. She was afraid of the words she would say if she was forced to look at him. All she would see was what he had robbed her of tonight, even if she understood why. He had made it very clear that he thought the river was a death sentence. Underneath all the pain and resentment, she knew that he had been scared tonight. That everything he did was because he loved her, but none of that mattered while she lay on the floor with her soul shattered.

After a while, her sobs gave way to exhaustion and she fell asleep with her arm around Cerberus. She was dimly aware of strong arms lifting her and being cradled against Hades' chest, but it was as if it was too much for her body to open her eyes. Maybe she was a coward and hiding from the pain she knew would be on his face. Pain she had put there tonight, but they were both hurting and their burdens weighed heavily on them.

When he laid her down on their bed, she felt him slide out as if he would give her space. As if he thought that she wouldn't forgive him. She reached out her arm for him and she heard his heavy sigh as he settled behind her and wrapped his arms around her middle. She clung to his arms and tried to memorize what it felt like to have him hold her. Fighting sleep as long as she could, she committed to memory each rise and fall of his chest. However, there was only so long one could fight against the inevitable.

CHAPTER SIXTEEN

IT'S A SAD STORY

PERSEPHONE

Persephone woke up groggy and with her body aching. It was as if the atmosphere was too heavy and she was being crushed. She turned, expecting to see Hades, and found Cerberus on his back with his legs up and snores radiating throughout his body. Despite her melancholy mood, she let out a raspy chuckle. Closing her eyes, she concentrated on the awareness that was Hades. Disappointment washed over her as she realized how far he was.

They hadn't talked at all about what had happened last night and soon they wouldn't be able to. As much as Persephone knew her mother couldn't keep him away from her in the mortal world, Hades had been sure that Zeus would make it nearly impossible to leave the Underworld. When she pressed him on how Zeus would manage it, Hades had shaken his head and a heaviness settled over him. She understood the unspoken words. Mortals would die so that Hades was kept busy. It made her blood boil that the gods used lives so frivolously.

Her mother had done it, and now Zeus would do it for his own petty means. Killing men, women, and children because it suited him. It would all fall on Hades and she wouldn't be here to share in that burden. It made her want to fight and scream, which were welcome emotions after the despair she had felt last night.

Putting on a midnight blue blouse and black pants, she left in search of her husband. Cerberus jumped from his sleep and struggled to roll over a moment before following close behind her.

"I want to be mad at you, but it's really hard." He licked her hand, and she rubbed his head. "You know it too, don't you?"

The walk to Asphodel felt long and overwhelming, and yet as the awareness of him grew, the more she found herself relaxing. She needed him in a way that was carved into her soul. The city was finally settling after the influx of souls from her mother's influence as they had worked tirelessly to move along those who were ready to Elysium. The expansion of Asphodel meant more buildings littered the city, but the souls who went about their day hardly seemed to notice. Asphodel was whatever they needed it to be and it was always right in their mind.

Many greeted her as she walked by, and the knowledge of the turmoil of their soul flowed into her at each encounter. It was one of the ways the Underworld claimed her in her marriage contract. She could sense how far a soul was from reaching Elysium, but after a few test runs, they learned it was not even close to Hades' ability, but it was still something.

Coming around the corner, she found Hades leaning back in a chair across from a middle-aged man. Persephone recognized him as someone Hades had been trying to push out for a while, but the man had witnessed the death of his wife and children and despite the fact that they were all in Elysium, he clung to his pain. If she hadn't known better, she might have thought Hades was relaxed as he spoke with the man, his hand gesturing quietly. Yet the tightness in his jaw and the way his eyes were haunted told her differently.

Sensing her, his eyes snapped up to her, and he ran an assessing gaze over her. The distance and the loss between them felt too large. She watched as Hades stood, clasping arms with the man before making his way to her. His steps were long and his body tense, as if he didn't know whether she was about to attack him again or not.

Cerberus had no such trepidation and jumped, landing his massive paws on Hades' chest. The corner of his lips quirked up as he pet Cerberus, who slobbered happily before jumping back down and curling up between them as if he couldn't decide which one of them needed him more.

"Hi," Persephone said, breaking the silence between them.

Hades' jaw ticked, and he slid his hands into his pocket as if warring with himself. "I know you want me to tell you I'm sorry, but I'm not and I never will be."

"I know," Persephone breathed out and watched as some of the tension left his shoulders. "And I'm not sorry for trying."

He gave a slow nod. Maybe they would both always be a little angry with each other for their actions last night, but in the end, it didn't matter. Deciding that they didn't have the luxury of time,

Persephone swallowed her remaining anger and stepped past Cerberus to wrap her arms around Hades' waist. He quickly followed suit, and she relished the way he pulled her tight against him.

He pressed a kiss to the top of her head, and a tear slipped down her cheek. Her heart was shattering over and over.

"For a minute I thought you hated me," Hades said quietly.

Lifting her head to his, she shook her head. "Impossible. You are as essential to me as the air I breathe. I could never hate what gives me life."

His face softened and his chest was heavy with the breath he had been holding back. He ran his knuckles over her cheek and down her jaw.

"You kneed me in the balls, Persephone," he said with a small quirk of his lips.

Despite everything, Persephone laughed at the sudden change in conversation. "I'll make it up to you somehow."

His eyes flashed, and he tilted her chin up. "You also hurt my foot."

"Is the god of the Underworld so very fragile?" she teased.

His thumb ran over her mouth and she fought back a shiver. "Is the Queen of the Underworld always so smart-mouthed?"

Persephone rolled her eyes. "You know the answer."

He hummed. "Indeed, I do." He pressed a kiss to her lips that was slow and promising.

Their peace offerings exchanged and accepted.

When he pulled back, he brushed a piece of her hair away and tucked it behind her ear. "I have something for you."

"Oh?" she said with a coy smile.

Hades chuckled and shook his head. "You are insatiable."

"Can you blame me? I mean, have you seen yourself lately?" She grinned.

"It's true, I *am* very good-looking."

"And humble too." Persephone winked.

With a broad smile, he sank his face into her neck, nuzzling into her. She laughed and tried to pull away, but he lifted her easily. She wrapped her legs around him a moment before he shifted them into the library. Cerberus hardly seemed to notice his change in scenery as he gave a contented sigh.

Hades set Persephone down gently and went to the fireplace, where he took out a small box. He handed her it, watching her carefully, as if eager to drink in her reaction. Taking the box from him, she gave him a wry smile.

"What's this?" she asked.

"A present. Something to remind you of who you belong to in case you forget," he said quietly, with a hint of a smile.

Persephone rolled her eyes and lifted a finger to trace over her collarbone. "Is this not reminder enough?"

He watched the movement carefully. "No."

Clenching her thighs together from the heat in the single word, she lifted the lid and found two rings side by side. Both were made of dark obsidian, but the one for her was smooth with a black diamond at the center. His was a tangle of vines.

He reached over and plucked out the diamond one and slid it onto her finger before lifting her hand and pressing a kiss to it.

Emotion tugged at her and threatened to undo her, but she took her hand back and took out the ring that represented her magic, and slid it onto his own finger. He took the box from her and set it on the mantle before coming back and wrapping her in a tight embrace.

"I will always protect you, Persephone. If you need me, I will feel it and I will come, no matter the cost," he said into her hair.

"I know," she answered honestly.

Hades stiffened beneath her and for a moment she wondered if that had been the wrong thing to say, but he pulled back and cupped her face with his hand. "Hermes is waiting at the gate."

It felt too soon. "He can come back later. We have more time."

"No," Hades murmured. "You are nearly at the end of the month and it's not worth the risk."

"Hades—" she began, but her protest was stolen as he portaled them to the gates of the Underworld.

Hermes stood to the side, a frown playing on his lips. She knew he didn't want to do this either, but they were all bound in some way or another.

Cerberus whined at her feet, and she bent down, dodging his slobbery kiss. "Take care of him, okay?" In answer, he left her to sit at Hades' feet.

Her eyes watered, but she bit the inside of her cheek to keep them from following as she met Hades' gaze. "Don't let him get used to my side of the bed. You know he takes up all the space."

He tried for a smile, but it didn't reach his eyes. "You've become very demanding recently."

Persephone's resolve fractured beneath his voice, and she crossed the distance between them in a flash. He lifted her easily, and she wrapped her legs around his waist, burrowing her face into his neck. All she had wanted was to live, but it had been more than she had ever dreamed. He had been more.

Too soon, he set her down and pressed his lips to hers. A long and claiming kiss as if part of him truly was afraid that she would forget that he was the other piece of her soul. She answered his kiss, hoping he would know that she could never forget. When they broke the kiss, both of them were left breathless.

"I love you." He murmured quietly, a hint of silver lining his eyes.

"I love you," she reached her hand up to his face, but in a flash, she was on the other side of the gate and Hades was gone.

The shock and hurt were palpable a moment before her stomach wrenched with pain. She clutched it and was vaguely aware of Hermes at her side.

"You haven't eaten in almost a month. Now that you are on the other side of the Underworld, your body remembers," he explained gently.

"Let's just get this over with," she said through gritted teeth.

Hermes nodded and wrapped his hand around her arm, and a moment later, she was standing at her lake. The curse wrapped around her as if it had hungered for her and was desperate to claim her. Her bones snapped, and she cried out in pain as they broke and reformed into something unnatural. It was violent, and it was consuming. No matter how long she lived, she would never get used to this pain. It was slow and agonizing as her body turned into something it wasn't. When it was over, she panted, but even that was wrong. Foreign. And all at once, the world felt too small, and she was trapped once more.

CHAPTER SEVENTEEN

A LOW BLOW

HADES

Fuck Zeus and fuck his demigod offspring. It had only been two weeks since Persephone had left him, and in that time, he had been balls-deep in whatever shit Zeus felt like throwing at him. First, it was a lightning storm that claimed hundreds of lives and now it was a demigod on a quest to invade the Underworld. If he wasn't in such a piss-poor mood, he might have admired his brother's creativity in keeping him busy. As it was, he was just fucking annoyed.

"How did he get in?" Hades growled.

Minos, who had never feared him, shrank back into himself. "One of the gods helped him."

Hades ground his teeth together to keep from exploding his office into smithereens. "I'll bet they fucking did. When I find out which one, I will personally pay them a visit."

Minos nodded as if that were perfectly agreeable. "Do you want me to deal with him?"

What a stupid fucking question. "What are you going to do against a demigod, Minos?"

Minos put up his hands. "I'm just trying to help. You've been—"

His assistant choked on the damning words which likely saved his life.

"Go do a sweep of Asphodel and bring back a report of over-crowding and at least two fucking solutions unless you want to join them."

Minos nodded and backed up into a wall as he tried to leave. Hades watched as he turned on his heels and practically ran out of the manor. Hopefully, Cerberus was keeping their intruder busy enough. While he'd happily end this demigod's existence, he knew that would only piss Zeus off more, and that was the last thing he needed.

Wrapping his magic around himself, he felt for where the too-bright aura came from. Fucking Elysium. How had he made it that far in such a short time? Someone was helping him and that meant he would get to take out his wrath on more than one person tonight. The marble steps of Elysium formed before him, with Cerberus fighting off a bronze-skinned man with a lasso in his hand.

Cerberus, who had taken his true form, was all menace. Three heads grew from his now-massive body and worked together, each trying their turn at the demigod, who dove and lunged to avoid his bite. Making it to the right of Cerberus, the demigod shot his rope out and it wrapped skillfully around Cerberus' joined neck. He pulled and Cerberus fell on his feet with a yelp.

Hades' blood was made from pure fire as he took in the sight before him. The would-be hero smiled with victory and started trying to drag Cerberus down the path. Understanding lit his veins and Hades shot out a tendril of magic, wrapping it around the boy's neck. His eyes bulged, but he held onto the rope.

"Are you trying to steal my fucking dog?" Hades ground out as he came closer.

The boy's veins pressed against his neck as he fought for air. Oh, right. He couldn't admit to his crime if his airway was cut off. Small detail. Hades released the tendril the smallest fraction and the idiot before him gasped for air.

"King Eurystheus," the boy choked out.

Hades was sure the sickly king hadn't come up with this little task all by himself. Though proving that would be time-consuming, which was likely what Zeus was counting on. He would be happy to disappoint. Unlike his brother, he had restraint when he needed it. If Zeus thought he was keeping busy on an investigation, that suited him just well. Fuck, he missed her. How had he gone his entire existence without her and been fine, but one month with her and it was like there was a giant fucking hole in his chest?

Cerberus groaned behind him, and he was brought back to the task at hand. Hades wrapped his magic around the rope and it dissipated into nothing. Cerberus quickly regained himself and prowled towards the demigod, but Hades held up his hand.

"What's your name?" Hades asked, venom lacing each word.

"Her-her-Heracles, my lord." The boy stammered out.

This was the best Zeus could do? Hades reached out and wrapped his hand around the boy's throat, enjoying the way it felt as he lifted him off the ground. The boy's eyes widened, and he clawed uselessly at Hades' hand.

"Next time you think about walking into my underworld and stealing my dog, remember that I am all too happy to rid the world of you and throw your miserable soul into Tartarus with the Titans. Do you understand me, Heracles?"

The boy nodded frantically and Hades threw him on the ground before banishing him to the upper world. Good riddance and fuck Zeus. He would figure out who was behind this interruption, but he would take his damn time about it.

An awareness filled his mind, and he half welcomed it and half wanted to rage because of what he couldn't have. Cerberus righted himself to his former size and came over to Hades' side, sitting at his feet. Hades patted his head and shifted, coming back into his office with Cerberus now happily padding over to the corner to take a well-earned nap. Stealing his fucking dog. That was low, even for Zeus.

Hermes watched him warily from across the room as Hades fell into his chair and ran his fingers over the ache in his head.

"You better be here to tell me something good, Hermes," he said through clenched teeth.

Hermes took a seat across from the desk and leaned forward. "Depends on your definition of good."

Hades sighed. "How is she?"

It was really the only thing he wanted to know, and he hated that Hermes was able to see her when he was stuck wasting away down here.

"Giving them headaches and making them wish they hadn't wronged her," Hermes said with a broad smile.

Despite the storm raging in him, his own smile found its way to his lips. "Oh?"

It was the only comfort he found in being away from her. He had been so worried that she would succumb to her grief like that night she lay sobbing on his carpet after he stopped her from running to her death. Never in his existence had he felt as helpless and miserable as that night when he watched her drown in her pain, knowing he had played a part in it. She thought the river was life, but she was blinded by her desperation. The river could only mean death, as that was all it was made of.

"Demeter is losing her mind, saying that you corrupted her daughter—"

Hades considered and then shrugged. "It's a little true."

Hermes shook his head and rolled his eyes. "She wants retribution, as usual. Keeps begging Zeus to break Persephone's tie to the Underworld, to you."

"Impossible," Hades mused, finding his spirit slightly soothed by Demeter's turmoil.

"Try telling her that. She's had suitors over to sway Persephone, but she sends them back wishing they had never heard her name."

Even knowing that Persephone wasn't entertaining them, jealousy reared its ugly head within him.

"That's . . . annoying," he said, flicking his fingers.

"She said to tell you she loves you," Hermes said quietly.

Hades took a deep breath and tried to fight against the immortality that was constantly making him forget what it was to feel anything other than rage and boredom.

"I think her current tactic is to make Demeter miserable enough that she agrees to send her back, but Demeter would rather be miserable with Persephone than miserable without her."

Hades nodded, knowing it was true, but hating it all the same.

"Zeus send another demigod?" Hermes asked.

"Tried to steal Cerberus," Hades said, waving a hand.

The part of his mind that was dedicated to Tartarus groaned, and he clenched his fist. Wasn't that just the fucking punch line? He had threatened Zeus with freeing the Titans, so now Zeus messed with his prison walls. He had half a mind to let them go and direct the Titans straight to Zeus, but knowing they wouldn't stop until every Immortal was gone stayed his hand.

"That's low," Hermes said.

The knot in his mind unraveled slightly, and he stood and wondered how there was an ache in his bones. He was being worked constantly without more than these small reprieves. If it wasn't one thing, it was another.

"Tell her I love her too," Hades said with a sigh.

Hermes just nodded in understanding before seeing himself out. There weren't words for how much he missed her and how much he wanted to fucking kill Zeus, but then again, his brother knew that. It was the main reason he was keeping Hades busy so that he wouldn't have time to plot, but the thing about Hades was that he was excellent at multitasking.

CHAPTER EIGHTEEN

A CASE OF BEING PROBLEMATIC

PERSEPHONE

T he night air was a welcome reprieve from the sun's rays that kept her imprisoned. As the curse eased its hold on her, Persephone found herself in her rightful form. It was as if her body was stretching after being cramped too long. She glared at the water's edge where her mother stood with a robe. That meant another pitiful excuse to throw men in front of her, as if Persephone's love was easily forgotten. It was as if her mother didn't know her at all, which was in many ways true.

As she neared her, her mother held out the robe, but Persephone walked right by her. She took special comfort in her mother's frustrated sigh.

"We have company," she said, coming up beside her.

"Then I guess you shouldn't have cursed me, else I wouldn't be naked and about to greet them," Persephone said with a wave of her hand.

"Persephone," her mother hissed.

Sighing, she stopped walking and turned to her mother. "If I put on the robe, will you send whoever it is away knowing that I will never give up my husband?"

"He's not your husband," Demeter growled.

Persephone ran her hand over her collarbone where she was undeniably marked by him. "I think they call that denial, mother."

Her mother's face twisted with a mixture of fury and loss. "I know you have been under his influence, but its effects are only temporary."

Huffing out a breath, Persephone took the robe only because the night air was cold, and despite how angry she was with her mother, she found she could only push her so far. "And who is to be my victim tonight? What number is this? Sixteen? I hope they last longer than the last two. Makes it more fun when I send them away crying."

"Zeus," her mother said, and Persephone tripped over her own feet, barely catching herself.

"He's here now?" Persephone asked, turning to face her mother.

The fresh anxiety on her face told her that was, in fact, what was happening. Fuck. Of all the gods and demigods she had been forced to endure, Zeus was a presence she had avoided until now. Ignoring her mother's string of advice, she made her way to the castle at the top of the hill.

She missed her power that would have helped her get there faster, but none of the benefits of being Queen of the Underworld had followed her into the mortal realm. Even the awareness that was him was dormant, as if he didn't exist at all. If it weren't for Hermes and Hecate's updates, she would have been more worried than she already was.

She could read between the lines of what they said about him. He was losing himself beneath the work Zeus was thrusting on him. The ache in her chest grew every time she thought about how much she missed him. It was worse when she knew he was struggling.

"Persephone!" her mother yelled.

Twisting, she faced her mother, who was red-faced with hands clenched at her fists.

"You can't treat him like the others."

Persephone watched her mother and did nothing to hide her disgust. "Are you trying to sell me off to Zeus now, too?"

"You can't refuse him," Demeter said quietly.

Disbelief coursed through her. "Are you fucking kidding me? What kind of mother curses her daughter to keep her safe from one god only to tell her she has to throw herself at another? If I wasn't convinced you were insane before, I am now."

Demeter drew in a steadying breath. "That's not what I mean, Persephone. I am telling you not to bait him and push him to where he asks for more than you are willing to give. I'm trying to help you."

Persephone leaned forward till their faces were inches apart. "You are pathetic."

Hurt crashed over her face and for the faintest of seconds, Persephone regretted the words. Regret was quickly replaced by the knowledge that her mother still wasn't sorry for what she had done. She still saw Hades as an enemy who had corrupted her precious daughter. Everything Persephone did or said that was disagreeable, she laid at his feet and his influence rather than seeing the truth of it.

Her mother stood back as Persephone made her way to the castle she used to call home before she realized what a real home was. Now there could only ever be one place she would ever call home, and that was where he was. Her mother had been bolder lately since Hecate had been asked to search her for any trace of sorcery. Persephone believed her when she said she had found none, but part of her wondered what it would mean to possess some of her father's ability.

Taking the back way into the castle, Persephone followed the corridors till she made it to her room. She knew she couldn't ignore Zeus' presence. There was a hierarchy to the gods and she would not give him more reason to encourage his treatment of her husband.

Persephone stared at the clothes that had been left her. All carefully tailored to hide the mark that sealed her marriage contract. Yet she had altered them all so that there could be no doubt to whom she belonged and where she belonged. After replacing her wardrobe three times, her mother had finally given up.

Putting on a teal dress that clung to her shoulders and draped low enough to show her mark, she slid on the ring that Hades had given her. If she must entertain Zeus, she would do so as the Queen of the Underworld. Following the main hallways, Persephone found Zeus and her mother in the main sitting room with a roaring fire set among lavish red and gold furniture. It was gaudy, just like the rest of the house.

Her mother inclined her head and spoke quickly to Zeus, who sat back in one of the oversized chairs with his legs spread wide and a glass of liquor in his hands. His large frame took up most of the chair that should have fit two people. She could see why people found him intimidating. He radiated strength, but it was too loud as if he were trying to command the space around him, whereas Hades commanded a room effortlessly.

Her mother's head turned to her and relief washed over her face, as if she had truly thought Persephone would refuse Zeus' calling. She should have known that Persephone would do anything to protect her husband, even if it meant tolerating the immortal who stood at her entrance.

"You look even more beautiful than I remember," Zeus said, setting down his glass and watching her much like a predator would watch their prey.

"To what do we owe such an honor of your visit?" Persephone said with attempted neutrality.

Her mother flashed her a glare that said that had been the wrong thing to say, but Zeus wore a small smile as if he were immensely enjoying himself.

"Do I need a reason?" He said, stalking closer to her.

"I suppose not," Persephone answered, reminding herself who she was.

Zeus loomed over her and, much like he had in the Underworld before Hades intervened, he trailed his finger along her collarbone. Persephone fought back the urge to slap his hand away.

"It's a shame such a mark mars such beautiful skin," he murmured.

"I must disagree as would my husband," she said with more calm than she felt.

Zeus chuckled. "I'm sure he would, but he's rather busy at the moment."

Before Persephone could tell him what he thought of that, her mother stepped in next to her.

"What can be done about it?"

The effort it took to not roll her eyes was one of epic proportions. Her mother was obsessed with the idea that the bond could be broken.

"We will see," Zeus said with a flash of something Persephone could not name in his eyes.

That was enough to make her stand a little straighter. Up until then, Zeus had denied any way to break the bond, but the way he watched her said he was hiding something.

"Given that I am bound to the Underworld three months of the year, it seems a futile discussion," Persephone tried.

Zeus arched an eyebrow. "Do you doubt my power, Persephone?"

Her blood ran cold while her mother nearly bounced for joy next to her.

"She would never question you, Zeus."

Zeus turned to glare at her. "I don't recall asking you, Demeter. Leave us."

Her mother paled as if she was only just now understanding the danger she put Persephone in. As if she had spent so long blinded by grief and despair that she failed to see the real danger in front of her. Even still, her mother bowed her head and slunk away, leaving Persephone with Zeus.

"Well? Do you doubt my power, Persephone?" he said as he lifted a strand of her hair and twirled it. It made Persephone draw inward, as it was something Hades often did to her.

"Does my opinion matter so very much when your power is uncontested?" she said sweetly.

Zeus bent and whispered in her ear, "Is it?"

Her heart raced in her chest as she tried to appear unaffected. "That I am here is evidence of it."

Zeus pulled back, wearing a smirk. "I suppose it is, and would you like it if you were no longer bound by any curse or contract? To be free?"

The flash in his eyes lit again, and Persephone's blood ran cold. "Is that possible?"

Zeus ran his hand over her collarbone once more, chasing each part of her mark. "You would forsake him so easily? I admit, I am a little surprised."

"You mistake my eagerness to break the curse with eagerness to be rid of my husband. They are not one and the same," she clarified.

Zeus' smile faded. "But they could be, sweet Persephone."

His breath was warm on her and wreaked of liquor and stale air.

"How is Hera feeling? I imagine you must be excited about your newest son or daughter."

The way his eyes roamed over her told her he hadn't even heard her question. Fighting the urge to step away, Persephone knew that no matter what the cost, she was not willing to let the being before her touch her. She would rather die than be one of his playthings.

"Imagine this coincidence. I finally get away to call on our newest goddess, and I find my brother as well."

She had never thought she would be grateful to hear that voice.

Zeus pulled away with an irritated noise caught in his throat. "Poseidon."

The god of the oceans and sea casually strolled to them and lifted Persephone's hand to place a kiss on it before slapping Zeus on the back.

"So what are we talking about?" Poseidon said as he sat down and patted the cushion next to him. "Come sit, Persephone, you must be tired after being a swan all day."

Gritting her teeth, she did as he asked only because she saw it for the rescue it was. The only question that remained was why.

Poseidon made a show of looking around before calling, "Demeter? Where is Demeter? Demeter!"

Even though he was incredibly annoying, she was quickly finding that she owed the immortal a favor. Her mother hurried into the room and when she saw Persephone as she had left her and sitting with Poseidon, she let out the barest breath that said she was relieved. She took the spot next to Persephone, as if she wanted to pretend she would protect her when she had been ready to give her up moments ago.

An awkward silence stretched as Zeus glared at Poseidon.

"I hope I wasn't interrupting. I was just curious to meet the goddess on everyone's lips," Poseidon crooned.

"And yet you chose today after it's been two weeks," Zeus said dryly.

"It is hard to get away sometimes. Anyway, how long are you up with the living before you scurry on back down to the darkness?" Poseidon asked cheerfully.

"That remains to be seen," Zeus said, his hand tight around his glass.

That made Persephone pause. She knew that they could draw it out and make her stay for months, but the way he said the words made her think there was more at play.

She opened her mouth to ask what exactly needed to be seen, but Poseidon gave her the slightest shake of his head, making her snap her mouth shut.

"Zeus has graciously left the decision up to me," Demeter said with a bright smile at Zeus.

It made Persephone feel sick. What wasn't her mother willing to do to pander to him? Selling her daughter wasn't out of the question, so the options were truly limitless. She had spent her whole life knowing that her mother was complicated, but seeing how she interacted with other immortals was entirely enlightening. How many hours had she spent convincing herself that everything her mother did was because she loved her? Yet with every day that passed, Persephone realized it wasn't love, but control.

From the moment her mother heard the prophecy regarding Persephone's fate, she did everything in her power to maintain control without ever considering how Persephone would feel. She would have rather seen Persephone trapped her entire life than lose her control over her.

Despite knowing all of this, Persephone still said, "I would think after having me cursed you might take into consideration my wants."

Demeter heaved a long sigh and pinched the bridge of her nose. "Persephone, this is not the time for this discussion. Will you never take into consideration anyone but yourself?"

She could have caught flies as her mouth fell open. "Myself? You are calling *me* selfish?"

"Oh my," Poseidon muttered unhelpfully.

He might not have existed, as Demeter glared at her. "You have no idea what I went through for an entire month. I was worried sick about you. I have never felt such despair in my entire existence, yet all you care about is yourself."

"You cursed me!" Persephone shouted.

"Okay, you little tsunami. Time to settle down," Poseidon said, reaching for her arm.

Persephone glared at him but saw the warning in his eyes enough to take a slow, steadying breath.

"I'm sorry, Zeus, you see what sort of influence he's had over her. She used to be quiet and kind, now she's . . . this," her mother said, waving a hand in her general direction.

"Excuse me?" Persephone seethed.

"She is certainly something," Zeus said, his eyes raking over her. It felt invasive and unwelcome.

"You know what we should do? A party! All right, all right, you win. I will throw one. Next week. Under the sea. You will love it," He whispered the last, leaning towards Persephone.

The tension in the room simmered to a low boil as Zeus watched his brother, considering. "Not a terrible idea. Demeter, you will bring Persephone so she may officially meet everyone."

Demeter swallowed back her urge to say no, visibly struggling, but settled for nodding.

Poseidon stood and clapped his hands. "Very well then. Come, Zeus, I've been meaning to pay Hera a visit, anyway."

To her relief, Zeus nodded and with one last look towards her, both the gods left them in peace. Silence fell throughout the room as they both struggled to work through what had happened and what could have happened. Both shaken.

Persephone pressed her hand to her chest, feeling the rise and fall of her chest grounding her.

It was her mother who recovered first. "How dare you speak to me like that in front of Zeus?"

The venom and sheer audacity shook Persephone to her core. She stood, putting a welcome distance between them.

"You gave me to him like I was nothing more than a grain to be planted at your will." Her jaw ached from being clenched together.

Demeter stood and threw up her hands. "What would you have me do, Persephone? Refuse Zeus?"

"Yes!" Persephone yelled. "For someone who claims to want to protect me, you are only set on protecting me from the one immortal I am safe with!"

Demeter scoffed, putting her hands on her hips. "That is absurd, Persephone. Honestly, I am growing tired of your theatrics. You are being willfully ignorant. You were not in any danger tonight. That you continue with this temper tantrum is a testament to the effect the last month has had on you."

It was unfathomable. That her mother would rather make Persephone feel like she was crazy than admit she had done something wrong. Persephone strode towards her mother and peered down at her.

"He would have raped me tonight if Poseidon hadn't come and you would have sat by and allowed it to happen. Hades would never have let that happen. I was safer with him than I ever was with a mother who is too blinded by her own greed to protect her own daughter."

She watched as Demeter's eyes widened and then a hardness fell over her as her mind worked to twist Persephone's words and actions into something more desirable.

"And why hasn't he come to you, Persephone? If he actually cared about you, don't you think he would leave his cave for you?" Demeter said with cold unfeeling.

Persephone tilted her head, warring against the words that fought for purchase inside her. After two weeks, she and her mother had only gone around in circles, never finding peace or reconciliation. They likely never would, and Persephone would need to make peace with that.

"I pity you, mother. You seek to sow doubt where there can be none to soothe your own shortcomings."

Demeter's lips thinned. "You think you know him after one month?" She released a short, rueful laugh. "I have known him for thousands of years and I could tell you stories that would make you beg Zeus to break the bond he forced on you."

What was meant to be a threat only ended up being exhausting.

"I am going to my room." Persephone twisted on her heels and began walking to the stairs, but her mother shouted behind her.

"You want to hide from the truth, but you know I'm right. It's why you run."

The words meant to bait her only eroded the good memories they shared before Persephone had become *problematic*.

"Good night, Mother," Persephone said without turning back.

She refused to sleep in her human form once more, but she would still lock herself upstairs and try to pass the time without sinking into despair, like she did every night.

CHAPTER NINETEEN

DON'T LOOK BACK

HADES

"I swear if you play that song one more time I will personally let you join your wife in the Underworld," Hades said, pinching the bridge of his nose.

The boy tucked his lyre behind his back and stared at Hades as if he were Medusa herself.

"I only thought it might help you to understand," the boy said.

Hades leaned back in his desk chair and closed his eyes to fight through the urge to flay the intruder and send him into the river just so he would forget to play that godsdamn melody. Taking a grounding breath, Hades leaned forward, tapping his finger on his desk.

"Listen Dorfus—"

"Orpheus," the boy corrected.

"Sure," he said. "There are fundamental rules that cannot be broken in the Underworld. Rule number one. What comes into the Underworld stays in the underworld. Rule number two. The dead stay dead. Rule number three. No one makes demands of the god of the dead. Now you, Erepheus, are attempting to break all three of those rules."

"No, sir, my wife—"

Hades held up his hand, ticking off his fingers. "Is in the underworld, is dead, and you are here demanding I release her and yourself back to the mortal realm."

"But you don't understand—" the boy began.

Fuck Apollo. It had taken a total of ten seconds for the boy before him to confess which god helped him in his little quest. He would have some words to share with the sun god next time he saw him. Even if it was at Zeus' encouragement, he could have sent anyone except this lyre-playing incompetent boy.

"And how did she die?" Hades said, running his hand over his temple.

"A snake," the boy said.

"I bet it was," Hades murmured.

Amidst all his annoyance, there was a sliver of him that felt a little sorry for the boy and his wife. They were nothing more than pawns caught up in a bigger game. This was a shitty game, though. If he let them go, then it would lead to more demigods and mortals taking it upon themselves to come claim their loved ones. The order of his realm would be put into chaos and essentially he'd have a large fucking mess to clean up. Yet, he was tempted to give the boy whatever he wanted if he stopped playing that ridiculous instrument.

"Please, if you only listen, Apollo said if you heard my song—"

Apollo was going to beg for forgiveness when Hades was through with him. Sending demigods down to plague him with their incessant quests was one thing, but this was entirely another.

"Look, Tepheus, I'll make you a deal." This was a terrible plan, but at least it would cut out the image that people could just walk in and take the dead.

"Anything." He nodded eagerly.

Hades had the dry thought that he should order him never to play the lyre again, but hopefully, he would be out of his realm soon enough.

"You can take your wife with you on one condition. You don't look back until you leave the Underworld." Simple instructions and hard to fuck up.

"But how will I know if it's a trick? Once I leave the Underworld, I won't be able to get back. I could just walk out and then Eurydice will be trapped down here forever," he said, anxiety making him rub his hands together.

That was a decent point and honestly not a bad plan for him, however, even he wasn't that cruel.

"I guess you'll just have to take my word for it. I have somewhere to be and I'm not prepared to give this any more of my time. Walk or no walk?" Hades said impatiently.

The boy watched him as if he could find some hint of whether Hades was telling the truth or not, but that might take all day.

"Listen, kid, I don't hand out opportunities like this very often, but you just so happened to find me at a difficult time. However, the longer you take, the longer I consider taking back my offer," Hades growled.

The boy stood up too rapidly and slammed his hand on the desk. "I accept."

"Delightful," Hades said.

He stood, portaling to the edge of Asphodel. Shuffling through the souls in his care, he found her. Her soul answered his call and Eurydice appeared next to him.

"Orpheus?" she asked in disbelief.

"Eurydice!" he yelled as they embraced, happy to be reunited.

Well, if that didn't just poke at his frozen heart. It was an effort to push Persephone from his mind and what it would be like to finally have her back once more.

"Remember the rules. You walk, she follows. If you turn around, she stays, you go," Hades said.

The boy clung to his wife and pressed a kiss to her lips, murmuring to her. It was annoyingly heartwarming. Hades genuinely hoped that he didn't fuck this up. Either way, he was done here. He could keep tabs on their progress easily enough without watching them. Hades portaled to his room that always felt too empty. He had gotten used to sharing the space with her and every time he was here, it reminded him what he had lost. His only consolation was how little he actually slept, thanks to Zeus.

"Cerberus, you have one job. Just one. Guard the Underworld. That was not even a demi-god this time who got through. It was a mere mortal." Under the weight of his accusations, Cerberus rolled over onto his back and wiggled into the bed further.

Useless. He would probably have less work to do if Cerberus was even a fraction more helpful.

"Please, at least try to not let anyone else in unless they are dead," Hades said as he ran his mind over the underworld. He had spent a week ironing out every facet of this plan. Apollo had almost blown it with his lyre-playing friend, but Hades was good at finding solutions most of the time.

Hades opened his portal, and for the first time in three weeks, he left the underworld. He could have picked a better place than Poseidon's home, but beggars could not be choosers, or so they said. Poseidon had better fucking keep his end of the deal. The room around him was much like all the castle under the sea. It was crafted from glass made by Hephaestus that could withstand the pressure of the sea. The glass encapsulated every room and allowed for those inside to watch the ocean around them as if they were almost a part of it.

A large ray slid across the glass, its belly showing gills and a mouth desperately searching for food. It was unsettling. Ignoring the hungry creature, Hades put his hands in his pockets to keep from fidgeting and began pacing instead. Poseidon's office looked like he had just grabbed bits of the sea and called it a day. A large clam had been shaped and reformed into an excuse for a desk and a giant coral made up his chair. It was obnoxious, much like his brother. At the far side of it, a fireplace held a flickering flame that was a direct juxtaposition to the ocean just outside.

Footsteps down the hall drew his attention, his chest fluttering, which was what he imagined dying felt like.

"I don't care if I owe you, I am not going to see your creepy office with you," his wife growled.

It was the most beautiful fucking sound he had ever heard.

"Why are you always so godsdamn stubborn?" Poseidon barked back as he opened the door.

Instinctually, Hades' eyes were drawn to his hand wrapped around her arm where he was dragging her, but Poseidon seemed to have some sense of self-preservation and let her go.

"She wasn't listening," he explained.

Persephone glared at him. "Are you talking to yourself?"

She was incredible. Her dress was a navy blue that draped over her body, barely clinging to her form as if it were slightly too big, but her shoulders were bare and the dress dipped enough that his mark on her skin was plain to see. It was all he could not to fall to his knees.

"You have ten minutes. He will notice any more than that and then we will both have to deal with him."

"You have your favor," Hades said, sealing their deal.

A favor, to be called on whenever Poseidon decided, for ten minutes with his wife. Some people might have considered it a poor bargain, but they weren't married to her. At the sound of his voice, Persephone twisted, her mouth falling open. She only needed a second to register what was happening before she barreled into him. The way she slammed her body into his open arms might have killed a mortal with the impact alone.

Hades closed his eyes and fell into the feeling of her body tucked into his. It was an effort to not run his hands over her like an animal just to make sure she was fine and in one piece. She pulled back and searched his face, always seeing more than anyone should.

"Hades," she said, a tear slipping down her cheek.

He ran his thumb over the loose tear and she leaned into his touch. "I missed you," he said, his voice too rough as emotion caught in his throat.

Persephone laughed, but it was a strangled sound. "I missed you too."

All his restraint was lost as he grabbed her face and brought her lips to his. It was a kiss of desperation and need. She was life to him. Without her, everything was darker and held less meaning. It was as if he had gone so long without any sense of living that now that she had shown him, he couldn't stand to be without her. His wife answered his kiss a thousand times over, and he knew she had felt lost without him.

Knowing their time was short, Hades pulled away. Lips bruised and breathless. Her eyes were wide as she drank him in.

"Are you all right?" he asked.

She knew well enough what he meant. "No. Yes. I am struggling, but it's not forever."

He didn't care for that answer. "What aren't you saying? We don't have long, Persephone, you need to tell me."

She frowned, running her hand across his chest as if needing to touch him. "Zeus. He tried to—Poseidon came in and stopped anything from happening, but I feel his eyes on me everywhere I go."

His blood boiled, and he fought back the urge to storm into the main hall where he knew his bastard of a brother would be. Persephone reached up on her toes and pressed a light kiss to his lips.

"Stay with me," she murmured.

Despite the call to arms radiating throughout his body, he nodded. "Has your mother not made it clear you aren't to be touched?"

That shouldn't even be necessary given that she was his wife, but that meant little when they all knew Zeus had him like a mouse in a maze.

Persephone shook her head. "She let him. She makes it sound like it's my fault, as if I've made my own bed."

Fuck. He had counted on Demeter loving Persephone enough to protect her, but he should have known better. Demeter cared about herself more than anyone else, which meant letting her come to the mortal realm had been a mistake. Either he would need to visit The Fates once more, or he was about to owe Poseidon a lot more favors. Probably both.

"Hey," Persephone said, running her hand along his jaw, her touch spiraling through him. "You are scheming in your mind. I know that look."

That she knew him well enough to know that made him want to take her back to the Underworld and damn the consequences, but it wasn't just a power-pissing contest anymore, it was about her life. She was bound to the lake and until they figured out how to break it, their hands were tied.

"I'll have to work on my tells then, since you've figured them all out," he said.

Persephone smirked. "A waste of time. I'll just figure out those, too."

He wanted to wipe that smirk away with his mouth, but time was of the essence, which seemed to be the theme lately. He tucked an errant strand of blonde hair behind her ear.

"I'll make sure he doesn't touch you. I promise." No matter the cost.

Persephone nodded as fresh tears bloomed in her eyes. "I miss you so much. You look so tired, Hades."

"I'm fine," he lied.

Persephone wrapped her hands around the back of his neck, clinging to him. "Take me to the river. Let me try."

"Persephone," he warned. Her and that damn river and death wish. He understood her need to hope, but every time she brought it up, it was like being consumed by ice.

"Fine," she whispered, running a hand through his hair. "Fine. I don't want to fight."

Hades relaxed a fraction. "Me neither."

The door opened, and he quickly thought of creative ways to torture Poseidon. "It's time."

"That wasn't ten minutes," Hades growled before pressing a kiss to the top of her forehead.

"Yeah, well, she's popular and her absence has been noticed," Poseidon said.

Hades drew Persephone into him, and she buried her face in his chest. When he pulled away, she lifted her head, and he kissed her as if his immortal soul depended on it. She parted her lips, and he consumed her like he could keep her. She met his pace just as eagerly until Poseidon cleared his throat.

Persephone ignored the god of the ocean and seas as she met Hades' gaze. "I love you."

Hades choked on the emotion constricting his throat. "I love you, too. You'll be safe," he reminded her.

She nodded, and he stepped back into the Underworld, his arms empty. As if it weren't bad enough that he had to leave his wife, the awareness that spread through him grated against his bones.

It had been almost impossible to fuck up, but he should have known better. The damn kid turned around.

CHAPTER TWENTY

THE THING ABOUT POWER

PERSEPHONE

She needed a second to mourn the loss of him, but Poseidon was already demanding she go back into that den of vipers. When he pulled on her arm, Persephone felt her fragile control snap.

"Give me a minute," she snarled.

Poseidon tilted his head and took a deep breath before releasing it. "You don't get a minute because every second we are in here they start getting a little more curious and if my brother starts getting curious, then what I just stuck my neck out for will bite me in the ass."

The self-righteous act was a bad look for him. "Don't act like you didn't get anything out of it. What favor did you ask of him?"

"It's to be determined," Poseidon said with an irritated huff of breath.

She didn't like it. It was an exploitation of their suffering and while she knew all the gods schemed; it was unsettling. Hades was exhausted and the fact that he had given up such a dangerous prize for ten minutes with her fractured her remaining patience.

"I don't trust you," she said with narrowed eyes.

Poseidon wore a sly smirk. "You shouldn't." He leaned forward, his face inches from hers. "Consider this my wedding gift to you—All of us have our own agendas and our own interests at heart. Sometimes they might align, but never make the mistake of thinking any of us are your allies. Even Hecate and Hermes, for all their time spent with Hades, would turn on him in a second. Did either of them speak up for you when Hades' party went to shit? No. No immortal is your friend, Persephone, and as much as Hades is focused on you now, someday he won't be. He will get bored and all you will have is yourself to watch out for, so might as well start now."

Her breathing was rapid as his words caused equal parts disgust and worry to flow through her. Not thinking, she reached out and slapped him hard enough that it sounded like a shot throughout the room. In response, he merely cracked his neck and met her gaze.

"I would prefer if you didn't do that again."

Her surprise at her own actions receded, but the anger that had fueled it remained. "Then don't say shit you don't understand."

Where she expected him to show emotion, there was a hollowness in his eyes as his lips quirked up. A shiver ran through her as she remembered what Hades had told her about living long enough to lose whatever humanity the immortal began with. It was unnerving seeing it in Poseidon, but at least he was right about one thing. She couldn't trust him.

"You've been alive for what? Thirty years? Less than that? I get your bright-eyed outlook on life, but stick around for a few centuries and then come tell me what I don't understand."

"You're an asshole," Persephone said, glaring at him.

Poseidon shrugged. "I've been called worse."

Deciding this was a useless game, Persephone shoved past him and down the long corridors made of glass. Being under the sea should have been incredible, and it was, but everything felt less than in the mortal world, as if her soul knew it didn't belong there. Even still, a whale larger than the entire corridor swam above her and she stilled. Her whole body seemed to sing for the incredible creature that continued on its journey as if she was insignificant.

"You know, for as long as I have lived, the ocean is the one thing that never ceases to amaze me," Poseidon said, coming up beside her and watching the whale pass by.

Two more followed behind, while one had a calf swimming beside its large flipper. Their song hummed in the air even through the impenetrable glass. It was a low sound that coursed through her with its infinite mystery.

"But you are the god of the oceans and sea," she said quietly, still mesmerized by the scene before her.

Silence stretched, but she didn't dare take her eyes away from the whales as they began to disappear into the ocean depths. "The ocean keeps her secrets, even from the gods. She transcends even immortality."

The reverence in his voice made her turn her head to him and there she saw it. The part of his humanity that he still clung to. It was as if the whales had called him back from the depths of his immortality and realigned him.

Blinking his eyes a few times, he turned to her, renewed clarity shining in their golden brown rings. "There will be questions about where we've been. Though it may be distasteful to you, a lie would be less problematic than the truth."

Persephone wrinkled her nose in disgust. "Can't we just say you were giving me a tour?"

He shrugged. "Sure, but they will infer something else into that."

"Hades—"

"Knows that even I would not cross that line. There is only one you need to worry about on that account, but I think you already know that."

Gods, how she wished she didn't. "Thank you for helping me the other night."

Poseidon narrowed his eyes and patted her on the shoulder. "Already forgot my lesson, I see." He bent down to whisper in her ear, "No one does anything for free, Persephone."

Her blood ran cold as he stepped away and gestured for her to follow him. Poseidon was an enigma that she wasn't prepared for. Who he was and what he wanted was likely as much of a mystery as the ocean's depths. She followed him into his main hall, which was a sprawling dome with a scattering of chairs, tables, and sofas made of coral. A fireplace that was eight feet tall and at least ten feet wide that was the shape of a great white shark's open mouth, its endless teeth bared to the room. Dark blue carpet lined the floors and paintings of various creatures and nautical scenes littered the glass walls.

The immortals in the room continued talking, but she felt each of their eyes glance over Poseidon and then her. Her eyes fell on Hecate's, whose mouth fell open before she recovered. Irritation ran through Persephone that the immortal she had dared to call a friend would think that of her. Hecate knew more than anyone there that she loved Hades. In one smooth motion, Hecate pressed a kiss to Aphrodite's cheek and made her way to Persephone.

At the same time, she was aware of Zeus' unwelcome gaze on her, but Poseidon moved to his brother and said something that earned him a boisterous laugh. Her blood simmered as she imagined what had earned such a reaction.

Hecate linked arms with her, drawing away Persephone's attention. Leading her to a table of refreshments, Hecate handed her a glass of champagne.

"Are you all right?" Hecate whispered, though the smile on her face was light.

"I'm fine," Persephone said defensively.

The lines around Hecate's eyes creased. "Did he hurt you?"

The undertones of anger in the question made Persephone pull back into herself. Her anger receded as she realized she had misjudged her friend. Poseidon's words had worked their way into her and already she was ready to believe the worst in someone she trusted. If that was what immortality meant, she didn't want it.

Persephone softened her tone. "He didn't do anything."

The inhabitants of the room still watched her with careful smirks and suggestive whispers. Her mother was pale, her hand white around the cup she was holding. That was enough to remind her of her anger. Her mother thought the worst had happened, and she hadn't done or said anything, hadn't even come to check on her.

"Persephone, your hair," Hecate whispered.

Reaching up, Persephone realized her carefully bound hair had been partially pulled from its confines and she realized with horror what Poseidon had done. She had been so distracted after Hades left she hadn't thought about his hands in her hair, disheveling her appearance. Poseidon could have warned her, but instead, he let her walk into this room knowing what they all would assume happened and that her hair would only confirm their suspicions. She caught his eye, and he winked at her before taking a sip of champagne.

That was it. She was fully prepared to make a list of the immortals she would happily see locked in Tartarus and his name would be the first. She would hand it to Hades as her own wedding present. At the judgment all of them watched her with, she imagined he'd be all too happy to comply.

"Hades," Persephone breathed out.

Misunderstanding her, Hecate pulled the tie from Persephone's hair and smoothed out the errant strands so they fell over her back and shoulders. "He will not be angry with you."

Persephone shook her head. "That's not what I mean, it was—"

"Next, we will host you in Olympus. What do you think of that, Persephone?" Zeus said, coming up beside them.

He wore a self-appreciating smirk that said he was thoroughly pleased with himself. It grated along her skin till she longed to tell him exactly what she thought of him. Instead, she plastered a small smile and dipped her head.

"I have always wanted to see Olympus. I would be honored." The first part was at least true and something to work with.

Zeus hummed, his lips curling. "Your mother was remiss in keeping you away all these years. I wonder at how things could have been different for you had she not been errant in her responsibilities."

The thought had often crept into Persephone's own mind and she used to imagine what it would have been like to be born into the world of immortals and to grow up among them. Now that she had met them all, she was almost grateful for her mother sparing her that fate. They lied, used, and schemed in an endless circle. Yet she couldn't help but wonder what would have been. Would Hades still have fallen in love with her? Would she have only seen his cool arrogance and disdained him? Part of her wanted to claim they were two parts of a whole and would have found each other, but she doubted even the Fates could say.

Persephone was saved having to answer by Hera coming up beside Zeus and threading her arm through his. "Darling, I wondered if I might have a moment with Persephone."

Zeus raised a brow, and his broad chest rumbled with a chuckle. "Of course," he said as he walked away, shoulders shaking.

His arrogance and self-worth were worse than all the immortals combined. As Persephone turned to Hera, she saw exactly what Zeus had seen. A challenge. Hera knew that Zeus coveted Persephone just like they all did, but what was surprising was that it bothered Hera. Zeus' exploits were well known and his infidelity was on the lips of every mortal and immortal alike. Though it might have been misguided, Persephone had thought Hera would be used to it by now, but that had been naïve. Why should a woman have to be used to her husband's flaunted infidelity? She would welcome Hera's displeasure with the respect she deserved.

Hera pursed her lips and turned to Hecate, who dipped her head and scurried away. Despite knowing that it wasn't worth Hecate's energy to stay with her, Poseidon's warning that all immortals were only looking out for themselves reverberated in her mind.

"You have caused quite the stir," Hera said, eyeing Persephone as if she were an insect.

She was beautiful in the way all immortals were, but her beauty was more refined. Her dark hair fell over her shoulder and her eyes were more almond-shaped that sat perfectly on her narrow face. Persephone understood the pregnancy made Hera's divinity more profound, but she couldn't imagine the goddess being anything other than stunning. More importantly, it was her presence that commanded Persephone's attention. Hera held herself proudly, with shoulders straight and her chin always tilted slightly up.

"It has been . . . challenging," Persephone said, trying to choose the least offensive word.

"Oh?" Hera tilted her head. "In what way?"

A strange question, but then again, perhaps not. "I've spent my entire life wanting to be among all of you. Now that I am here, all I want is to be with my husband. While I am grateful for the welcome I have received, I would be happier in the Underworld."

It was meant to be an exchange of peace. Hera would see that she didn't covet Zeus and was not a threat to her. Yet as Hera considered her, she saw the wariness of mistrust bloom in her cheeks.

"You say that, but you are also content to spend the evening in the company of . . . others."

All at once, it made sense. Hera had believed exactly what Poseidon had wanted her to believe, and it destroyed all of Persephone's credibility. It was irritating in every way. She and Hera could have been allies, but they were being pitted against one another. Persephone longed to say that she had been with her husband and that she actually disliked Poseidon, but her mouth stayed firmly shut. Hera would exploit her as quick as all the rest. She would happily sell Persephone's truth to Zeus in exchange for her perceived justice.

So Persephone merely said, "Not even his mark on my skin seems enough to convince others of my loyalty, but then, as the newest goddess, what power do I have?"

Hera's chest barely rose with the breath she took as she ran a hand over her rounded belly. "Power is a difficult thing among Olympians."

Persephone nodded, feeling the ice thaw around them slightly. "The more I learn about this world, the less I think I have of it."

Her face smoothed. "Power is taken, but rarely should it be done so."

While Persephone thought she followed the trajectory of their hidden meanings, doubt was alive and well within her. "I'll be sure to remember that."

"There are, however," Hera began. "Times when it is the only course of action. Everything can change in a single moment. In a single prophecy."

Her eyes were haunted as she said the last and Persephone wondered what could have created such ghosts in the immortal's eyes. Recovering, Hera drew in a large breath before arching an eyebrow and turning away. Leaving Persephone feeling like she had passed some sort of test, but at the same time, Zeus' eyes were on her like an unwelcome guest.

CHAPTER TWENTY-ONE
NOTHING HAS CHANGED

HADES

The wrath burning through Hades' veins promised vengeance and retribution. His control was quickly fracturing with each update Hermes and Hecate brought with them. It was quickly becoming clear that playing Zeus' game was no longer an option, which meant he needed to be smarter. The idea of butchering the hierarchy of the gods would be enticing if there weren't so many damn consequences.

Even still, he wasn't prepared to leave Persephone up there much longer, and he now had a deadline. Zeus was planning on having a gathering on Olympus in one week, which meant his wife was coming home before that.

"Whatever you are thinking is a bad idea," Hecate murmured over her glass of wine.

"Thinking I could trust Poseidon was a bad fucking idea," Hades growled.

Hermes grunted where he was sprawled out on the couch. "If you would have asked, we would have told you that."

Hades continued his pacing while he managed five minutes of respite. Zeus and Hera had a fight after Poseidon's party and the result was an overcrowded Underworld once more. The fact that they couldn't manage to hate each other without ending mortal lives was exceedingly annoying.

"In his defense, he did cover for you," Hecate said, her legs crossed and her posture relaxed. If only they could all be so calm.

"By insinuating he had his way with her!" Hades shouted. "All that did was convince them he won't face consequences for trying."

"Or you could punish Poseidon. Send the Furies after one of his heroes or even his son, Theseus," Hecate offered.

The notion was enough to stop Hades from his incessant pacing. It would be within his right, and Zeus never intervened when Poseidon and Hades fought. It was a welcome scenario for the god of thunder to have his only rivals at each other's throats. Despite his presented easy-going attitude, Poseidon had a temper that had brought nations to their knees. It was easy to forget when he was obnoxiously charming.

Hades tugged on his connection to the Underworld. All at once it was overwhelming if he didn't maintain each thread meticulously separate from the others. The dead, the guardians, the Titans, Tartarus, Elysium, Asphodel, the Furies, hellhounds, the goddamn river. All of it and more took up too much space in his mind, but there at the center was the small knot that belonged to her. It was dimmed and barely anything with her outside of his realm, but knowing she was there was still a comfort.

Focusing on the task at hand, he grabbed onto the thread that was the Furies and let his will sink into it. With a resounding snap, he felt their acceptance and movement. Theseus would not enjoy his evening tonight. It was a small consolation for the shit his father had pulled with Persephone. Hades should have known better and fixed her hair, but his control had been fracturing and he knew if he didn't leave then, he wouldn't have been able to. Still. It was his failure not to protect her.

"You could have thought about it before you sent them after Theseus," Hermes groaned.

Hades shrugged. "It was a good idea."

Hecate grinned. "He deserves every second of it."

Raising a single brow, he stared at Hecate, who wore a pleased smile. "You could have just asked and I would have done it, regardless."

He knew her well enough to know that the glint in her eyes said that she had a personal vendetta against Theseus. It could have been something minor, like an altercation with one of her heroes, or it could be that she had found him a wanting lover. Either way, it was enough for him to be sure he would enjoy the report his furies brought back.

"Still doesn't help with Zeus, though," Hermes said unhelpfully.

No, it didn't. One week to decide how to free Persephone. Once she was in the Underworld, she would be safe. Fuck Demeter for not watching out for her and protecting her. When he figured all this shit out, he would pay Demeter a visit and he would enjoy every second of it.

Grim understanding fell over Hades as he realized what he needed to do. He would not have done it for anyone else, not even himself, but for her. For her, he would do anything. Sighing, Hades pulled at his shirt, righting it of any wrinkles from long hours of working.

"Hades!" Hecate shouted, her mouth falling open.

She was always perceptive to a fault. It was one of the reasons he could tolerate her when everyone else drained him or bored him.

"What's happening?" Hermes sat up, his eyes darting between them before his eyes widened. "Don't do that. You know he will use it against you at every opportunity. He will know she is your weakness above all else."

"She *is* my weakness." The only one he had, as a matter of fact.

"He *will* use this against you, but it's also smart. If you are willing to cross that line for her, then he will know you will be willing to do anything if he touches her. It loses some of the impact after your little get-together fiasco though," Hecate considered.

As usual, she was right. He was running out of options, though. "Don't light the place on fire or anything while I'm gone. If any demi-gods show up, feel free to entertain them till I get back. It's been a minute since the last one, so I imagine we are overdue for company."

Before they could say anything, Hades stepped into his portal and into Olympus. His skin crawled with the pristine marble and ostentatious decor. It was such a stark contrast to the Underworld that it was nearly unsettling. He knew Zeus would have sensed his presence as soon as the portal opened, but he would not be receiving a warm welcome. They both knew why he had come and his brother would draw it out as long as possible.

Shoving his hands in his pockets to keep from clenching them, he dragged himself to where he knew Zeus would be receiving him. This was a repayment for Hades' attempt in the Underworld. All positioning and power struggles as if that was all immortality was made of. Until recently, it was even for him. Now there was more.

Zeus sat sprawled across his throne, a lightning bolt resting on his lap as he idly ran a finger over it. Subtle. Hades ignored the threat and walked till he was a few feet from the grand dais, letting the silence shift between them. The longer it went on, the more Zeus' face tightened with irritation. Probably a bad start.

"I suppose I should thank you for all the recent entertainment I've had to look forward to lately," Hades drawled.

Zeus' lips quirked. "A small punishment, all things considered. You deserve worse."

A string of words crossed his mind that he would have liked to call his brother, but instead, he shrugged his shoulders. "Probably."

Zeus arched an eyebrow. "Probably?"

Taking a step forward, Hades fought to regulate his emotions. It wouldn't benefit him to test his brother's patience, but after so much work and little rest, it was hard to separate his anger. Putting

Persephone at the forefront of his thoughts, he met Zeus' hard gaze.

"You and I both know I was pushed into a corner and did the best with what I had to work with. At the end of the day, we both know that Demeter is the real problem here. She hid a goddess from you for thirty years and then had the audacity to punish the mortals and take from *you*."

Zeus ran a caressing finger over the lightning bolt. "You are trying to minimize your part in all of this while placing all the blame on your wife's mother. Do you think Persephone would thank you for that?"

The urge to rip out his throat for even uttering her name was almost too much, but he had worked to still his rashness for too long to fall victim to it.

"I certainly don't think she'd fault me for it," Hades said.

Zeus leaned forward, gripping the lightning bolt in his hands. "And what have you come here for, Hades? This hardly seems like you are begging for forgiveness like you should."

True enough.

"I want my wife back, and I want it to be made abundantly clear that she is not to be touched. She is mine," Hades said with quiet wrath.

Fuck. That wasn't helpful. So much for having worked to still his rashness. He was no better than a human, with no control over their emotions and words.

Standing, Zeus stepped down from the dais and fixed his gaze on Hades. It was the same gaze that he had worn when he sentenced

Prometheus to torture, when he had bound Ixion to a burning wheel, and when he condemned Tantalus to an eternity of wanting.

"You are testing my patience," Zeus growled.

Hades didn't back down. "Do you blame me for what you would and have done? Didn't you sentence Ixion to his fate for wanting Hera? Why do you fault me for something you understand well?"

The haze of power lifted from his eyes a fraction as he considered Hades' words. "Are you saying I should punish Poseidon for his actions in regard to what you see as yours?"

The insinuation that Poseidon had touched Persephone was enough to draw his darkness from him. He felt it swirl around him, stretching out like the morning mist. It contrasted with the purity and ostentatiousness of Olympus, but it was too much a part of him to banish. Zeus stepped back, running his eyes over Hades and the wisps drawing from him.

"You are more unhinged than I've ever seen you, Hades." Zeus leaned forward and whispered conspiratorially, "It makes me want to know what exactly about her is worth risking everything."

Hades lashed out, a black tendril of power reaching towards Zeus, but the bolt of lightning Zeus held, cut through it as if it were nothing. He realized his error a moment too late as Zeus' face reddened and his face twisted with rage.

"You dare!" Zeus bellowed.

The overwhelming force of Zeus' will fell over him and Hades strained against it. "Why do you bait me? I have never asked anything of you except for this one thing. Leave her be."

Part of him wondered if Zeus had even heard him as the pressure around him forced him to his knees. Never had he had this much will exerted over him and he wondered if his brother meant to kill him, except that was not his preference. Zeus liked to punish, and this death would be too simple.

Even still, the rage that Zeus was radiating that Hades would dare to raise a hand against him was enough to cloud his judgment. Gone were the eyes of his brother, and in their place was an immortal set on vengeance. If Hades fell to Zeus, what would become of Persephone? Never once had Hades considered Zeus would actually do anything to him outside of his busy work. There was no one else to run the Underworld, but Hades failed to consider Zeus' temper and the fact that logic might escape him. Hades opened his mouth to remind him, but nothing came out, swallowed by the pressure.

"Isn't it a little early to be having family squabbles?" Hera's lilting voice broke through the haze in his mind.

As if her voice had been the cure, Zeus' eyes cleared, and he blinked several times before withdrawing his will. "Fuck, Hades. Why do you push me like this?"

It took a moment for Hades to gather his mind enough to stand while Hera threaded her arm through Zeus' and gave a small smile to him. "Because he's affected by the same affliction you and I have, darling. You know how jealous we both get."

There were two things Hades knew since coming to Olympus, and neither one set well with him. One, Zeus was willing to sacrifice Hades, and two, Hera was helping him. Never, not once in all their shared existence, had Hera ever come to his aid. In fact, he was fairly certain Hera hated him more than any of the other immortals. Which begged the question of what she had to gain from this. Even though everyone knew she raged against Zeus' infidelity, it was rarely a reason for her to speak out with the exception of punishing those cursed by Zeus' affections.

Zeus took a long breath and chuckled deeply. "I suppose that's true enough, but I hadn't thought him capable."

"Nor I," Hera said, cradling her stomach and eyeing Hades as he brushed off his shirt.

"That makes three of us, but my request remains the same," Hades said.

Zeus' eyes darkened. "You are lucky I don't punish you further. Nothing has changed today except you should tread carefully moving forward. Go."

He caught the flash of Hera's purple eyes before he was banished from Olympus and returned to the Underworld. The room came into focus and Hecate and Hermes stared at him with their lips turned down in identical frowns.

"What the fuck is Hera playing at?" He fought the urge to slam his fist through the wall.

Always quick of mind, Hecate said, "Hera and Persephone talked at Poseidon's place. I don't know what was said, but I'll bet it had something to do with that."

"Find out," Hades ordered, and couldn't bring himself to regret it.

To her credit, Hecate just nodded, disappearing in a flash. He resented how easily she could go to Persephone, but he would rectify that soon enough. Feeling Hermes' eyes on him, he waved a dismissive hand.

"Say what you want to say, Hermes," he ground out.

"That didn't go well, which means you are about to go to more drastic measures. I understand how you feel about her, but you are making a mistake. Three months isn't that bad. You can't protect her from all the gods, Hades. Sooner or later, Zeus will take—"

Hades shot out his hand. "Don't say another fucking word."

"You are being irrational," Hermes ignored the warning.

He was. It was unlike him and left him feeling wild and dangerous. Either way, Zeus' message was clear. He intended to pursue Persephone and Hades would be damned if he let him, which meant this time, when he made his power play, he wouldn't fail. The world would thank him when he was done. They had gotten rid of the Titans, which meant it wasn't impossible to ruin an immortal. One week to plan. It would have to do.

CHAPTER TWENTY-TWO

A BARGAIN AND A FAVOR

PERSEPHONE

Hecate was there the moment the sun went down and the curse released her. Her friend held out a robe to her, but Persephone hardly cared.

"How is he?" she asked quickly, throwing on the robe.

"I'm great, thank you for asking." Hecate rolled her eyes.

Persephone searched Hecate's face for what she wasn't saying, and yet the immortal had long since learned not to give anything away. Frustration burned in Persephone. The last time she had seen Hades, he had been exhausted and with Zeus' attention on her more and more, she worried it would only get worse for him.

"Please," Persephone whispered.

The sigh that broke from Hecate was infinite. "I can't decide if you two are the best thing for each other or the worst."

"Probably both," Persephone mused.

Hecate grunted in agreement. "He sent me to find out what you and Hera discussed."

Wrinkling her nose, Persephone thought back to that night and how much *more* the goddess seemed. There was cunning and intelligence there that she doubted Zeus even realized. Underneath even that, there was a darkness that hovered beneath the surface. As if she were capable of anything.

"Why does he need to know?" she countered.

The groan that left Hecate was excessive at best. "You are always so difficult. Just once you could make it easy for me. Fine. Hades went to see Zeus and I don't know anything really except that Hera stepped in. Which she never does and certainly not for Hades. Which means it was for you."

There wasn't time to unravel what that meant, or what Hera intended by it. They weren't allies by any means. Maybe Hera empathized with Persephone's unwanted attention, but at the end of the day, Hera still watched her as if she were a threat. If there was one thing Poseidon had taught her, it was that she couldn't trust Hera.

Pulling the robe around her tighter, Persephone took a steadying breath. "Tell him to keep his head down low and to not do anything stupid."

Hecate eyed her as if she were a wild animal. "Why? What are you going to do?"

Persephone turned and followed the walkway. "I am going to save my own damn self."

***

The only regret that lingered in Persephone's mind was that she should have taken the time to put on actual clothes. Yet she had been so frustrated with Hecate's news that she could only think about how to get them both out of this mess. Persephone had always known the answer since the day The Fates came, but now it was time to stop putting it off.

The ocean waves crashed along the rocky beach as Persephone searched the stormy sea in front of her. It had begun last night and her mother had sat on the lake's edge and told her it was never a good sign when the sea began to writhe. Maybe it was foolish of her to come with the skies gray and the waves white with rage, but if she was going to save herself and her husband while she was at it, the time was now.

Crouching down, she placed her palm flat into the seawater, letting its icy kiss surround her. Pushing out her power into it, she pulled back to stand and wrapped her arms around herself to ward against the chilly winds. She didn't have to wait long for her request to be answered. She watched in awe as a black and white whale of enormous size erupted from the water, the ocean around it receding in its wake. On its massive back rose a large dorsal fin that Poseidon, god of the oceans and sea, held onto. Even from afar, she could see the rage that lived on his face. Gone was the mischievous god who enjoyed instigating and in its place was the god who had long earned the title of earth-shaker.

When he was close enough, Poseidon leapt from the creature and stalked towards Persephone, the waves caressing him as if they longed to be a part of him. The tempestuous sea in his eyes made

Persephone feel as if she had made a grave mistake. She had been prepared for the god she had known or, at worst, the one devoid of life and happiness she had witnessed in his home. This was something else entirely.

"Here, I thought you were smart beneath all that sheltered nativity," Poseidon seethed.

It was an effort to not take a step back from him as he loomed over her, vengeance burning in his bulging muscles and veins as if his power were writhing beneath the surface.

"I need a favor," Persephone said without betraying any of her nerves.

Poseidon's face twisted with rage. "You are insane. Do you know what *he* has done?."

Shit. Never once had she considered that Hades was the reason for the sea god's anger. Yet even as the thought entered, she realized that she should have. Hecate and Hermes would have told him about the insinuation Poseidon made at his gathering, and Hades would not have let that go lightly. Maybe this was a monumental fuck up, but she'd be damned if she let the opportunity pass her by.

"What is between you and him is not me," Persephone said.

Poseidon tilted his head, looking more like a god than she had ever seen him before. "He sent his Furies after my son, even after I helped him. I gave his sentimental ass the time to see you and this is how he thanks me? By torturing my son?"

Fuck, Hades. She understood why he had done it. Poseidon had sent a dangerous message by letting the others think she could be touched and Hades would have wanted to make sure to send his own message. Touch her and the fires of the Underworld would lie in wait.

"I understand you are angry and you are entitled to it, but as I said, your fight is with him, not me," Persephone tried.

Poseidon took another step forward till their chests were touching and Persephone was reminded that she was only wearing a robe. Stupid. This had been a stupid idea. He lifted his hand and threaded a wave of blonde hair through his hand.

"Did you listen to nothing I taught you, Persephone? How do the gods move against each other? How did your mother strong-arm Zeus into getting you back?"

She didn't pull away from him, recognizing that something ancient in him wanted her to be afraid. "Mortals."

"Exactly," he growled. "And right now, you are low enough on the hierarchy of immortals that you might as well be considered a mortal."

Her blood ran as cold as the sea air. "So, you would seek vengeance through violence against me instead of procuring not one favor from the Underworld, but two. Hades already owes you one. You could add mine to it."

The rage in his eyes dimmed a fraction as reason fought for power within him. "Do you know what it is you offer me?"

No. Only that if Hades had been willing to pay the price for ten minutes with her that she would pay it for this.

"Does it matter?" she countered.

Poseidon tilted his head, considering, as he dropped her hair and stepped back, giving her precious space. "What is it you want?"

Persephone fought the urge to smile. She knew this would be a problem later on, but at least the bigger issue would be solved.

"Information," Persephone answered.

Poseidon gave a small snort. "Sometimes that is worth more than a favor."

"It's just one question. One answer," Persephone said.

It was an effort not to cower under his consideration, but she saw the moment he let go and accepted the bargain.

"One question. One answer. A favor of my choosing to be called on at any time," he summarized.

"Deal," Persephone said, feeling the finality of the bargain settling over her as if it were now ingrained in her bones.

"Ask," Poseidon ordered.

"What would make a god sleep for at least two hours?" she asked.

His eyes danced over her, searching. "That's dangerous information, Persephone, Queen of the Underworld."

"Will you relinquish our deal?" Persephone goaded.

"Lotus blossoms are potent against mortals, but even gods feel their effects, though it would not be enough for what you ask."

"Are you saying there is nothing?" Persephone felt defeat burrow into her.

"I did not say that," Poseidon said quietly. "You would be wise to divulge the plan you've whipped up in that pretty head. I guarantee there are a thousand holes within it that will lead you to grave consequences."

"And you would council me?" Persephone raised her eyebrows.

"For a price," Poseidon said.

It was time to recall his wedding present to her. She would not trust him. Not in this. "I will keep my own council."

He shrugged as if it were her loss, but she saw the hunger in his face at what price he would have collected had she chosen differently. She always owed him and being in debt already sat poorly in her stomach.

"Morpheus. Bring a lotus blossom to him and he will create a sleeping potion that will do what you seek," Poseidon said gravely.

Persephone could practically hear the words and warnings he left unspoken. "Where can I find him?"

Poseidon clicked his tongue. "That's two questions, little Persephone."

She couldn't afford another favor. That meant she would have to delay her plan longer in order to find the answer one way or another.

"However," Poseidon drawled. "I confess I am interested in seeing this all play out and perhaps I even like you a little bit. Morpheus sleeps in a cave. In Erebus, which, perhaps conveniently or inconveniently, is located in the Underworld."

Shit.

"I studied the maps in the Underworld. Erebus wasn't listed."

"Would you advertise directions to a place that could compromise a god?" Poseidon chided.

No, she supposed she wouldn't and Hades was too careful to make a mistake like that. It might be impossible, depending on how close it was to the river. Hades wouldn't let her get anywhere near the river and she couldn't ask him for help with this.

Poseidon chuckled, seeing a dilemma whether he understood all the pieces or not. He turned back to the sea and stepped into its icy arms. "North of Asphodel, behind the city."

With the gift of words, he stepped on the back of the incredible creature and returned to the depths of the ocean.

She may have bargained something precious, but she gained something invaluable. Persephone was going home.

Chapter Twenty-Three

Two Unwanted Visits in One Day

Hades

Hades stood at the walls of Tartarus, staring at them as if a better plan would come into view. What would the Titans do with their freedom? It was a stupid question. They had been imprisoned with only their hatred and anger for company. It was a shit plan, and he doubted he was even stupid enough to go through with it. If he only freed Helios, would his freedom be enough to stay his hand after he took revenge on Zeus?

He ran his hands over the barrier only he could see, feeling the fury of the souls behind it. How much was he willing to give for Persephone? At least that question was easy. Everything. He would give everything for her. Maybe she had become his obsession. Maybe he was no better than the other immortals who committed terrible deeds in the name of love. Maybe. In the end, it wouldn't matter.

The awareness of a new soul brushed against his senses and he mentally reinforced the bonds holding the prison together. He knew he would have to deal with this sooner or later, but he would have preferred later. Usually, there was a back-and-forth of vengeance before it came to this. Either way, it was better to be done with it. One less thing to worry about.

Stepping through a portal, he found himself in his dining room where Poseidon sat with his legs up on the table, tossing a pomegranate up in the air and catching it. Where he had expected to find rage, there was distant amusement radiating from his brother. The seas had been violent, and many souls had found their way to the Underworld at their hands. Shipwrecks created from the wrath of the immortal before him.

Hades said nothing as he took his seat at the head of the table a few seats down from Poseidon. Was he here to call in his favor? That seemed unlikely since Hades was sure it would be used to intervene in a squabble with another god. Poseidon wouldn't waste it on petty fights.

"You are surprised I am not angrier," Poseidon said, catching the fruit once more.

"Your temper tantrums usually last longer," Hades said with a raised eyebrow.

The god of the seas and oceans caught the fruit and leaned forward, fixing Hades with his too-blue eyes. "That was a really shitty thing to do."

Hades mimicked the movement. "You made her vulnerable."

Poseidon scoffed and cracked the pomegranate open, the juices dripping over his hands. "She was already vulnerable. I merely picked the lesser evil, unless you wanted Zeus to know you had put your hands on his latest obsession."

"She's *my* wife," Hades seethed, feeling his darkness seep from him.

"Nothing belongs to us, Hades, and you know it damn well. You are too lovesick to remember that. I did you a favor and you punished my son. Like I said, it was a shitty thing to do."

"And you came all this way to tell me this?" Hades said, knowing there was more. Hating that there was more.

Poseidon took his finger and dug into the flesh of the pomegranate, ripping out the seeds slowly and letting them fall to the ground between his legs. "No, brother. I came to tell you we are even."

Without hesitating, Hades felt for the awareness of her that was dimmed while she was in the mortal realm, but not gone. There was no change in her aura of life, and Hades gave a mental sigh of relief.

"What did you do?" Hades asked, knowing that Poseidon was gloating.

Poseidon lifted his finger, stained with the red of the seeds, and studied it. "That remains to be seen. These things tend to have a life of their own. I only know that whatever it is that the cost will be as great if not greater than the one my son paid."

It was an effort not to reach out his magic and wrap it around Poseidon's neck. Whatever he had done was involving Persephone. That much was clear. His Furies had torn apart Theseus' skin and waited for it to heal before beginning again. In his torture, he cried out for his father and cursed Hecate. Though Hades still didn't know his crime against her, he knew it was enough that Theseus blamed her for his torture.

"Poseidon—" Hades began, but his brother stood, setting down the ravaged fruit.

"Save the dramatic threats, we all know you are pulled too thin to be a real threat and now that you've used your Furies, we are all watching ours carefully. The same thing will not work twice. You had one card to play, and you wasted it on petty jealousy. I hardly recognize you," Poseidon said with distaste.

Hades' fists tightened, and he imagined which depraved tortures would suit his brother best. "You set a precedent that she could be touched. There needed to be consequences."

Poseidon arched an eyebrow. "And there will be. Love does not look good on you, brother."

With that, Poseidon stepped through his own portal made of the ocean itself, its endless depths stretching out before him. Hades contemplated throwing out his own power and forcing Poseidon to stay, but there was no use. He wouldn't get any other information. He watched as the portal closed and he was left with the mangled fruit and threat of a scorned god. This cycle of vengeance and fury was endless, and while it had satiated the immortals throughout the eons, it was occasionally exhausted.

As if one visit from his kin wasn't enough for one day, another awareness filled his mind. One he had never felt in the Underworld before. Precedents, indeed. The day Persephone had come into his life was a beacon of chaos and emotions he hardly recognized. Still, he couldn't bring himself to regret it.

Opening his front door, he found Hera in all her radiance facing him with cold eyes, as if she had retreated far into her godhood. Her bright white dress and porcelain skin seemed too bright for his Underworld, making it clear she didn't belong.

"I'd say I was pleased to see you, but seeing as I have no idea what game you are playing . . . " He let the words trail off as he eyed her.

Hera eyed him with contempt. "I have never liked you, with your arrogance and unearned self-righteous bullshit."

Hades raised an eyebrow. "That seems a little hostile for someone who is knocking on *my* door."

"I'm already regretting it. Are you going to let me in or not?" She glared at him.

As he stepped to the side and held out his arm, he thought how this was the real Hera everyone failed to see. She had crafted her image perfectly. Goddess of women, marriage, and childbirth. She was regal and refined. A dutiful wife, no matter how far her husband strayed from her bed. Her jealous rages on his lovers justified and a symbol of her unfailing love.

No, Hera was more than a scorned wife. Behind her eyes lived an intelligence she kept hidden from her husband. If news ever came that Hera had overthrown Zeus, he would not blink twice. In fact, it felt more like a prophecy than a fantasy.

He watched as Hera eyed his home with scorn, running her hands over priceless artifacts and woodwork as if they were dirt. "This isn't what I expected."

"Happy to disappoint as usual," Hades drawled.

Hera turned, her beautiful face drawn in a scowl. "I didn't help you for your sake when you foolishly angered Zeus."

"That thought never once crossed my mind," Hades said honestly.

Hera pursed her lips, considering. "Good. I did it for your wife, who, by the way, you do not deserve in the least."

"Finally, something we can agree on," Hades said, the mirth receding from him at the mention of Persephone.

The way Hera watched him now left him feeling naked and thoroughly seen. It was unsettling and he could have done without it. When she was satisfied, the immortal crossed her arms.

"I believe you and I share a common goal. I would rather not see her fall into Zeus' hands and I am inclined to believe you feel the same given your reckless behavior of late."

The way his mind processed and worked through the scenarios that Hera could be orchestrating was proof of how treacherous immortality could be. He should have been gladly welcoming her help, given she was the one immortal who could likely see this through.

"Why?" Hades asked.

Hera clicked her tongue. "While I understand your trepidation, it's still annoying. Despite myself, I like her. She is passionate but capable. All the best of Demeter and none of the worst."

He could have argued that there was nothing good in Demeter, but it felt counterproductive.

Crossing his arms, he leaned against a nearby wall. "What is it that you propose?"

"That depends. I know you summoned The Fates for her. What did they say?"

Hades pulled away from the doorframe and let Hera see all of the contempt he felt for her. "How?"

Only Hermes, Hecate, and Poseidon knew. It wasn't hard to guess which one had sold him out given the recent visit, but he needed to know.

"None you suspect, but that is beside the point. If you want my help, you will tell me what they said," she commanded.

Hades held out his hand towards the front door. "Turns out I don't want your help."

Hera tilted her head. "That bad? What could they have possibly said that would make the god of the Underworld *fear*? Because that *is* fear I smell on you, Hades."

Everything inside Hades begged him to force her to her knees and wipe the knowledge she carried from her mind. Hera was nothing compared to his power and he could easily subdue her. The consequences of that were a different story.

Hera sighed and turned the golden bangle that clung to her wrist. "I know it doesn't seem like it, but I do want to help her.

I can't do that if I don't have all the information. You can keep it to yourself, but know that in less than a week, I am sure Zeus plans to have her, and I think you know that. Time is of the essence."

A strange sentiment for an immortal, but nevertheless, it was true. He was running out of time and his ideas were firmly rooted in chaos and world oblivion.

"To break her curse, she must enter the River Styx." Hades spat the words like the poison they were.

Hera's eyes widened a fraction before she recovered. "A death sentence."

His chest felt heavy as he nodded. "One she would gladly give herself over to if I let her."

The way Hera's mouth fell open was the most surprise he had ever seen from her. "She would try?"

"Has tried," Hades corrected grimly.

Hera recovered and shook her head with a small smile playing on her full lips. "At least I know I was right."

"About what?" he asked.

"That she is different and that it certainly was that bad." She pressed two fingers to her lips, thinking. "The only way to protect her is to bring her back to the Underworld."

"You don't think I know that?" Hades growled.

"Yes, but you are going about it all the wrong ways," Hera murmured, her mind still working.

"And just how should I be going about it?" Hades seethed.

"By going through Demeter," Hera said, as if it weren't the stupidest fucking thing anyone had ever said.

"Yes, because Demeter, who cursed her own daughter to keep her away from me, would be very accommodating. She practically handed her to Zeus!"

"Yes, well, you were never going to get very far, that's for sure. I'll speak to her. You need only be ready when I say," Hera said, clasping her hands in front of her as if it were all well and settled.

"And then what happens when she's forced to go back at the end of the month?" Hades felt his restraint slipping.

Hera took two steps towards him, meeting his gaze. "Then you let her try to break the curse."

"The fuck I will!" Hades said, his power leaping from him and billowing out in waves of smoke.

Hera gave a small, disappointed shake of her head. "Fear is not a good look for you, Hades. If I stick my neck out for you, it's because you will let her try. Otherwise, it's a fool's errand."

"You said yourself it was a death sentence," Hades reminded her.

"So I did. Nonetheless, it should be her choice, not yours. Do we have a deal or not?"

He'd be damned before he let her dip a toe in the river, but it wouldn't be the first oath he had broken. When he nodded his head, he got the feeling both he and Hera knew he was lying.

As she turned to leave, she said over her shoulder, "You should consider the witch Circe."

"I'd rather listen to Apollo's music all night," Hades said with disgust.

The truth was that making deals with sorcerers didn't sit well with Hades, especially knowing who Persephone's father was.

They were powerful, but they were plagued by all the side effects of immortality. It made a dangerous combination.

Hera merely clicked her tongue and left.

CHAPTER TWENTY-FOUR

THE THING ABOUT MORTALS

PERSEPHONE

Perhaps The Fates were finally on her side as her mother was called away to Olympus. Persephone neither knew nor cared why, only that this was her opportunity. Throwing on one of the least ostentatious gowns her mother allowed her, she made to leave her false home for what she intended to be the last time.

She had ten hours before the sun rose and the curse claimed her once more. Ten hours to be human and make it back to the Underworld. There were two destinations she had in mind, and she hoped she would only need the one. The Olympians called Hades cruel for his task he'd given Orpheus, but Persephone had seen through it. He had given the lyre player a chance, and that had been the best he could do. Even still, the way the Olympians went on about the poor man's suffering had been meant to taunt her, but she had turned it into a weapon.

Persephone's power was small in comparison to the others who had feasted on generations of worship. Where Hecate and Hermes could portal at will to the Underworld, it was not a skill Persephone could boast. However, portaling in the mortal world was something she had been practicing every day of her imprisonment while she waited. The portal that opened before her was made of black roses that left a lingering smell in the air. Stepping through, she found herself in the city of Thrace.

It could hardly be called a city as the buildings were decayed and the smell of smoke and rot hung in the air. Beggars sat on every corner, their emaciated bodies clinging to life. It was enough to make her stomach roll with nausea. That they should be living like this when one blessing from the gods would see them well and cared for, but therein lies the secret of the gods. Suffering and pain were an aphrodisiac for worship. Just the right amount led to plentiful sacrifices that worked to increase the power of the gods. Yet too much suffering, as her mother had recently demonstrated, led to a lack of faith and despair. It was a careful balance and the city of Thrace looked to be on the precipice of the latter.

It only took two beggars to give her directions to the inn she needed. As soon as she stepped in front of it, a mournful tune drifted beyond the broken walls and nearly brought her to her knees. Persephone wiped a tear from her eye and stared at it in wonder. Reminding herself why she had come, she pushed open the door.

The inn was desolate except for one man, who wore tattered clothes and whose beard was overgrown and poorly maintained.

It was hard to say if the smell that wafted from the room was from him or just in general. His fingers strummed his lyre while his eyes were glossy, as if seeing something that wasn't there.

The innkeeper eyed her warily, but she met his eyes and he averted his gaze. That was another thing about mortals. They feared immortals as much as they loved them. Persephone's aura might not have been as strong as any of the others, but there was no denying that she was other. When she took the seat across from the broken man, he didn't even glance at her, too lost in his mournful tale.

"I'm sorry for what you've lost," Persephone said.

He didn't respond and continued to play as if she weren't there. All at once, she saw the truth of him. He was merely existing. He had left his soul in the Underworld along with his wife. Another tear fell from her eyes and she wiped it away.

The music stopped. "Does my pain amuse the gods?"

The words that were meant to hold fire merely sputtered and lost their flame.

"Some," Persephone said honestly.

"But not you," he said quietly.

"Not me," Persephone answered.

"Then why have you come?" Orpheus asked, setting down his lyre.

"To ask you how you made it into the Underworld."

Orpheus sighed and picked up his lyre once more, as if he had entertained her long enough. This song was haunted, as if an ominous presence loomed just ahead. Persephone tilted her head.

"You wrote this song for Hades," she guessed.

The chords sang out in errant synchrony. "Does it matter?" he said as he righted his fingers.

"It matters to me, as does your pain," Persephone answered.

Orpheus watched her for a long moment, and Persephone knew that there was nothing she could say that would convince him to help her. She could not promise his wife back or give him reprieve from his sorrow. More than that, she would not force her power or divinity on him. He had suffered enough. She had known there was a chance this would not work. Heracles would be harder to track down, but she would try.

"Apollo showed me a cave not far from here." He said the words as if they were nothing when they were everything.

"Would you show me?" Persephone asked, her heart soaring with hope.

"No," he answered.

It was as if the world had shattered into a million pieces. Hope there in one moment only to be taken in the next.

"But I'll tell you." His words, though covered in grief, were music to her ears.

Chapter Twenty-Five

CALL OUT TO YOUR GOD

Hades

If he were a mortal, he would have long given up and drowned himself in drink. Instead, he was drowning in too many souls. Zeus had created a lightning storm that conveniently took out enough mortals that Hades was stuck rearranging Asphodel once more while the mortals prayed for forgiveness and cast offerings to their murderer. It was exhausting.

A young girl walked aimlessly past him, and he reached out grabbing her arm. "This way, Selene."

The girl looked up at him with large brown eyes that were lost amidst a life of pain. Hades winced when he searched her soul and found the root of her torture. Fury that was vast and far-reaching clawed at the surface of his skin. Instead of giving in to his baser instincts, he searched the influx of souls and allowed himself a self-satisfied smile at what he found.

Hades gestured for Minos, who left the older gentleman he was speaking to and ran his hand through his hair.

"This is a lot," he said, his eyes searching the masses.

"It is," Hades agreed. "Asphodel will be whatever they need it to be. I will move along the souls that are close, but there is something I need to see to first. Please help Selene to get to where she needs to be."

Minos did not question him as he took the girl's hand, which was why he had survived this long as Hades' assistant. Stepping through the portal, he stood at the banks of the River Styx, which had long become his least favorite place in the Underworld. Bending down, he reached his hand into the murky depths and coaxed the soul forth.

Greedy as it had been in life, it barreled through the river and into his waiting hand. When Hades righted and released the soul, it changed from a silvery thread into a six-foot man with a receding hairline and eyes that were too big for his face.

"Atrius," Hades said with disgust.

The man scrunched up his eyebrows and confusion flitted through his features. That was the thing about the river. It was a punishment, but a kind one. It robbed mortals of their memories and doomed them to an eternity of meaningless existence. It was too generous for the black soul before him.

This normally wouldn't have escaped his notice, but when he was busy, he was careless. Had it been any other time, he would have gladly sent Atrius to where he belonged. However, he was not the god of the Underworld for nothing and he reached out his power and ordered the river to release its feast. For the river fed on memories and emotions. If he had waited much longer, it would have consumed Atrius' till there was nothing left, but the generosity of Zeus saw that the river was sated.

He made sure to have each depraved memory in hand that shot out of the river like icy shards and into his hands. When he was satisfied, his hand glowed with the stolen memories. Placing his hand on the man's chest, he shoved them all back and watched as the feeling and humanity seeped back into him. His eyes widened and then he fell to his knees, clutching Hades' shoes.

"Thank you, my lord Hades. Thank you." The rest of his murmurings were lost on Hades as he picked the ill-fated mortal up by his neck.

Atrius' beady eyes bulged as he fought to adjust to his new fate. Hades could only imagine what his smile looked like as he stepped into the portal and carried them into Tartarus. It was a barren wasteland filled with scorching heat and the screams of those locked in endless torture. The breeze that blew by could have been comforting, but instead, it was significantly hotter than the air, burning where it touched.

Atrius screamed as Hades released him and threw him down on the hard sand.

"Please, there must be a mistake, Lord Hades," he stammered, tears falling from his eyes.

Hades pulled on the string that was his furies and their call echoed in the dry air, making the man in front of him whimper.

"Your soul is as tattered and rotting as the rest of you," Hades sneered. "For the crimes you have committed, you will live out eternity amongst the damned with a torture of my pleasure." He knelt down, resting his arm on his knee. "And I can be *very* creative."

Hades might have been offended that the man jerked his gaze up to the sky and whimpered as if Hades wasn't the most terrifying thing here, but then again, he knew better. Three winged creatures soared above and landed with a flourish, sending the ground rumbling in their wake.

Alecto, Tisiphone, and Megaera folded their wings behind them and stared at the man before them as if he were all they had ever longed for. In answer, they smiled, showing large canines.

"Atrius here is happy to meet you three," Hades purred. "He—"

The awareness in his mind pulsed, as if testing its awareness. Everything in him went taut as the sensation grew louder.

"Hades?" Tisiphone asked.

Thoughts of torture and maiming quickly left his mind as the awareness ceased pulsing and burned bright. He waved a hand in dismissal and as one the three Furies turned on Atrius, whose screams echoed even as Hades' stepped through the portal to the gates of the Underworld. There, bending down and scratching Cerberus' chin, was his wife.

He felt as if he were made of stone as he fought to understand the sight before him. Cerberus seemed to have no trouble as he rolled onto his back and his tongue rolled out the side of his mouth. Persephone laughed and scratched his belly. She was as perfect as ever and her laugh made the darkness that had been swallowing him recede.

"Persephone," he said, his voice thick.

She stilled and stood; the gates opening to her. Cerberus groaned and rolled back over to sit at her feet, but Persephone's eyes drank him in as much as he did her.

After an era had passed, she shrugged her shoulders. "I saved myself."

He just bet she fucking did. Walking would have taken too long and so he stepped through the portal and wrapped her in his arms, breathing in the scent of her like it was the source of his power. She melted into him and damn, did it feel good to have her arms around him. All at once, there was nothing left except her. There would be consequences for that later, but he didn't care.

He pulled back and ran his hands over her face. "How?"

Her smile sank into a small frown and he wished he hadn't asked. "Orpheus helped me."

He didn't appreciate the feelings that erupted in his chest at the boy's name. Ignoring the gathering feelings, he brushed a blonde strand of hair from her face.

"I was working with Hera to get you back. I should have known you didn't need help," Hades said.

"Here, I thought I was coming to save you." Persephone smirked.

The rightness that settled over him was followed by a lurking truth. "Why did you come back, Persephone?"

Her eyebrows furrowed, and she was a really terrible actress. "For you."

Despite the fact that she had a penchant for trying to kill herself, she was fucking perfect. Still, he eyed her suspiciously.

"No, you didn't come back just for me. You are smarter than that," he accused.

Persephone tilted her head up to him and parted her lips, making all conscious thoughts go directly to his cock. "You make me dumb." Her voice was sultry and commanding.

He knew perfectly fucking well what she was doing, but he also didn't care. He caught her lips with his and dove into her mouth. Claiming and feasting on her like he had longed to do for so long. His body sprang to life as she opened for him and clawed at him as if she were just as desperate. One of his favorite pastimes had been to imagine how he would take her once he had her again, but all of those fantasies faded behind the need to be inside her right fucking then.

Before he could open his portal, Persephone slammed her hands on his chest and pushed him back into the scent of fresh roses. She followed closely after him and before he had a chance to register what had happened; he realized he was in their room. Pride clung to lust as he took in her beaming face.

"You've been practicing," he said with unmitigated pride.

She stepped into him and ran her hands up his arms. "Do you want to see what else I've been practicing?"

"I honestly don't know what the fuck that means, but yes." Hades grinned.

Her laugh was his best dreams come to life. If he could have captured and bottled up that sound, he would have.

"Kiss me, Hades," she ordered breathlessly.

It was one order he was happy to comply with. Her mouth tasted like champagne and cinnamon. His cock throbbed, and he had the unfortunate understanding that he would not be taking his time with her. He let his power gather around them and whereas he might have preserved their clothes; they disintegrated with the force of it. Persephone pulled away, eyes wild and chest heaving.

She took his hand in hers and stepped back towards the bed. He could only imagine how he looked to her, like a man starved and desperate. She was the other part of his soul. The twin to his fire. He drank her in as he followed her lead, gently lowering his body over hers.

Persephone reached up and ran a hand over his face, searching. "I missed you so much."

He was choking on the emotion threatening to undo him. "I merely existed while you were gone."

There was a beat of sorrow in her eyes as she reached up and pressed her lips to his. "I love you, Hades. I'll always find my way back to you."

And he believed her. The woman that had come to him lonely, but fierce and more than capable. She was a force of nature that bent the world to her liking. He had a million questions for her, but none of them mattered while she was beneath him. Yet that wasn't right either. She was his queen and his savior.

Hands on her hips, he rolled them until she was straddling his hips. Everything in him wanted to plunge his cock into her and sink into the feeling of being inside her, but he would wait on his Queen's command. Thankfully, she was a benevolent deity and raised her hips till her heat teased him with the promise of more. He was practically shaking from restraint, his hands digging into her hips.

Her eyes locked on his, she lowered herself onto his cock, stretching and molding to him perfectly. He threw his head back and groaned at the pleasure that built in the base of his spine. Nothing felt as good as her. She was made for him.

"Hades," she breathed as she rode him.

The pleasure in him was building too fast. He would be spent like some god in his first decades of life.

If he was going, then he was damn well taking her with him. He pressed his thumb to her clit, and she cried out his name once more. Fuck, he was almost there.

"That's right, Persephone. Call out to your god. The god who worships at your feet as you ride his cock."

Her blonde hair cascaded around her, making her look like some sort of painting. She was a masterpiece.

"I am going to make you come so many times that you will be begging me to stop. Your body sings for me, Persephone." He felt her contract around him and it was an effort not to spill himself into her right then.

"Yes!" she cried, hands digging into his chest as her hips fell into an erratic motion.

"Tell me your truth, Persephone," he ordered.

"I love you!" she shouted as her body contracted around him even as he continued to flick her clit, drawing out her pleasure.

"And I fucking love you," he said as the pleasure in his spine barrelled through him, leaving him raw and breathless.

She collapsed on top of him, and he held her tight to his chest. They came down from their high slowly, both content to be with the other. It was as if he were whole once more. The Underworld seemed to relax around them, as if it had missed her just as much. There were things they needed to talk about, but fuck if he cared. She was home.

Chapter Twenty-Six

LESSONS ON INSULTING GODDESSES

PERSEPHONE

Curled up in Hades' arms and thoroughly spent, Persephone sighed contentedly. She knew their peace would fracture at any second and her disappearance would be noted, but she refused to not enjoy every second of this. His finger idly ran up and down her side while she was draped across him.

The silence stretched, easy and familiar. She knew he was taking in every second as well. They had been forced apart and their souls had paid the price. Wild and restless without their home. Yet, like all good things, it had to come to an end.

"How do you think this plays out?" Hades asked, his voice gravelly.

She was tempted to deflect the question, but there wasn't a point. She lifted on her elbow and looked up at him. "I stole myself. They can't fault you for that."

"You still are bound to the lake, Persephone. Even if Zeus doesn't intervene and drag you back to Demeter, the curse will," Hades said, watching her carefully.

She frowned at him. "Here, I thought your spirits would be a little higher with me in our bed once more."

"Don't," he warned, tension coiling him. "Don't for a second think that I don't know you came back for that damn river."

She wanted to yell at him for ruining the beautiful illusion they had created, but she found where she thought there would be anger, there was only heartbreak.

"You have always given me the choice, Hades. It's one of the reasons I fell in love with you. Let me choose this."

She shouldn't have asked for things she knew he couldn't give her. It was only setting them both up for failure.

"No."

Persephone sighed, pressing her forehead into his chest. "This will never end if I don't. This was one month, Hades. We can't do this forever and expect that he won't come for me eventually. Either I resign myself to that fate or I choose my fate."

Hades sighed and ran a hand over her hair. "Your tenacity is aggravating."

"You are evading the matter at hand with compliments." Persephone eyed him.

The rumble of laughter that broke from his chest lodged itself into her heart. "Only you would call that a compliment."

Her attempt at mock seriousness failed as she felt the smile lift her lips. "Tell me about Hera."

Hades' amusement faded quickly like a fire snuffed out. "What did you two speak about?"

"Power," Persephone supplied.

His hand ran over her cheek, and she closed her eyes, leaning into the touch. "She claims that she has taken a liking to you, which, while I can appreciate, seems . . . unlike her."

She frowned, considering. It had been difficult to ascertain whether Hera had seen her as a threat at the end of their conversation, but hope clawed at her all the same.

"You are plotting," Hades accused.

Feigning innocence, Persephone sat up abruptly. "That's a very rude thing to say, god of the Underworld."

He rolled his eyes, and it made her core tighten with need. "I'm not sure whether I should be amused at your tactics or annoyed."

Persephone wore a feline smirk as she shifted, straddling his hips once more. His hands found her hips and his eyes darkened. Always eager, her god.

"Why not both?" she asked.

He growled and jerked her entire body up his chest, capturing her in his mouth in one swift motion. The startled yelp that let loose from her chest quickly transformed into a moan of pleasure as he licked his tongue up her clit as she straddled him. Sensation after sensation worked through her as he pulled her hips down, consuming her. Whatever discomfort she might have had at the strangeness of the position faded under his ministrations.

He groaned against her, and the vibrations sent shivers through her body. Only he could worship her like this, drawing pleasure from every skillful maneuver. Banging on the door had her lifting off him, but he growled in protest.

"They can wait. You, Persephone, are going to ride my face until you scream my name. Do you understand?" His voice was midnight gravel.

It was deliciously wicked, and she loved the way it flared heat into her every surface. He would know who was here, but if he didn't care that they would hear her scream for him, then she couldn't bring herself to mind. Lowering herself back onto his mouth, he murmured his approval, his hands holding her in place as if he refused to let her go.

Knowing that they were being listened to set off a new sort of need in her and she ground her hips against him, chasing that feeling. Hades sucked and licked as if he had only ever wanted this. It was hard to breathe, but she gulped down air as she moaned. Throwing back her head, she reached her hands up and rubbed at the peaked nipples, which earned a groan from her husband. His eyes feasted on her just as much as his mouth did. It was sensual and everything.

Persephone rolled her hips and his tongue flicked out, sending her careening against the pressure building. She was close, but she didn't want it to end. She fought against the tide that threatened to carry her away, but it claimed her all the same, slamming into her. Crying out his name, she rode the waves of pleasure and he continued his efforts, drawing out her pleasure. When the last of it broke, she collapsed onto the bed in a heap of bliss.

Hades bent over her, pressing a languid kiss to her mouth as if they had all the time in the world. She loved the way she tasted herself on his lips, as if they were ensnared body and soul. When he finally broke the kiss, she protested, but he was already sliding off the bed, his cock hard and begging for her mouth. As if he sensed her thoughts, he pulled on a pair of pants and met her gaze.

"Later. Later, Persephone, I'll let you suck my cock to your heart's content," he said with hunger.

"Or now would be fine," she said, sitting up.

Hades grunted as he pulled his shirt over. "It's not just Hermes here. Ares is too."

That drug all the lust from her veins as she quickly sat up. "The god of war is in our house."

The shrug from Hades made her slightly less alarmed. "It's fine. Zeus hates Ares. If he sent him, it was just as much to annoy him as much as me. Now, if it were Athena he had sent, that would be a different story."

Her favorite stories that Demeter would tell her were all of Athena, and when she had finally met her in person, it was the first time she was truly impressed with an immortal outside of her husband. The goddess radiated intelligence and a shrewdness that was intimidating. From what she had seen of Ares, she found she was less impressed. He was loud and arrogant. Always laughing, as if he were in on the joke when she was fairly certain he never understood them.

Persephone rose from the bed and chose a black ensemble lest anyone question her place in the world. Next to Hades, she was his queen in every way that mattered. Twisting the ring on her finger, she turned to her husband, who watched her like a man starved.

"What should I expect?" she asked.

His lips thinned. "Posturing."

He crossed the distance between them and pulled her into him, pressing a kiss to her forehead. She melted into him, finding strength in his strength.

"Are you ready?" he asked.

She nodded her head, and he opened the portal that led them to the dining room. As always, the table was littered with endless food and wine, but Ares stood at the head of the room, red-faced beneath his helm. Hermes sat with messy hair with his head in his hands over an empty plate. While power radiated from the war god, all she could feel from Hermes was his overwhelming anxiety.

As Hades and Persephone entered the room, both sets of eyes lifted to them. Ares' bulky form turned and assessed her as if she were nothing before he glared at Hades.

"Whatever amusement I found in this game of yours ended the moment I became a fucking messenger dog," he snarled, fists clenched at his wine.

Hades smirked and spread his hand out toward the table. "Have some wine gifted by Dionysus. It will soothe your bad temper."

In answer, a glass of white wine appeared at the head of the table. It was as if Ares couldn't decide what he wanted more as he shifted his glare from the cup to Hades. Giving in, he lifted the cup and drained it in one gulp. When he finished, he slammed it down and took a long breath. He was a short man who Persephone quickly learned was motivated by three things. Drink, sex, and war. Anything else would not hold his attention for long, which was why Persephone guessed he was angry about this new appointment.

"Zeus wants her to go back," he said with an absent wave of his hand towards her.

"Or there will be war. Message delivered. As always, you excel at your work, Ares," Hades said as he pulled out a chair for Persephone at the opposite head of the table.

"This isn't a joke, Hades." Hermes groaned into his hands.

"Have I ever told you that you worry too much?" Hades asked as he took the seat next to hers, his legs kicked out as if he hadn't a care in the world.

"For once, his nervousness is well deserved," Ares said with a gruff voice. "While I do enjoy war with the mortals, we both know it would be very different among ourselves."

"I would think you would enjoy the change of pace," Hades said.

Ares snorted, amusement dripping into him as if the wine really was a cure-all. "Maybe."

Hades clapped his hands together and sat forward. "Excellent visit. You can let my brother know I'll expect his declaration of war at his convenience."

The god of war shook his head. "It's a war you won't win, Hades. You'll end up in Tartarus right next to Kronos and the rest."

All the false humor tore away from Hades as his face drew into all straight lines and severity. "Then tell my brother to draw his own barrier around Tartarus because I swear on the River Styx, I will drop the walls and throw everything I fucking have at him if he touches me or mine." The air swelled with the power he held at bay at all times, and Persephone let it wrap around her, basking in its comfort.

Ares and Hermes grunted underneath the pressure of it, and strain pulled at their faces as they fought against it. The tension dropped from Hades' shoulders and he leaned back in his chair, lifting his power from the room as if nothing had happened. Hermes leaned forward, gasping for air while Ares clutched the broadsword at his side while taking strained breaths.

Hades caught Persephone's eye, and she nodded at the question there. She was fine. Even if he had wanted to, she doubted his power could affect her the way it did others. It was a part of her. The Underworld was hers just as much as it was his. Hades turned his attention back to Ares and tapped his fingers on the edge of his chair.

"Is there anything else you would like to convey, Ares, or will that suffice?" His voice was as sharp as the end of a knife.

Ares shook his head as if to clear it from the haze of power, but there was a fire glinting in his dark eyes that glowed at the prospect of what Hades offered. Even if he had cautioned against war, he longed for it like another might long for love. It was the thing that made him feel alive when immortality threatened to numb every nerve. Despite what Hades said about Ares not being a threat, Persephone found herself inclined to disagree. An immortal who lusted after blood or ichor was a fear worth sheltering.

"All this for a pair of—"

Shadows swarmed down the table, knocking over dishes and glasses until they reached Ares and shot down his open mouth, disappearing into the immortal.

Persephone stared in muted horror as Ares' opulent skin grew dark, with black veins working their way down his body and up his neck. They pulsated with energy as Ares writhed beneath them, grabbing at what was lodged deep within his body. Enough. It was enough and even as she thought it; she knew it wasn't. Could never be.

Standing on legs that felt steadier than she had expected them to be, she set her hand on Hades' shoulder, breaking his focus on Ares. He looked up at her and she could see black circles around his blue eyes that seemed to pulsate just as the shadows did. He was far away from her, but at the same time, his presence was firm in her mind, unwavering.

Taking another step, she continued towards Ares while Hermes reached out for her.

"You need to get him to stop. He's not thinking," he begged.

Poor Hermes. He deserved better than what he got. Even still, she ignored him and continued until she stood before Ares who was on his knees, golden ichor dripping from where he had clawed his skin open. His eyes were wide, pleading with her. Raising the palm of her hand to his mouth, she called to the magic she shared with Hades. What he had offered her alongside his marriage vows. What he would never give to another. His shadows answered her call like a beacon in the night as they drifted from Ares and into her waiting palm, where they danced contentedly.

Ares gasped out a breath with his hands on the floor as he fought for purchase against the power that had ravaged him. She imagined it was something akin to feeling death inside of you, eating away at your flesh slowly and purposefully. It probably felt terrible for someone who didn't understand the darkness.

When Ares finally composed himself, he stood, and Hermes blew out an audible sigh of relief. Ares was a few inches shorter than her, but he straightened his broad shoulders and stepped forward, imposing himself on her as if she would be intimidated when he was in her domain.

"I hope you aren't waiting for a thank you because—" he began.

"Finish what you were going to say before Hades stopped you," she said calmly, despite the rush in her blood.

Ares' mouth opened slightly, his only sign of surprise before he set his lips in a determined line. His eyes darted past her to where Hades sat, but Persephone sidestepped to block his view.

"Not to him. To me. Finish. Your. Thought," she said.

Ares was a god of war. He had fought in thousands of battles and killed countless mortals. His happiness was tied to the act of killing and battles for power. Not in a million years would he let some newborn goddess let him feel anything other than the powerful

Olympian he was. Fixing his eyes to hers, he pressed his lips into a sinister smile.

"Ares—" Hermes began, but the god of war would not have heeded him even if he had been able to give warning.

"All this for a pair of tits that are as good as the next." His voice wrapped around her.

Persephone let the words marinate in the room while Hades' wrath gathered behind her. That he held it back was a testament to his love for her. He gave her the space to deal with this on her own, and she longed to show him his faith was not misplaced. Her body filled with divine anticipation as she stepped forward, her body pressing against Ares as she lowered the darkness gathered in her hand and gave him a small smile.

"Thank you for your honesty, even if it was inaccurate." With her words, she coaxed the darkness into his mouth and watched as his eyes bulged.

Hades had let it feast upon his whole body, but that was not her intent and the power knew it. As much a part of her mind as her immortal spirit. Stepping back, she watched with satisfaction as the power gathered in his right arm that struggled to grab the hilt of his sword. Satisfaction rolled through her as his arm grew gray and then a sickly black. The smell of rot and decay potent in the air. Ares clawed at his arm with a pale face behind his helm. She wondered if he had ever felt such horror in all his immortal life. She certainly hoped not.

The arm began to decay; the skin sinking into the bone in a disturbingly wet concoction. Ares roared in rage and it was music to her ears. When the darkness had finished consuming his flesh, only bone and rot remained. She called it back into her waiting hand and let it slide through her body, welcome and warm.

Finding his voice, Ares opened his mouth to speak, but she shook her head.

"Remember this next time you think my *tits* are only average," she crooned.

Red-faced and reeking of death, the god of war sneered at her, but the effect was lost on her while his arm hung uselessly by his side.

"You will regret this, bitch," he spat.

She shrugged her shoulders. "I doubt it. I think it more likely your screams and horror will lull me to sleep most nights."

Ares struggled against the dullness of his own mind. She could practically see him trying to think of something clever to say, but he was made of brute strength and force. As if he understood the same, he created a portal of red flames and stepped through. Running home to tell Daddy of his abuse in hopes he would avenge him. Maybe he would. She liked to think it was worth it either way.

"By The Fates," Hermes breathed behind her.

Persephone twisted and found Hermes staring at her open-mouthed and Hades reclined in his seat, his eyes smoldering flames. Pushing down the heat searing her veins, she turned to Hermes.

"I need you to send Hera a message for me," she said, as if nothing had happened.

"Persephone." Hades' voice was hoarse, but there was no mistaking the warning in her name.

Hermes groaned. "You know, I used to be fun. They called me the trickster god and everyone delighted in my stories and cleverness."

"You were annoying back then," Hades said.

"Yes, but I was happier. Shit like this is the reason I'm not. You two get to terrorize and maim gods, and I'm the one that has to witness the aftermath," Hermes said.

"It's not maiming if he will just heal in an hour or two," Persephone clarified.

"Eh, it'll probably take four or five," Hades said.

Persephone couldn't help the smile that broke out over her face and found Hades' own lip quirking at the side.

Hermes darted his eyes between them. "See. This is exactly what I'm talking about. You two get to play your cute little flirting game and—" His words dropped off and his face fell. "Shit."

"That quick? Oh, my." Hades smirked.

The glare Hermes shot him would have been more intimidating if it was anyone else. "I'm remembering why everyone hates you."

Despite the words, Hermes winced, and Persephone knew she didn't have much time.

"Tell Hera that I would be grateful for her time should she be willing," Persephone said.

"Don't tell her that," Hades ordered.

Hermes turned to him and gave him a wicked smile that made her see a glimpse of the one they called the trickster god right as he disappeared into a portal of white wings.

Chapter Twenty-Seven
QUALITY TIME
Hades

Hades had never faced such a dilemma in all his years of immortality. To demand she tell him exactly what her plot with Hera involved, or to bend her over the damn table and fuck her senseless. His cock was hard with the need that drove through him, making his thoughts murky at best. The way she commanded his magic as an extension of his own and the way she used it was enough to drive him to madness.

Ares had meant to intimidate her, and he had left crawling back to his father. She was fucking perfect. Her eyes were alight with the rush of power and her blonde hair cascaded over her shoulders. Pressing her hands to her hips, she tilted her head.

"It's been at least a minute since Hermes left and you've said nothing," she said.

"I'm having a crisis," Hades ground out.

Her perfect mouth tilted up and the way she sauntered over to him had him seeing stars. Just as he thought she meant to slide onto his lap, she twisted and plopped herself onto the table in front of him. Hades made a sound low in a throat that sounded feral, but it only encouraged her smile more.

"I liked that," she confessed.

Damn if he didn't know it. Her body practically vibrated with the endorphins she released torturing Ares, but it was more than that. She had defended herself and shown that she wouldn't cower or be cowered. All of Olympus would hear how she had used the god of war and all would know that she was not the simpering victim Demeter had tried to make her. Today, Persephone had made a name for herself and when immortals and mortals alike heard the title queen of the Underworld, they would pause.

"It will be one of my favorite memories," he said, running his eyes greedily over her every curve and taking enjoyment when she swallowed hard.

"So violence is what does it for you, huh?" she grinned.

"You are what does it for me." He stood and tilted her chin up so she would understand every word he said next. "However, Persephone, it's witnessing you carve out your own name and setting your own boundaries that have me contemplating all the things I'd like to do to you."

Her cheeks flushed with heat. "And here I thought I would have to distract you from being nosy."

"Oh no. I am going to bend you over this table and fuck you senseless, and then you are going to tell me what shit you are trying to achieve with Hera," he growled.

Just as he bent to take her mouth in his, she pulled away and slipped off the table to move past him. When she was a few feet away, she turned to him with a sickly sweet smile.

"Sadly, that plan is not going to work for me. While I think I would enjoy the former, it's the latter that is the problem," she crooned.

She could not be serious. While he enjoyed her asserting herself against others, he was not about to have her throw herself in danger for some misguided attempt at trying to get past him for the damn river.

"Persephone," he warned.

Pursing her lips, she raised an eyebrow. "How about this? I let you fuck me over that table, but then you let me create my own alliances, and just trust that it'll all be fine."

Hades ground his teeth together as irritation and love warred against each other. "I will build a wall around the river before I let you in it."

"You are assuming that everything I do is to break this curse, but it's more than that. I will never stop trying to break it. Fifty years, a hundred years, a thousand. It doesn't matter. You can make whatever attempts you want, but I will find my way to it. In the meantime, I have to exist in this world with and without you, so while I love you, I will make choices that benefit and protect me, even if they go against your wishes."

"While I respect that, I am asking that you not go into it blindly. I know Hera. Use me. Let me help you." Hades held out his hands in offering.

Biting her lip, she considered him. "Unfortunately, our interests don't align in this, so I will keep my own council for now."

Irritation lit throughout his body. Not that she would deny him, but that she would choose death over immortality. He couldn't begin to imagine the imprisonment she endured and the abuse at Demeter's hands, but this wasn't the answer.

"Would you swim even if you knew it was your death sentence?" he asked quietly.

She blew out a long breath. "They wouldn't have prophesied it if it was a death sentence."

Darkness rolled from Hades, but she did not back away.

"That is your isolation and naivety speaking. The Fates and gods alike delight in prophecies that reek of hope when they foretell death. You and Prometheus discussed Odysseus, but what was his fate? What prophecy did he carry with him that bespoke tragedy veiled as peace?"

Persephone sucked in a breath and for the first time she wavered in her conviction, her sharp eyes dropping for a fraction of a second. "That he would die of the sea on land."

"But instead it was that his own son murdered him using a weapon of the sea. There is no peace in prophecy, Persephone. Only tragedy. You would jump in that river and the curse would be broken because you would be bound to it, unable to remember or live. Freedom from one curse for another. Give me time. I will find a way to keep you safe. There are other ways to break a curse. Give me time." He had never begged in all his years, but for her, he would.

Silence stretched between them as she considered his words and for one fleeting moment, he thought she might finally see reason, but instead, she pulled her shoulders back and clenched her jaw.

"Time means laying myself at Zeus' altar and I won't do it, Hades. Even if you found a way around this, it would be in blood and ash. There would be nothing left of the world after the war you would champion."

"Your life would be worth the cost," he said with dark promise.

"For you. Not for me," she said, sadly.

There they stood, only a few feet from them, but their lines drawn clearly without hesitation. While she was the compliment to everything he was, in this, they would remain divided. Always on opposing sides.

"I should lock you up and never even give you the chance to throw your life away," he said.

Persephone crossed over and reached her hand up to his face. He melted into her touch that somehow felt infinitely more fragile and precious.

"But you won't because that would make you no better than my mother," she said confidently.

The sigh that cleaved from his chest was a mix of desperation and exhaustion. "We would be stronger together if you let us."

Her smile was soft, with a hint of sorrow. "I imagine we would, but until one of us concedes, it will not be."

Lifting his hands, he tangled one in her silk hair and the other around her waist. "I would spend eternity with you if you would let me."

"And I you," she said as she pressed against his chest.

***

The summons was long in coming and that alone made him wonder if Hera wasn't interfering. She would be expecting him to fulfill his side of the bargain, even though she did nothing to get Persephone back to the Underworld. He should have known she would do it herself. Even still, their time was limited. The curse bound her to the lake and so she would always return to the mortal world, no matter how clever she was.

Never one to leave anything up to chance, Hades had secured a temporary solution to his wife's death wish for when the summons finally came. As soon as he felt Zeus' pull, he called in his favor. Hecate appeared in a portal made of stone, with the night sky peeking through the gaps and arches. The thin line of her lips told him she was still displeased with him for calling in an old favor.

"Prick," she said as she slid past him. "Where is she?"

"Library," he answered as he cracked his neck against the ever-growing pressure of an unanswered summons.

"She's going to be pissed," Hecate said for the tenth time.

"Better than the alternative," he said through clenched teeth.

Hecate fixed him with one of her deathless stares that made mortals and gods alike think twice about displeasing her. However, he was immune to her intimidation, having known her for long enough to know that she was all bark and no bite. Mostly.

The pressure berated him, making his ears pop and his mind fumble. Gritting his teeth, he fixed Hecate with a warning glare, but she merely waved a hand at him.

"A favor for a favor. Honestly, I don't even remember what I liked about that mortal I had you shuffle into Elysium. Hardly seems fair to call in a favor when I can't remember how I accrued it in the first place."

They both knew she remembered, but he wouldn't be the one to say anything. Hecate had made the cardinal sin of falling in love with a mortal only once, but it followed her well into eternity. The problem was that the mortal had been born into a shitty family and she had done less than honorable things to survive. It wouldn't have mattered in the end, but when she killed a demigod who was supposed to be Athena's champion, it became controversial. Athena wanted to see her soul wither in Tartarus, but Hecate loved her. Unfortunately, getting on the wrong side of Zeus' favorite child was something they all avoided. Hecate had promised him a favor to secure her lover's soul, and he had accepted. The truth was that he would have done it regardless, but a favor among the immortals was not something to turn down.

"She doesn't go to the river," Hades repeated the agreement.

Hecate rolled her eyes. "Go, you idiot."

Part of him wanted to argue, but the part that was being pummeled by Zeus' summons was louder. He made the portal and found himself on Olympus for what felt like the hundredth time in a short period of time. Zeus was sprawled out on his throne, one finger tapping along the side.

"What do you have to say for yourself?" he intoned.

Hades had expected anger or more threats, but there was an undercurrent to Zeus that said this was not going to be at all what he expected.

"That Ares deserved a lot worse," Hades said.

Zeus bellowed his laughter throughout the hall. "He probably fucking did."

This was the thing about Zeus. He was erratic in his moods. There was either this nonchalant attitude or his desperate need to be loved and obeyed. Hades had spent lifetimes learning to navigate them, but it was treacherous. One wrong word or gesture and he would find himself on the receiving end of a power trip.

"How long did it take for his arm to heal?" Hades said.

Zeus grinned. "Five hours. Whined about it for the entire time."

Hades shrugged. "I'm sure Aphrodite consoled him just fine."

"The day I figure out what she sees in him is the day I cease being immortal," Zeus said with a wave of his hand.

While Hades enjoyed not being threatened and abused by his brother's magic, it all settled wrong on him. Zeus was in too good of a mood and he had never, not once, been summoned to Olympus for brotherly bonding.

"You want to know why I summoned you?" Zeus' self-satisfied smile made the hairs on the back of his head stand up.

"It had crossed my mind," Hades said dryly.

"Even the god of gods must bend the knee sometimes. You and I are going to spend quality time together, little brother."

Fuck.

Chapter Twenty-Eight

THE PRICE OF DREAMS

PERSEPHONE

The Underworld was obnoxiously large. Too much space filled the distance between each of the major parts of it. Persephone stared at the map in her hands and ran her finger along the west side that she hypothesized was where she needed to go. She only needed an opportunity. As if she were an offering from the gods, Hecate shuffled through the door and threw herself on a chair.

Persephone grimaced. "You are my babysitter again."

Hecate gave an exasperated sigh and nodded. She had felt Hades leave the Underworld moments ago, but knew it would be Zeus' summons. He might have saved the cloak and daggers act with Hecate, as Persephone had known he wouldn't leave her unattended. Still, she knew an opportunity when she saw it.

"He made you swear not to let me go to the river," Persephone guessed.

Hecate raised one hand. "On the River Styx itself."

"Then if I swear not to go, you won't interfere?" Persephone asked.

That was enough to get the goddess' attention as she sat up in her chair and leaned forward. "What are you up to?"

"Plausible deniability usually requires a level of ignorance," Persephone said sweetly.

"You know who doesn't give a shit about plausible deniability?" Hecate said with narrowed eyes. "Your husband."

Part of her knew this wouldn't be that easy, but another part of her had hoped, nonetheless. She had a small time frame. Two hours, to be exact. That was the message Hera had sent with Hermes a few hours ago. While she hadn't known what form that would take the moment Hades left, she knew her clock had begun. It would have been nice if Hera had taken into account Hecate, but she knew she was lucky for even getting an ounce of her help.

"You know, I recently decayed an immortal's arm," Persephone said. Despite her attempt at being serious, her mouth quirked up to the side.

"I've heard."

"So you know I am just as scary as my husband," Persephone clarified.

Hecate barked a laugh. "Hardly. If I have to pick one of you to be on the wrong side of, I'll take my chances with you."

Persephone groaned. This was proving to be more challenging than she anticipated, and time was of the essence. She would just need to adapt.

"Listen, Hecate. I swear on the River Styx I will not step foot into its waters on this day. Now, I need you to let me go do something."

"Is it something that will get me tortured for all eternity when he finds out?" Hecate asked with a raised brow.

Maybe. Hopefully not. Probably. It should have taken at least a century to become a heartless immortal, using and discarding those around her like husks of grain. Yet, here she was throwing the first being she ever called friend into peril. Unfortunately, there was nothing Persephone wouldn't do to be free of her curse and to secure her future.

Hecate watched her carefully before sitting back in her chair. "That's what I thought."

Standing, Persephone closed the book and put it on the shelf before turning back to Hecate. "Hera gave me two hours to get what I need to do done. She thinks that means going to the river, but we both know that Hades has one eye on that river. I would never make it there in time. You more than anyone know what it's like for me being a swan during the day and my mother's prisoner during the night. You saw how quickly she was willing to sell me to the highest bidder. Let me save myself, Hecate. Please."

The moments that passed by were eternities as she watched indecision play over her friend's face. They both knew that whatever Persephone was about to do was not going to make Hades happy, but they also knew what it meant to want to have control over your own life.

"That river is a death sentence, Persephone. Only you think it's the answer," she said quietly.

"I know."

She wished she didn't know. In her moments of self-doubt, she considered the possibility that they were all right. Hades had asked her for her eternity, but what was an eternity of imprisonment with only stolen moments for comfort? Maybe if they understood what it felt like to have your bones snapped and pushed into something unnatural each night. Maybe if they knew what it meant to have no control over your own life. But they could never understand because they were immortals who gambled and played games with human chess pieces. She wouldn't be a pawn in their games any longer.

"Hecate," Persephone pleaded.

Running a hand through her dark hair, Hecate grimaced. It was an impossible situation for her to be in. She cared for both Hades and Persephone. No matter what she chose, she would be making an enemy of one.

"The river will hold you to your oath," she said solemnly.

Persephone's chest fluttered as she breathed out her relief. "It will."

She wouldn't waste her thank you's on the goddess because she knew it wasn't what she wanted. It was enough that she created this space for her, and both of them knew what it meant to Persephone.

Without another word, Persephone conjured her portal and left, knowing that this was the easy part of her task.

She stepped into a rocky terrain that was entirely different from the rest of the Underworld. The air was thick and ripe with the smell of lavender mixed with eucalyptus, but it smelt off as if it were not quite natural. What should have been calming had her muscles tightening in anticipation. In all her research, she had found very little on her destination. The only mention was that of a price. While it was unsurprising, it was unsettling.

A massive cave rose in the distance, the entrance black as a starless night. A soft rustling breeze ran past her that sounded like wind passing through trees, but when she looked around, there were only rocks. Only one hero had survived the quest she was about to embark on, but their name that should have been memorialized among the greats was lost to time.

All that was written was that he had gone in search of a cure for his wife, who lay in an endless sleep. What he found in the cave was a vial that released her from her slumber, but his mind was irrevocably fractured by what he endured that he descended into a comatose state, withering to nothing under the weight of his mind. For his sacrifice, his wife left him for his best friend, and the hero was lost to time.

Persephone might have let herself fall into the fear the story elicited in her, but she was not here to claim a cure. Her purpose was darker and less forgiving. The question was, was her mind strong enough not to break against the sinister forces lurking just ahead? Was a life of imprisonment better than the fate that she could be walking into? There was no doubt in her mind. A fate chosen was a fate she could endure, anything else was intolerable. Even if it was the wrong choices that led her to it, they were hers and hers alone.

Scaling the terrain, Persephone let out a shout as she slipped on one of the dragged rocks and golden ichor dripped from the palm of her hand onto the tip of the gray stone. Her mind felt foggy as she fought to register the pain that ran down her hand, but as she tried to flex her fingers, no movement came to pass. She stared at it, willing it to move, but it remained defiantly still.

If she had been mortal, the injury would have been devastating. Somehow, the jagged peak had sliced through nerves and tendons alike, rendering her hand useless for the remainder of her life. However, her godhood slowly seeped into the wound, sealing it and restoring what was broken. The moment her fingers curled in answer to her mind, she breathed out a sigh of relief.

It was the first time Persephone felt truly grateful for her divinity. Up until that moment, she had only felt the weight of the cost of her mother's immortality. The parts of her that were decayed and broken from living too long. Hades had spoken of the numbness that follows an endless life, but that wasn't the case for Demeter. Something terrifying lived in the goddess of the harvest and it made her insatiable for control and perceived power. She would do anything to maintain it and call it love.

As Persephone pulled herself over a ridge, she found that the cave was surrounded by a small lake. Familiarity and nausea bloomed inside her as she took in the steep incline that ended in the still water. Panic clawed at her as she desperately searched for a way into the cave that would not mean her entering the lake, but nothing was forgiving in the game of fates.

Scaling the wall, she slipped her boot into the water and felt the darkness surrounding her. Fear sliced through her as she fell into it. Not fear for her flesh, but fear of failure. She knew in an instant she had made a grave miscalculation. Despite every immortal's warning to not trust them, she had believed Hera would help her. Her own arrogance would cost her an eternity of servitude.

"This is the price you are willing to pay for your death wish?" Hades' voice was violent and full of wrath. "You are no better than the rest of us."

Persephone spun, her boots sinking into the murky water. The face she had come to love was devoid of any affection as he watched her. His lips pulled back in what almost looked like a snarl, but beneath it all was disgust. It was as if he had punched her in the gut as she clutched her stomach and tried to suck in a breath.

Hades took a step forward, the lake splashing around his feet. "Now you want to pretend that you feel pain at the consequences of your selfishness? I offered you what I had never offered another. I would have been content to make you my equal, but you chose yourself. You are no better than Demeter."

Amongst the pain ricocheting through her was a thread of truth that clawed at her mind. "You have always admired my tenacity. Is it because it was never wielded against you it was okay then, but a fatal flaw now?"

Hades took two smooth strides and wrapped his hand around her throat, stealing the air from her lungs. "The problem is in that you dare to wield a weapon against me and scorn the gifts I've laid at your feet. I asked you to trust in me and instead, you abused my affection."

Clawing at his hand, she felt the pressure build in her chest as it fought for breath that wouldn't come. The edge of her vision filled with black spots and she was filled with the knowledge that her chosen path had cost her everything. Maybe he had been right before. A half-life that saw her bound to the whims of lecherous gods could have been more than a life devoid of love. She had known Hades would be angry with her, but she could have never predicted this wrath.

Just as her head gave way to the darkness surrounding her, he released enough pressure that she sucked in a breath, desperately clinging to each molecule. Her breath rasped as she fought for equilibrium.

"You are a treacherous snake unworthy of love." He leaned forward, whispering in her ear.

Persephone knew it was true. Despite how she hid from it and pretended otherwise, Hades saw her as he saw everything. Clearly. It had only taken him a little longer than usual. If she had been capable of instilling love in others, her mother would have seen her misery and fought to release her from the curse. For a small moment in time, Persephone had begun to believe the lie. Laughing with Hecate, teasing Hermes, loving Hades. All of it made her feel like she was capable of being more and giving more, but when it came down to the moment, she chose herself. She used all three of them to get what she wanted, no matter the cost.

Victorious knowing glistened in Hades' eyes. "I had thought you would fight against the truth a little more, but you couldn't even manage that. You know what you are. A manipulative bitch not worth anyone's time or effort."

Tears fell down her cheeks as she sank into the words. He had seen her more clearly than anyone ever had or ever would. She had allowed him into the very fiber of her being. If this was how he saw her, then who was she to argue? The world seemed to cave in upon her all too similar to when she was forced into the swan's form. Too small. Too suffocating.

Yet amidst the despair that threatened to undo her was a hint of a larger truth. It was in the way he always watched her with such pride when she would defend herself or speak her mind. It was in the way he laughed whenever she would say something clever. The way he made her believe she was capable of anything. That he would love her despite all her flaws.

Gathering her voice and her courage, she looked up at him and refused to give in to the hatred she saw. "You saw who I was from the very beginning. I have never been anything other than who I am. I am not my mother or the sum of her love. I am the same woman you made love to and told me I was brave. Now you curse me because it didn't play in your favor. It was fine when my power was wielded against others, but now that it's against you, you call me snake. If that is what you call love, then I have severely misjudged you."

The air shimmered around them, but Hades merely snapped his fingers, and she was falling. Cold water wrapped all around her and she struggled to swim to the surface. Everything felt too heavy, and her body was already exhausted from the pain of losing him. Even if his love had been fragile, hers had not. She had loved him with every capable cell in her body. Love given in error is still love. Even if she had misjudged him, it didn't matter. She had loved.

Persephone broke the surface and instead of relief, despair cascaded over her and she let out a wail of grief. He had sent her back. He had found her wanting and had sent her back to her prison, her lake. Moonlight glistened over the water, while the night sky twinkled with the promise of joy far away from its depths.

"Persephone!" Her mother's voice was clear and without waver.

Turning towards the sound of her voice, Persephone found her mother at the edge of the bank, crouching down and holding out her hand. It was as if the world had reversed and Hades cast her away while her mother reached for her. None of it made sense, but then the world rarely seemed to. Shoving her grief and loss down, Persephone swam till at last she was being drawn into Demeter's arms. She couldn't remember the last time her mother had held her like this.

"Oh, darling. I'm sorry, love," she crooned as she smoothed back Persephone's wet hair.

Pulling back, Persephone met her mother's eyes that always seemed cold and distant. "You know what happened?"

Demeter frowned and there was a level of concern she couldn't recall ever seeing on her youthful face.

"Of course, sweetheart. Everyone felt him cast you out. I wish I could have saved you that fate, but you always were so stubborn. If only you had believed me."

Maybe she was right. If Persephone had listened, her heart wouldn't be shattered into a thousand pieces.

"After everything I did for you, you still didn't believe me," Demeter said softly, running a hand down Persephone's cheek.

How much time and energy had she spent wishing her mother had been different? Protection and love were different for everyone, but maybe that was what Persephone had failed to understand. Her mother loved her in the only way she knew how. She had given Persephone the best that she had and, like a petulant child, she had scorned that gift.

"I'm sorry," Persephone said, defeated.

Demeter ran her eyes over Persephone, consuming her submission eagerly before clicking her tongue. "Well, it's done now. I've given up everything for you, Persephone. It's been so difficult all these years with your moods and your defiance, but I never wavered in my love of you. Even when you ran away and made a mockery of me."

Persephone nodded and fell into her mother's chest. Demeter awkwardly placed her arms around her, but then it was impossible to blame her for that when Persephone was soaking wet. All the hurt and the loss they had endured seemed to wrap around them. The question nagged at her like an incessant fly. What was it all for?

"The curse. It didn't matter in the end," Persephone said, her throat dry.

Demeter stiffened beneath her. "It isn't a curse, Persephone. What I did saved you from binding yourself more than you did. I am sure I can speak to Zeus and find a way around the pomegranate seeds. You never have to go back there again."

Persephone disentangled herself from her mother and narrowed her eyes. "It's a curse, mother. It's torture to be made to fit into something that shouldn't fit. It's a half-life."

Rolling her eyes, Demeter stood and looked down at Persephone with contempt. "Already you treat me with such disrespect, even after knowing what the sacrifices I made for *you* cost me."

Wasn't that just the way of Persephone? To have realized that her mother had loved her the best she could and then to throw daggers at her the first chance she had. This was why Hades had cast her out. There was nothing inside of her that deserved love. She was cold and heartless. Only thirty years of life and she had become the worst of the immortals.

"I'm sorry," Persephone whispered.

The sigh that broke from Demeter was long and born of weariness. "I just don't understand why you insist on being so cruel."

That made two of them. It was as if it were a part of what made up her. A crucial piece to her biology that made her cut before she could be cut first. To always find a way to put distance between the people who tried to love her, like her mother. Yet, even as the thoughts passed by, she grasped at tendrils of truth.

Moments with others where she was nothing but herself. Speaking to Hera, asking Hecate for help, working beside Hermes, and even fighting with Hades. She remembered standing next to Poseidon and looking out at the vast ocean surrounding them. How their truths had been laid bare despite the walls between them.

They had all seen her as she was. Not cruel, not cold, but something more.

Something loud and urgent rose in her. "I am not yours to demean and coerce."

Demeter threw a hand to her chest and her eyes hardened. "Persephone! How dare you speak to me like that? You know how much it hurts me."

Persephone stood, pushing her hand up off the ground. As she rose, Demeter watched her with her hands on her hips.

"Honestly, Persephone. No one else would put up with the way you treat me. You are lucky to have me."

"Love shouldn't feel like this," Persephone said, meeting her mother's eyes.

Demeter barked out a laugh. "Oh? And am I supposed to take your expertise on that? You are a child, Persephone. What you called love tossed you out like trash and then you have the nerve to tell me I'm the problem?"

With every word, Persephone felt the truth settle in. "Love shouldn't feel like a burden. It shouldn't feel like a debt. Love is empowering, it's a partnership, it's peace. Your love is a cost I will never be able to pay. I will never be enough for you, Mother, and that . . . that's not love."

As if the words meant nothing, Demeter scoffed. "And where will your love take you, Persephone? You have no one and nothing. You only have me."

It was as if there had never been any other course. "I have me."

The air shimmered and all at once Persephone was back in the Underworld, the cave entrance just before her, but the lake she had been standing in was entirely dried up.

"It's not often someone's greatest fear is themselves." A deep voice intoned.

Persephone raised her head to find a hooded figure before her, hands clasped in front of him.

"Morpheus," she breathed.

He held out his hands, his face entirely obscured by the dark. "Well, Queen of the Underworld was the price worth paying."

All at once, understanding dawned on her. "They were dreams."

"Yes, and no. They were based on your greatest fears. Your fear of being unlovable and your fear of being unloved. Some never escape their fears." He gestured to the space around her and found countless human remains surrounding them. "They lose themselves in them and forget to live. Only one has ever made it through as you have."

"But he was broken after," Persephone said.

"Yes, but that will not be your fate, I believe," he said.

"You know why I have come, then?" Persephone asked, fighting the urge to clutch at her chest.

Despite his confidence that she would not be broken, the dreamscape had wrenched its cost from her. Her body felt foreign and wrong, but her mind was worse. She struggled to know what was real and not real while fighting to hold onto her sense of self.

"I know what it is that you seek. Dreams are places of truth. The night feasts on the lies of the day." Morpheus spoke solemnly, as if it were a sad truth.

She wondered what a burden it would be to watch everyone's fears and truths without relief. How frustrating it must be to see people hide from their unhappiness over and over again. To see memories relived in different narrations, but the pain always the same.

"There is joy too, Queen," he said. "Reunions and fulfilled wishes. Some find relief in my dreamscape."

"But it's never true," Persephone said.

Morpheus inclined his head. "Yet it is an escape all the same."

"Will you give me what I seek?" Persephone asked.

Time was running out. She had no idea how long she had been in the dreamscape, but her awareness of Hades was still outside of the Underworld, which meant she still had time. The memory of the dream flooded back to her and for a moment she wavered, not wanting to escape the dream for something similar. Yet, she knew even if he could never understand her choice, he would never treat her in that way. Forgiveness was another story.

As if he had heard her thoughts, Morpheus said, "You are risking more than your life, Queen, I have seen the god of the Underworld's dreams. He will not forgive such treachery, even from you."

More than anything she ever knew to be true were the words she spoke next. "So be it. I will choose myself."

Chapter Twenty-Nine

MY FAVORITE FATE

Hades

He had spent lifetimes carrying out and ordering tortures, but he had never been a victim of it before. That was until Zeus held him hostage for two hours to regale him with tales of his exploits, of which there were many. The more miserable Hades felt, the more delighted Zeus was to continue on. It was a much more sinister punishment than sending demigods into his home. Even the overflow of mortals into Asphodel was less of a curse than this shit.

"So because she was locked in a tower . . ." Hades began.

Zeus roared with laughter. "That prick Acrisius thought he was being clever, but I made myself into a golden rain."

Hades ran his hand over his face, feeling the weight of all his years of existence. "I can't imagine that even feels good."

"It's about the chase, Hades. You've never understood that," Zeus boomed.

"No, I have not." Hades sighed.

Zeus frowned at him as if he were an orphan, alone and abandoned and in need of love. Fates be cursed. This was complete and utter ruination.

"At least you aren't completely hopeless. I hadn't pegged you for a swan—"

Hades stood abruptly. "Please, Zeus. I've been a fairly unproblematic brother. Please release me from this." He gestured to the room.

Zeus roared and slapped his knees as if this were the funniest experience of his fate's damned immortal existence. "You could have left at least thirty minutes ago, but I must tell you I have thoroughly enjoyed this quality time together."

The summons released from his body and he had never made a portal so fast in all his years. Zeus' laughter followed him into his library, where he collapsed onto a chair and threw his head back with a groan.

"That bad?" Hecate said, amusement dripping from her raspy voice.

"I will never sleep well again," he said without even a hint of dramatics.

"Do tell. What was it that finally broke Hades himself?" Hecate asked.

The despair riding his bones was palpable. "Two hours. Two hours of hearing him talk about his exploits."

Hecate made a disgusted noise, but nothing from his wife. He cracked one eye open and found her sitting on the floor, her legs tucked under her and an open book at her feet. She had been distant since they had drawn their battle lines, even though she didn't need to be.

He understood her determination and respected it. It was only its execution that he refused to allow. Whenever he began to doubt his own position on the matter and wonder if he was being a controlling asshole, he remembered it was her life he was trying to preserve.

"Persephone?" he asked, cracking the other eye open.

She practically jumped at her name and there was a paleness to her that wasn't there two hours ago. Sitting forward, he rested his elbows on his knees and studied her.

"What happened?" he asked, feeling the crack of anxiety that only she could provoke in him.

Hades liked to think he knew his wife fairly well and so he knew she would try to persuade Hecate to let her go. It was unlikely Hecate, who agreed with him, would, but even still he had kept one eye on the river. It had remained blissfully empty of goddesses in his absence.

"I'm fine," she lied.

"You're not." He eyed her, looking for what he was missing and finding nothing.

"I'm going to go now that I'm done babysitting," Hecate said, standing abruptly.

If he wasn't already suspicious, he sure as fuck was now.

"What did you two do?" he asked.

His mind grazed over his territory, seeking out any disturbances and finding nothing. It was hardly a reassurance.

"Hecate," he warned.

The goddess looked between Hades and Persephone, biting her lip. Hecate was always cool confidence, and he had rarely seen her concerned, but in this moment she reeked of anxiety. Before he could question her further, she stepped through her portal and left him alone with the source of his problems.

Never one to be intimidated, Persephone met his gaze without flinching, but there was something there that was foreign.

"Are you going to tell me what happened?" he asked.

"No," she answered quickly.

At least she wasn't lying to him anymore.

"You're pale," he said.

Fuck, why did he say that? It was unhelpful and stupid. The truth was, he didn't know how to navigate this barrier between them. Despite the fact that it shouldn't exist, it felt like an insurmountable canyon.

"I love you," she said.

Silver lined her eyes, and her nails dug into her palm. Fear, similar to the night she had almost made it to the river, filled him. He moved quickly from the chair and dropped to his knees before her. A tear tracked down the side of her cheek and he reached for it, wiping it away as if that would vanquish her demons.

"What did you do, Persephone?" he asked, quietly.

She shrugged, more tears falling. "I just love you, Hades." Her vibrant blue eyes were muted as she met his gaze. "I didn't know what it meant to love before I met you. I thought love meant conceding parts of yourself for another as if it were transactional. You showed me what it could be. With you, I feel strong and capable. Safe. Happy. Of all my fates, you are my favorite."

His chest cracked under the weight of her words. A millennia had passed without him understanding what she spoke of. Time passed over him without ever knowing what it meant to live. In a short period, she had wrecked him entirely. He felt as he had never felt before. It was addictive and terrifying. A rush he wanted to drown in, but a lifeline he clung to.

His thumbs brushed away her tears as he cupped her face, seeing the incredible being she was. He was luckier than any immortal had the right to be. Even when that happiness came with fear of the unknown and certain difficulty, it was worth all his days.

"You are entirely unprecedented. You are everything. I love you, Persephone. Whatever it is, we will face it together," he said.

Her tears fell faster, but she pushed up, pressing her lips to his. The kiss was soft and tentative, as if she were unsure of him. Of all the things he could endure, that was not one of them. He pressed his hand to the back of her neck and drew her deeper into the kiss, coaxing her to settle into him. She gave a soft murmur that would have made him wonder if it weren't for the darkness invading his mind.

Pulling away, he brought his hands to his head and tried to stand, but the world was bearing down on him, forcing him further and further to the floor. He had never experienced anything like it. It was as if the darkness were swallowing him whole, as if he were—No.

"Persephone, what have you done?" he asked as horror reached down his throat and gagged him.

Among the darkness was the knowledge that she had been saying goodbye. She had said her farewells because not even she was confident she would live. He reached for her and she caught his hand as she gently lowered him to the ground. He couldn't reach for his power. It was as if every part of the Underworld had been tied up, maintained, but out of reach of him.

"Per—" His voice faltered.

"I'm so sorry," she said, voice fractured as she ran her hand down his face.

Her face, beautiful and broken, was the last thing he saw as he fell.

CHAPTER THIRTY

THE WATER'S FINE

PERSEPHONE

Everything in her felt like it was splintered and sickly as she looked down at the sleeping form of her husband. Tucking a strand of beautiful blue hair behind his ear, she bent down and pressed a kiss to his forehead, the powder from Morpheus spent on their kiss. If her greatest fear was being unlovable, this only furthered the anxiety it provoked. Morpheus said that Hades wouldn't forgive her betrayal, and she knew it was a possibility. Even if she survived tonight, she might have lost the one who loved her best. Who she loved in return. Was freedom worth that price? It was too late now. What was done was done.

Cerberus padded over and whined as he nudged Hades' face with his nose. It felt like even more of a betrayal than it already was. The guard dog turned his head up to stare at Persephone, a question in his too-intelligent eyes.

"I'm sorry," she said through a haze of tears. "He'll be all right."

She hoped it wasn't a lie. There wasn't time to ponder it further because she didn't have much time. Morpheus' potion was powerful, but it wasn't enough to hold Hades for long. He was the most powerful Olympian and there wasn't much that could detain him. Standing, Persephone made to leave, but Cerberus grabbed the bottom of her pants and pulled as if he could prevent her from going in lieu of his master.

"I'm sorry, buddy," she said, reaching down to disentangle herself from him.

She knew Cerberus' true form would have caused her significant delays or even kept her from her destination, but she also knew he wouldn't. Reaching down, she pressed a kiss to the top of his head and left. It wasn't long ago that they had made this same trek and even still, Cerberus padded along beside her, just as he had then.

By the time the river came into view, her nerves were a jumble of erratic, pulsating threads. Anticipation, anxiety, fear, hope. They all battled within her for dominance. Regret. Doubt. Her hands shook, but she wouldn't waver. She was no one's prisoner, least of all herself. Zeus would not have her. Demeter would not have her. She was her own and the water flowing with silver souls would ensure that, for better or for worse.

To trade one fate for another. One last moment to spare for the consciousness that was him, she let herself feel him. Cerberus barked behind her, a last plea. Unwavering in her conviction, Persephone leapt. The water was warmer than it should have been. As if it were an unnatural spring. A thousand pinpricks bombarded her skin, taking and maiming. The dull pain changed to something sharper: knives. Opening her mouth to scream, water rushed in, choking and burning her.

There wasn't time to consider the implications when all she knew was pain. Everyone had told her it was a death sentence, but she had refused to listen. Her fear of being trapped more powerful than her self-preservation. Swinging her arms, she tried to make for the surface, but something wrapped around her legs, pulling her deeper and deeper into its murky depths. Panic grew and thrived in her chest as she fought to escape.

When she looked down below her, she saw silver tendrils wrapped around her ankles. Souls. Souls doomed to an eternity of obscurity and wanting. They grabbed at her, ensuring her mind would follow theirs into oblivion.

Reaching down, she tried to disentangle herself, but there was nothing solid to hold on to. Her fingers slipped through them every time. If Hades woke now, would he be able to save her? Would he want to? She reached for the part of her mind that belonged to him and found nothing. He was gone. What had she done? With renewed fervor, she kicked and swam, the surface still feet away.

The curse didn't matter, all that mattered was him. She would endure any fate as long as he was safe. When she tried to remember why the curse had been enough for her to enter the cursed waters, she fumbled over the answer. Something about the world being too small pricked the side of her mind, but that wasn't quite right. Deeper and deeper into the river, she sank. Thoughts of her mother passed by without the normal emotions they provoked. Usually, she felt something more. Was it love? Somehow, it felt complicated.

Persephone stopped kicking when she couldn't remember why she had begun in the first place. It felt like a release. All her muscles relaxed and her mind cleared. The pressure around her ankles evaporated, and she was able to swim effortlessly. An existence like this was not a cruel fate, after all. A fate.

The word triggered something inside her chest. Hadn't she just said that something or someone was her favorite fate? That was before the river's blissful emptiness ran over her. Now there was only the feel of the water cocooning her in its warm embrace. Never would she be broken or too small again. Yet . . . never again would she feel anything else, because among the pain and the cracking of bones was another. Something new. Something infinite.

Him. A sense of belonging. Home. Power. An eternity if only she took it. There, at the tip of her mind, was a small wave of consciousness. Not hers. Someone else. Him. Persephone reached, yes, that was who she was. Persephone reached for him and the river sensed the change in her resolve. Tendrils of souls wrapped around her ankles once more, determined to add her to their oblivion, but she had known long ago that she was made of darker things. The river couldn't hold her. This wasn't sacrifice, it was conquest.

Hades. Her fate chosen for her and chosen by her. The river pulled her deeper, but it had made a grave miscalculation. She was not a mortal ripe for the taking. She was a goddess. Releasing her divinity, a flash of light burst through the space around her, and the hold on her evaporated into nothing.

Persephone swam. She swam for him, for love, for herself. She swam for all the times she couldn't. For all the times she would. Persephone swam.

Chapter Thirty-One

How to Trade in a Fate

Hades

Shit. Fuck. How had he not seen this as a possibility? Because no one was fucking desperate enough to go to Morpheus' cave, but she was. Of course, she fucking was. He should have seen this a mile away. Should have suspected Hera's influence when Zeus held him hostage for two fucking hours. *Even the god of gods must bend a knee sometimes.*

He had just thought it was Zeus being obnoxious at the time, but now he understood. It was Hera. Hera had strong-armed Zeus into summoning him to give Persephone time. Hades had only been focused on the river and she had known that and planned for it.

The dreamscape formed and broke around him as he forced it back. The dream would take him if he let it, but he wouldn't. Morpheus' potion would make him sleep, but he could fight the effects easier if he didn't give in to the lure of the dream. Images of her flickered in and out and it was an effort not to fall into her, even if it wasn't truly her. To pretend that she was safe and not throwing her life away on a fatesdamned prophecy.

How had she even known about Morpheus? He knew how much time she spent in the library, learning the landscape of the Underworld and its points of interest, but Morpheus was not a subject well stocked. She would have had to go searching, which meant someone had pointed her in that direction. Poseidon. He had said they were even, and now Hades understood why.

Poseidon had known exactly what Persephone would do with Morpheus' power, and he had led her straight to it. Led her straight to her death, or what was as good as death to an immortal. Persephone reached out her hand to him and his own twitched as he fought the urge to take it. He knew he was too late. No matter how he fought the dreamscape, he would still wake up too late. It would have been better to give in and enjoy these last moments with her, even if they weren't real.

Yet he couldn't risk it. If there was even a chance he could make it to her in time, he would take it. Beneath the fear living inside him was something darker. Betrayal. Anger. He wasn't fucking stupid; he knew she would do anything to get to the river and that she would never stop, but this still fucking hurt. Because that was the thing about Hades. In all his existence, he had never let anyone close enough to hurt him until her. Only she had the power to do so, and she had knowingly done it.

"I told her that the price could be your love," Morpheus said, forming in front of him.

Draped in his robe, his face obscured him.

"You can drop the mysterious act," Hades seethed.

What almost sounded like a sigh left Morpheus as he lifted his hands to his hood and revealed his scarred and unnatural face. One red eye, one brown eye, and three slashes running down from the right side of his face all the way to his chin. Never quite healing, they were open and yet scarred. Half his lip was split open and swollen. A consequence of perceived heroism.

Morpheus had been a mortal once. His daughter was taken and devoured by the result of Zeus' infidelity. Lamia had been Zeus' mistress once, but Hera cursed her and turned her into a monster after slaying all her children. Lamia was a shapeshifter and used her power to devour children as if that were recompense for her own loss.

When she killed Morpheus' daughter, he set out to hunt her. Famous for her seduction, when he found her she had transformed into a beautiful woman and lured him into her bed, but Morpheus was stronger than his desire and he ran his dagger into her chest. Lamia then transformed into her monstrous form of a woman mixed with the body of a lion and talons that stretched out half a foot. In her dying rage, she had attacked him, her poison killing him almost instantly.

When he had come to the Underworld, Hades had recognized his service in ending what had been a vicious consequence of Zeus' infidelity and Hera's rage. He offered Morpheus a position as dreammaster, knowing that he would never be able to remove the scars of her poison. Knowing his daughter had already moved on to Elysium to be reborn, he had agreed and done his job dutifully. Now he proceeded over the dreamworld, keeping nightmares and dreams in line and maintaining the barrier between the waking and the dream worlds.

"You knew what she would do with it and still you gave it to her," Hades said.

Morpheus held out his hands in supplication. "I am bound by the agreed-upon price. She passed the tests and faced her greatest fears. It was not for me to deny her request."

Her greatest fears. Now he understood why she had been so pale and haunted. She had faced the worst of what her mind could create and did so knowing the potential cost. In the distance, she came into view again, and the urge to wrap her in his arms was palpable. Still, he fought against it.

"What did she see?" The sadist in him needed to know.

"Our fears are ours alone, god of the Underworld," Morpheus said.

"You are bound by your appointment by me, Morpheus. I should remove you from your position for this. Why did you tell her I would not forgive her for this, knowing damn well I would? You sent her to her death believing a lie. I would have done the same thing if I were her." Hades wanted to reach out and end Morpheus' existence, but the memory of his service stayed his hand.

"It was the final test. The cost was the thing she treasured most. Your love. If she had not been willing to pay it, then she would not have been worthy of the power given to her," Morpheus said in his monotone, obnoxiously matter-of-fact way.

"Let me out, Morpheus," Hades ordered in the way only one borne of power could.

The thing she treasured most. Not freedom, not power, but him. His love. He should have been livid. Should have gladly let her drown in the river after choosing this, but he couldn't. She was his equal in every way and with that; he understood her. No, he would not fault her for choosing this path, and he couldn't hide from the part he played with it. He had given her no other options.

"You know I cannot," Morpheus said.

"Then why the fuck bother coming at all?" Hades wished he could access his powers and cause the made immortal pain.

"To keep you from falling into the dreamscape. You need only wait for the potion's power to work through your divinity," Morpheus explained.

All at once, Hades was reminded of why he had granted Morpheus his power. He may have been bound to give Persephone the potion, but he would ensure if there was a chance to help her it would be done.

"Does she live?" The words came out mangled as if they would strip him of air.

"She does not dream," Morpheus said in way of answer. "There is still time."

Morpheus had once explained that when a being falls into death or even a pseudo-death like the river, they fall into his dreamscape first. As long as he did not see Persephone there, it meant there was still a chance.

Morpheus cocked his head as if listening to something and Hades' heart sunk into his stomach. Would he be too late to save her? The thought of immortality without her by his side was a thought he couldn't tolerate. Would not endure.

"She is close. Slipping into the dreamscape, but she fights against it," Morpheus said.

Never. Never in all his years of existence had he felt so helpless. She had bound him and made him useless, but he was aware of every moment. Every breath. It was a torture not even Zeus could dream of. To know the only thing that brought meaning to life was slipping away into oblivion. It was unbearable.

"How much longer, Morpheus?" He gritted out.

The question was two-fold. How much longer she had and when he could be released. Morpheus grimaced, which made Hades want to burn it all down. And he would. If she was lost trying to break Demeter's fucking curse, he would start with that narcissistic bitch. He would torture Demeter till she didn't know her own damn name. When that was done, he would come for Poseidon. Then Zeus for cornering her and making her feel like she didn't have the time to find another option. If he hadn't already been thrown into Tartarus by then, he would punish Hera next for her part.

"Not long, but she is slipping in and out of the dreamscape," Morpheus said quietly.

Persephone.

"There will be nothing left if she is lost," Hades promised.

"I know," Morpheus answered. "Hera has dreamt it."

"And still she helped make it come to pass?" Hades spat.

Morpheus' mangled lips thinned. "There is something more pressing her forward. She fights for the same as you, only the vessel is different."

"That makes no fucking sense and you know it," Hades growled.

Holding out his hands, Morpheus said, "It is not for me to divulge the truths found in dreams. While I am no oracle, I would see you both succeed for the fates that could be."

He didn't have time for this shit, except he did, and that was exactly the problem. Trying to pull at his divinity, he fought to bring down the dreamscape, but locked inside, he might as well have been a mortal.

"There is time, God of the Underworld," Morpheus said. "Go."

The dream snapped around him and he bolted up right where he had fallen asleep. There was no thought, no consciousness as he stood and portaled to the edge of the river where he had saved her once before. Its calm waters lined with silver spirits flowed before him without any sign of her. He reached for her awareness and found it faint, flickering in and out, but she was close to him.

Hope and fear warred within him and he thought that if he gave into either, he would be lost. For all his power and his dominion over the Underworld, even the River Styx was beyond his command. What it took belonged to only it. Except her. It could not have what had been given freely.

As if she had heard him, a flash of light caught his eye and his breath caught in his throat. There, only a few feet down, was Persephone. He could see the souls desperate to take her, but she was more determined. Without thought, he bent over the river and reached in his arm. The effect was instantaneous. The cold water wrapped around him as if it had long wanted to feast on him.

The lure of oblivion was strong, even with only his arm affected. How Persephone had fought against it fully submerged was an impossible question. The small bundle that was her in his mind pulsed, reminding him of who he was and what was at stake.

Silver tendrils wrapped around his hand and he anchored himself on the river bank, refusing to give in. Though if she didn't climb out of this damn river, he might just let them take him too. An eternity of oblivion was better than remembering what he had lost.

The thought evaporated into nothing as the familiar pressure of her hand thrust into his, strong and unwavering. Hades pulled with every godsdamn inch of his strength. Using his other hand, he reached out, and she took it. He shoved his weight behind him and in a rush of cold water and the howl of lost souls, Persephone gave way. He landed in a heap on his back while she lay on her side, choking on the river.

Crawling over to her, Hades sat her up and ran his hands over her, searching. Whatever he thought he might find after so long in the river, he wasn't sure. Was it too long? Would she remember anything?

Persephone gagged and wretched, the foul water leaving her body. It was as if everything moved too slow and too fast all at once. Cerberus came up beside her and nudged her shoulder as she finished heaving up what was left in her. Her breath was ragged, but she was breathing, and that fact alone was enough to make him lose what control remained in him.

Her eyes lifted to his and for a fraction of a moment he thought that was it, she was fine, but then her eyes rolled back and he shot out his arms to catch her. The breathing he had just been grateful for turned erratic and her skin paled to an almost bluish color. No. She had made it out of the river. That should have been enough.

"Hermes!" He bellowed as he cradled his wife in his arms.

The summoned god appeared in an instant, eyes quickly assessing. "Fuck."

"Go to Aeaea and fetch the witch," Hades demanded.

"Hades," Hermes begged. "Circe is temperamental and not likely to—"

"Do it." Hades threw all his godhood into the command and not even Hermes could argue.

The messenger god disappeared in an instant, leaving Hades to watch his wife fight for her life.

"Please," he pleaded, but she did not answer.

Hermes entered in a white flash, a goddess in tow behind him. She was not traditionally pretty, her nose too big and her face too small, but she held herself in a way that made her seem more than she was. She had been exiled to her island for crimes against Zeus. The truth was that Zeus feared her power and had her banished for it. There would be consequences for calling on her if he survived it.

"Help her," Hades ordered.

The goddess merely raised a single eyebrow. "There is no cure for the river."

"Enough with the shit, Circe. I will owe you if you do this," Hades seethed.

"And what can you offer me, god of the Underworld? Will you end my banishment?" She asked.

"You know that is not within my power," Hades growled.

"Then *what* will you give me if I save her?" she repeated.

That was the way of immortals. Never give what you can sell. Even banished for centuries, Circe knew the game well.

"Your love of mortals is no secret. I will guide one soul of your choosing to Elysium. Only one," Hades said, his mouth bitter with the offer.

Circe cocked her head. "No matter their crimes?"

Hades grimaced. "No matter their crimes."

If she chose an unworthy soul, it would threaten the balance of the Underworld. The work he would have to do to maintain order and rewrite the foundation would be extensive, taking weeks. Possibly even months. Yet, there was no price he would not pay.

"Two," Circe said.

Persephone convulsed in his arms and her color turned dusky. Her immortality not preserving her against the river's effects. All at once, he understood. The fates had said she would be free of her curse if she swam in the river, but it was through death. The river would strip her immortality, and she would die if there was no intervention. Fuck.

"Deal. Fix her, witch," he yelled.

Reaching into the pockets of her dress, Circe held out two potions. She set them on the ground and pulled out a series of herbs.

Persephone's chest rose and then fell, paralyzed with the absence of her breaths.

"Now, witch."

Circe glared at him. "Witchcraft is all about intent, god of the Underworld. If you want her to live, you will let me do it in peace."

The urge to lash out with his power was strong as the witch tinkered with her herbs and potions, muttering words and breathing over them. Witchcraft was unique to only four beings, Circe and her siblings. The others were corrupt with power and achieving what should never be achieved. They would have refused his request based on arrogance alone.

Circe gave a satisfied huff and pushed back her dark curls before bringing the potions over. It was an effort not to grab them from her and force them down Persephone's throat, but witching was precarious. He only knew what Hermes had divulged about Circe and her siblings, but it seemed as if the magic was purposeful. One ill thought or half-focus could undo an entire spell.

The strange woman thrust Persephone's jaw open and slid the sweet-smelling amber liquid down her throat. The fact that she didn't even gag or fight against the liquid had fear gathering like tendrils of fire in his chest. Persephone was stubborn, strong, assertive. Just because no one had ever survived the river didn't mean she wouldn't.

Hades opened his mouth to beg, barter, yell, but Circe held up a finger and whispered a word he had never heard of. It was almost like it had come from her soul, a deep knowing.

Persephone's body convulsed in his arms, and her head was thrown back, her eyes rolling. Fuck. No, no, no. The word reverberated through his skull until he realized he was screaming it. He gathered his wife close to his chest.

"I wouldn't do that if—" Circe's words were cut off as Persephone expelled dark black river water all over his shoulder and chest. It was purulent, and the texture was thick, like sludge. Even still, he didn't pull away from her, couldn't find it in himself to be disgusted. Her chest heaved as she sucked in the air her lungs were long since denied. Twisting his head, he looked at her and found her color gradually returning.

A choked sob escaped him, and he buried his face into her neck, feeling her pulse beat miraculously beneath him.

"Hades." His name was hoarse on her lips, but it was her voice.

"My love," he answered, unfamiliar liquid coursing down his cheeks.

"I'm so sorry," she said.

"It's all right. It doesn't matter anymore. You're all right," he said, smoothing back her hair and taking in the sight of her stunning blue eyes as she fought to keep them open.

"Morpheus said—"

"I don't give a fuck what Morpheus said. You are as much a part of me as my own ichor, Persephone. Nothing you did could jeopardize my love for you." He nearly choked on the words at the crack in his chest.

It felt as if he were breaking and being reformed over and over again. She was alive. Everything else seemed to fade away against that singular fact. Persephone's mouth twitched up as she let out a ragged breath and shut her eyes, exhaustion pulling at her.

"She is no longer immortal," Circe said quietly. "It looks like you and I have more in common than we would have liked to believe."

The truth of her words hit him squarely in the chest. He had known the river had stripped her of her immortality, but when she was dying, it had felt secondary. Now that she would live, the reality of what it meant would have brought him to his knees if he hadn't already been there.

"You made an immortal once," he said.

Circe gave a sharp, bitter laugh. "You would remind me of the reason for my banishment? The reason your brother fears me enough to force me into exile?"

"Please." Hades didn't know if he had ever said the word before and yet he had said it to this witch twice.

"How do you know she would thank you for it? Immortality is more a curse than a blessing. Are you so arrogant you think her love for you would weigh against everything else?" Circe stuck up her nose. "Of course you are. All Olympians are."

"What do you want?" he bit out. He would give it. Whatever the price was, he would pay it.

Circe's eyes narrowed. "She must ask it of me when she is fully recovered. It must be her choice."

The words were sharp and biting as she had meant them to be. To reprimand him for taking a decision away from Persephone that should have been hers alone. He knew better, but he would have done it had she allowed it. Did that make him any better than Demeter?

"I will go home now. Two souls, god of the Underworld," she reminded him before turning to Hermes, who was remarkably pale and sickly looking.

As if nodding to himself, Hermes took Circe's arm, and they stepped through his portal together.

Gathering what was left of himself, Hades rose, cradling Persephone's body against him. He stepped through the portal and into their bedroom. In a thought, her wet clothes were removed and a light nightgown replaced them. Steeling himself, he gently placed her on the bed, but she hardly stirred. Shifting her body, he made himself look. To see the truth of what had been done. There on her back, where the white wings of a swan had been, was only smooth skin. The breath that left him was heavy.

She had done it. His tenacious and impossible wife had done what should have been impossible. Even though he knew she wouldn't grieve the cost, he was amazed by her. Changing his own clothes, he tucked her under the covers and pulled up a chair beside the bed, watching her sleep as if she might disappear at any second. Cerberus hopped onto the bed and curled up into a ball, laying his head on Persephone's stomach.

She was alive. Mortal, but alive.

CHAPTER THIRTY-TWO

EVERYTHING HURTS

PERSEPHONE

Every muscle hurt. Every breath hurt. Bone deep weariness that shouldn't exist carved itself into her. Persephone rubbed at her eyes and found the world too bright. Too much.

"Easy," his deep voice said.

A thrill went through her at the sound of his voice, even as anxiety crept in behind it. She didn't know if she had imagined him saying he forgave her or if it had been real. Morpheus' omen clung to her all the same. When she tried to sit up, her back cracked, and she moaned in pain. Why did she feel so fragile all of a sudden?

Hades let loose a low growl and she jerked her head towards him. He watched her as if he could end her existence in one fistful. Her blood ran cold. There was no mistaking his anger for anything but what it was.

His aura washed over her, strong and intrusive in a way she had never experienced before. Almost like it hurt to look at him.

"Fuck," he said before the air around him shifted. "That should be better, I'm sorry."

Despite the heavy air between them, Persephone laughed. "*You* are sorry? Hades, I betrayed you."

It was the strangest apology she had ever given. She opened her mouth to try again, but he grabbed her hand that was cradled in her lap.

"I told you that nothing could jeopardize how I feel about you, Persephone."

So it hadn't been a dream then.

"Did it work?" she asked, unsure she wanted the answer even though something in her knew it had.

Hades heaved a loud sigh, his lips in a thin line. "Yes."

She had done it. She had changed her fate and saved herself. A feeling she had never known washed over her. It was heady and alive. It was freedom. Never again would she be too small or forced to be something she was not. Freedom. It was as exhilarating as it was terrifying. All she had ever known was the curse, but now . . . now she would live.

The smile that formed on her face was born of accomplishment and possibility, yet when she expected to see her joy reflected on Hades, there was only grim resolution. Her smile fell, and she reached out for him, but his hands were clenched on the arms of the chair. He said he was not angry with her, but rage seemed to boil out of him.

"What is it?" she asked.

Hades' narrowed eyes ran over her, searching. "You are mortal, Persephone."

Her mind couldn't work through the words. The implications. Even as she cataloged the way her body felt and how difficult it had been to look at him. His divinity. She had struggled against his divinity because she had none of her own. A fate for a fate. Part of her wanted to rage. To break everything she could and to scream, but the voice that she had lived with all her life was too loud. *So be it.* She knew the truth before she ever thought it. The cost was worth the price. Years spent in freedom were better than an eternity in chains.

"Just like that, you accept your fragileness?" Hades' voice was lethal.

Gathering all her conviction, she met his gaze. "You knew I would."

Hades clicked his tongue in irritation. "Forgive me for thinking you might resent a short lifetime, but then again, you were willing to risk my love for you, so it shouldn't surprise me."

Persephone flinched against the harshness of the words, the hurt that rode just beneath the waves. Pulling back the covers, she slid out of the bed, her body protesting the movement. When she stood, the world weighed down heavily on her, but she placed herself between his legs and ran her hand down his stubbled cheek. Despite how he was feeling, he leaned into the touch.

"I love you, Hades. You are the best thing that has ever happened to me."

"To be fair, there are very few good things that ever happened to you. Your life has been shit," Hades said, still leaning into her touch.

Persephone snorted. "That's true, but even if it weren't, you still would be the best. I don't regret a single thing except one. I wish I had never had to hurt you to free myself."

"It's not really a regret if you would do it again," Hades said dryly.

"Hades." Persephone blew out an exasperated breath.

His chest rose and fell with a long breath as he reached up to cup her hand with his. "I understand, Persephone. I know why you did it and I don't fault you for it, but this . . . it's not a logical feeling. It's one thing to know and understand a thing, but another to feel it. I will get past it over time, but I also can't pretend I feel nothing, not with you."

That was, perhaps, the highest compliment and testament to his love that he could give. That he wouldn't pretend to be anything other than what he was. Even when their agendas did not align, they were always honest with each other. Minus the part where she drugged him and schemed with Hera. It was hard to feel misery beneath the euphoria of knowing she had freed herself.

"You saved me again." Persephone smiled.

Hades lifted his head and ran his hands up her bare legs, sending shivers through her.

"You saved yourself, as always, but there is something I need to ask you." His eyes locked onto her and she knew that what he said next might as well have been a test.

Steeling herself, Persephone nodded.

"The river stole your immortality, and you were dying. I didn't know what to do, so I called on the one person who had ever created immortality," Hades said slowly.

"Circe. The witch you refused to ask for help in breaking the curse because Zeus would not allow it."

"I would have done anything. You were dying in my arms. After she saved you, I asked her to restore your immortality."

Persephone's heart fell into her stomach as a hope she had been harboring slowly died within her. Knowing he had tried and that it couldn't be done broke something in her, even amidst her victory.

Hades' hands tightened on her thighs. "You wish she had?"

The corners of her eyes burned as she fought back unwelcome emotion. She didn't want to mourn when she would sacrifice it all again and yet it was grief she felt in her chest. Grief for time lost and for what could have been.

"Of course, Hades. I would live a thousand and one lifetimes with you if I could. Did you think I wouldn't?" she asked, irritation creeping in at his deliberate obtuseness.

Hades heaved a large sigh as his face smoothed some of the tension that had been lingering.

"She refused me, but she said that you could come to her and decide for yourself."

All at once, the grief shed from her and she realized that against all odds, she could have it all. Her freedom, him, and immortality. It seemed impossible, and yet here it was in the palm of her hand.

Except, the way Hades was watching her made caution rein in her joy.

"What is it?" she asked.

"Circe drove a hard bargain to save you. I gave up more than I should have, an imbalance of the natural order. She will ask for more in exchange for your immortality," he said.

That was expected and unexpected. "What does she want?"

"An end to her banishment, which Zeus will never allow. He fears her. Hermes swore to keep her summoning a secret, but if Zeus finds out that she played a part in saving your life ..."

Persephone shivered against the weight of the words. That meant no one could ever know what happened. She understood well enough.

"You should probably be nicer to Hermes if you want him to keep your secrets," she teased.

The low laugh that left him was music to her ears. "Probably."

"So we go to Circe. No one except Hermes knows I am mortal. It's now or never," Persephone said.

Hades smirked. "Always so eager, so determined."

"It feels like the world is a giant weight on my bones and everything hurts. Being mortal is rather uncomfortable." She pouted.

"First, you are going to bathe. You smell like death, and while I am aware of the irony of that statement, it's unpleasant. Then we will go see the witch."

Even as she laughed, heat ran over her skin. "Will you be joining me?"

His eyes darkened. "No, Persephone. The things I need to do to you will be only suitable once you are immortal again."

The shiver that ran over her at the dark promise was enough that a cold bath sounded very promising, after all.

CHAPTER THIRTY-THREE

THE MORTAL, THE WITCH, AND THE GOD OF DEATH

HADES

Hades pulled Persephone into his side tightly as he created the portal to Aeaea. It took all his willpower to not carry her as if her mortality would become immediately fatal at every moment. How many mortals had come into his halls with inexplicable accidents? He hated knowing that whatever Circe asked of him, he would pay it. Yet a nagging feeling told him the witch had demanded the order come from Persephone, not out of respect for her autonomy, but because the deal she wanted was from her.

The second they walked through the portal, the sun and nature wrapped around them. The bustling of wind running through the trees and the smell of spring was palpable. They entered on a paved pathway that rolled up the mountain until it met a small house with a thatched roof and a smoking chimney. He knew what to expect of the island as Hermes had spent some time there on occasion, but Persephone stared open-mouthed as her wide eyes took it all in.

"It's incredible," she breathed.

Sometimes Hades wondered what it would be like to see the world through her eyes. How she breathed it all in with a fervor that only one starved could appreciate. Just like that, he felt the urge to go to Demeter and make her pay for the isolation and torment she put on her daughter.

"I don't know that banishment would be so terrible here," she said.

"It's the isolation that is the true punishment," Hades said.

"With her crime being that she was different. Powerful."

Hades nodded once, feeling as if all the eyes of the creatures and trees were on him. Maybe it was his own superstition, but the island felt as if it sang for its mistress. That, while it had been a punishment, she had claimed it all the same. What would Circe do if she ever achieved her freedom? It would never happen, but he wondered all the same.

A branch snapped nearby and Hades shot out his power, wrapping it around Persephone. His heart felt like it would beat out of his chest, but Persephone only laughed and grabbed at his hand.

"I don't think a stray branch is going to kill me, Hades. Let's get this over with before you make yourself ill with worry."

It sounded like a great plan, given the way adrenaline was coursing through his every cell. A large pen of pigs lay at the base of the house and Hades eyed them with disdain.

"They used to be men, right?" Persephone asked, eyeing them as well.

"Most of them," Circe said from the doorway, nearly making Hades jump.

The faster Persephone got her immortality back, the better. It was an effort not to draw his eyes to where her shirt dipped over her shoulders and down her chest. To where the mark they shared should have been. His own was missing as well. The river broke all bonds, apparently. That he had been able to sense her at all had been an inexplicable boon. Even now, he could sense her, but it was faint, almost like a haunting of what had been. Just another reason to fix this and reassert their vows. Then he would be able to breathe easier once more.

"Did they deserve their fate?" Persephone asked curiously, entirely unbothered by any of it.

Circe arched an eyebrow. "The pigs or the men?"

"It seems rather impossible to differentiate the two at this point," Persephone said.

The snort that came from the witch was one born of amusement. "Well enough. Come in, let's get this over with."

She turned through her doorway and disappeared. All of this left a bad taste in his mouth. He didn't like things he didn't understand and he sure as fuck didn't like needing things from immortals. It made him feel vulnerable in a way he didn't relish.

The house was as charming as the rest of the island, which was just delightful. It had a well lived-in sense that he was sure some would appreciate, but it made him feel slightly claustrophobic.

"I expected you here hours ago," Circe said as she pulled a knife off the kitchen counter and began chopping and crushing various greens.

"What do you want, Circe?" Hades growled.

Persephone elbowed him, earning a laugh from the witch. "Know your place, god of death. The Underworld may be your domain, but Aeaea is mine."

"Hardly something to brag about," Hades said.

The chopping stopped, and both Persephone and Circe stared at him. Fine. He heaved a sigh, his chest tight.

"Forgive me for wanting to get this over with. Mortals are remarkably fragile, as you well know," Hades said.

She was formidable, with her dark skin and pale eyes. There was a sense of drive and determination he had only ever seen in one other.

"Thank you for saving my life," Persephone said.

Circe shrugged her shoulders and continued chopping. "No one does anything for selfless reasons. You want your immortality back."

It wasn't a question. They all knew why they were here.

"Name your price," Hades said.

Persephone elbowed him again, and he fought the urge to tell her it felt like he imagined a flea bite would.

"My price is for her and her alone," Circe said as she set down the knife and scooped up the finely cut herbs.

"That—"

"Is fine." Persephone glared at him. "I do not have much to bargain with, however."

Circe's pale eyes traveled from Persephone to him and back to his wife. "You have much. My only request is this: there will come a time when I will need to keep something safe. You will do so for me for twenty years. *If* you should fail to do so, the spell will retract your immortality, and you will be mortal once more."

It might as well have been an ill omen for the way it wrapped itself around Hades' throat. It felt like a trick. A trap.

"Why didn't you ask it of me when you bargained before?" Hades asked.

Her lips quirked up. "Because I knew you would be back."

That made his ichor chill in his veins. The way she said it made him feel like he was missing something important.

"What is the item?" Persephone asked, quietly.

He sensed her hesitation and was grateful for it. She was clever enough to see there was a larger game at play.

"Nothing that will harm you or yours. Do we have a deal?" Circe asked, an eagerness in the words.

What could she have that could possibly need protecting? She was isolated on this island and while she formed attachments to mortals that passed by; they were not in need of protection. She had even had children with them in the past, but they lived out lives of demigods.

Persephone turned to Hades and all he could see was her body convulsing in his arms. How helpless and broken he had felt. How he would do anything to never feel that way again. He nodded.

Squaring her shoulders and her face smoothing with acceptance, she turned towards the witch. "We have a deal."

There was no imagining the short breath the witch released or the drop of her shoulders. She was relieved. Whatever this item was, it was important to her.

"Come here," she ordered.

Hades might have protested, but he was certain Persephone was safe with the woman. Now that he knew how badly Circe wanted this, he was sure she would see the spell through. He only wished he knew what they had bargained for.

Persephone walked towards the woman who held out her hand. "A drop of mortal blood will be necessary."

Placing her hand in Circe's, Persephone made a small hiss of pain when the knife sliced through her palm. The red blood seeped into the cup Circe held below it. When she was satisfied, she set the cup on the counter and sliced her own hand, despite her immortality, her own blood ran red as well. She added the leaves and herbs she had been chopping and then a drop of dark liquid before handing the cup to Persephone.

Part of him still wanted to take it from her, but the image of her dead and dying was too permanent an image in his mind. As in everything, Persephone didn't hesitate. She downed the contents in one swallow, though her face paled under the taste. Circe's eerie stare bore into Persephone's as she whispered a single word.

The effect was instantaneous. The wound on Persephone's hand dripped gold a moment before it sealed itself. Her skin took on its natural luminescence that made her radiate health. Everything about her spoke of strength and infinite life. The pressure in his chest eased.

"Do not forget the price of failure, goddess," Circe said.

Persephone nodded, but didn't bother to thank her this time. She had finally learned the lesson that there were no favors among immortals, only debts.

CHAPTER THIRTY-FOUR

SURRENDER TO ME

PERSEPHONE

The first thing they had done upon returning to the Underworld was to renew their vows. Persephone ran her fingers over the dark lines on her chest that had become a comfort to her. With her immortality and her place as Queen of the Underworld reinstated, no one would ever know that anything had happened. Except for one change that was more than welcome. Angling herself to the side, Persephone stared at the smooth skin on her back, unmarred by the wings of a swan. Free.

Her eyes stung with tears, but she didn't fight them. She wanted to feel this. She wanted to feel every overwhelming emotion that belonged to this victory. It was an intoxicating thing to be proud of oneself. Having lived her entire life just surviving, she never knew it could feel like this. It was hard to look away from the mirror when the marks she loved were boldly displayed and the marks she hated were nowhere to be seen.

The door opened, but Hades stood frozen in the doorway. Despite the tears flowing down her cheeks, she clenched her thighs together at the heat in his gaze. He drank her in, taking his time. She stood with her shirt clutched in her hands, nude from the waist up and whereas she might have been uncomfortable with his undiluted attention, she relished it.

When his eyes finally made it up to her face, his lips fell. "Are you all right?"

She gave a shaky laugh. "Yeah. Just admiring my backside."

He grunted in appreciation. "That I can understand."

"Was Hermes all right?" She really didn't want to talk about Hermes, but it felt important to get an update.

"Fine. It seems Hera has been staying Zeus' rage over your elopement. Using her pregnancy as a weapon, saying his rage is upsetting her and the baby," Hades said.

"I owe her a lot," Persephone said quietly.

That earned her an irritated huff of breath. "You owe her nothing. What she has done has been for her own interest, even if that's not immediately clear."

"What could she want?" Persephone had wondered from the beginning and she knew it was naïve to think that Hera saw something in her that made her want to help, but part of her still wondered.

"Persephone," Hades said.

"Hm?" She turned her head from the mirror and found his eyes dark and searching.

"I really don't want to talk about any of that right now."

That was convenient because she couldn't even remember what they had been talking about with the way he licked his lips while looking at her. As if she were something he could eat. Oh, Fates. Warmth pooled low inside her.

"I'm not mortal anymore," she said breathlessly.

"No. You aren't," Hades said, voice thick.

Persephone swallowed. "What will you do with me?"

A dangerous glint entered his eyes. "Take the rest of your clothes off."

Was that a whimper that left her lips? "Can't you just do the—" She snapped her fingers for demonstration.

He arched a single eyebrow. "Don't make me ask again."

Oh. The part of her that had fought to claim independence fought against the command, but another very real part of it loved everything about it. She did as she was told, but she took her damn time about it. Almost imperceptibly, the side of Hades' mouth quirked up, and she knew he loved her insolence as much as her obedience.

When she was finished, she held out her hands, letting him feast his eyes on her. It wasn't hard to be confident in herself when he looked at her like that. When she knew how much he loved her. He had been willing to destroy everything and everyone for her. His love was chaos and brute force, and she surrendered to it with open arms.

"On your knees," he commanded.

That was well enough, given her legs were shaky, anyway. Her body thrummed with nervous energy mixed with desire so potent she could taste it. Her knees hit the soft carpet of the floor and she watched as he slowly came towards her, drinking her in.

"I have never felt so utterly helpless or out of control the way you made me feel, Persephone," he said darkly.

Of all the things she expected him to do or say, that wasn't it.

"Hades—" she tried.

He held up his hand, effectively silencing her with the unspoken command. "I need—I want to do something different with you, but there are a few things we need to discuss."

Her breath caught, the anticipation in her returning even as she wanted to shift uneasily against the unknown.

He crouched down in front of her and it was an effort not to reach for him. He was devastating in every way. Her fingers ached to touch him, but somehow she knew she shouldn't.

"I want you to give me complete control."

She shivered. "Is this a punishment?"

"No and yes," he answered, and for some reason, the hollow at his throat was terribly distracting. "Eyes on me, Persephone."

The command in his voice was intoxicating. "What does giving you control entail?"

A slow smirk spread across his face. "You surrender your body to me. You follow my orders. If you agree, I will begin by binding you with ropes. I will have complete and utter control of your body and your pleasure."

"Oh," she said, her mind working through the implications.

It felt like everything she should hate. To be constrained, to be subjected to feeling too tight. Yet, even as panic began to work its way in, she saw what he was offering her. A way to take back her own control. To claim this.

"What if I don't like it?" she asked.

He tilted his head to the side. "Then we stop, Persephone. You say the word, and it all stops."

Control without control. The thing was that she trusted him explicitly. She knew he would do anything for her and would never hurt her.

"I agree," she said.

Hades sucked in a breath. She realized he had thought she wouldn't agree. He should have known better. Should have known that she would follow him anywhere.

Recovering, he stood. "On the bed. Same position."

Again, she obeyed but took slightly too long. It made her body shoot with fire, eager to know his reaction.

"Persephone," he growled.

Fuck, the sound of her name like a threat was thrilling. She quickened her pace and took up on her knees. Hades held out his hands, and a long threaded rope appeared. She swallowed. Maybe she had agreed too quickly.

"Choose a word to say if you want to stop. You say that word and everything stops, no judgment, no consequences," Hades said.

That was all well and good, but her head was entirely empty of words at the moment. Except it wasn't. All at once, she knew.

"Swan," she said, her voice even.

Hades' composure slipped and his hands stilled over the rope. He watched her, searching her. She knew that look better than most. He was proud of her. It settled against her own pride like a twin flame.

He swallowed hard and came to the edge of the bed, where he laced the rope around her hands. From there, he worked methodically, careful not to touch her skin. It was a different kind of agony. She wanted him, needed him, but he was focused on his labor. She held perfectly still as he looped the rope under her breast before crossing over her shoulder and repeating the motion on the other side.

The rope rubbed against her sensitive skin, making her want. Making her need. He moved behind her and tied her feet together. The urge to test the binds was strong, to push against them, to prove she could find her way out. Yet underneath all of that was a trust that went deeper than her past. Past the pain and the confinement she had endured. A truth in *him*. That he would never ask more than she could give and that he would always set her free when the time came.

When he was done, he stepped back and ran his eyes over every inch of her, both admiring his work, but also drinking in her.

"Stunning," he said, breathlessly.

"And what will you do with me, god of the Underworld?" she said, her voice raspy.

In answer, he stalked forward and gripped her thighs and turned her on her side. She felt so helpless and so safe. The competing emotions sent a barrage of lust through her. Not knowing what he intended was tantalizing, but then she didn't have to wonder long.

His mouth landed on her swollen clit with dangerous precision. Persephone cried out in shock and pleasure. She had expected him to tease her, but instead, he moaned against her as if she were the best thing he had ever tasted. He licked and sucked, building a tendril of flames low in her stomach that grew with every second of his attention. Her hands itched to latch on to something, but at the same time, she surrendered entirely to him, laying herself into the bed of sensations until there was only him and the pressure building in her. Just as her own sounds of pleasure neared a crescendo, he pulled away, ripping her from her release.

She would have protested and called him an ass, but he settled behind her, his hard length pressing against her in promise.

"Please, Hades, I need you," she pleaded.

"You have me," he said, as he pulled her in tight to his body and entered her.

Free from their opposite goals, there was nothing they couldn't be together. She arched her back against him, taking him as deep as she could. His heady breath ran over her neck and shoulder, and it was divine. That she should be lucky enough to have an eternity of this seemed impossible, but it was hers. Theirs.

Her breath became erratic as she crested near that release. Hades moaned behind her and she lost her control as release barrelled through her. It was violent and consuming. The sound of her name on his lips followed her over the edge, and when they were both spent, she lay limp in his arms. She would have been content to stay that way, but Hades pulled away and began work on her binds. His hands were slightly shaky, but with each fall into his precision, he gathered himself.

When she was free once more, she held out her arms for him and he settled his head onto her chest. That was how they stayed for as long as time would allow. Whole and together.

CHAPTER THIRTY-FIVE

NOTHING

HADES

The peace they found was always going to be disturbed, at least temporarily. With Demeter throwing daily tantrums at Zeus' feet, he was bound to demand Persephone leave at some point. Hades might have been more annoyed if it weren't for the confidence he had in his wife. She was bound to no one and nothing.

"Are you ready?" he asked her, holding out his hand.

She took it without a second thought, looking every inch the queen and goddess she was. Mistress of the Underworld. It answered to her, unfettered by curse or loyalty. She wore a turquoise blouse that made her eyes brighter and simple black leggings, but she had never looked more beautiful. Her immortality and strength radiated from her like a beacon in the night.

"More than ready," she said, her face smoothing into something unreadable. "Let's get this over with."

So she decreed, so he obliged. Hades threw open the door to the Underworld's dining room with tendrils of power that leaked and seeped into the room with dark intent. Zeus sat at the head of the table with his arms crossed, a faint smile of amusement playing on his lips. Good. At least his tumultuous moods worked in their favor today. To his right, Hera sat, radiant with a near-golden aura around her. As her belly grew, so seemed to her divinity.

To the left of Zeus sat Demeter, in a horrendous brown and orange dress that seemed to leak life from it. Her dark eyes bore into him like they could flay him alive, but as usual, he was happy to disappoint her.

Persephone took the opposite head of the table and he to the right of her. Only because he was watching her closely did he notice the small twitch of Hera's lips. He knew what every immortal in the room wanted except for her. It made her dangerous.

"You stole from me again, Hades. No one would fault me for calling for war," Demeter said, dramatic as fucking always.

"Let me be the first to correct you, Demeter. Persephone came home all on her own. She didn't need my interference in the least."

Demeter's mouth fell open, and she turned to Persephone, who was tapping her fingers on the table.

"I am tired of this. Let me be clear, I am not going back with you, Mother. Maybe, centuries from now, I might decide to visit you, but I will not be bound to you any longer," Persephone said.

Demeter scoffed. "The lake—"

"Is no longer a concern," Persephone said. "My curse is broken, as is my tie to you."

If he could have, he would have commissioned a painting of Demeter's shock. It was everything he ever hoped for. Zeus leaned forward, his amusement faded to interest. Hera was the only one that showed no emotion, which only added to his growing suspicion.

"How?" Demeter sputtered.

Persephone tilted her head to the side, looking absolutely predatory. "You are still under the impression that I owe you anything. I do not."

The shade of Demeter's red face contrasted beautifully with her hideous outfit. It was turning out to be a *very* good day, but there was still room for improvement. In the meantime, he would thoroughly enjoy watching his wife finally get the closure she deserved.

Zeus recovered enough to feign disinterest, leaning back in his chair. "And I suppose you now want to stay in the Underworld and have me disregard Demeter's claim to you."

It was everything he could do to hold back his power, his darkness. The idea that anyone had a claim on Persephone was enough to make him see stars. The small, satisfied smirk on Zeus' lips told him he was doing a shit job of concealing his emotions. Hopefully, this was over quickly and they could put some distance between them and Olympus.

"I would leave that choice up to my mother," Persephone said, her voice strong, sure.

Even Hera's eye twitched at that. It was the last thing they had expected her to say, which was why they would always end up outwitted by her. Persephone was as cunning as she was beautiful. Tenacity like a second skin to her.

"Of course, I will choose to have you with me, sweetheart," Demeter said, playing at the doting mother.

Persephone turned to Zeus. "Do I have your agreement that my mother can choose?"

Zeus practically purred, enjoying whatever game was happening, even if he couldn't begin to comprehend the intricacies.

"You do," he said, running his thumb over his chin and lip.

There was a plan. A very good plan, but there was also a very good chance Hades would fuck it up if Zeus kept looking at his wife like that. A tendril of warmth wrapped around his leg and pulled abruptly. It took all his years of existence to not react, but he recognized the power well enough. Hera. When he lifted his head to her, she gave a very subtle shake of her head. Whatever game Hera was playing required that Persephone succeed. That should have made him feel better, but dread coiled low in his stomach.

Focused on the task at hand, Persephone ignored Zeus and turned to her mother, waving a hand. Smoke gave way to a bowl of nine plucked pomegranate seeds in front of Demeter. Disgust rippled over her face as she slammed her hand against the bowl, sending it flying off the table to shatter with a loud crash.

"How dramatic, Mother." Persephone clicked her tongue and waved her hand.

The shattered bowl repaired itself, every last seed returning to its place before it floated on dark smoke right before Persephone.

With a raised eyebrow, Persephone plucked one and raised it to eye level as if inspecting it.

"Persephone," Demeter begged.

In answer, Persephone met her mother's eyes, coldness reverberating over her beautiful features. "I am bound to the Underworld for three months. All I have to do is eat nine more before I am lost to you entirely."

"You wouldn't—" Demeter scoffed.

Persephone's lips tilted up in a cruel smile. "I assure you, Mother, I would do this and more to be free of you. As it is, maybe in a few centuries you will cross my mind. Maybe in five hundred, I will think of the moments of kindness you showed me. Maybe in a thousand, I'll decide I wish to see your face. This is your choice. If you force me from my husband and my home, the next time I return, I will make sure you never can again. Do you understand?"

Demeter gritted her teeth. "That's no choice at all."

The truth was that part of him hoped Demeter forced Persephone's hand and she took all nine. It would make it impossible for Olympus and Zeus to touch her, but it would make her a prisoner in one of her own making. She would never see the sun or what the world had to offer. She deserved more than just the Underworld and him for company. The fact that they were letting Demeter choose at all grated along his bones, but it was a calculated risk. They needed Zeus to be in agreement, and this had been the only way.

"Persephone!" Demeter yelled, panic creeping onto her ageless face.

Persephone lifted the seed to her mouth slowly.

"Fine! I relinquish my claim on you!" Demeter shouted.

The air left his chest all at once as he struggled to realize what they had achieved. What *she* had achieved. The last chain around her wrist torn apart and reduced to ash. He could practically feel her relief in the back of his mind, but she merely gently placed the seed back in the bowl. Out of the corner of his eye, he saw her hand shake lightly where it gripped the edge of her chair, out of sight of everyone else. She was fracturing, her control wavering.

"I believe that concludes this delightful get-together. Please see yourselves out and feel free to not come again," Hades said, rising from his seat.

Demeter's face twisted into a scowl before she stood and turned towards Persephone. "Sweetheart—"

Hades waved his hand, and Demeter disappeared in a dark mist. That was also incredibly satisfying. Sadly, the same trick would not work on Zeus and Hera.

"I think we've seen enough, darling," Hera said, rising and reaching out her hand to Zeus.

He chuckled and stood. "It was certainly more entertainment than I expected, although Hades rarely disappoints."

It was as if his lusting after Persephone and everything that had come before meant nothing, but then again, it was typical of the god of gods. To want and try to take what was dear to others when it meant very little to him. Not having Persephone was an inconvenience, despite the anxiety and terror it had caused her.

One day, he would happily see his brother languish next to their father in Tartarus. One day.

Hera met Persephone's eyes a fraction of a second before Zeus and she disappeared in an eruption of lightning.

As soon as they were gone, Persephone let out a mangled cry, her entire body giving way to shakes. Hades knelt at her feet and pressed a kiss to her knee.

"Tell me what you need." He would do anything if she only asked.

Her answer was breathless as she turned to him. "Nothing. I need nothing."

And it was beautiful.

EPILOGUE
A Promise of Chaos

The garden she had begun months ago was coming along beautifully. It had grown into a field that the residents of Asphodel could see and enjoy. Every flower and tree that grew under her touch gave her purpose and satisfaction. Olympus had been content to leave them be for the time being and it was all she could have asked for and more. The peace they found was like a dream.

"Do you think we should try to convince Hermes that you are planning a coup? It's been boring around here. I need some entertainment." Hecate whined from where she was spread out in the grass, twirling a yellow flower in her fingers.

Persephone snorted. "You and Hades are so mean to him."

"It's *entertainment*, Persephone. You refuse to do anything exciting except grow flowers and have mind-blowing sex. Some of us aren't so lucky."

"I think I do a little more than that." Persephone grinned. "Also, you could do both of those things, too. I'm sure there's someone willing to have you."

Hecate stuck her tongue out at her. "Happiness is annoying on you."

Persephone shrugged. "Happy to disappoint."

Her mind felt him a moment before he appeared before her, wrapping her in an embrace and dipping her low with his kiss. Hades righted her, and she gave a breathless laugh while his own smile was bright. Months of respite from the games of gods and he appeared every inch the powerful immortal he was.

"See? I told you!" Hecate groaned. "Go away, we are busy."

"Bored again, Hecate?" Hades smirked. "I'd offer for you to join us, but I'd rather not."

"I would rather pluck my own eyeballs out and gift them to The Fates. Not because of you, obviously, Persephone. You are perfect," Hecate said.

"Isn't she?" Hades crooned.

Just as Persephone opened her mouth to speak, Hades' smile fell. She felt it only a moment later, her time in the Underworld having added to her powers.

"Hades—" she began, but he waved a hand and Hecate was gone in a haze of smoke.

"We cannot go back on our deal, Persephone, but we've talked about this. Do not give more than you gave. Do you understand?" Hades' blue eyes bore into hers, willing her to understand.

Anxiety that she had been blissfully free from for months crept back in like an old friend.

"But there are three—" she began.

"I've wondered for months what she had to gain from it, but now I see it. Fuck. Persephone, your immortality is worth the risk, do you understand me?"

There was real fear in his words that she had only seen twice before.

"Hades, you are scaring me," she said.

He wrapped her in an embrace, holding her tight to his chest. "Tell me you understand, Persephone. You will not sacrifice your immortality. Swear it."

She knew she shouldn't have without knowing the source of his fear, but he was her weakness.

"I swear it," she decreed.

The sigh of relief that left him was ancient and born of selfishness.

Hades stepped away and gripped her hand tightly in his as he portaled them into the dining hall where Hermes stood looking practically green, his hands erratically rubbing together as if he could soothe his own anxiety. Circe stood next to him, cradling a small bundle wrapped in blue linen. Divinity seeping from beneath the blanket in a translucent orange glow.

All at once she understood, and she whirled to Hades. "We can't."

"We will," Hades said, his jaw set.

"I call on you, Queen of the Underworld, to uphold your oath or be damned as an oath breaker to mortality," Circe said with a confidence that made Persephone think Zeus was right to have feared her.

"She offered you an end to your banishment," Hades said.

"What has been promised is of no concern to you, god of the Underworld," Circe said dismissively.

"I like to know exactly what I sold my fucking soul for," Hades said.

"We both know what your price was and that even knowing you would have still agreed to it," Circe said.

"This will mean war," Persephone said, staring at the small bundle.

"Don't do it," Hermes pleaded. "It's a death sentence."

"The immortal don't fear death, Messenger," Circe snapped.

"No, what lies at the end of this road is far worse than the mercy death offers," Hades murmured.

Despite the fear that made her bones heavy, Persephone took the damning steps forward. Circe watched her with cold certainty, but she hardly noticed her as her eyes latched onto the small babe that slept soundly. A small spread of red hair over her little head as she sighed sweetly in her sleep.

"What is her name?" Persephone asked.

"Artemisia," Circe answered.

Forcing her eyes away from the child, Persephone shot an accusing glare at Circe. "You swore what you asked me to protect would not hurt me or mine."

Circe gave a cunning smile. "And she will not. I imagine she will grow to love and protect you. There is a reason Hera chose you to raise and protect her child."

"More likely we were the easiest mark," Hades growled behind her.

"This child will bring death and ruin," Persephone said, though she was no seer.

Circe inclined her head. "It has been foretold by The Fates and the oracles alike. Hera learned of it during her pregnancy, but Zeus—"

The ground underneath them shook, and a rumble filled the air. Persephone's heart beat rapidly in her chest.

"There is only so long you can hide a prophecy from the god of gods. That time has just come to an end. Choose now, Persephone. There is no time left. He has heard the prophecy, and he searches," Circe said.

Hermes shook. "He's calling for me. I cannot withstand the summons, and I am not strong enough to hold against his demand for knowledge. I will tell him the child is here whether I want to or not."

Persephone ignored him. "Tell me the prophecy."

"A child of Zeus and Hera will grow to one day be his downfall."

"He has four other children with him. One of them being the god of war, which seems more of a red flag than an infant," Hades speculated.

"We all know the timing of the prophecy matters. While it won't stop him from making sure the others are not threats, he will know it is the babe," Circe said.

Artemisia would destroy everything as they knew it. If Zeus found her now, Hera would be tortured in Tartarus for trying to hide the infant, and Hades would be rewarded for not accepting her. Persephone would die old and gray as her immortality succumbed to the breaking of her oath. Everything would continue as it had been.

Yet if she upheld her oath. Everything would change, and even though it would be wrought in chaos, there was hope. Persephone reached for the babe and the weight of her felt right. The promise of her. She would be chaos, but she would be everything.

"Artemisia," Persephone whispered.

She snuggled deeper into her swaddle, and Persephone smiled. "Do what you must, Hades."

It all happened in a flash around her, but it might as well have not mattered for the possibility she held in her arms. Circe and Hermes disappeared in a flash and the Underworld shuddered with the wave of power Hades released. The air felt heavier, and it was as if a door sealed around them.

She was trapped once more, but it was for everything. Hades came up behind her and wrapped his arm around her shoulder, looking at the chaos she held.

"He will summon me any moment and I will not be able to resist either. His entire divinity is unleashed. The power I will have to use to maintain the Underworld makes me weak," Hades explained, and she wished there had been another way.

"He will torture you," she said, lifting her eyes to him.

"Mercilessly," Hades said with a sigh, as if they were discussing the weather.

"But he cannot get her." Persephone didn't know if it was a question or a statement.

"I have made the Underworld inhospitable to all life, with the dead as the only exception. You remain because of the bond and shared power. The same for Artemisia," he said.

"But she—"

"You gave her some of your darkness the moment she came into your arms. It was a side effect of you deciding to uphold the oath. You gave her what she needed to be protected," Hades said.

Persephone felt for the power that she had grown used to and found it less than it had been before. Hades reached for her hand and lifted it where a bow and arrow imprinted on her wrist. Somehow she had known, just as she had with Hades. She pulled back on the swaddle and there, on the infant's wrist, was the small twin to her own.

"You are bound to each other," Hades said grimly.

Persephone placed her finger in the tattooed hand, and Artemisia gripped tight around her. "So we are."

The End

ACKNOWLEDGMENTS

Gratitude is such an important part of who we are. When I think of the times I have been truly grateful in my life it's always three people that come to mind. Always my mother. My mother who sacrificed and was brave enough to create an entirely new life for us. Without her judgment and her courage, none of my stories would exist. Thank you, Mom, for everything you were and will ever be. Your spirit is alive in well in those that you loved and who loved you as well as in your grandchildren who ask about you all the time. The second part of this equation is Jennifer and Cory. There are a million ways my life could have played out after Mom died, but I should have known you both would make it the most ideal and smooth. Neither of you has ever missed a beat when it came to stepping up. You both have a place in my heart that is much like Mom's in the sense that it is completely unique. No one else could ever fill the place you take up and that is just how it should be. You both shed light on every life you touch. The world is a better place for having you both in it.

Rebecca Fazzio. There are a million things I could say about you and what you mean to me. Probably none of them are appropriate. You are infuriating and perfect all at once. My soul recognizes yours. I really am so grateful to the Universe for conspiring to bring us together. It lowkey probably regrets it, but no takebacks so . . . Love you more than words could say.

Veronica...listen, everyone, she has a sassy side to her. You think she's all sweet and innocent and you are right, but also she has a dark side. I love every second of it. You are literally the perfect human and the world is lucky to have you. I cannot wait to see how much people love your stories. Also please write Lace 2. K Thanks, love you.

My husband. Gerald, you are something else. You are so supportive and I love you so much. You have faced hardship that no one should have to, but you didn't let that harden you. You are kind, generous, and thoughtful. You deserve a love that is infinite and timeless. I am grateful that you let me love you and be who I am. There is no greater gift. Honestly, you deserve the most credit for this book or as you like to call it, The Honk Honk Heist. It's thanks to you that it exists given that you sparked all the ideas for it. I am grateful you let me go on and on about my books and provide such amazing ideas. You are the best. I love you so much.

Henry. Darling, you are the sweetest and most interesting little boy. I know you love straight lines and practical things, but you work so hard to find your place in all of it. Your laugh is infectious and your love for cats is inspiring. I love you, Henwiggle. Mommy will always be so proud of you and so grateful for you.

Elli. If you don't end up being a writer someday then I guess that makes me a monkey's uncle. You tell the best stories with the most emotion. The world is full of infinite colors for you and you boldly seek every one of them out. Your passion and courage will take you far. I love you, sweet boy. You make me so happy and I love you effortlessly.

Danielle. I appreciate all the years of endless entertainment. I really like your kids. They are the best thing you ever did. My only complaint is that Brendan is unnaturally good at Mario Kart . . . like not real-life good. Haley is perfection (no pressure HaeHae's). Maddy is basically me so I think she's really great. Basically, what I am trying to say is, well done. Oh, and I love your dogs in this order: Kali, Lily, Maple, Blue, Dexter. Lily would have been first, but she gives too many kisses and she only has one eye.

Justin. I am so excited to move next door and bug you every day. I hope you are using this time to mentally prepare. It's going to be great.

Jason. I used to get so sad when I thought about the hurdles you've had to face in your life, but you have never let any of it hold you back. I hope that you find the happiness you both want and deserve.

Caaaaaaaalcifer Catbus Clum. I could not have asked for a better cat. Your purrs and sweet cuddles are everything. I love you in a way that is vast and precious. Stay with me forever. I love you.

Belle, thank you for continuing to edit my books and saving me from myself.

Becca. This is your second love note. Thank you for selflessly editing this book as well. You are amazing and I am proud to be your first customer even if I didn't pay. I'll buy you dinner though.

Fairy Porn Book Club. From skin care to smutty books, I know I can count on you all!. Sam, I am so proud of you for making Seattle work and pushing your career, but also plan on moving to Maine. Adela, I like your choice of smutty books. Keep up the good work. Emily, that era's tour outfit was bomb af. Love you all and I am so happy we started our traveling books!

Heather! I am so happy that you signed up to ARC read my debut. Your support means everything to me and I swear on The Fates and the gods themselves if I ever make it in this industry enough to hire a PA you have a job. I don't care if you are already working for someone else . . . you will need to quit. Ok, phew, got that out of the way. You are such a beautiful person and I am so grateful for you.

Katrin, you have become so integral to my books and I am so grateful for your time and your beautiful feedback. Thank you a million times. Can't wait for you to meet Katrin in Threads 2!

Tina, thank you for all of the time that you put into reading these books. I am grateful for you!

To my ARC team. You make the world go round. Kat, Sabine, Mellissa, Sara, Amanda, Abby, Lynn, Monica your posts and reactions are everything. This group really has made me so happy throughout this journey so please know I am grateful for every single one of you and that you stay and sign up for ARCs is the highest honor. Thank you so much.

To my readers. Thank you for being here and taking a chance on a new author. Your support and energy are a symphony on my darkest days. There aren't words for the gratitude that I feel.

ABOUT AUTHOR

J.A. Good is a northerner living in Florida who's love of books and new worlds inspired her to create her own. She is a pediatric intensive care nurse at night and a writer, mom, wife, and cat enthusiast during the day. When she isn't naming all the dinosaurs with her toddlers you can find her staring at her book collection with her cats lamenting her lack of castles and magic.

ALSO BY J.A. GOOD

The Forged in Fire Series

-NA Fantasy Romance-

Forgotten Embers

Revenant Flames

Divine Inferno

A Thread of Fate

-NA Fantasy Romance-

Stand alone

Enemies to lovers

The Threads That Bind Series

-Paranormal/Dark Academia-

Of Blood and Magic

Of Shadows and Magic (2024)

Made in the USA
Columbia, SC
04 December 2024

48402234R00248